THE KNIGHTS OF JATALI

Kelly Thomason

SWANHEART PRESS

For everyone who supported

and believed in me.

The Glory be to the One True God in the Highest.

CONTENTS

the high Kingdom of Jatali

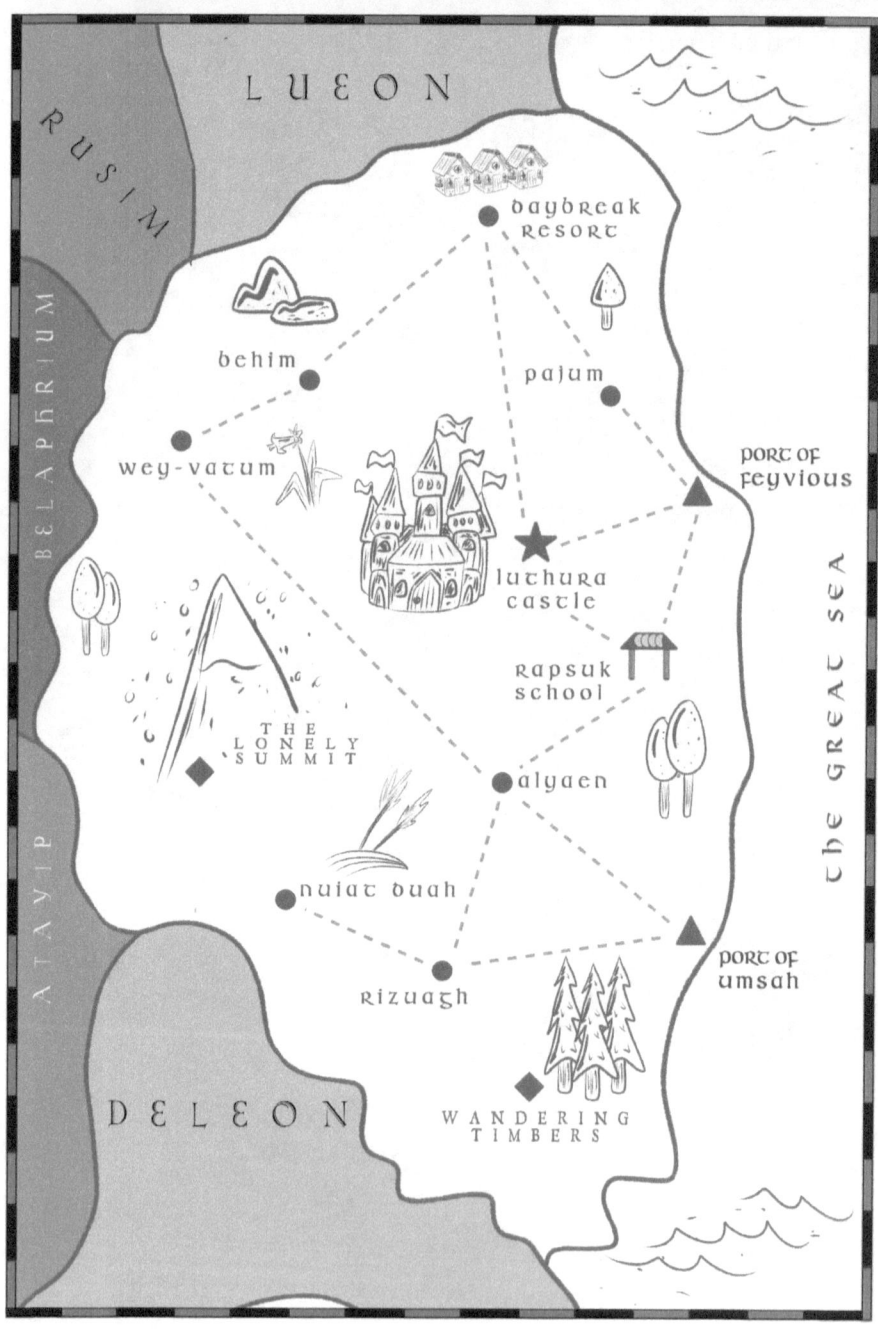

The High Kingdom of Jatali

AZUEFAE-yoh

Rulers: Great King Elin-rah Ventash Gantus and Prince Azufae-yoh Zintah Gantus

Capital: Luthura

Ports: Feyvious, Umsah

Other Cities: Daybreak Resort, Alyaen, Behim, Nuiat Duah, Pajum, Quania-leh, Rizuagh, Wey-vatum

Key Locations: The Lonely Summit, Wandering Timbers

Alliances: Rusim, Lueon, Belaphrium, Mutamay

Dominant Species: lion, jaguar, leopard, and other large cat species. They are considered a melting pot of other kinds of animals.

Nationality Name: Jatalians

Country Flower: *Tash-nev Roch*, also known as the Fireheart flower, is prominent around their nation specifically. It blooms purple until the end of its life and then turns red-orange as it dies surrounded by sparkling dust. In its death many more flowers are born.

Summary: They are truly a melting pot of the many nations. This is the place where many animals can fill different roles that what might be the traditional expectations in their home nation. The Great Castle of Luthura in the center of the country. After beings finish their training in Belaphrium, they further their training here. Those taken in from other nations just start their training at the castle. If they are younger, they start their learning at the Rapsuk School.

Not every solider becomes an elite Knight of Jatali, but there are plenty of positions in the army. They often have to send troops to the other nations for support from bandits, and the other dark forces that look to infiltrate them. There is mostly town and cobblestone roads. There is a single mountain peak in the south called the Lonely Summit. There is a lake with sandy banks to the north called the Daybreak Resort that is often a vacation destination. There are also cabins for extended stays.

Common Phrases

Eatiref!— **good tidings;** a greeting and also parting phrase

Jokan, Mutiem, lus Haoyut tav Jatali!— **the chant at the end of training;** Justice, Peace and Glory to Jatali

Tayaeme— **rats/curses;** something has gone wrong, sound of frustration

Artivah— **That's it!;** sound made when breakthrough is made, like Eureka

Zellum Yus— **get well;** akin to prayer, that the recipient will be blessed with good health once more

CHAPTER ONE

The Time Before

INDESSAH

My name is Indessah-yah Brantum, fox being, Belaphrium native, and a teacher for the Rapsuk school located in the High Kingdom of Jatali.

For as long as I can remember, our world has been breaking apart.

The continent of Ituvoh was once a paradise. We had no separate countries and only one capital— Jatali.

So many different beings made their home here but there

was harmony. All of them came and went as they wanted.

The High Kingdom of Jatali ruled the continent under the Great King Elin-rah Ventash Gantus, a golden-brown lion with a shimmering silver mane. The former Queen— may she rest peacefully in the Void. Their son, a tawny colored lion with a bronze mane, ruled at his side, Azufae-yoh Zintah Gantus. It was the heart of our once great nation.

It started small with new rivers forming or mountains rising out of the sea. But then as the arguing increased, the different beings could no longer find peace with their unique qualities. They started dividing the land into new nations.

A new being came to our shores. A kind we'd never seen before. They seemed like allies for a time before they found a forbidden magic. The birth of a shadow in these shining lands. Their leader used it and urged others to do the same. To believe that the Kingdom of Jatali was keeping great power from them. We may have been divided before but that lie sliced through the heart of Jatali.

So many beings embraced the shadows that day.

The beings we once called friends, had turned their backs on the High Kingdom of Jatali. They would pave their own way and forsake friendship to foster pride.

The foreign beings were driven from our lands, and their leader corrupt with power was banished by our King to what we call the Abyss of Garaev.

But it was too late.

Some of these new nations, it wasn't enough to just do

what they wanted. Some nations wanted the High Kingdom to perish.

War was coming.

The beings of Ituvoh had little idea it was their actions that were causing the shadows to continue to grow. The highest rule of Jatali is to love other beings as ourselves. But they saw too many differences. Too many ways the others were wrong. They were fed up with the very teaching that was protecting them. They felt like all they had been taught was a lie.

The Great King Elin-rah founded the magic that had built them up all these years. He knew everything about it. We call it the Magic of Jatali. The Spirit that rules these lands and gives those who respect it power. But times were growing desperate to save his beings from further division. He feared they would all be lost to the shadows forever.

He knew of one more sacrifice that could be made. A work that would keep the shadows suppressed for at least a time.

A sacrifice he wasn't sure he could make.

He questioned his son— even though he didn't want to even ask at all— what he might give up to save our beings?

Azufae-yoh said, "I will do whatever you ask of me Father, no matter the cost."

Elin-rah said, "Even at the cost of *everything* you are?"

The Prince hesitated, "Might there be another way?

Something else to counter the growing darkness?"

But Elin-rah said, "Sadly, it is the only way."

A way to purge the darkness and so that they might be able to see into the hearts of beings, to know their whole possible future so that they might change it to make them new. To keep them off the broken path.

Azufae-yoh nodded solemnly. He loved the beings just as much and if there was even a small way to ease the burden of the shadows, he would do it.

What we call the Great War was finally at our gates. We gathered our soldiers to meet them as they surrounded the whole castle.

But as those soldiers formed lines, and those against us raised their swords, an unbelievable thing happened—

Prince Azufae-yoh walked onto the field. He cut a path straight to the heart of the burning conflict.

He pleaded to speak with the divided nations once more. That we didn't have to fight but that peace could be ours if we work out our differences.

The division between the countries burned ever brighter as he spoke. Like a flame in the woods, calamity had come to a head.

A bird from the Tribe of Ikouvan had heard enough. His heart was hardened as he struck the defenseless Prince down in cold blood. Then beings from the Nations of Mutamay, Nidah, Esakivh, Sekulan, Zutaom and Guth joined in before any being could come to his aid.

Prince Azufae-yoh was dead.

This caused the Great Sea to form. A split straight down the middle of the continent. The lands who had turned their backs on us drifted far from the once mainland. This is now called the Eastern Continent.

But as the Jatalians mourned, the heir to the throne cut down so young—

A brilliant light erupted from the center of the battlefield. The forces of both sides thrown back from each other.

The young prince rose from his spot. His coat should've been bloody and tattered from his wounds, but it had been turned from tawny to pure white. His mane flickered in a golden light. Never had such a brilliant white ever been seen until that day.

Many hearts were changed.

The light that came from him washed over all the beings of all the Nations.

And those who had hate in their hearts, shadows were born in their souls.

A darkness they might never escape—

Those who rose against Jatali fled that day in terror. Azufae-yoh's sacrifice had brought forth a magic that had never been seen before or since. A magic to come back from the dead. To live forever and read the hearts of those he touched.

He turned to his troops—his allies—his friends, "I know it's hard to understand now, but all of this had to happen *this* way."

His subjects were in total awe. How could this be? How could he live after such fatal wounds?

"I will bring back all our lost beings. We will be whole again. This Promise has been given to me: As sure as this heart beats in my chest, so too will the lifeblood of this continent beat once more. The Peace we lost will re-form, and the flame of Love will burn hotter than ever."

The other Nations who followed Jatali were disheartened. Even after witnessing such a miracle, doubt grew in their hearts.

He urged them further, "Even when all seems lost, a light can still shine in the darkness. Even if the whole world faded, the tiniest star will be enough to turn everything back."

Maybe the Nations couldn't live in peace.

Maybe they were better divided. They were too different after all.

Instead of one almost border less continent, the Nations of Rusim, Lueon, Belaphrium, Atayip, and Deleon made their own territories too. The land left over now belonged to Jatali.

The cracks in the territory lines have been filled with shadows ever since. Watching, waiting, hoping for more strife to form.

The once shimmering continent now many broken pieces of rock.

Some of the Nations are still holding onto their own beliefs.

Other Nations are waiting for the Promise to be fulfilled.

The Promise that the Prince of Jatali will rise once more as the true Ruler over all and reunite the countries of every being under one banner.

The Promise that there will be Peace, Light and Love throughout the Nations once more. That we won't have to fear the Shadows ever again!

But it's been such a long time since those words were spoken.

It's hard to understand that the Prince and the King have lived for many generations since this happened. King Elin-rah being the first and only King of Jatali. Many Rulers have faded away, but our Rulers stay constant.

So long in fact, it's hard to know if it was a *real* Promise?

Or just a *Fairytale* bringing false hope to the beings of Ituvoh?

CHAPTER TWO

Creed of Zutaom

TATCHATHURA

My name is Tatchathura Devantum, fox being, thief and assassin working under the banner for the nation of Zutaom. When I was a cub, I lived in a country called Belaphrium in a little rock of a city near the coastline called Fusaim. But then the Kingdom took *everything* from me. Any reason I had to stay taken in the blink of an eye. My parents killed by raiders who decimated our little fishing town.

Beings that die go into a dark, empty place. What we call the Void. No motion. No talking. *Pure* stasis. Their soul energy still remains. But it isn't in a place that anyone can reach. Re-kivah and his beings are drifters. They took me in when I had no one. I owe them everything. And even though I haven't agreed with all our methods, I know it'll be worth it in the end. I'll get my parents back from the Void and the revenge on the Kingdom I seek.

Zutaom has been at war with Jatali for as long as I can remember. Many of the countries on the Eastern Continent have joined our side. I wouldn't say it's all because they really wanted to— it more of a *business* transaction. You know? Join us or we burn down your towns.

It seems harsh now because they don't understand what we're doing— but they will in time. It won't be just my family that's brought back, but anyone else who wants their family back. The Rulers of Jatali have lived for five hundred years since the Great War. They clearly have the magic ability to do that for themselves but let the rest of us perish into the Void.

They *say* they care, but does that sound like a being with a heart?

Our continent is overrun by what we call shadows. They are beings that gave themselves over to a strong negative emotion and let it consume them. Now they have what you call a one track mind— desperately trying to fulfill their one purpose in life— whether that be sowing seeds of jealousy or spreading lies and panic around the towns.

It brings a *tear* to my eye. Not really but *at least* they still have dreams anyway.

Most of these shadows run rampant until a Knight of Jatali uses their frilly magic to banish it to the Abyss of Garaev.

Some of those shadows are weak on their own, and they offer themselves up to a living being— a trade— another business transaction if you will. I trade something I own— a part of me, and the shadow gives me all the extra power I need without having to bow down to Jatali's magic. The shadow I made *friends* with was given to me as a cub. His name is Vengeance and it seems fitting given the way my life has gone. All I had to do was give him my arm and suffer through a night of agonizing pain as his soul twined with mine.

But hey, now I can throw trees across valleys, and silence anyone who gets in my way. So worth it, I guess?

They say the shadows in the Abyss are suffering. Writhing in a torment that craves energy from others to exist— A place where their soul can never rest. Every terrible physical calamity you can imagine will follow a being into this place—

But that's not the most important thing, the Drake is sealed there. Our Master. The only being who ever led a rebellion against the Kingdom and actually had the *Great* Elin-rah himself on the ropes. The only reason that rotten lion won is he cheated at the last moment.

So much magic was used that day, the sun didn't rise for almost three days. All of the forces from both sides were in some kind of weird stasis— or so they say—

Our commanders have a plan to break the seal on the Abyss. Free the Drake and all the shadows. Our forces will have quadrupled! And then Jatali won't know what hit them.

"Yes, sir?" I push open the broken slat wooden door.

Re-kivah looks down his snout at me. There's a scar down the middle of his face, and his ears are torn. His rippling shell cracked in many places with a spindly rat-like tail curled around his clawed feet. He says he's an armadillo but I'm not seeing it.

He says, "Did you get the western troops their orders?"

"Yeah, I told the rock brains their work." I fold my arms, *It was grunt work. I don't even know why he sent me...*

"Thank you—"

I clutch my chest, "I'm sorry?! Did you say 'thank you'? *Great* now you have me showing *concern*."

"Don't get sassy." he flicks his working eye in my direction, "I needed someone who could strike a little fear into those brats."

I let out a scoffing laugh and lean back into the door frame. If it can even be called a door.

Re-kivah shoves himself out of the seat. His short legs shuffle across the floor. A scroll in his claws before he slaps it into my chest. Another dark look before he returns back to the desk.

I notice wisps of his shadows oozing from his tail. He looks worse than usual— as if that's even possible.

"What Vanity and Bluster didn't want to *help* you work today?"

"We're **not** talking about me. That scroll has the schematics to Luthura Castle. Every nook and cranny you could imagine has been painstakingly marked. And the poor fool who's been spying on your target for months just now got it back."

I skim over the paper only half listening to the old being rattle on.

"All you need to do is be where the X is at the time marked." his lips curl, a few broken teeth come into view, "I'm sure even a mutt like you can *manage*."

"Psh, I'll be in and out before you can get your tea ready." I shove the paper into my leather jacket, "I'll even buy it for you. Pick your *poison*."

"You're *poison* enough for me, **cub**. Now go on. It'll take you long enough to get over there."

"What of Lu-kan?" I shoot him an even look. She's my usual partner in these kinds of missions. The one being in this rotten place I can actually trust.

"Don't worry about her. She'll be around that location too."

I bite my tongue. In cases like this, it's better not to argue.

Re-kivah glares at me, "Don't screw this up Tatchathura. You've got *one* chance."

I smirk, claws scrapping against the door frame, "Do I *ever* miss my mark?"

Re-kivah nods slowly. For once he seems uneasy but goes back to writing his reports anyway.

I let out a huff as I shut the door behind me. It's true Jatali is a little different than most countries I go to, but every place has it's weak points. Even if it's the strongest castle around, it's still made with mortar and bricks—cracks all around just waiting for a shadow to pass through.

CHAPTER THREE

Perfect Execution

ALTIKUA

My name is Altikua Talous, a wolf being that, like most of my kind, hails from Belaphrium. I am the Commander of the entire Jatalian Army. I work mainly at Luthura Castle alongside the Great King Elin-rah and Prince Azufae-yoh. Ever since I was a cub, I was taught to do what's right by Jatali and I always strived for that. The Magic of the land protects those who respect it. It's a sacred power that directs our hearts and minds so that we all may know a greater peace.

I'm settled in the center of my training room. It has a smooth floor with a few pieces of workout equipment. I'm wearing a loose shirt and shorts. The Tome of Truth is in my lap. It's one of the 12 volumes of Virtue Magic. The Virtues make up the Magic of Jatali. There are many qualities a being may hone, but for me it's always been Truth. Because without the truth we have nothing.

I read through the pages with my gaze sharpened on every word. I've read this Tome a hundred times easily but refreshing my mind at the start of each day is what keeps my power strong. You can't use what you don't know. The only way to strengthen a Virtue is to nurture it.

I close the book. I set it on the ground as I rise up. Taking in a deep breath, I fan a paw out wide. My other paw lowers to clench at my side. I stare straight ahead, "Jatali knows the Truth inside us all. There's no heart he doesn't know."

A subtle glow forms around my raised paw. I close my eyes for a moment picturing my Father instilling these life lessons into me from a young age. My eyes open sharply. They focus on a target on the far wall. The glow beams brighter. A flickering string of lightning circles around my paw before blasting into the target. It shatters and pieces fly everywhere.

I let out another breath pulling my paws close to my chest, "Thank you for having been with me, Jatali."

* * *

After my morning training, I change shirts. I'm reminded of the magical markings on my chest right over my heart, and one on my forehead that's usually hidden by my hair. They look like comets. Our kind may come in many different colors, but we all have one thing in common, something we all call Magical Markings. It's a natural part of our life cycle. They are usually basic shapes, or can be symbols that represent things in our culture such as specific trees, or flowers.

I got these markings when I was only a cub. Many beings believe it represents the amount of times a being has gone against the Magic. Now that I've matured in my studies, I know better. It's a mark of a changing heart. A being who's growing. But I guess I haven't changed much from my youth.

Every being in Ituvoh has some variation of these markings except for the King and Prince of Jatali. They never had a mark to begin with. But after their royal sacrifice their coats were sealed in perfection by the Magic.

My desire for Justice and Truth has always been strong. Justice is another Virtue a being can learn. But since our kind must align our wills with the Magic, our hearts must match. I've never been able to get Justice quite right. You would think with a title like Altikua the Just I'd have it all figured out, but there's still some changing that needs to happen under this dusty old pelt.

I take a few moments to slide on pieces of my golden armor. Even though the streets of Luthura are mostly safe, I never know who might be lurking in the shadows ready to take their revenge. As Commander I've made it my number one priority to keep the beings here safe but in doing so I've also made my share of enemies. So many beings in Zutaom despise me based on my record alone.

My armor is a bright bronze color with yellow trim. A sun emblem covers the chest plate. I have wing like blades on each shoulder. My orange arm pieces have more golden prongs that are dangerous if others aren't careful around me. I wear a thick golden belt with a fire-like shape to it. Armor covers almost every inch of my body. A blue striped tunic covers the remaining small section of my legs. My helmet is orange with blue feathers of every shade coming out of it. I look in the mirror for another moment before heading out the door.

* * *

As I walk through the streets of Luthura, I'm greeted by most beings I pass. Subtle compliments and chattering amongst the common folk. A few of the girls seem interested in getting to know me— I give them a polite nod and keep heading on my way. I only have a heart for my late wife and there won't be another being who changes that.

I pass another road and a being comes fumbling out of the alleyway with armfuls of stuff. They stumble slightly on the cobblestone. I throw my arm out to help curb their descent. It takes a moment for me to steady them. They huff and stand awkwardly next to me. I slide half of their boxes into my arms. Their face comes into view and I recognize them, "Xai-ten, how *many* times have we talked about this?"

Xai-ten, an older, and gruff looking salamander waves a paw at me, "Eh, you know I is a stubborn ol' fool."

"That much is apparent." I half-chuckle. I can still recall the last time I bumped into him like this— half a shipment of fine dishes ruined all in one go because he refused to make more than one trip.

"C'mere, I got dis here new on's. They are might beaut." He slides on ahead of me towards his restaurant.

His purple tail swishes back and forth as he walks uphill. A subtle trail of slime drips from his pores. He told me he wasn't always like this— it only started after he had a shadow. Ever since the King saved him, he's had a "leak" he says. Further proof that a being trades more than a temporary existence when they make a deal with a shadow. He actually used to live in Esakivh before I found him.

We push our way into his closed restaurant. He settles the boxes on a table before shuffling across the floor towards the bar side.

I push on the front door, "I'll be on my way. Please consider hiring some help—"

"No ye ain't." He waves a commanding paw at me, his thin digits beckoning me closer.

"I'll have to see the dishes later. I can't keep my Masters waiting."

"Bah, it'll onl' takes a second, it will. Come, a drink for ye."

I narrow my gaze, "As long as it keeps me awake *this* time."

He cackles. A few tears spring to his fading black eyes, "I is so'rr for dat. 'Tis only a newt's error. But dis is a brew from da rabbits across tha road."

Well, that gives me a little bit of relief. At least they know how to make a morning tonic. I reluctantly cross the floor to the bar side.

He quickly shuffles the cups around under the cupboard. He curses slightly shifting the jars around as if he can't find it. I roll my eyes good naturedly.

He calls, "Artivah!" which is our language for "That's it".

Excitedly he slaps the cups onto the counter. The jug slops forward pouring out the liquid, "Ya these rabbits know how to make'er a good un. It keeps this ol' guppie going fer sure."

I take the glass and give him a thankful nod. I duck back a sip of the warm liquid. It's faintly woody with floral tones. A nice spicy zing right at the end. In fact, I think I feel more awake already.

He's humming a jaunty tune and rifling through the drawers for something else to go with it. I can tell already—

it's on the tip of his tongue— "Jus stay a moment long'r."

It's not like I don't want to see him— it's just being punctual is important to me.

I say, "Thanks, Xai. I really must—"

He shoots me a serious look, "I heard thar be shadows on the Western Moor. Do ye know a ting about it?"

The Western Moor. That's a new rumor for me. It's true Luthura has been getting a few more "shadow sighting" reports. Most of those investigations have ended with a shadow that was passing through a location and that was promptly dispatched by the teams sent to investigate. The Western Moor is quite far from Luthura. No beings really live out that way so I figure I'll alert the Prince as soon as we are done with our morning trials.

"I can't say I have. Did they give any details?"

He sighs deeply. A tenseness forms in his neck, "Aye, t'was three of dem. They were jus floatin' along as if look'n fer somthin'."

"Has anyone informed the castle yet?"

"Hmm, a young mutt were supposed to tell the guard, but I know not if ye did so."

"I'll be sure to look into it."

He nods feebly. He starts to walk around the bar side, but before he can make it too far, his knees buckle and he crashes to the ground.

I quickly slide to his side, "Xai!" I take a careful moment

to hoist him into my arms. Slowly I settle him onto a chair. I keep him steady as I kneel before him, "Are you alright? Shall I take you to the medical—"

There's a bit of a snuffle in his voice, "Aye. Jus tha past rear'n tis ugly mug."

"You sure? I can take you down the street—"

"Bah!" he swipes playfully at me.

I give him a half-smirk, concern at the back of my mind, "You better not be *stalling* for time."

He scoffs again, "Be on ye way. But if ye could, look in ta dat shadow. I gots a terrible feeling, I does."

"Of course, my friend."

His eyes get mistier than usual, "Yer always the hope of dis town, you is."

"Great King Elin-rah saved you. I just follow my Masters and Jatali. Nothing more and nothing less."

"Aye, tis the King who saved a lot such as I, but ye were the warrior who laid me at such a throne as der's."

I give him a warm smile, my chest swollen, "Thank you Xai-ten."

* * *

After I left Xai-ten's place, I made sure the rabbits across the road will go check on him later. He's getting up there in years and I worry about him often. He refuses to hire any help even though it's long past due. But still, I'm thankful for beings like Xai-ten. They help ground me. Remind me of why I do what I do. Remind me of why I get up everyday. A sharpened sword is nothing without a house to protect.

I knock on the Prince's study. It takes a moment before I hear him call me in. I slide the door open with a drink in paw. I finished mine awhile ago but had decided that maybe Prince Azufae-yoh would like some as well. (After I was sure it wasn't sleep inducing.)

He turns from his podium. It holds a book that has a translucent map of all of Ituvoh. For the moment the map is quiet. His eyes are practically glowing as he meets my gaze, "My dear friend, Talik, how are you this morning?"

I chuckle, "Same as usual Sire." I offer him the drink, "Would you like something for this morning? I've already ensured it's safe."

His eyes flash in excitement as he takes the drink, "Thank you. Where is it from?"

I scratch the back of my head, "Uh, I got it from Xai-ten but he said it's from the rabbits across the street— I forget what the name—"

"Bunarium Heights? Miskav makes the *best* home brews." He seems even more pleased, "I do wonder how her and Ten-quah are doing. I must call them later."

"Of course, but we should probably get to this business first."

He sighs, "Yes, of course. Duty first."

He leads the way out of his study. I follow him down the

long, winding hallway. The legends said that the Prince gained a connection with all the beings of Ituvoh when he sacrificed himself in the Great War. But who would've known he'd be able to actually remember each being in such detail? It's fairly impressive to me. The Bunarium rabbits aren't exactly first on the guest list. And it's not just them but so many others. I have no idea how he's able to keep track of it all.

As we walk towards the throne room, he starts telling me about some other new beings he's met in Ituvoh. It brings a warm smile to my heart. He has such a love for our beings. And not just the beings of Jatali, but from all of the countries. We've had plenty of transfers from his travel encounters and he's always so excited to meet a new being.

Like his father, he follows the Magic of Jatali. It speaks with him on a personal basis too sometimes. For me, I know Jatali is there, but I've never heard his voice. They say that the Magic will only speak to true rulers who have the purest heart for Jatalian ways. But anything is possible with the Magic we serve. We reach the Great Hall Throne Room and I push the door open for my Master.

He nods subtly as he walks inside. The King is already seated on the far wall. A pristine and perfect white marble throne. There's almost a subtle glow to the area around it. The Prince walks closer to the throne.

King Elin-rah stands up with his arms thrown wide. They meet in a giant hug, "My Son. How I've missed you."

"Father, it's only been a few hours." There's a look of mirth on his features.

"I know but it feels like forever when you're in that room." He tilts back to give him a look full of pride, "You're doing an excellent job. I hope that you might have some time for us this afternoon?"

"Of course, Father."

The King twists from his son and starts walking towards me.

I kneel before him and bow my head, "My Liege, may you reign under the rule of Jatali forever."

He leans down and hoists me to stand, "How many times must I tell you? Altikua, you are like a son to me. Please don't feel the need to be so formal."

I glance up, "At least two hundred times more, Master."

He warrants me a warm look before compressing me in a hug. A tightness in my chest rises. Slowly I wrap a paw around his waist for the briefest moments before pulling back.

King Elin-rah sighs but seems to understand, "Let us get to work then."

He settles onto his grand throne and motions towards a pair of the guards. They go scampering off towards the other set of doors. The Prince beckons me closer. I straighten out my tunic and stand at the Prince's side.

The guards come back through the door. A group of three

criminals in chains at their sides. They look terrified. A couple of them seem bruised as though there was a struggle. The soldiers walk them across the Great Hall to halt in front of the Prince. All of the jovial nature has left King Elin-rah's face. He subtly nods to Prince Azufae-yoh.

The Prince wears a serious expression, his bright blue eyes steely calm, "Do you three know what you stand charged with?"

I fold my arms and shoot them all an intimidating look. I've been as loyal to the Kingdom as I can be but I don't always agree with my Masters' methods. I know this routine like the back of my paw.

Before the Prince can even explain to them what their charges are, one of them throws herself at his paws. She's a weeping mess begging for mercy. Another one of their group gets a good look at me before following suit. The third bows his head as if in agreement. The Prince's gaze softens as he turns to glance at his father. The King nods almost knowingly.

Prince Azufae-yoh kneels to the one crying, his paws lift her to look at him, "I can tell you are sorry for all that you have done. You have all offended the Magic." He glances at the other two, "There still must be a reformation in order. I'd like to keep you around. I have some important jobs for you three."

They all seem startled with the words coming from my Master's mouth. So stunned they've stopped crying and fussing. Completely speechless.

"So what do you say?" his gaze now slowly gentle, "It won't be easy—"

The crying one hugs his foot, "Thank you! Great is your mercy, Prince Azufae-yoh, and Great King Elin-rah! Long live our gracious rulers!"

I sigh and suppress an eye roll. It's not like I want anyone in trouble. In fact, it would make everything easier if the Promise was fulfilled already and Love healed the land. But instead I have to bear witness to such things. To me sometimes its as if the criminals have gotten bolder because the Prince and King always seem to dole out mercy at the first sign of tears— actually— even at the first sign of *cooperation*.

The Prince starts telling the soldiers what he intends for our new recruits. Firstly explaining that they should all get a bath and a hot meal and of course comfortable living quarters in the barracks. They were only caught for petty theft so I guess I shouldn't expect anything less. My paw seems to itch as I open and close it.

We go through a few rounds of criminals like usual. Their actions all rinse and repeat. My Master's grace knows no bounds. Some get actual prison time down in the metal cells. Some get new jobs. And some still need more time to come to terms, so they are sent to our higher level prison cells that are more like apartments rather than cells.

They bring in one of the last criminals for the day. He

looks annoyed and like he's been thrown under a cart one too many times. My paw twitches in anticipation.

The Prince clasps his paws together, "Do you know—"

The criminal throws himself off the ground. The guards holding his chains are caught off guard. He's strong enough to yank free of their lazy grips. The chains clang across the ground.

I grumble, "There's always one in every group."

He's making the other guards look like fools as he scrambles towards the door. I take in a deep breath. My paw subtly raises.

The criminal is almost to the door. He's been half caught and bangs his head against a smaller soldier. They go tipping backwards holding their new wound.

The Prince sighs and nods to me.

The glow around my paws ignites, "Jatali knows the Truth inside us all. Conform your heart to will of the Magic."

Instantly the being halts. His feet frozen to the stone under the control of my golden glow. It's not a power I like to use. Verity is a Branch of Truth that allows a user to control the actions of another temporarily. It only lasts at most half a minute, nothing more or less. It is meant to be a defensive power that lasts about a minute. Long enough to allow a being to get away or to halt an attack. Using it for other purposes becomes shady territory fast.

The being turns on his heel and walks back to stand before the Prince. His eyes are wide and all rebellion is lost in his gaze. I wave the magic away with a silent prayer in my mind thanking Jatali for his aid.

And then the tears from the criminal start flowing. He now understands this is his best chance.

The Prince kneels to meet him where he is—

The criminal recoils backwards. He bows lowly practically clinging to the ground, "P-please, S-sire. M-mag-gnificent One. I—"

The Prince's gentle paw rests on his shoulder, "I know you have suffered. I only want to help you. Please don't run again."

The criminal shakes even harder and more tears are shed. Even at my Master's gracious hand the criminal doesn't accept his paw. He thinks himself unworthy, and he'd be right. None of us are worthy of the Mercy Jatali brings.

After a few long moments the throne room finally settles. The criminal is taken away to serve his sentence. The other soldiers have tended to the injured or sent them downstairs to our Medical Bay.

I turn towards the Prince, "Sire, now that we have a moment. I heard a rumor this morning about the Western Moor. A *trio* of shadows."

His eyes widen a moment and he glances towards the King. The King keeps his gaze focused on us.

"We should investigate it immediately."

Prince Azufae-yoh's brow creases, "That is strange indeed. Do whatever you think is best."

Another soldier tentatively approaches us. He half-covers his snout, "Sire, Commander, we've also heard rumors of a potential attack by the—" he suddenly closes his mouth as though he's too mouse-hearted to speak.

I say, "Well, out with it."

He whispers behind his paw, "*The Shadow Fox of Zutaom.*"

There are a few quiet gasps around the room, but it seems most of them haven't heard.

I lean in closer, "Where might you have heard such a thing?"

The Prince's tail starts swishing. His ears raise and eyes seem to glimmer in excitement. Only he would get excited about such a thing—

The soldier lets out a breath, "Some intel from Zutaom was leaked this morning. I was told that Admiral Ray-tah intercepted chatter from some seafarers that brought the Shadow on board. They were paid to keep it a secret but I guess that's Zutaom for you." He lets out an awkward chuckle.

The Prince seems to puff up, "Of course Ray-tah would intercept knowledge like that! He's always so reliable."

The Prince seems to gush like a proud parent over their

child. I'm less impressed— Ray-tah may be my friend, but the being looks like a pirate so of course beings from Zutaom would be confused and hand over precious information. It's cheating is what it is.

The Prince turns towards me, "I have to do some research but do you think your beings would be ready for such a capture?"

I watch him for a moment. It's true our castle has been fortified a hundred times over. Training is always rigorous under my command. But the Shadow Fox is a notorious war criminal. He's not like the petty thieves and liars we find in our town. He's also got a lot of power he shouldn't have. They say he was bonded with a shadow as a cub— way younger than any normal being— and still he hasn't turned full shadow yet.

The amount of will that being has to have must be *astronomical*. They also say he makes the will of other shadows bow down to him at Zutaom's behest. As for the other reports I've read on him— he sounds like a being with no conscious—

"Altikua?" the Prince repeats, "Will your forces be *ready*?"

I shake my head, "Sorry Sire. If it's what the Magic wills, then it shall be done. But what would you have us do upon capture?"

The Prince glances towards the King for input.

King Elin-rah stands up, his gaze like fire, "Once you have

him in our possession, bring him to the Great Hall **immediately**. I don't want any unnecessary struggles."

I'm quick to say, "I'll make sure every being in my guard knows."

The Prince's tail swishes, "I'll go do my research now." He puts a paw on my shoulder, "Don't be afraid my friend. This means it's time for the *Promise* to come to pass."

My eyes widen for a moment, before they narrow, *"Really?"*

"Well, not the first Promise, but another one the Magic gave me about a week ago. I have to make the proper arrangements! This is so exciting."

I shake my head somewhat amused by his display. He hurries off towards his study once more.

The King sighs slowly slumping into his throne, "Altikua, please help him with this difficult task."

"Consider it already done, Most High." I bow my head to him before heading out of the room.

Today has been nearly perfect. It's the way things are supposed to be. I'm in control. Criminals bowing at my command. Keeping Luthura safe through any means necessary. The growing shadow reports have been enough to keep me up at night. But now this rumor of the Shadow Fox potentially heading for our borders? It's enough to make me never want to sleep again. It's bad enough he has been loose in his own country.

I half-growl and shake away the dark trajectory of my thoughts. It matters not. The Magic of Jatali always has a plan and will keep his beings safe. And I'm experienced enough to know how to handle *one* measly fox.

CHAPTER FOUR

A Typical Day

INDESSAH

I wish I could say I'm a morning being— or that I'm someone who makes it everywhere on time— but I'd really just like to embrace my averageness. I tumble out of bed just early enough to do the basics and grab my lunch. I dart out the door and almost smack face first into my best friend —Kyltia.

To be fair she's hanging from the archway of my doorway — like a bat— because she's a huge bat.

I roughly brush her fur out of my face, "Do you *have* to do that?"

She snickers and shuffles down to the ground, *"Finally awake, eh?"*

"It's easy for a being when you've been up all night." I start heading towards the main school campus. It's called Rapsuk.

She's amused but follows me without another word.

At least I live on campus, so it won't take too long. The cubs may come and go but we're dutifully stuck here.

Kyltia glides just slightly above me. Her broad leathery wings misting a cool breeze down onto my head. I glance up at her. Her coat is shimmery mix of salmon and pinks. Her chest fluff is a complimentary violet blue. She has broad ears and eyes to match. Her eyes are dark and shimmer with an undertone of greens and browns like the stars.

She glances down noticing I'm distracted, "You know nothing has changed since yesterday?"

I'm not getting into that conversation today so I give her the simplest answer I can, "Right."

"You got mist in your brain today?"

"It's nothing." I half-bite, *She just won't leave it alone...*

"Whatever. Keep it to yourself."

I smile softly. To a normal being, they'd probably think she's was irritated with me, but I've known her long enough to know better.

Kyltia has been my best friend pretty much since I got here...

When the Prince first brought me to the Rapsuk school, there was so much whispering as I walked onto the campus.

Even though I know he didn't say anything about what had happened in my past (he never does about anyone). It seemed plenty had heard what happened at the castle. And that someone else was aware of some of the intricate details and had loose lips. The day after the Prince left— the gossiping just got worse. I was barely there a few days before the whispering turned into full blown rumors. Things that had no weight at all. Some beings were so oblivious that they talked about me straight to my face.

I thought that our country was supposed to be all light and love. But it seems I was in for a rude awakening. They acted like all of their coats were so perfect, as if none of them have ever done anything against the Kingdom either. Although I tried to ignore the rumors, and whispers, trying to make friends with my co-workers was mostly in vain. Sure, they had a bright smile on their faces when I spoke with them. But as soon as I would walk away, they were back judging me all over again. I know what I did was wrong. I know all the things I did I can never take back.

None of us can.

Late one night, I was upset from the day. Anxious, and

unable to sleep. I'd only been there a couple of weeks at this point. Although the students were great, all of my peers talking about me weighed on my chest. My tail dragged. My ears flat. I wanted to sink into the ground. I wanted to call the Prince and tell him that I couldn't do it anymore. There had to be some other job for me. I'd do anything else— even clean the castle floor! **Anything** was better than hearing all of this.

These lies about me.

Because that's the thing about rumors and gossip, they don't just stay next to the truth. They start to mutate and twist until they're not recognizable anymore. I had my bag slung over my shoulder. My feet had dragged me all the way to the front gate. It was quiet and I didn't see any of the guards around. Not that they would've stopped me but still I wondered where they might be.

I slipped through the rusted metal gate. The latch clicked behind me. I stared up at the gate, eyes watery, 'Sorry, Prince Azufae-yoh. I don't want to do this but I feel like I have to. I'm not cut out for this job even if it means running away again...'

Just as I started to walk down the hill, a figure whooshed by me. Out of the darkness came an incredibly fast winged figure. They swooped down to stand before me shrouded in the darkness of the night.

I panicked. A fist raised and tail lashing "What are you?"

"Relax." said the voice, "I was patrolling and just wondered who you were. But I see you're just a teacher."

The figure walked closer to me. Finally the moonlight hit her broad glistening wings. They were powerful and leathery. Almost perfect bat wings until I see the scar that's down the middle of her left wing.

I narrow my gaze, "A guard? You weren't at the gate."

"Honey, I've got wings. I'm not staying bored by the gate. Besides, I'm super fast." She raises her wing towards her visage to look around like she's on the hunt, "So I was just you know, **rolling**."

For some reason that makes me laugh, "**Rolling**?"

"Yeah, because it's faster than saying **patrolling**." She seems proud of herself, all puffed up, "Now why are you out wandering in the dark?"

"Uh, early assignment."

She narrows her gaze and looms over me, "Uh-huh. Now why are you **really** out?"

I bite my lip. It seems I'm caught.

She waves her wing wide, "So you're just gonna run away in the middle of the night and disappear without a trace? How original."

'How dare she...' I stare at her dumbfounded, "No, I wasn't. I'm just going for a night walk. It's cool outside."

"I thought it was an early assignment?"

"It is— I— just wanted to stretch my legs— why do you

care anyway?"

She settles on a nearby rock, "Look I get it, the Welcome Wagon hasn't been very welcoming."

I sigh and grip my bag tighter, "I guess things aren't going like I expected. No one is like the Prince after all."

"Ah, that's true. I was talking more about myself actually. You see when I was just a teenager," she spreads her wings wide, "I had the world figured out."

I covered my mouth and try not to laugh. I'm supposed to be sad aren't I? There's just something about her that makes me— calm. It's like—

"I was living in the Severed Peaks of Atayip. It's pretty rough parts over there ever since the gryphon King Tiphan-rah took over."

"The only family I had was my brother. We did everything together until we didn't. He did something foolish. A deal with a gryphon from Tiphan-rah's court who double-crossed him. Now, I was all alone. It was hard to lose him. But I was about to do something foolish too."

My paws tighten. She's treating me like I'm her own. Like how all of Jatali should be.

"I left in the middle of the night. My wings flapping furiously. I was approaching the gates ready to swoop down and have my revenge. Fly straight into the gryphon court. It didn't matter to my little pea brain that there were millions of guards!"

I say, "**Millions**?"

"Okay, thousands!"

"Aren't the gryphons all out for themselves? And doesn't King Tiphan-rah only have a few close guard?"

She puts a claw to my lips, "The point is— there was a lot of bad beings there and I was about to make myself a roasted bat."

I smile behind her claw, 'It's been so long since I had... maybe...a friend.'

She throws her wings wide, "There I was— vastly outnumbered. No magic. No recourse. But I didn't care. They took my brother and I wanted him back even though I knew it would never make him come back."

I watched her carefully. She's so animated. And ecstatic. I can't believe she's almost happy talking about such a thing. She's odd to say the least.

"I slip down into a tree line not far from the castle walls. I peek around the bark noting my surroundings. I tried to get a good view on the lay of the land before I strike."

"Suddenly there was rustling in the trees behind me. I turned quickly— my wings ready to go. I almost lashed out. A set of blue eyes stared back at me. And then a shiny white coat came into view. He was practically glowing in the moonlight.

"Prince Azufae-yoh! What are you doing here?"

"I could ask you the same thing." He said evenly.

"I didn't have to tell him my plans. He already knew exactly what I was up to. And he'd come there to stop me. He stopped me because he obviously knew how it was going to end up."

Suddenly she's quiet. Meek even. Her wings folded in close. Her eyes glossy and downcast, "I haven't done a lot of— good things in my life. There's stuff—well— I can't take it back."

Realization hit me like a ton of bricks. She's just like me. I know we all have our issues, but the way she said it, it's exactly how I feel most of the time.

She rubs her wings together, "It was strange to me. Why go to so much trouble to meet me in the middle of the night and stop me? Why not just stop King Tiphan-rah himself?"

"I don't know."

*She threw her wing, eyes wounded, "And why hadn't he saved my brother when he had the chance? Why **me**? I didn't deserve it but he came for me in my moment of weakness anyway."*

*I slowly slink onto a nearby log, "I keep asking myself the same thing. I'm supposed to stay at the school until the right time, but **when** is that? How can I even be ready for such a time? I don't even know what to prepare for."*

"He told me to wait too." Her gaze is sympathetic, "I didn't have the best time starting here either. I had no

idea Jatalians could be so— uh— biased."

"Yeah, they're **not** supposed to be."

"Well, the point I'm making to ya is we've got destinies! You and me girl. It doesn't matter who we were. Don't let those fools cheat you out of it." Her claw points to my heart, "The Prince chose you! It has to be you or you wouldn't even be here."

"I guess you're right."

"I am **right**." She shines her claw against her chest fluff.

"But I've been alone so long."

"Not anymore you're not. Name's Kyltia."

I offer a paw up, "Indessah-yah Brantum."

She bumps paws with me, "Oh you're that being. **Never mind**." She wears a cheeky look. Her white fangs glistening in the dark.

I smirk in return, "My friends call me Indy. But only the best ones."

"I see. You'd better get back to your bunk. We've got work to do."

"We?"

"My shift is almost over. I'll go to bed early so I can be with you in the morning."

"You'd do that for me?"

"Hey, Jatali is light and love right? We gotta stick

together against the shadows."

I nearly jump, "You too!? Everyone I meet doesn't think shadows are a thing!"

"I know. I've seen my fair share. So naive."

We must have talked for hours that night. Both of us standing guard at the gate until her relief came. It's hard to imagine a world without Kyltia. She and I are each other's anchor. A rock to lean on and a castle to make our stand. As we walk through town on our way to school, Kyltia keeps rattling off about every random thing she sees or hears. She's a bit of a gossip— something I don't like for obvious reasons— she says it's 'keeping in the know' as she wants to be a reporter some day.

She's practically gushing at this point. I shake my head.

She raises her brows with a knowing look, "Have you seen *red-fur* lately? He seems interested in you, you know?"

He's not around at the moment but I know who she's talking about. I fold my ears at the very idea, "Stop. None of that is important anymore."

She rolls her eyes heavily, "Yeah, yeah. Des~tiny!"

We stop by the front gate.

I say, "Hey, you're the one who said it *first*."

"I'm just saying there is more to life than waiting for the future. And even then it might not be the future you're imagining."

"And what exactly am I *imagining*?"

"Probably you gallivanting off to destroy the shadows by yourself." She waves her wings around like they're swords while ignoring the looks of each passerby.

"Not likely." I give her a half-smile.

"I don't know!" She ruffles my hair, "I'm not in Indy-B's head— but what I do know is you think too much. Just *do* already!"

I sigh, gripping my bag strap tighter, "Look, I have to get to class. Still want to do dinner after work?"

She raises her claw to tap mine, "You know it. Have fun girlie. I'm going back to sleep."

I turn to walk into the curling metal gates. The sight of them reminds me of my first time here.

I'm originally from Belaphrium. It's common for foxes and wolves to live there. It's also where the most of our military strength is built up. The terrain there is mostly flat but just harsh enough that it makes it easy for us to be conditioned to any kind of environment except for the cold. Not that there are many cold places in Ituvoh. I hadn't even finished my training there when I first met the Prince. My Father is a politician in Belaphrium and is a close friends with the Prince. But through a chain of events, I didn't end up going to the Kingdom right away.

Instead I tried to carve my own path, do some of my own things— it didn't end well. The Prince actually bailed me out in my time of need. He was even gracious enough to put me through Basic Training at Luthura and give me this position at the Rapsuk school. But even after I had done so much wrong, I'll never forget what he told me that day...

I stare up at the school. The two looming columns seemed ready to crush me at a moment's notice. Cubs are running all over the place being followed closely by their teachers. It's such a positive and strong energy here. It feels so different after stumbling around in the dark.

Prince Azufae-yoh walks to my side. His white coat seems to glimmer in the sunlight, "Indessah, I'm glad to have you back."

"Yes, of course, Sire. Are you sure I'll be able to do this?"

"I have full confidence in you. Never forget that." he puts a paw in his mane, "However, I have to tell you this now. In the future there will be something special I need your help with— a task only you can complete."

"A task that only I can do? I seriously doubt that. You saw how much of a mess I was."

He puts a gentle paw on my shoulder, "Your heart isn't the way I need it now, but teaching these cubs and staying with these beings at the school will give you the skills I need."

I watch him for a moment. My heart pounding out of my chest. I'm such a mess and he's given me an important responsibility to these cubs. And then another task in the future that only I can complete? How can he have such faith in me when I have no faith in myself?

*"Indy, don't worry about it for now. When that time comes, you'll **still** have a choice. So, try to enjoy your time here. Who knows? Maybe some beings' choices will change and your mission won't be so dire anymore?"*

I fold my paws together, *It's alright I don't have to think about what my answer will be. When he calls me again, I'll be ready this time...*

It seems so long ago. So I press onwards, I tell myself again what's been getting me through these days; *Keep waking up. Drag your paws across the floor. Keep opening that door. Never back down.*

* * *

I walk down the main dirt path towards my classroom hut. A group of my co-workers are chatting next to their huts as they fill up with students. I take in a deep breath and walk towards them. They were laughing but at my approach I can see their joy diminished.

"Eatiref!" They almost become guarded at the traditional greeting phrase, "How are you all today?"

Finally the goat says, "Fine. We should be getting ready for class though."

The other two nod along and start heading elsewhere.

"Okay, we'll catch up later. Have a good day." I wave and keep going on my way.

I'm not naive. I understand what's happened. Some part

of me can't blame them. After what I've done— it's hard to forgive myself too. I'll probably never fully reconcile with those decisions but I have to live with my choices just like every other being. That's why I like cubs—they don't judge you and they don't care who you were. They just know who you are right now. I don't get very far before three of my cubs come rushing up to me. They're all panting and motioning towards the nearby forest.

My ears flat, "What's wrong?"

Finally one catches their breath, "It's Betavon!"

I let out a sigh, "Alright, let's go see what he's done *now*."

The cubs dash ahead of me as we head towards the woods. I keep a steady pace behind them. We slow at the edge of the thicket. The rest of the class is hovering around the base of a rather large tree. I already know what the problem is. I sigh and slowly part the sea of cubs. I stare up into the leaves. Sure enough, on one of the higher branches, a young tiger cub is clinging to the wood. His eyes are clenched shut and his tail is twisted around the branch.

I call up, "Betavon, what have we talked about?"

"We're fine! Those cubs just had to be wet-cats."

I glance to the side of his branch and realize that not only is he stuck but two of his other classmates are clinging to branches partly obscured by the leaves.

One of the cubs from the tree, a raccoon calls down, "Sorry Ms. Brantum, help us!"

"Yes please!" the other calls while Betavon stubbornly stays silent.

The cubs at my feet seem flustered. They're all murmuring and trying to figure out what to do.

"We told him not to do it."

"He just had to prove himself."

"I'm scared."

I let out another breath. Sliding my bag down to the ground, I urge the other cubs to back up. They clear a wide space. I wave my paw and a green glow starts forming, "A Knight of Jatali is brave, strong, and true. Let these vine help my kin."

I spread my paws wide. Green and purple vines glistening like crystals emerge from the ground. Slowly a few large leaves form. Each vine reaches a cub and wraps gently around them. The other two come down easily, but the vine is having trouble coercing Betavon. A spark of fire flashes off his coat and the vine recedes.

He yowls, "I don't need anyone's help!"

Once I know the other two are safe, I tell the others to stay put. I walk to the base of the tree. I need to hurry up because we are way behind schedule. Digging my claws into the bark, I quickly scamper up the tree. The branch he's on is too small for me to crawl onto, so I hold myself out a little from the tree. It's a good thing Kyltia and I get a lot of practice in these woods.

My paw extends to him, "When are you going to understand you can't do these things yet?"

He glares at me, "My Dad says I'll never know if I'm ready if I don't try."

I think about what he's said for only a moment, "There's also wisdom in knowing your limits and practicing at a lower level."

He seems ready to protest some more, but I've already wrapped an arm around him. Stubbornly his little claws clack against the bark. I compress him to my chest as I slide back down the tree. Some stubborn tears form on his cheeks. He seems ready to shove me away the minute we hit the ground—

But instead he hugs me. More hot tears down his cheeks.

I brush his hair in a comforting way, "I know it's hard now. But someday this will be easy for you. Just enjoy the now Betavon."

* * *

It takes a little bit of time but I finally get the cubs settled into my hut. It's finally time to teach them an important lesson— but it's one I've been dreading.

I stand at the front of the classroom. We have a broad wooden wall that I project magic onto. It's a clear white screen for the moment. I wave my paw and a picture of the continent of Ituvoh from long ago appears. It's back before we were divided. It can't be emphasized enough to the younger generation how far we've fallen. The unity we once shared.

Some of the cubs let out sounds of excitement and wonder. They start whispering and pointing.

I look them over, "Does anyone know what this place is?"

A chicken squawks, "Ituvoh!"

"But Ituvoh *when*?"

A deer raises her hoof, "Before the Great War."

A viper slithers out of her seat, eyes wide, "Back when the Prince sacrificed himself!" she pretends to be attacked with a dramatic show of "spurts of blood" coming from her. She flops onto the ground.

Another cub cries, "No! Not Azufae!"

The viper makes a homing kind of sound like a light glowing as she slowly rises again, "It is I, the future King of Ituvoh! Love wins!"

The cubs all giggle and start breaking out into our national anthem. I shake my head amused but knowing there's more to it than that.

The sacrifice that the Prince made all those years ago has allowed them to live for almost five hundred years now. They have been working through the magic to try and find a way for all of us to live together forever. A place where we don't have to worry about death anymore.

We've been at war with Zutaom for as long as I can remember. History books are filled with our conflicts and still our King and Prince are always leaps ahead of them.

But still there's a problem in our country— an almost unspoken agreement between us all— why hasn't the Promise been fulfilled yet? Has it not been ages since that moment? Do the shadows not grow everyday?

I wave my paw and they slowly fall silent, "You all know the Great War well enough. But there was a time before this, a war even more tragic— do any of you know it?"

The cubs are silent for a moment. Some of them look to each other for answers.

Betavon hops up, his ears twitching, "Is it that one war with the leg lizards?"

The other cubs giggle and the viper seems offended.

I wave for them to settle, "Yes, it was called the War of the Achitions. And it was how the first shadow was born."

An owl snorts at this, "My Dad says there's isn't any such thing as a shadow. Just beings with bad attitudes."

"If only it could be true."

A sand cat half-growls, "It's more than that. My Uncle lives in Sekulan. He sees shadows outside his window all the time."

The owl hops up, flapping his wings, "You're uncle is probably *crazy*!"

The viper smugly adds, "There's no such thing as a shadow. At least not anymore— Deleon would know if there was. We uphold the law after all."

I fold my paws and give them a moment to work it out.

A unicorn finally speaks, her voice quiet as she tugs on her hair, "My cousin lives in Mutamay and she knows a guard captain there. They're always trying to protect the border from Esakivh's shadow problem."

The other three look ready to wind up further. I wave for them to calm, and they find their seats again.

"You've all made valid points." I narrow my gaze at the owl, "Except for you Pethus. We don't call other beings crazy."

He shrinks slightly.

"In fact, in a way you all are right. Shadows do exist. Some countries have more shadows than others. And some beings don't believe in shadows at all. But they are very *real* my dears."

All of the cubs' eyes seem to get wide at once. Another hushed flurry of conversation fills the room.

Pethus says, "That means beings are *really* getting turned into shadows?"

He starts to shake and some of his feathers litter the ground.

I sigh and realize that some parents may have told their cubs they don't exist because they think they're protecting them. But that couldn't be further from the truth. You can't fight what you don't know. And the beings that slowly turn into shadows, are beings who don't understand the Code of Jatali.

And beings who chose to partner with a shadow—

I will never understand how they let it get so far.

Giving up parts of who you are to gain temporary power? Or momentary prestige? That sounds like an empty deal to me. Of course, I've wrestled with my own shadows in the past— everyone has— but those shadows were never a part of me. I had no idea they were stalking me until it was almost too late— all because I didn't understand the Code. The Prince saved me at the last moment. I've been forever grateful since.

And those who become shadows, their fate is not so pretty. They may be able to live as shadow for a time but they suffer every minute of it. Constantly craving energy and eating other beings to stay alive. The beings who invite a shadow to live inside of them may be "fine" for a long time, but sooner or later the price is paid with their whole soul. The fully formed shadows that are caught are condemned to what we call the Abyss of Garaev. It's the ocean to the east of Zutaom. The Abyss is a terrible place of torment. Surrounded by shadows and a dark place where every pain imaginable invades a being's soul.

There is no rest in the Abyss.

The sand cat hits his desk and the others startle. He stands up on his chair, "But see that's why we moved to Jatali. The King protects us here. No shadows can ever breach our borders!!"

The classroom seems to be placated with that notion.

They start to sing songs praising the Kingdom of Jatali.

I sigh because I hate crushing their enthusiasm. There was a time I believed such a thing.

My brows tilt, "Cubs, don't be afraid. It's true a shadow hasn't been sighted in our land in some time, but that doesn't mean it can't happen— again."

They all seem to echo 'Again?'.

"Long ago, before the War of the Achitions was started..."

Back when we were whole, long before the Prince was born, a neighboring continent sent a ship full of their kind to visit. They called themselves Achitions. They were upright walking, lizard-like beings. These newcomers had arms and legs along with wings. Sometimes they had wings for arms. They aren't like our beings the Delie of Deleon which only have arms on the upper half of their body and a snake tail for the rest.

Their leader was a green Achition named Senteia Rakous. He was very wise and happy to have met us. He and Elin-rah became friends and there was a peaceful time between us all. We shared technology, crafts and established a trade route. We even shared how our magic works with each other.

They had a different kind of magic that came from their breath and their wings. But the magic they had, you were born with one kind. Senteia was amazed at our ability to choose the power we wanted to have. A magic based on will and emotion.

Senteia pleaded that his people might learn this skill. They wished to acquire it to aid in their current war with the Cekantus. These were the scaled titanic beings of the southern oceans. Giant water creatures with many tails, and leather skin. Too many fins to count and holes in every side that allows the water to shift through them. It's as if they become one with the ocean. Lightning fast and silent.

Elin-rah considered what they were asking but wasn't sure it was even possible to share even if we had wanted to. That the energy of this continent seemed to be one with the beings born here. Senteia claimed he understood. That he would continue their friendship in the hopes that a way could be found.

Even though we freely shared with the Achitions, there was a part of the King's study that no one can go. Its locked and sealed with a strong magic. Senteia worked day and night to learn how to open it. And once he did, he buried himself in learning everything he could. He learned a lot of magic that no being was supposed to have. Magic from other lands.

He stole this different magic and used it for his own selfish purposes. What Senteia didn't understand is that the magic that had been hidden away has a dark twist. It wasn't a magic that comes from Jatali but from something else.

It seems like any other magic, but to use it fully, you have to sacrifice more and more of who you are until your *soul is depleted...*

The sand cat seems too excited to yell, "*Osekou! Shadow Magic.*"

The unicorn covers her mouth. Pethus and the viper stare at him. The rest of the class seems unsure what to do with that information.

Betavon's brows are set deep, "Then that means— the Drake— he brought that magic *here*?"

The viper half-hisses, "Weren't you listening? He stole it from the King."

Betavon sticks his tongue out at her.

She twists to glare at me, "Why would the King have such a magic and hide it away? Why not destroy it?"

I give her a sympathetic look, "Sometimes it's hard to understand why our Rulers do what they do. But they always have our best interests at heart. We must always cling to that..."

It turns out that they had already won the war with the Cekantus species. That we were just next on their conquest list. A ploy used by their leader— befriend and then betray after all the knowledge had been exhausted from that continent. All the knowledge that can never be gained by books.

Enraged at their betrayal, Elin-rah sought to protect his beings the way he knew best. His knowledge of the ancient magic knew no bounds. The Achitions that tried to make war with us— most were destroyed in the battle. Those that fled were allowed to leave.

But those that stood with Senteia, refused to give up. Even some of our own beings from various countries believed him. They felt lied to and betrayed that the King would keep something from the rest of us. They didn't understand he had done so to protect us.

They didn't understand that those who use that magic would pay dearly for it. They too only saw power and greed and not all of the destruction a shadow brings. The birth of the first shadow was Senteia. He became so corrupted we now call him the Drake. His followers fell soon after. A whole army of shadows.

Elin-rah sealed the Drake and all of his followers into the Abyss. The sun wouldn't rise for three whole days after that. The King was so distraught he hid himself away for weeks. The fear of what might have been. Since that day visitors from other lands are rare. Some say it's because they heard the rumors of the conflict and they find our King too scary to approach. Others claim the King used his magic to make a barrier around Ituvoh's boundaries.

But whatever the case, there are only a few Achitions left in our land. Isolated and preferring to hide away in the caves and swamps. Or maybe there were some stray Cekantus that reclaimed the land of the Achitions while their ruler was away giving them nowhere else to live.

Who could say really?

Even though there was peace for a long time after that, the fighting between the beings started to rise. The peace talks futile. The Drake may have been sealed away, but the damage was done. The words he'd said had stirred up division. He had infected the land with his shadows. Some beings had believed the lie that the King was keeping important things from us.

And that lie grew and grew. More shadows started to grow where they hadn't before.

So many were convinced of that lie that they started to form their own nations. Many of the same species agreed with each other and borders started to form. Some of them still followed the rule of Jatali as the High Kingdom while others did not. Soon these new nations chose their own rulers and the Great War began. It ended with the Prince's sacrifice. Although it granted a temporary peace, there were still more shadows to defeat.

The division between the nations grew ever more since that point. And with every passing year, the seal on the Abyss has weakened allowing more shadows to come out. Weaker ones slipping through the cracks. It wasn't long after the Great War that Zutaom made it's new declaration. They would never yield. They were a free nation.

The King yielded to their wishes until they started to encourage the shadows— actively inviting them in and using their power for every horror imaginable. The King could not let such a thing stand. We've been at war with them ever since. Their rulers have formed coordinated attacks against Jatali and all we stand for...

The cubs seem spellbound. Their little eyes focused on the screen before them. It seems many of them had never been told this part of our history. To them, the Drake is just a bedtime story to make little cubs behave.

I say, "So on that note, everyone lets go over the Code of Jatali together."

The cubs start rolling their eyes. Some stand up in a begrudging manner. Others half-lean on their desks.

"I know it's boring, but it might save you one day."

Honor the Ruler of Jatali above all.

Help every being that you can, no matter the cost.

Treat every being like family even when they are your enemy.

Honor the family you're born into, and also treat the community likewise.

Do not steal, for all trinkets serve to bring life to another.

Do not murder, for all life has value.

Beware, Jealousy will make your heart and soul rot.

I clasp my paws together, "Very good everyone! Now can anyone tell me which countries are our allies?"

A rabbit raises her paw high before blurting it out

anyway, "Rusim— my home country— Lueon, Belaphrium, and Deleon!"

The unicorn lets out a chuff, "You forgot Mutamay."

"Oh yeah, cause they're far away from us." She rubs her ears in embarrassment, "I forget about them."

I say, "Okay then, and those who are against us?"

I can tell this is a little harder for them. Some of them seem to know the answer but are afraid to make their classmates upset if they hail from that country.

"It's okay everyone. The countries that are against Jatali aren't a reflection of everyone who lives there. Many beings are in the countries they were born into because they are trapped by Zutaom's forces. Or they don't think there's a problem with the country they're in. We can't judge any being by the country they come from— always remember that. Light and dark can come from anywhere."

The viper scoffs at this and puffs out her chest, "That will *never* happen to Deleon. Without the courts, there would be criminals everywhere!"

The rabbit sits up taller, "Well, my country supplies all the medicine to the Kingdom. Without us, you'd all be sick in the streets."

I wave for them to settle again, "Cubs, we all have our *roles* to play in this Kingdom. And they are **all** important."

I can tell the tensions are starting to raise in the classroom. Everyone there is starting to think about their home country as the best. Seeing only the differences as their ancestors did. It will take more time for them to fully understand.

"Alright, let's quit focusing on how we're different. We **all** want what's best for Ituvoh. And we all love each other here in Jatali. Let's focus on that as we head outside for play time."

They all seem to forget the quarrel from before and dash out the door. I shake my head and let them all pass ahead of me.

The unicorn pauses a moment, her hooves tugging her hair into her face, "Ms. B-brantum—"

I kneel down next to her, "It's alright, Av-thianus. Ask me anything."

She parts her hair, eyes glossy, "Do you think my cousin will be okay in Mutamay?"

"Of course. The King has sent extra guards there too you know? Knights of Jatali in glowing armor to help them uphold the Magic there."

She seems brighter at this. A small smile forming on her snout.

"Run along and play. We'll talk more about it after playtime."

I stand and watch her go.

It's true all of the countries are different. And the countries on the Eastern continent all have different roles in relation to Zutaom too.

Sekulan became their fast ally since they are next to each other on the map.

Guth has great power and strong leaders. But they too have allowed themselves to be dragged into this conflict. They could fight back but chose to actively help our enemies because it was easier.

Nidah hates the Knights. We're never allowed to go there. Not that you'd want to—it's a raging Savannah and a lot of its territory has been eaten up by what's called the Endless Burning Desert. A place with no water and no mercy.

Ikouvan likes to do things their own way. They don't follow the teachings of Jatali anymore. They think what they're doing is *close enough* but they couldn't be more wrong.

Esakivh as a strong producer of our food. They are one of the nations that work tirelessly to keep the beings of all nations fed. But since Zutaom started their assault, they quickly caused a choke hold on the food supply they provided. The beings of Esakivh are so dedicated to working on their farms, they never took the time to build a military.

They haven't been bothered to worry about if their food stores are helping fund the enemy. They've allowed the occupation with little complaint. Any suggestions of freeing Esakivh from occupation have been met with scorn from their rulers, so we've stayed away from there too.

Mutamay is one of our true allies. The unicorn leader there may be young and inexperienced but she always relies on us for strength. She's done her best to instill the teachings that will keep our continent from going completely dark. They have fortified their borders from the other countries in hopes of keeping the flame alive.

But it's hard to be the only light in a pit of darkness.

The destruction of our world has been slowly caused by our own actions and sadly I've been guilty of this too. A debt, if you will, that I want to repay more than anything.

That new purpose I will have to fulfill—

I was told to wait.

I wonder— when will that time come?

What could Prince Azufae-yoh could possibly need me for?

* * *

It's the end of another long day at the Rapsuk school. After a late dinner with Kyltia, we head out to the woods like we usually do. We're perched on top of one of the higher trees. The two of us stare out at the horizon. If I squint hard enough, I can almost see the faint outline of Luthura castle from here.

Kyltia stretches before leaning back, "So, how's the magic coming?"

"Fine. I told you I had to use Patience to get those cubs out of the trees today."

"No, I mean you're other magic. You know, the Courage based one."

"Oh, that." I stare down at my paws, "Well, I get it mostly but it's the last, most powerful part that I don't get. It's like I can't have the right feelings."

She shrugs, "I guess that's why it's the hardest. I'm sure you'll get it soon enough."

My paw extends to Betavon, "When are you going to understand you can't do these things yet?"

He glares at me, "My Dad says I'll never know if I'm ready if I don't try."

I stare out at the navy sky. The green stars twinkle brightly.

"Yeah, let's hope so."

CHAPTER FIVE

Shadows

CATCHATHURA

I thought the ship would never hit the shore. Those slimy furballs took their time. That's the last time I use a bunch of pirates for my means. It was about a day's walk from the port of Feyvious to Luthura Castle. I would've taken another form of transportation but I didn't want to risk any further delay by unreliable drivers. It's not like we're trying to win this war or anything.

My partner should be around the castle grounds

somewhere. I'm supposed to meet at our rendezvous point after we've completed our missions. If everything goes right, she should be done with her mission the moment I start mine. I'm in and out. Target down and Luthura has one less pain in the neck running around. Then we jump the next ship back to Zutaom. It's simple and there's a beauty in that.

The hill I'm perched on gives me a great view of the Southern wall of Luthura Castle. I start pushing off my usual clothes to reveal my counterfeit Knight of Jatali garb underneath. I glance over the handiwork. It took a few specialists to replicate such a convincing copy. It's a dark brown leather garb with red buttons with red, and yellow flame markings on the arms. They even made a dark belt with a gem centered in it just like the *best* Knights wear. Yuck.

Sure we could've probably nabbed a few but it gets sticky trying to steal from a Knight. Plus Jatali has this pesky rule of the garb matching the user. Trying to hunt down a fire-looking one— that also fits me— good luck.

I take another moment to pull out a jar from my pocket. I unscrew the lid and start rubbing the makeup onto all of my fur. It's a coating made of sparkling mushrooms from the Eastern Glades in Zutaom. It's not perfect but a pretty convincing fur sparkle for any quick glance a being might give me. Sure I won't be able to hide my energy signature, but most of them are so rock brained they can't even sense a thing like that. My target is the only one who might sniff me out before I strike.

But by then I'll make sure it's too late.

* * *

I've been flawless. My steps completely silent. It wasn't hard at all to slide into the inner castle wall and follow the courtyard hall all the way down. As expected the soldiers may pass a stray look over me, but still can't be bothered to question me. I keep my gait casual as I inch closer and closer to my target. I can see his glimmering golden pelt from where I'm standing. I walk into an offshoot from the main path. I lean against a wall trying to look casual. I need a moment to steady my breath and assess the best way to attack.

You see the unfortunate thing about Luthura, is it's pretty good about keeping shadows out. That includes shadow powers. The good thing for me is that my shadow is one of the strongest ones around. But still my timing will have to be perfect. I only get one shot at this. I clench my fist and focus hard on the target ahead of me. He's surrounded by soldiers and he's scolding them about something.

I'm so focused I barely notice the crack and chatter behind me. SPLASH! A giant blast of water drenches me. Sharply I turn to growl at the rock-brains who doused me in water. The two soldiers start apologizing— oblivious for a moment— then one realizes I'm not one of them—

This is bad—

I strike to try and silence them— but my foot slips. The water forces me forwards just between them. I scramble to catch my footing but it's too late— CLANK. CLANK.

My world is spinning and I hit the ground.

It wasn't supposed to happen this way.

* * *

"You're dead."

I squint up at an armed solider. His sword right at my throat.

"Or you would be if I had *my* way."

I spit, "Just do it. *Coward.*"

He seems as though he might lunge for me but another guard holds him back. They share a look.

"Fantias, think of what Altikua *will say.*"

He scoffs, tail lashing, "That old wolf is scared of his own *shadow* let alone this being— He's going to be so impressed we put him away on our own."

I can't believe this! Water of all things. I slipped and then I'm caught by these two fluffballs. Can I fail any harder?

The other solider still seems unsure and holds me tighter, "I hope we can do this."

"Come on, just think of the promotion we'll get after this."

"We really should've told him directly—"

"The others saw what happened. He'll find out soon enough—"

"But didn't the King say to bring this one directly to him?"

"He's going to the dungeon, what's he gonna do?"

I glance between them, *That name...I know of Altikua well...*

They keep dragging me down the cold cobblestone dungeon hall. Altikua Talous the Elite Commander of the Knights of Jatali. He's so pure and righteous— even the Prince granted him the title, Altikua *the Just*.

Makes me want to vomit.

The first guard looks me over again, "Why are you so ready to kill him? Shouldn't he get a trial first?"

Fantias narrows his gaze, "Normally I'd agree, but this is Tatchathura Devantum. *The Shadow Fox of Zutaom.*"

The other guard looks perturbed, "What?! This is —
him!?"

He looks like he might crumble in the hallway. His arms shaking and weapon trembling at his hilt, "Oh this was a **bad** idea! What if he conjures a shadow? Then what?"

"We're on castle grounds. He can't do that. Here *monster*," Fantias slings me into the metal cage, "I saved a spot for you."

My back hits the mossy stone wall but I barely feel it. This place is cozy compared to where I'm from. The door screeches shut and Fantias paws shake as he locks the door. His companion tries to hold it together but there's a twist in his tail as it wraps around his feet.

I slink to my feet. My snout pressed through the gate, "You're just afraid of what *I would* do to you—"

"You can't do *anything* in this castle." Fantias turns. A sneer on his lips, "You had all that time in the hallway."

It's true. I did have time. I reveal nothing as I press into the metal, "Then why are you're being such a *coward?*"

Fantias growls and takes a step towards me.

His companion pushes against his chest, "He's just trying to bait you. He's already locked up. Let's just go upstairs—"

"You're *right*." An almost self-righteous smirk plays on his lips, "There's nothing he can do."

I glare at my captors through the bars. I can feel his energy. That darkness we all share.

The guard lunges his sword through the bars and it grazes my shoulder.

A normal being would have winced— but I hold steady.

I level my sharp gaze with him, "You have *no idea* what I can do. And you just placed me in the darkest place you have."

"So ***what?***" He digs his sword into my shoulder. Blood spurts out. Red flecks against my dark leather jacket.

The other guard's voice is a shrill whisper, "***What*** are you doing?"

I summon the energy I have. A wispy, dark cloud ebbs from my shoulder. It grows tendrils and wraps around the sword. It crushes the metal before flashing against his neck. His eyes flare wide as he realizes his mistake.

For him to give into his Rage— Vanity— His twisted sense of Justice— which is really just *Vengeance* wrapped in a bow. All negative emotions. All things that go against the teachings of Jatali.

And just enough gas to light my fire.

The other guard drops his sword and crashes out the archway. His cries will meet deaf ears.

I *already know* there isn't anyone else in the hallway.

No one else nearby.

And he knows it too.

And after I break this guard apart, I'll be a free bird again.

But just as I was about to crush him completely— the light draining from his eyes— a powerful force comes careening down the hallway.

A being too strong. I have no doubts *who* it is. My shadow weakens and curls backwards at the force. Fantias crumples to the ground winded and unconscious.

As soon as Altikua steps into the room, all of the shadows fade. This golden furred wolf has destroyed all the darkness. He's glowing like a comet that's crashed and ruined the party.

It's not like that pompous guard didn't have it coming to him. Did they expect me to just *accept* punishment? To just go into a cell without a fight?

Altikua stares me down.

He looks so disgusted in me.

What terrible sight.

I can't imagine being so full of myself— like he's never done a thing wrong in his life.

I know he has.

The underworld has plenty of rumors on his perfect golden fleece.

"Hey Blondie, *just* in time." I click my teeth, "That guy is sleeping on the job."

Altikua snaps around to see Fantias on the ground and turns a sharp eye on the other, "*What* happened? Why didn't you bring him directly to *me*?"

The guard cowers, "We wanted to put him in the cell so you'd be impressed with us—"

"Try *again*." He half growls, "What else?"

The solider is shaking in his boots, "The prisoner kept taunting Fantias. I told Fantias to stop but he wouldn't listen."

I rotate my arm with a smirk growing, "Also, I think I did something to my shoulder—"

"Silence." Altikua's voice is like a beacon.

His light is so powerful my knees weaken. I curse internally and try to play it off. What a terrible predicament

I'm in.

This wasn't what was *supposed* to happen.

I don't make stupid mistakes anymore. I'm not a cub.

"What's done is done." Altikua sighs, "Tell the others to come down here. We'll keep him in line one way or *another* at least until I confer with the Prince again."

I slowly fade to the back wall. I've got a clue as to what he might do. And I'm definitely not going to like it. Altikua stands watch.

The one guard scoops Fantias off of the floor to drag him out the archway. I stare at them as they leave. Their coats are all so shiny and bright. The guards aren't as bright as Altikua, but still glossy enough for me to call them *Rainbow Brights*.

In fact, that's pretty much what we Zutaomese call all Jatalians— Rainbow Brights because their coats are just *so perfect*. Their rulers are *so perfect*. Everything is just so fuzzy and *wonderful* in Jatali.

Give me a break.

* * *

You see that's the thing about Jatali. Full of light and love. Frilly happy stuff. It's a place where shadows have a hard time growing. Wrong soil and all that.

However there's weakness there. Plenty of bones to pick like the guard from before. Their faith was weak in the teachings they proclaim to protect. It was easy to pick him off.

Try to anyway. I've been told he's in the Med Bay recovering.

But get a room full of weak Rainbow Brights together and well— let's just say I'll need a scene change. Their combined energy will keep my shadow extinguished.

Tayaeme...I curse mentally, *I overplayed my paw*... I almost beat my head against the wall, *How did he get to Altikua so fast? Was Altikua already on his way? That's not an energy signature you can just ignore...*

A few of the guards lean against the metal bars. They're staring at me with their little swords raised and whispering like I can't flipping hear them. *Hello,* I'm a fox, remember? I have *great* hearing.

I throw a glare in their direction and they scatter like the bugs they are. As I harden my look, I notice that there are more than foxes or wolves there. Oxen, tigers, hawks, and even a few little bunnies.

Jatali really is a melting pot after all..

I feel like I've been put in a jar.

I wonder if my partner Lu-kan finished her job— or is she stuck in a cell like me?

CHAPTER SIX
The Calling

ɪnɒessah

It's been a long morning at school and I'm more than ready for the cubs' play time. There's only so many interruptions you can take before it's time to let everybody burn that energy off.

I lead my students outside. They barely make it to the edge of the clearing before they all scatter. It's a good place for the young ones because there's plenty of trees and bushes to hide in. There's even a lake for them all to get their exercise in. I find a log to sit on. Usually there are a few other teachers who bring their students here around this time but maybe I'm a little bit early today.

I put my paws on the coarse wood. Leaning back slightly, I look up at the sky. It's a clear lilac blue today. Plenty of misty clouds block some of the bright sunshine. I start to dream about the future.

Before I can get too deep, a being appears through the thicket. A female cheetah approaches me. She's decked out in a tight leather jacket coat. A golden and black belt around her waist with a blue gem in the middle. She has square pattern markings on the jacket in gold and green. There is a hammer axe attached to her back.

A Knight of Jatali... what is she doing out here? Surely there's no danger? I glance around, shifting my ears to try and see if there's any other sounds that I'm missing. But all I hear are the sounds of the cubs' raucous laughter.

The cheetah bows her head slightly to me, "Are you Indessah-yah Brantum?"

"Indessah is fine. What brings you to my neck of the woods?" my lips curl up into a chuckle.

There is no joy on her face. In fact, she looks solemn.

My ears flatten. Maybe I'm jumping to conclusions too fast— but most Jatalians are full of light and love and happiness. It's very *rare* to find someone who's too upset. She looks like the whole world is ending right now.

"I was told to escort you to Luthura Castle. The Prince

said it's time for you to fulfill your obligations to the Kingdom."

I'm frozen a moment.

She wrings paws together, "I'm sorry to have to be the one to bring you this news— I know how much you love being a teacher here, but the Prince said it was *urgent*."

It's like the world is slowly going silent. Time to fulfill my obligations?

"I've already informed the other teachers. Someone will be here to take over for your class. You're going to have to come *right* away. So pack your bag and I will meet you at the gate."

She watches me curiously.

As my brain turns over the new information— I'm reminded of a moment when I first came to this place—

When he calls me again, I'll be ready this time...

I spring to life, my paws on her shoulders, "What are you talking about? This is great! I'm finally gonna get to fulfill *my purpose*."

She looks at me with a raised brow, "Haven't you been fulfilling your purpose *here*?"

"Yes, and it's important— but this is the other **most** important thing!" I finally let go of her and turn towards my class, "Everyone! Come here for a moment."

It takes a long moment for all of the cubs to rejoin us. They look up at me in confusion. Some of them are pushing each other. I can hear some whispering towards the back. I look over each of their tiny faces.

My chest tightens. I'm going to miss them all so much. So much I could say to them all but a few stand out—

I say, "Pethus, never stop seeking the truth. Remember to ask the right questions."

Pethus ruffles his feathers and puffs up proudly, "Yes, of course!"

"Av-thianus, the best thing you can do for your cousin is to believe that the Magic of Jatali will win this battle."

She nods meekly as her classmates try to encourage her too.

I look to the viper, "Remember just because a country represents something doesn't mean they don't have issues. It also doesn't mean their kind are infallible."

She seems annoyed at being singled out. I lean in closer to crouch before her, "I say this because I love you. Pride is a terrible shadow you don't want around."

She covers her mouth as though realizing her mistake from the other day.

I glance at the rabbit, "That goes for you as well."

All the cubs seem to understand what I'm saying.

One of the cubs says, "We won't do it anymore. Jatali is one nation and one being!"

For as excited as I am, I know this mission won't be easy. But I've changed a lot since I first came here and I know that if the Prince is calling me now, he knows all those changes are exactly what he needs.

I say, "I have to go away and serve the Kingdom at the castle now to finish my training to be a Knight." There is an uproar from the students before I can finish what I'm saying, "I love you all and I'm going to miss you so much! So please *promise* me when you get a new teacher you don't drive them *crazy*."

Most of the cubs grumble at the notion. There are pouts on many of their faces and a few are even crying. I kneel on the ground and motion them all closer. Slowly a group hug forms.

Doubt claws at the back of my throat.

What if I can't do this?

Betavon growls above the others, "Enough crying! You're going to be **warriors** ain't ya!?"

His stubby paws climb onto the log to stand above us, "And you Ms. Brantum— when the Prince calls you— it's time to go to battle! RAWR!"

He swishes a stick around with reckless abandon. The other cubs giggle and join in grabbing sticks and leaves to fight the battle with each other.

"*Betavon*." I say sternly with an undertone of affection.

His ears flatten and he bounds down from his post to my side.

I put a gentle paw on his shoulder, "There's only *some*

beings that can handle your level of energy, please keep that in mind."

His whiskers twitch in amusement before he's absorbed by the other cubs' antics. They're all caught in their new play battle, oblivious to my internal struggle. There's a bittersweet feeling in my gut. He'll grow up to be a resourceful and brave warrior one day. In fact, they all will.

* * *

The castle isn't that far from the school but we're taking what we call a Blazewagon. These machines are magical. All you have to do is contribute some fire magic to the wispy interior. Then find the location that you would like to go. The only drawback to them is they have to stay near the road to use automatic mode.

Most of the common locations are already programmed into it, so all we have to do is select Luthura Castle. There is also an override seal on the side of the wagon in case you have to drive it manually. The cheetah and I talk a little bit on the drive over but I'm too distracted by the window to have a meaningful conversation.

For as excited as I am, there is still that feeling at the back of my mind.

That doubt that's clawing at my brain trying to overwhelm me—

To tell me I'm not good enough—

It's a mistake all over again.

That all I'm going to do is bring everyone down and ruin any chance we have of *finally* bringing the peace we all crave to the Kingdom.

* * *

After a little while, the glimmering city of Luthura comes into view. I push my face against the window. There are wide, long walls that enclose our capital city. Towers loom every few hundred feet with guards at their posts. A giant metal gate comes into view. At our approach, it slowly raises to allow us in. My tail is swishing so fast as I gaze out at the city. It's been so long since I've been here and it's even more beautiful than I remember.

The cheetah taps my shoulder, "Want a real view?"

I turn to look at her. She motions to the ceiling.

I practically jump out of my fur. The two of us stand in the center and a platform pushes up about halfway out of the wagon. My ears immersed in the sights and sounds of the bustling city. Beings walk up and down the sidewalks as more wagons and creatures with beings on their backs speed down the roadways. There's thick bronze cobblestones for the road. Smooth, paved ruby colored stones for the sidewalk. Along the sides of the roads is every kind of building and shop you could imagine.

One of the best things about Luthura is that most beings own their own shop. The things bought and traded are almost exclusively with individuals. There are only a few major businesses like the Fireheart Papers and Tanelle's

Grocers.

The wagon finally rolls up to the main gate of the castle. I stare up at the giant castle for a moment. The walls are sweeping with towers on every corner. Each tower has a sparkling golden peak with sloping rooftops. The walls have pathways on top with soldiers calmly patrolling back and forth. Behind those walls are more towers. The one on the left corner reaches far higher than the others. It's the Prince's study.

My heart clenches for a moment. I'm back in the city. We talked a few times through a Soul Link. This is basically a way we communicate with other beings using our magic. It's just like the projector I use in class only you can see the other being on the screen. You have to have a connection to a being before you can call them this way. But I haven't seen him in the fur since he brought me to the school.

The platform slowly lowers and the Knight nudges me to attention. I shake my head free. I can't get distracted. The Knight and I step off the wagon and into the main archway of the castle. It's dark for a moment as we pass under the stones. Then we walk back into the light. The main courtyard is before us. Many soldiers are training here. There are instructors calling out drills to each regiment. It's been a long time since Basic for me. I stretch slightly and feel a kink in my back. The Knight looks at me in confusion. I laugh awkwardly trying to straighten my back again. I'm sure I'll get back into the swing of things.

There are many long covered paths that surround the

courtyard on each side. Each path has bronze stone column pillars that turn into decorative stone archways on each side. There are pairs of soldiers walking the paths. Each group seems absorbed in their missions. My Knight starts heading down one of the paths. I follow her realizing we are heading towards one of the northern courtyards. Most likely the one the Prince spends the most time in. That sharp feeling of dread clutches my gut as we walk ever closer to the courtyard.

She stops short of an archway. She peers inside for a moment tail twitching before motioning me onwards.

Stiffly, I walk to the small archway.

"Best of luck. Maybe we'll get to work together." She heads away from me back towards the main courtyard.

"Yeah, maybe. Thank you for getting me here." I glance at her a moment before focusing on the task ahead.

With a deep breath, I push myself through the archway. It's quiet for a moment until faint talking tickles my ears.

It seems as though we are in a side courtyard behind a tower. There are bushes filled with fire heart flowers getting ready to bloom. Some other flowers scattered throughout in almost every color you could imagine. The vines for the plants even seem to be holding up the stone to the wall. Everything here is growing in perfect harmony.

I walk slowly and try to tame my inner struggle, *The Prince called me here, didn't he? Nothing is wrong. I can do whatever he has planned for me...*

As I pass a tall topiary, the stone benches come into view. Perched atop one is Prince Azufae-yoh. A perfect white lion. His brilliant golden mane shimmers more brightly than the walls of this place. He's speaking warmly to a golden wolf that's standing off to one side. I recognize that wolf as Altikua. It's been a long time since I've seen my Brother-in-arms too. He's always had a protective streak over me. We bonded over my stubborn nature whenever I was here for Basic training. I always figured some of it was because he felt sorry for me. After what had happened—

"Indessah!" The Prince calls, his smile warm as ever, "There you are. So great to see you."

My slow steps screech to a halt. It's like I'm on display.

He bounds off the bench and rushes towards me. He scoops me into a hug. My paws awkwardly hug him back. My face is flush. I wasn't expecting such a warm welcome.

He settles me back on the ground, eyes full of a family kind of love, "My cub, how I've missed you. I would've come myself but—"

"It's okay, Sire. I understand."

"I also apologize for not having visited the school. I'm sure you've done brilliantly though?" His gaze is leading.

He already knows.

He's just giving me the opportunity to talk about it. My cheeks burn. I knew he was there for me to talk to—

I never took the opportunity.

I didn't want to bother him even though I should know better than that.

Altikua comes to my other side, he places a strong paw on my shoulder, "How have you been Indy? Ready to knock back some shadows?"

My face falls a little, "Oh right. Is that why you've called?"

They have courtyards full of soldiers and I know there are even more recruits ready to deploy at a moment's notice from my homeland of Belaphrium. So why exactly call me?

Prince Azufae-yoh and Altikua share a glance with each other. The Prince takes a step towards me again, "I want to remind you first that everything in the past is forgiven."

I nod (even though I don't fully believe it), "But still, I have to pay my debt to the Kingdom."

He shakes his head 'no', "I paid that debt for you already. Remember?"

"Right. Then why me Sire?"

He narrows his gaze, "The Magic of Jatali gave me a vision."

I cover my mouth trying to hold in my gasp.

Altikua leans over me, "You see we have a *certain* prisoner in our holding cell."

The Prince says, "I need you to understand that whatever I ask of you, you can say no. You're under no obligation. However, if you can bear a week with this prisoner, it would be enough to change his wretched heart."

"Another thing to consider is he might remind you of the past too much. He's already given my soldiers quite the issue."

I glance at them both. I can tell they are trying to give me an honest picture of what I might be signing up for. A normal being might have asked more questions or just declined outright. After all my debt has been paid. Why should I risk my neck? But I just don't work that way. I've never worked that way. Another reason my past haunts me — there was another being with a checkered past I thought I could change— but the joke ended up on me.

It ended in heartbreak and destruction.

I must be out of my mind.

I say, paws on my hips, "Sire, how could I say no to such a request? If the Magic told you something about me, then I need to listen."

He chuckles lightly, "Just like *that*? It won't be easy Indy."

"It's just a week. How hard could that be?" I ham up my performance because inside there's a little cub shaking in my heart—

But my duty, and responsibility is to the Kingdom that saved me from a grisly fate. Maybe now I can help another escape such a thing. Maybe.

Prince Azufae-yoh turns to pull something from his robe, "Hang on, I brought you another old friend." He pulls out a chrome colored sword out of a crimson colored scabbard. It has a standard black handle with a red octagon shaped pommel. My old sword. I'd used it during Basic and left it here because I didn't see the point in bringing it to the school. After all, I believed this life was behind me. I reach for the hilt and hold it outright. It's heavier than I remember. I try to think of the words I need to ignite its magic glow but my mind is still working on that. Slowly, I practice swinging it to and fro.

Prince Azufae-yoh seems amused, "Just let me know if there is anything else I can do to help you, Indy."

I nod slightly still absorbed in my sword swings.

Altikua sighs, "Master, forgive me, but are you sure she's ready?"

I bristle slightly. It's true he has every right to question when I'm clearly having the same internal conflict— but I don't need him bringing me down. Old worry wolf.

The Prince says, "Indy, would you be able to retrieve the prisoner and bring him to my Father's throne room?"

"Yes, of course."

Altikua's ears flatten, his voice quieter now— like I won't hear him, "Sire, maybe it's best if I take care of it—"

The Prince puts a paw up, "I understand your concerns old friend, but you shall be with her. I know the two of you will be fine."

I send the wolf a challenging look, "Come on Altikua, let's not leave him alone too long."

He rolls his eyes but is slightly amused by my tenacity. The Prince seems to wish us well as we depart. I start heading towards the dungeon without another glance in his direction. I'm going to prove myself. To everyone!

* * *

Altikua and I walk down the winding hallways towards the dungeon. It's pretty sparse down here as most of the criminals are rehabilitated upstairs or banished to the shadows forever.

Before we walk the last leg of our journey, my old friend stops me. There's a concerned glimmer in his eye.

I say, "I can do this—"

He raises a paw, "Don't *underestimate* this one—"

"I won't—"

"I'm serious. I'm not just saying this. He took out several of my guards this morning. Even when he was chained, he was able to conjure a shadow."

I stare at him wide-eyed a moment.

"You don't need me to tell you twice why that's *extremely* rare."

I stare down the hallway and my tail starts to twitch.

He sighs and brushes past me, "Better not linger."

I follow him with less determination this time. The muscles in my feet seem locked in place. Every step is like a stiff piece of wood dragging the ground. We reach a stone archway. I stare inside noticing all of our other soldiers within. I can smell their fear and I don't stay on that thought for long either.

The dark furred fox is reclining against the mossy cobblestone wall. I'd barely be able to see him at all if he didn't have those bright red markings on his ears and feet. The flash of his tail is still clear white so that's something right? He can't be all bad or he'd be a shadow for real already— right? His clear blue eyes catch mine. He knows I'm watching him. But he doesn't linger. His appearance reminds me of— him.

Of the one from my past that hurt me—

A shiver runs up my spine. My tail sweeps the ground.

Can I really do this?

Really?

CHAPTER SEVEN

Reading a Heart's Desire

TATCHATHURA

*Eight hours of these Rainbow Brights starting at me...
and not a brain in sight... my gaze drifts to the lone barred
window, I've got to get out of here...*

I let out a low growl and most of them tumble backwards.
Huddling together like the cubs they are. Pathetic. I shoot
them with a sharp gaze. My paws grip the rusted metal
bars. The grit cuts my paws but I don't care. My gaze
catches on a newcomer lingering in the hallway.

A stark purple fox with blonde hair and brown eyes. Her coat doesn't sparkle as much as the others. It seems darker somehow. Her eyes meet mine and I can't help but flash her a smirk before looking at the rest of the prey. This is what I've been waiting for? They call in a newbie to get me out of the cell? Just *how* dumb are these Jatalians?

More whispers float around the room about how scary I am, how dirty my coat is— my scars. And here I thought these fluffballs were *kindness incarnate*. The purple one finally starts parting the sea of nosy cubs. Their attention now drawn to her. They don't recognize her either. Nice.

She gives them all a sharp look, "And all of your coats are so *perfect*?"

The mass of fools slowly recedes. I hadn't noticed before but it's true, they all have what we call *Magic Markings*. You see the magic here marks our kind. Every time you go against the High Kingdom, another mark on your body.

Go against them too many times and your coat turns murky— like what's happening to me. And then the real fun part, you get to *become* a shadow. And not like the one in my arm. The kind of shadows a real monster is made of—

A bone crushing, soul tearing monster with no conscious that'll be condemned to the Abyss of Gareav when caught.

Another fun place.

It's actually outside my window back home.

At least what I've heard about the Prince being forgiving proves true. Every single one of them has plenty of marks and still he trusts them with swords. I glance over at her. A smirk plays on my lips as I keep my back to her. Her energy is strong like Altikua's but not quite so perfect. It's bright, but I can feel her shadows too. Those tiny little cracks— like bones ready to break.

I turn slightly to watch her out of the corner of my eye. There's something new there. Something I hadn't noticed before— she's carrying herself so regal. Even more pompous than Blondie.

I shoot her a hot look. My blue eyes absolutely venomous as they lock with hers—

But as our eyes meet, it's almost like meeting an opposite force. Like magnets I look away almost immediately.

Her brown eyes are so clear. So innocent. Like a babe lost in the woods.

What a dirty trick from someone so pure.

I keep my gaze on the wall, "Is that the *Queen* of the Rainbow Brights here to visit me? What an *honor*."

It's like tree bark on my tongue. Bitter.

"You know we only have one King and the Prince. But I admire your *enthusiasm* to flatter me."

Who is she? I twist slightly. There's mirth on her face. She's not intimidated by me in the least. But the room is so full of fear it may just be hard for me to tell.

She starts unlocking the door.

I lean on the bars, my snout pushed through the grate,

"You sure you want to do that Princess? I might be *dangerous.*"

Her ears twitch as she slips the chains around my wrists, "You're in chains now, any danger you pose will have to wait."

She shifts to kneel and place a weight on my tail. The kind of weight that latches into your fur and makes it *very* hard to shake.

Great.

I lean slightly to make things harder for her, "Didn't stop me before. What makes *you* so sure?"

Slowly I let myself sink to the ground. I'm obstructing her way.

She locks her gaze with mine, a fire there, "His soul was *weak.*"

"*Ouch!* Throwing your brethren under the cart? That's not very *nice.*"

She shifts sides. There's mirth in her gaze, "The truth hurts sometimes but it doesn't mean we shouldn't speak it."

She tightens the cuffs and tries to tug me up. I'm happily rooted to the ground. A smirk of my own.

"Besides," she says, "He'll get better as we all do. As you will."

"Awfully *confident* I see." but as I look her over for weak points, I can't see any. The cracks in the veneer of her coat have vanished. The others are shaking like leaves in the breeze. Even Altikua standing in the hallway can't ease their fears.

Every single one of them is afraid except for her. In that moment, she reminds me of Lu-kan—

I shake that thought away. Those two are *not* the same.

She has a sudden strength about her— a powerful glow as she lifts me stubbornly to stand. She must have been speaking some words of Jatali while I was distracted.

"There you go." she smiles up at me, "Let's go."

I snort and follow her leisurely. My tail flat to the ground as I purposefully drag down the pace. She glares back at me. I pretend I don't understand her while throwing a scowl at the others I pass.

The golden wolf looms over the archway, "What's taking so long?"

She says, "He's murkier than usual."

"Oh you noticed, did you?" there's an amused curl to his lips, "I'd expect nothing less from the Shadow Fox of Zutaom."

The purple one freezes mid step, "What! Th-his is Tatch-a— the one—"

I lean over her with a smirk, "Ah, so you have heard of me. I'm *charmed*, really."

She stumbles backwards as I walk closer to the wolf. Her chest is rising and falling like she's been shot.

"Prince Azufae-yoh called me to escort *Tatchathura Devantum?!*"

"*Indessah-yah*, please." Altikua grabs me by the scruff before pushing be down the hallway, "He's as harmless as a cub in the woods."

"Tayaeme!" I hear her curse behind him. A low growl on her lips, "That's not funny Talik! He is very dangerous. You didn't even warn me—"

He raises his paw, "I believe your words were 'I can do this.'."

She shakes her head still acting annoyed.

Altikua lets out another low chuckle while ushering me further along. If my predicament was different I'd probably be amused too. But now that I'm out of my cell again I can work on finding an escape plan.

I'll get out of this somehow.

* * *

Altikua and *Indessah-yah* walk me down the long corridor towards the Great Hall. There are many banners on the glossy stone walls. They have a banner for each of our countries. Even the countries that have gone against Jatali.

It's pathetic really—

To keep holding onto this ideal that we're all be unified one day. We're all too different. Only cubs believe in that fairy tale.

The banner for Rusim is first. The Land of the Reaching Forest. Nothing but a bunch of bunnies, ducklings, and other rodents. It has a rounded light purple flower with dark purple flame like tendrils. It's leaves are bright green with yellow and red stripes.

*Tash-nev Roch...A fireheart flower...*Absently I rub the mark on my forehead. That same flower is there in red and a subtle burning fills my gut.

It's supposed to be a symbol of loyalty to the Kingdom. It's a special flower to Jatali. A flower that at the end of its life literally burns up. And as it dies, it spreads its dumb seeds everywhere making even more of those flowers bloom. They say they grow even better because of its sacrifice.

The next banner that catches my eye is for Lueon. The Land of the Endless Waters. It's mostly turtles, and otters, things like that. I always thought that it was kind of a dumb name. They only have a small piece of land as most of their Kingdom is underwater. I've heard they've got a queen there now. A *dolphin.* Another brilliant choice by their brilliant Prince Azufae-yoh. On their banner there's a turtle shell in the shape of a shield flanked by many curly orange and pink Sak-tov flower— or weird lilies. They grow long vines from the ocean floors until they reach the surface. If you don't know where you're going, it's easy to get tangled in them. Many ships get wrecked on their vines.

Then there's Mutamay. The Land of the Unicorns. Another land with another *incompetent* ruler. The king and queen died not too long ago and Azufae let their young daughter take over— which normally is how a monarchy works but that's not always the rule in Ituvoh. Those who have aligned with the Kingdom have their rulers chosen by the Great King Elin-rah and as long as they fall in line they keep their Kingdom. But just because your parents ruled doesn't necessarily mean you're next in line to the throne. Elin and the Azufae can change their minds at any time.

Still. Most of that doesn't matter to the unicorns. They spend most of the time playing games and going to resorts. It's a wonder Zutaom hasn't eaten them alive yet— and then I'm reminded it's because Jatali has fortified their borders.

And then a banner I know very well. *Tried and true* Belaphrium. My birth land. It takes all of my strength to not scoff audibly. All it does is remind me of my past and what was taken from me. Sucking in a breath, I glare at the brown and orange tapestry. It has a black and blue wolf on a cliff face howling at our three moons; green, red and blue. The red one is broken. There's a myth in our land that it became that way in one of our past battles. That the Great King broke it to prove a point to the rebellious king in that area. It is said that the rebellious king yielded that day and that Belaphrium has been faithful to Jatali ever since.

There's also a picture of a castle tower. It represents the Cinnasuk Stronghold no doubt. The place where most of the High Kingdom's army is trained. Further proof of my being's oppression. That's why I had to get out of there and go somewhere I'm *appreciated*. Zutaom might not have the best beings to hang out with but everything I've worked for —everything I've done—has been rewarded.

I can't say the same for my home country or the High Kingdom.

It seems I've been staring too long.

Indessah watches me curiously. Her gaze following mine to the banners. She looks back at me with a small smirk on her lips, "The black wolf kind of looks *familiar* doesn't it? Even though you're a fox."

I snort, "I wouldn't be so sure about that. The being in this banner is a *coward*—"

She bristles, "Nulia-tah was a great warrior. She saved all of Cinnasuk because of her wit."

"She hid behind a stone wall while the **real** warriors fought."

"She used his enemy's weakness against them. By sending waves of warriors, and using the gryphons from Atayip to distract them—"

She sounds so excited and I can't stand it, "Don't you have *somewhere* to take me? I've heard the *Great* King doesn't like to wait."

She shoots me a sharp look, her tail sent thrashing again, "Come on then. We're almost there."

Altikua says nothing as he holds up the rear. I glare at the banners one last time before we enter the main hallway.

They're going to need more than bunnies and turtles to stop what's coming.

As we enter the main hallway, a few other guards take notice of us. Altikua nods to them and they start to follow behind us. It's evident the golden wolf doesn't trust me the closer we get to the King and the Prince.

And he would be right— usually.

Most of my compatriots would jump at a chance to be so close to either one of them— to try and strike them down in cold blood—

But most of them would be *idiots* because you see the thing about Azufae and Elin is—

Ever since the Prince sacrificed himself in the Great War, the two of them haven't been able to die. Any assassination attempt on them has always failed. They may get a mark or two but it heals so fast. And then that poor fool has done nothing but condemn himself to the shadows for *eternity*. There are two guards on either side of me. Indy towards the front and Altikua to my back. I noticed earlier there seems to be quite a lot of oil on their leather jackets. Stubbornly I lift my tail to try and wipe some off with my tail.

One of the guards glare at me, "Hey!"

I shrug as though I don't know what he means. If I can get enough oil on this device it might be enough to get it to slip off.

One of the guards starts whispering about my coat like I'm not even here. It's kind of *amusing*. Their whole creed is supposed to be about acceptance and unity or whatever.

One whispers, "Look at his coat. It's so *murky*."

The other says "And those *scars*— his ears— how is he *not* a shadow already?"

A wicked smirk plays on my lips. I tilt slightly so that I can look at them, "You know come to think of it— I'm starting to feel a little *weird* inside. Like this shadow in my arm," I raise my arms dramatically and stare at it like it's foreign, "It might just take over or something."

I swing my paw towards one of them— I wasn't actually going to hit them but it runs straight into Alitkua's arm. He grits his teeth at me. I give him another look of amusement. My ears twitching in a way that could be considered *happy* in some beings.

He says, "Stop *fooling* around."

"*Thank you.* I feel so much better. I guess all it took was a simple touch from the *perfect* golden fleece."

He rolls his eyes at me. He unsheathes his sword and points it straight in my back. It pokes me slightly and I pick up the pace.

I say, "There's no need to be rude."

Indessah says, "It's best to keep that temper under control—"

I look confused, innocent even, "*Temper?* Oh, you're

talking to *him*?"

Altikua snarls at this, "Indy, know *your place.*"

He twists the sword against my back. I ignore sharp stabbing sensation.

Indessah glares at us both, "We all have to work together, you know?"

I curl my lips, "Yeah, you wag your tail at Altikua's every command, *don't* you?"

She stops walking and I bump into her backside. The sword presses against me further. She twists to face me with her ears folded back and lips curling. Clearly I've struck a nerve.

"Alright, so you're going to be one of *those* criminals...as usual they have no idea what they've been given."

"I didn't ask for anyone's charity. Thank you."

She rolls her eyes and takes in a deep breath. We make it through the last stone archway and into the Great Throne Room.

The room is wide and sweeping. there are many stone pillars. Each pillar is decorated. On the back wall is a blue and gold banner with clouds, and flickers of magic like fireworks. This is a banner that represents Elin specifically as a ruler of Jatali. If the Prince ever gains control, the banner will change. A golden flickering pulse seems to run throughout the castle walls. Every stone alive with it's own energy.

There are many flower bowls hanging from every window. Sadly each of these windows are too small for me to sneak through. There are lines of soldiers against every wall. Most of them look forward with their swords at the ready. A few hold banners and try to sneak a peek at me. There's just too many beings and not enough options for me to slither away. I grit my teeth to brace myself for the coming judgment.

In the center of the room, the Great King Elin-rah sits on his huge stone throne. It's white marble with wisps of every color running throughout. There's pattern's of fireheart flowers printed throughout. He's a golden lion with a flowing silver mane. He has huge upper body strength with a stoic look to match.

Prince Azufae-yoh stands near his throne. A perfectly white lion with a golden mane. He wears a platinum collar with bright blue gems set inside of it. There's a platinum locket in the middle with a blue gem set inside of it. It's a collar that marks a being's loyalty to the Kingdom of Jatali.

All of the Elite Knights and those who are closest to the Prince wear one. So not every solider carries that *honor*. Those that have them are made with gold. They're all in a similar style but all have different colored gems. I'm sure they have some other weird rules about that, but I honestly couldn't say if it means anything.

The Prince is talking to a group of criminals. Their paws in shackles. There's several Knights on either side of the three of them. I find that odd because the three of them seem too pathetic to even move— frail even. Their spiritual energy is almost nonexistent and yet they're more chained than I am.

My teeth grit at the notion— *Blondie's* arrogance.

Almost as if on cue, the Prince looks over at us. Like he sensed my energy coming into the room even if we're still far away. He glances back at his current task. I notice a couple of the criminals are crying now—

What fools. If you're going to be caught, at least be brave about it. Accept your failures.

The Prince says a few more things before the Knights take the criminals away. He starts walking towards us with his arms stretched wide. He looks more pleased to see a criminal than anyone should ever look **ever**.

"Altikua, my friend! Indessah, my dear, this is the *one* I was telling you about— isn't this *exciting*?"

Altikua nods, "Yes, Sire."

Indessah looks less thrilled, "I remember what you said in the courtyard, but still I'm not sure I believe it your Highness."

The Prince is a space away from us. He leans towards Indessah, "I'm sorry he's probably been a pain in the neck *already,* hasn't he?"

There seems to be a small chuckle shared amongst them. Sure, laugh. Have your fun now. These Jatalians won't know what hit them. They've been sitting at the top for *too* long and now it's finally our time to knock them down several 100 feet into an abyss made out of the ruins of their nation.

The Prince takes a small moment to look me over. He narrows his gaze and some part of me feels like he's looking straight through me. It's even a little unsettling for me. I'm sure he's just assessing my soul quality.

I've heard what happens to criminals who get caught.

Most of the time they're just talked to by the Prince and the King. Sometimes the golden furball Altikua forces answers out of them with his Honesty magic.

But for a higher level, wanted war criminal like me— I doubt I'll get off so lucky with just a fireside chat.

The Prince has another power that was gifted to him—

They say that when he touches you. He reads your heart

—

And then he changes it—

He takes all your free will away and then you're forced to follow the Kingdom whether you like it or not. It's enough to make *even* me shudder a little bit. The thought of having no control over my actions— I'm sure it's enough to make *any* being's gut turn.

But if that is my fate, at least my personality died doing what I thought was right. Who knows? Maybe my partner will be able to save me. And if that happens, I'm sure there's a way to reverse the magic.

Prince Azufae-yoh tugs lightly at my jacket collar as though admiring the handiwork, "What *exactly* were you doing on the South wall, Tatchathura?"

"Well, you see Sir, I've heard that Luthura castle has the best flowers. Just figured I'd swing by and grab some. You know how Granny loves her fireheart flowers."

And strangely enough there's no rage, no annoyance—not even a flicker of frustration in the Prince. He merely looks up from my jacket at me.

There's an amused smile on his lips, "Tatchathura I *knew* your granny. She's already resting in the Void. Care to tell me your *real* reason?"

I watch him stubbornly. My brows are set deep. Of course, I knew he wouldn't buy it but what do I say here? I can't possibly tell them *why* I was *really* on that South wall.

One of the guards seems to get a brave streak, he motions towards my jacket, "Sire, it seems as though he was trying to impersonate one of *us* to get in close to our ranks."

The Prince says, "It does *appear* so, but I'd like to hear what he has to say for himself."

I mean they let in riffraff all the time. How was I supposed to know that they would figure me out so *simply*. I blame my energy signature. I mean, when you've got *it*, you've got *it*, right?

I let out a sigh, "I was just getting some information and I made a mistake. So if that's all you need from me, I'll be on my way. After all you've got plenty of other things to do, *don't you?*"

I slowly start to back away from the group. For a moment it seems I might just get to walk away from all this.

"You're all about mercy and giving beings second chances — so I think I've been fair enough to come down and answer your questions. So I'll just see myself out."

I back into a strong arm. Of course, I *knew* that wouldn't work either, but still it's worth a try. Especially since they're being so *calm* about the Shadow Fox of Zutaom literally in their quarters.

Altikua grabs me by my scruff and holds me up, "You haven't answered *any* of our questions. And if you want any chance of leaving here *alive*, you're going to start answering them. And you're going to be more respectful to our rulers."

I try to ignore the searing pain of his warm paw pressed against my neck. I hadn't really been paying attention. The Great King had been so quiet— which I've been told is usually what he does— but it seems that at the taunting of his son, his face had slowly started to turn into one of anger.

Before I have a chance to think about it too long—

Altikua says, "Let the stonewalls of Jatali stand forever. Let no brick be so weak that it makes the rest of us collapse. Honor your comrades, and speak truth *no matter* the cost."

A strong, golden glowing energy takes over and completely surrounds me.

You see the problem we've had trying to infiltrate their ranks is the fact that Altikua has the Virtue Power of Honesty. It's something that can only be used by a being with pure heart and intentions. It forces others to speak the truth no matter how they feel inside or whether they want to tell the truth at all.

I expected it but if I blab the truth here— it's safe to say our mission is over with **for good**.

I feel every word being torn from me like pages out of a book. I writhe against Altikua's grip but it's useless. Between his brute strength and the magic there's no way I can pull free. I start blathering on about all of Zutaom's secrets— even though I doubt these things are secrets to the Prince or King— they always seem to know everything somehow—

I struggle against his grip, "It was the Taoah-lut Glove. One of the thirteen relics. That's what my partner came to get. I know if she's been successful, she'll be so far away from here by now. You'll never catch her."

The Prince's eyes widen for a moment. He glances back at his father to which he nods for them to continue.

I dig my paws into Altikua's paws. He only flinches slightly, "We were gathering the items so that when the seal on the Abyss is broken, the Drake will have all the power he needs."

One of the soldiers repeats, "The *Drake*?!"

Another panics, "Breaking the seal on the Abyss?!"

There are more gasps around the room. It seems all of them are shaking in their boots now save for Indessah, Altikua and the Rulers. As one last ditch attempt, I try to pull all of my weight to get away. The main reason I was at the castle is burning up my throat. It's seconds away from being revealed—

Azufae says, "Stop, that's enough."

Altikua drops me like a bag of rocks. His eyes are on fire as he glares at me. There seems to be a primal rage in his every breath.

And for once the Prince seems to have an angry expression, "Altikua, always *remember* we have to control ourselves."

Altikua snorts and then bows his head slightly, "Oh course, Sire."

I'll admit it— I brace myself against to the ground panting— I can barely catch my breath, *I almost spilled everything...let's hope the Drake doesn't kill me for that...*

The ground is cold but my paws are hot. I feel like I'm burning from the inside out. What is it with these beings and fire? You know my name means 'born with fire', but sometimes I don't know if I believe that.

I figured they're waiting on me to recover. Watching me be pathetic on the ground.

Prince Azufae-yoh offers me his paw so he can lift me up off the ground.

My gaze shoots to his. My eyebrows are set deep. I twist away and shove myself forcefully off the ground. I'm lightheaded and my feet are crossed trying to stand straight. I see Indy out of the corner of my gaze but it's hard to tell if her expression is sympathetic or if she's just watching. Either way I don't need their sympathy or charity. I was here to complete my mission and I couldn't even get that right.

Prince Azufae-yoh takes a moment to speak with a few of the guards in hushed whispers. I can't exactly make out what he's saying but I assume it has something to do with me mentioning the Drake. It's been almost five hundred years ago now since the Great King fatally wounded him. Then he sealed him in the Abyss of Garaev.

But seals don't last forever.

Prince Azufae-yoh turns his attention towards me. Despite what I said, there's still no malice there. He steps closer and waves for everyone to back up.

"I'm going to read his heart now. If any of you are squeamish, feel free to leave now. Tatchathura is a special case and there might be some frightening things inside him."

"Gee, thanks" I give him a flat look.

"At least you're keeping your sense of humor." he says before reaching out to me.

He takes one of his paws and presses it against my chest right over my heart. I'm still winded from Altikua's energy but I hold steady so that I can stare Azufae-yoh down.

I take a moment to think about everything that's happened to me up until this point—

To think about all the beings I've loved and still love—

If this changes me forever—

Into something I'm not—

It's not like I had much choice in the matter.

Just *one* mistake is going to haunt me for an eternity.

Prince Azufae-yoh says, "Through trouble, or calm, may your heart beat true. May every pulse of your soul show me how you are broken."

Unlike Honesty which was a glowing, raging lightning storm, this magical energy turns into green vines and wraps around every single one of my limbs to hold me steady. The two of us are raised slightly off the ground. A pink aura of energy surrounds us next. And again more of me is ripped from the spines of this broken book— only I'm not speaking this time—

It's like every thought, every memory, every possible thing that's me has been yanked into a whirlpool. My life is on center stage. So much noise, colors, lights, and energy. A whole life full of decisions in the blink of an eye. Prince Azufae-yoh's eyes are glowing bright blue. Wisps of purple and gold seem to fog in his gaze as the images of my life reflect in his eyes.

Those below us are mesmerized or frightened. I can tell they don't have any idea what the Prince is seeing. There may be an active display of color, light and sound but it means nothing to those below. They **can't** see what he sees. It's a magic that only he has— that only he can understand the chaos of a heart—

And it's probably for the best.

Then as he digs deep— straight into the pit of my soul— a shadow comes out into the pink mists. A crashing, roaring being. A calamity of its own that destroys all the light and beauty in those moments of my life. We're drenched in shadow— all of those pretty images like a toxic black goo ebbing across the sphere.

I'm not afraid.

I know that shadow part of me well.

He's been a with me since I was cub. He's a part of me now.

And nothing can *ever* change that.

There's a gentle gasp of confusion down below. The others seem to become more erratic and upset. My shadow blocking out the light of the magic. Only the faint glow of his eyes and my orange heart are left in this pitch darkness. To the rest of them it probably looks as though I've devoured their precious Prince, but it couldn't be further from the truth.

We'd all been told the Prince had a terrible power—

I was ready for physical injury— ready to be clawed pieces by Altikua and his army.

Ready to be blasted apart by the Great King's magic for going against the High Kingdom.

But I wasn't prepared for the Prince to tear my heart apart like a puzzle.

I wasn't prepared for my soul to be in pieces on display like fine art. Like shards of glass reflecting the pieces of me that aren't shadows yet.

Prince Azufae-yoh breathes out. His eyes turn blue again and there's a warmth there as the shadows start to fade. His light shines and the aura of the magic fades. His paw is still prominently on my chest as the vines slowly lower us back to the ground. I can barely stand but stubbornly I try to hold myself up.

That magic could've killed me.

So why didn't he? Why spare me? A bargaining chip for later I suppose.

Azufae slowly lowers me to the ground.

I crumple the rest of the way. The pulsing heat from the magic fades into a sinister chill. I can tell the shadow inside me is furious for having been disturbed. Exposed.

I thought I was strong enough. I've been training my whole life for this.

Indessah presses her paws together, "Will he be *alright*?

He doesn't look too good."

Azufae nods solemnly. I can tell that what he's seen is starting to wear on him. That small amount of mirth he had when we were speaking is no longer there. He gives Altikua and Indessah a determined look and starts walking towards his father.

While the Prince speaks with his father, I find myself struggling to get off of the ground. I can't take another hit like that. I thought they were supposed to be the good guys or something. I can't imagine what their actual torturers are like— if they even do that here. I take quick note of the room again. There are guards on every corner. Every possible station— every windows which are still too small—

I twist to look behind me. Indessah and Altikua are talking about something probably related to me. They're so close together there's no chance of escape that way.

I've got to get out of this place.

I realize at this point if they had caught my partner Lukan, then I probably would have seen her by now. She's lucky that she got away when she did.

It's then in that moment that I realize— I have the choice to leave.

I'm actually *thinking* about running away.

In Zutaom, we were always taught that if the Prince used his magic on you like that, you would lose your free will— that you wouldn't have a choice *anymore*.

But everything inside me, the thoughts I'm having— they haven't changed.

I'm still me.

It seems either someone's misinformed or it takes a little while for that magic to take effect. Either way I'm not sticking around to find out.

Azufae comes wandering back with a smile back on his face, "Great news. He's a keeper."

There is some murmuring from the others around the room:

"He *always* says that."

"Not *once* has he turned someone away."

The Prince seems to ignore what they are saying until another solider approaches him. His head is bowed and ears folded back. He slowly seems to have the courage to look into the Prince's eyes.

"But Master, please My Liege. I'm so *tired* of showing mercy to the enemy."

His gaze narrows, "And all of your coat is so perfect?"

"No, I just worry. He will escape back to the others. He will know *our secrets!*"

The Prince is quiet a moment.

"He won't know anything more than they do already." The Prince turns back towards me.

The solider cries again, "*My* Liege—"

Indessah puts a paw on his shoulder, "He *knows* what's best. Come on now."

Finally the soldier seems to yield, he bows and backs away slowly.

Azufae reaches for me on the floor. I'd rather not have his help, but he's yanked me up before I've had a chance to protest. His grip is both inviting and powerful all in the same breath. It seems that they're not *all* talk after all.

He gives me a little push in the direction of Indessah and Altikua, "Indessah, I am putting him in your care."

"What!?" she and the wolf say almost at once.

Altikua looks positively frustrated, "Sire, you *can't* be serious. She's only just now come back from teaching cubs. She's *out* of practice."

Azufae seems to almost shrug, "Take her to training. Take them both and get them all up to speed. We'll talk more later. I still have questions for him. So *please* try to be nice."

I expected the two of them to protest more but it seems they know their place better than that other soldier. The two share a look and seem to collectively sigh. They take a moment to chain me back up before nudging me onward. We start heading towards the archway that we came through.

I glance back at the throne room one more time. The Prince and the King are in a heated discussion. It brings weak smirk to my lips.

Whatever has happened, whatever I've started—

It doesn't seem to be faring well for them no matter how they act for their subjects.

CHAPTER EIGHT
Choices

INDESSAH

After the Prince is finished speaking with his father, we are dismissed. The three of us cross the throne room and go through the archway out into the corridor.

Tatchathura is ahead of me. I take a moment to look him over in the light. He's got red markings on all of his limbs. Dusty orange hair, and a yellow and red fireheart flower on his forehead. The red markings and flower are his magical markings. It's a misconception of many beings that these marks mean you're going against the Kingdom. They actually mean a being is growing.

I wonder what he's actually learned though? Sometimes their learning involves turning murky. Some beings are just so stubborn they have to walk through darkness to know the truth. I'm guilty of this too.

Usually after their relationship grows with the Prince they become brighter and brighter. If they can truly change their hearts, and become like an ideal citizen of Jatali, then their coat will become purified.

Altikua is leading the front. He is good example. He will never be perfect— none of us will— but he's immune to a shadow's influence. They can never take him over. Maybe some day my faith will be that strong.

There are a few other soldiers next to us covering the flanks. My mind is buzzing with the news.

*Me in charge of a wanted criminal? Not just any wanted criminal but one of the most **notorious** criminals of Zutaom's army?*

You see the wonderful thing about the Prince's magic is he can see things we can't see. He can see the pathways that a being might take and has a good idea of the choices they might make— but he can't fully predict whether they will actually take those choices.

So if the Prince sees a pathway that a being can take to be redeemed then he says they're a keeper. But nothing is set in stone.

It's hard for the rest of us to understand sometimes especially when we dealt with some criminals that are the *absolute* worst. My friends Sukua and Heroh are a couple of the training specialists here at the castle. They told me about all the trouble they had with the last one the Prince approved as a keeper. They even started just referring to him as the "Last One" just to keep from validating him as a being.

So even though the Prince saw a way, the pieces didn't line up, the criminal didn't care to take the path. But we can't force anyone to make the right choice. The last I heard is he's still on the run.

I'm reminded of what Prince Azufae-yoh told me in the courtyard.

Interact with him for one week.

Just one week and it will be enough to change his heart.

Can one week *really* be enough to change a heart?

Can *one* moment really, and truly change someone?

I want to trust the Prince. He and the King have been right about mostly everything that comes our way, but still —

After some of the things I've heard about Tatchathura and Zutaom—

I'm not sure I'm cut out for this.

I'm used to making cubs behave— not adults who are *acting* like cubs behave.

Speaking of which—Tatchathura seems to be annoying Altikua once more. The soldiers next to me start whispering to each other. They have their weapons raised and keep watching the Shadow Fox like he's gonna explode at a moment's notice. They don't seem to understand that Luthura's power suppresses the shadows. There's nothing Tatchathura can do right now—

But Altikua mentioned him conjuring a shadow earlier didn't he?

What if— can he do it again? Or did the Prince and Altikua weaken him too much?

A rabbit soldier says, "My cousin told me he's seen shadows on the edge of Luthura."

A stoat leans in, "The Shadow Fox mentioned *the Drake* in the throne room. I've heard other beings talking about that lately. I wonder if it's true?"

I say confidently, "*Just* because he said they were trying to break the seal on the Abyss doesn't mean it's going to happen. He had to say the truth and it's truth *to him* but that doesn't mean that it's going to be *our* reality. The Great King's magic is too much for them."

The pair of them seem unsure and continue chatting.

"I heard if you spend too much time around a being that has a shadow you can get murky too."

"What if his dark heart corrupts the rest of us and brings *all* of Luthura down?"

I say, "You two are being ridiculous."

A rabbit says, "No way. I thought you had to *give up* a part of yourself— you know *invite* them in?"

Tatchathura turns, eyes wild, "*Actually*, I've heard all you have to do is look them in the eye and then they **take over.**"

Two of the soldiers jump at this. Another one raises his lance shakily.

Tatchathura has a snide look on his face. He looks incredibly *too* giddy to have startled them.

He says, "In fact, I've been talking to my shadow this whole time. He's got some friends if you guys would like some *actual* power."

It seems Tatchathura was listening the whole time. It's kind of crazy to me that he's able to keep up with multiple conversations. How was he able to listen to us and annoy Altikua at the same time?

I frown, "The last time someone used our power on you, I recall you falling to the floor."

He glares at me. His tail thrashes across the ground, "*That* was your precious *Prince*. He doesn't count. He'll count *even less* when you have a whole army at your door."

"Are you forgetting we have an army **too**?"

"Not *much* of an army if they shake in their boots when dealing with *one* single criminal." He rolls his eyes and waves his paws about, "It's kind of ironic. There are *actually* beings worse than I am—"

"I'm surprised you'd sell yourself short—"

"What can I say, I'm just a humble assassin at heart."

"Is that so?" my ears fold back.

"Some beings are far more terrifying too. Some beings even have the power of *multiple* shadows."

"That sounds *tragic* not powerful."

"That's a *matter* of opinion, isn't it, *Princess*?" as he shrugs, his ears are high and his tail is swishing playfully.

I can tell me being in charge of him is going to be an annoying pain in the neck.

But *why* me? What's so *special* about me?

What *was* the Prince thinking?

There's a low growl in my throat. Tatchathura is back to pestering Altikua. And the other guards seem very distracted. Even though, in his own dumb way, Tatchathura answered their question. They seem even more confused and anxious at the prospects of shadows being so close to our borders. It's like they've forgotten the Promise from the Great War. All of this is happening the way it's supposed to. We just have to hold on and get through the hard parts.

Altikua starts to converse with another soldier at the corner. The soldiers that flank him are still chatting completely focused on each other.

A split second—

Everyone's distracted-

One moment and then chaos—

Tatchathura sweeps his tail under the legs of one. His tail weight dripping in oil and slinging across the ground to bang the legs of another. He jumps up to dodge a slice. Those soldiers crash into me and each other.

Altikua turns to shoot a blast of Verity at him, but Tatchathura is faster— he twists a soldier into the way as a shield before jumping off of that frozen solider's shoulders. That solider crashes into Altikua knocking them both to the ground. Tatchathura lands on another soldier's shoulders. There's a yelp. And then he pushes upward and lands on the opposite wall. His paws clutch a small open window high off the hallway floor.

His metal cuffs slam into the window sill melting into a pool of molten goo as sparks of his shadow hiss around it. The soldiers' look horrified. I glare up at him struggling against the dog pile.

He smirks down at us flaunting his free wrists, "Later Princess! Have fun rotting in the tower."

He scrambles his way out of one of our small windows.

Everyone is still flustered. I'm still stuck staring at the window. Oh no! How could this happen? I let myself get distracted too. We all let our guard down like we've got fluff in our brains.

Altikua pushes himself up off the ground, "I never should have underestimated him. He was being way too *compliant.*"

The guards finally peel themselves off the ground. One turns to help me stand.

I throw my arm, "We have to go after him!"

Altikua growls, his paw thick in his hair, "What would you *suggest* we do? Anyone who fits through that window, is going to crash down the side of that stone wall. There was nowhere for him to go that doesn't end in injury."

I glance back at the window. My ears tilt searching for a specific bit of sound. All I can hear is skittering and maybe the sounds of a few soldiers outside but nothing that would indicate someone has been hurt or is disrupting others.

Unless he smacked all the way to the ground already.

I point at Altikua, "Get me through that window."

"Are you *crazy*? We'll go down to the bottom level and cut him off before he gets to the forest." He turns to yell at the others in the hall, "Tell every soldier you see to be on high alert for the Shadow Fox!"

Altikua dashes off with a few of the soldiers in tow. There's still a couple soldiers who seemed too upset to move forward. They're shaking and clinging against the wall.

Altikua will never make it in time. It's too far...Here goes everything! I narrow my gaze and take a deep breath, "Come on you two! Let me stand on your shoulders to get through that window!"

I point upward hoping my energy is enough to rouse them from their anxiety. They look at each other as though 'better her than us.' Slowly they lift me onto their shoulders. They grumble as I try to get my bearings.

My paws scramble at the edge of the window. I really am out of shape since I've been away. My claws dig into one of the cobblestones. I push off of my fellow soldiers and finally slide halfway through the window.

I stare down the castle side wall. Everything seems scary from this angle. We're very high up. I'm dizzy for a moment. I dig my claws in tighter.

Why did *I* think **I** could do this?

I search the castle wall and finally I see a black blob with a little flash of white. It seems he's skidded against the wall all the way to the outer wall for leaping over. It's incredibly dangerous for me to do this. And Altikua will probably kill me for this but I have to try. Slowly I twist around in the window. I'm hanging by my front paws while my legs dangle. I figure if he can do it, then I can too.

Shifting my weight, I press my back against the wall. Slowly but surely I start to slide. My claws graze over every last stone. It brings tears to my eyes. He made it look very easy— or maybe he's just very tough and I'm a just a fluffball like he kept calling us. I make it to the second ridge and the soldiers there help me over. All of them are fussing over me confused as to what I was trying to do. They somehow all must have missed our escape artist. Altikua really should scold them for being so inattentive.

One says, "Just what are you doing Indessah?!"

"The Shadow Fox is escaping!" I point towards the ground, "I need a ladder!"

A few of them grab a ladder while the first says, "This is dangerous."

"You're a **soldier**, aren't you?"

"There has to be a better way—"

I grab the rope ladder and latch it to the stone before throwing it down, "No time."

They still seem dumbfounded while I slide down the rope. Maybe all the protection Luthura gives has made them soft too. I clench my teeth. My paws are burning and absolutely aching at this point. Every last piece of my clothes are torn but I can't stop. How foolish am I? I don't see any of the others in sight, so it might just be worth it if I'm the one to catch him. After all, he's supposed to be my responsibility.

I run faster than I've ever run. Every fiber of my body seems to beat. Blood rushes in my ears. My tail is swishing like crazy. My ears flat against my head as every rush of wind makes it hard to hear. But then I see him. He's almost to the forest and then we'll lose him for sure.

"Tatchathura! Please wait. Don't do this."

He only looks back at me for half a second. A look of pure malice and disgust on his face. As if I'm a fool for chasing after him— as if I really *believed* asking him to behave was going to work. I just figured I'd take a page from his own book and try to distract him for at least a moment. He's so fast. I'll definitely have to brush up on my cardio when I get back to the castle.

I keep running and start reciting some words of Jatali, "Jatali lights my way. Like a fire, my light will shine even in the pitch darkness."

I start throwing fire in his direction. Glowing balls of red and orange energy whiz past him. A few flickers hit the nearby trees. He glares back at me again, and this time I hit him square on the shoulder.

He's startles to a halt just outside the forest's edge. His sharp blue eyes slice towards me.

I stumble to a stop. I'm a good distance from him but one last dash and he could be torn from my sight forever. I frown realizing we're very far from the castle now. The energy of Luthura's Castle isn't strong enough here to stop a shadow.

And now it's just me and him.

I edge closer to him even though every fiber of my being is begging me to cut my losses. But there's just something inside me. Something that won't quit.

He cracks his wrist, "Couldn't just stay in the castle could you, Light Bright?"

"Tatchathura, you don't know what you're giving up—"

"So what you're gonna do, **Indy?**"

"I told you not to call me that. You haven't *earned* it." I throw my paw, "Quit—"

"Earn *that*?" he lets out a wicked chuckle, "We *both* know how this is going to end."

There's something about the way he's looking at me that makes me freeze. A predatory growl on his lips he saunters closer.

He says, "You're **not** strong enough to take me out. And I'm **not** letting you take me back to that palace anytime soon."

He pauses a space in front of me. The arm with his shadow poised to strike, "But I'm in a charitable mood today. So why don't you just turn around and **go home**?"

I grit my teeth, paws clenched at my sides, "No."

I level my hot gaze with his.

He snorts backing up a space, "You really are a weirdo. You know in the dungeon, I saw what you were trying to hide."

What...My ears flatten, eyes shifting to look his face over, "What are you talking about?"

"I see the holes in your coat. Those dark cracks in your fur just ready to burst."

The energy shifts around us. A wafting red mist coats my fur.

Desperately, I look down at my coat. It's true. My

shimmery purple pelt is fading into a putrid, muddy black. My heart slams into my chest while my paws raise to touch my coat, *Is it true what they said in the hallway? Is he turning me into a shadow?!*

A faint smoke starts to roll across the ground. A foggy thick barrier makes our steps slow.

He sneers at me, "Quit pretending you're better than anyone else. You've been touched by shadows too."

"We all have—" I try to sound strong, but all I can think about is the overwhelming condition my coat is in. It sludge that's slowly infecting my heart and mind. A darkness that rages and covers the specks of light in my coat.

Memories of my past start flooding back. Every terrible thing I've ever done.

Every way I've ever betrayed someone—

It's like a terrible movie on fast forward with no pause button. Just every miserable feeling overriding my every sensation until my thoughts are a cluttered mess. Is this another power of a shadow-user?

He's looming closer. I don't understand why he hasn't struck yet.

His tail is lashing about, but his voice is a strange kind of calm, soothing even, "I know that there is darkness inside you. And it's just *dying* to come back out."

I clutch my head, "I'm n-nothing like y-you."

His snout is only a space from mine, a wicked glare on his

face, voice even darker than before, "That's why you're on leash and chain to the Prince. You're **afraid**."

More memories flood my mind. The memories of the one who hurt me the most coming to front. I clench my eyes shut. It's too much. I don't want to remember that. Any of it!

"Is your precious Prince worth suppressing who you *really* are?"

My knees start to crumple under the weight. My body is like a brittle frond in the wind. His paw is finally raised to strike.

"Jatali will never leave me." I shoot my paw outwards. It crashes into his strong chest. Flickers of Courageous Flame dance around my paw.

His eyes are wide for the briefest moment before they narrow again, "Fine, have it your way—but know this— if your precious beings ever knew how dark you are under all that sparkle— you'll be alone for ever. Maybe they'll even throw you in Abyss—"

My tail lashes out of control, a snarl on my lips, "Shut up! I serve him willingly. There was no condition to him saving me."

A blast of fire shoots from my paw. He's pushed backwards a few steps and he plants a paw to his chest. He seems amused at my attempt. But the truth is— I'm in over my head. But if I can stall him long enough then maybe the others will catch him in time.

I reach for my sword and raise it high. The metal tip brushes the edge of his chin. My paws start to shake. I expected him to move, run or block— something.

He condescendingly stares me down.

"Here," he peels the edge of his jacket collar down, "Someone already started it for ya."

I can't help but stare at the mangled scar that trails from the edge of his chin down to his shoulder. Any closer on that cut to his throat and it would've killed him easy. How did he even survive something like that?

I swallow my fears, "I'm not letting you get away—"

"I don't think you have to *worry* about that." His eyes darken, the blue color fading to an eerie grey, "Your light is never going to shine *ever* again."

A shadow tendril starts to creep from his paw. He clenches his fist, and then the shadow grows to devour everything around us like it's sucking up the ground. We're encased in darkness— just me and him in our own personal abyss.

I grip the hilt of my sword tighter. I'm not brave enough to use my fire right now, not patient enough for vines either, *What rotten luck! What would Altikua do? Where are they? Maybe they can't find us— maybe this smog has hidden us. Why did I follow him? Why?*

The darkness is so overwhelming. I can't see anything but the faintest of smog wafting around the ground. I can't smell anything. It's silent. His shadow strikes my neck. A raw heat unlike any fire. The smog grows thicker still. Slowly it constrains the air.

He sounds empty, "You should've gone back to the castle."

I struggle against his grip but it's useless. It's like all my strength has left my body. My bones are dust, every fiber screaming for relief from the burning pain. My mind growling in agony as the past crashes over me again.

For a moment his grip loosens, and some of my senses return to normal. His gaze turns faintly blue for a moment at he watches me. My paws clutch at the shadow trying to loosen it more.

He's hesitating.

Why would he do that?

I try to force words from my mouth.

His hesitation is shaken away and his grip returns, "This'll be over soon enough."

My brows furrow, and my breathing is shoddy as I close my eyes.

It's dark. Slowly turning colder.

So this is it, huh?

I couldn't even make it one day.

How pathetic am I?

CHAPTER NINE

Torn Apart

ALTIKUA

My legs lash out ahead of me. Every stride is almost painful as I force myself faster. The soldiers on the East wall mentioned they saw Indy come crashing down the wall after our criminal. I gallop over the last hill and stop at the top. Looking downwards I see the edge of our forest border, and at the bottom of the hill a pair of bodies surrounded by a charred patch of land. The unholy destruction of a diseased shadow fire.

My chest is tight as I slide the rest of the way down the rocky hill face. The others are hot on my tail as we make it to the bottom. My nostrils flare as I see the state she's in. His body is crumpled alongside her. For a moment I fear they've destroyed each other. A wheezy gasp from him proves me wrong. He doesn't move or open his eyes. She's perfectly still.

Sharply, I bark, "Everyone, get them to Med Bay now! Carefully!"

As the soldiers swarm around them, my mind is filled with that familiar fear. A deeply rooted past wound that rattles all of my bones, *She isn't ready...please let her be okay...*

* * *

It's frigid cold in Med Bay. There's a quiet shuffle of the healing staff as they finally leave Indy's side to tend to the other rooms. We are in a medium sized pale room that's separate from the other normal patrons.

Indy lays in bed. A subtle rise and fall of her chest the only indicator she's still alive. It's a miracle of Jatali that she's arrived mostly unscathed from her encounter with Tatchathura. A few burns across her ears and cut on her cheek and shoulder.

Tatchathura is recovering in a bed a few paces down from hers. He's securely bound with magic to the bed so he poses no threat to anyone for the moment. It took four healers to revive him.

141

A molten fire burns in my gut. A subtle rage dying to lash forward at that monster. Just the thought of him and what *could've* happened to my sister-in-arms, makes an ugly feeling rise in my throat.

There is some rattling footsteps near the hallway. My gaze shoots to it. A brief relief to see it's only Kyltia the bat standing there. There's water in her glossy gaze. She stumbles across the marble floor to flop into the seat next to her bed. I stand stoically next to her.

She bites her lip, "Will she be okay?"

"Hard to say. The healers seem to think so."

She gives me another somber look before she's completely focused on our friend. Kyltia turns strangely quiet. She's never been the kind of being to sit still for long. It's almost like she's contemplating.

Prince Azufae-yoh appears in the far doorway. His expression somber.

I stalk towards him. Kyltia shifts closer to take my place holding Indy's paw.

The two of us slip around the doorway just out of sight knowing that it's somewhat pointless. Kyltia'll probably hear every word anyway.

Prince Azufae-yoh says, "So any word *exactly* what happened?"

"The only witnesses we have are those two." I motion back to where Indy and Tatchathura lay, "The last beings that saw them were the guards on the East wall. But even they were too cowardly to follow her."

He nods slowly, "I wondered how this would play out. Altikua, make sure that you retrain everyone in the Virtue of Courage. We will need its strength more than ever in these coming days."

I nod. It's been on my mind lately and given these last few *incidents*, it's high time these recruits shape up— for what good is their power if they never use it?

"Sire, is it completely necessary to keep involving Indessah?"

"The vision I saw was for a week. So as long as she can handle it, then we must stay the course."

"Forgive me Master, but disobeying direct orders and ending up in the Med Bay barely alive doesn't exactly scream that she can *handle it*."

He sighs slowly, "I understand your concern but that is where I expect you to help her most. The spiritual energy she carries inside of her is strong but needs molding."

I watch him for a hard moment. Tail twitching.

He raises a paw, "I will speak with her also. It was dangerous what she did."

We both glance back into the room. She starts to stir. Her ears are twitching and eyes slowly open. She startles and clutches her chest, gaze darting around the room before it settles on Kyltia.

She says, "What *happened*? How am I alive? This isn't the Void—"

Kyltia dashes forward and hugs her tight practically crushing her whole body inside her wings, "You scared me fuzzbrain! I thought I lost my best friend."

It sounds almost like her bones have cracked under the gentle pressure.

Indy whines, "Kyltia, *too tight*."

Kyltia releases her hold while the Prince and I walk back into the room. We're all gathered around her bedside.

Indy says, "I'm sorry. I just didn't want him to get away he's my responsibility—"

I say, "He's everyone's responsibility. What you did just put other beings in danger. We just got lucky that he didn't exert his full power until you had him cornered." She stares down at the bed, while I scold her further, "I told you to stay with us. You disobeyed me and it *almost* cost you **everything**."

Her ears swivel sharply forwards, "He was going to get away—"

"Going out a **window** Indessah-yah?!" I throw my paw.

She growls lightly, "Waiting on you would've—"

I scoff, "I would rather have him lost in the woods— If *anything* were to ever happen to you—"

"That's never happening again." her eyes like a flash in the night.

I suck in a hot breath, "Fine. You're still in training. So in the morning, fifty laps."

"Fifty!" She lashes her tail.

I smirk, "Should it be hundred instead?"

Her ears droop and all the color drains from her face.

Kyltia and Prince Azufae-yoh chuckle lightly.

She stares at her paws, "Fine. I get it."

The Prince puts a gentle paw to the side of her cut shoulder, "How are you feeling?"

She puts a paw to her head, "Like a Bulzatin ate me for breakfast. Ug."

A Bulzatin is a native creature to our land. Giant, slimy, and full of claws and fangs. Definitely not a creature you'd like to meet ever. Luckily for us they've mostly died out.

Prince Azufae-yoh says, "Can you tell us what happened then?"

She looks confused for a moment before she starts to relay all the details of their altercation outside the castle walls. But then she gets to a detail in the story and pauses.

She scratches her head, "I thought he was going to kill me. But there was something in his eyes."

I say, "Something in his eyes?"

She shakes her head, as if she doesn't understand, "He looked at me weirdly and then I blacked out." She glances towards his bed, "Did he *spare* me?"

Kyltia throws a wing, "Not likely. He probably ran out of juice."

I think back to the state I found them in. It is possible— considering he'd already been weakened by the Prince and I.

The Prince looks her over again, "Indy, if you're ready to quit, I understand. Don't push yourself so hard."

"I'm not. I made a mistake."

Before the Prince can say another word, the Great King Elin-rah walks into the room. His long flowing robe swishes around his feet. There is a gentle look on his face for once.

Kyltia and I immediately bow and say, "Your Highness."

The Prince says, "Father?"

Indy can't seem to react at all. She looks frozen— terrified even.

The older lion gracefully walks to her bedside. She can't meet his gaze— forced to stare at the sheets.

"Indessah-yah Brantum, so you're alive." He sounds relieved.

She looks like she's holding back tears. Biting her lip and trying to look brave— but I know her better than that.

King Elin-rah kneels down to meet her distraught gaze. Gently he encourages her to look towards him. Stiffly her head turns to meet him. Her face is fiery red, completely embarrassed that the King himself is kneeling to look at her. His broad paw comes to gently rest against her shoulder.

"None of us want to see you hurt again. Please promise to be careful." His voice is caring but stern, like a parent toward their cub, "Promise this to me, or I will have to reassign you to a different mission."

Indy glances around at us, eyes wide and nostrils flaring, "No, please Sire, Most High, I *want* to do this. More than anything."

There's a gentle chuckle on his lips, "I know, my cub. But first you must learn how to drip."

We all look a little confused save for Prince Azufae-yoh.

"Not all water forms a stream or a lake, most of it ends up stuck as a puddle. Stagnant— unchanging because it can't learn to be the ocean. Not like that anyway."

Indy says slowly, "Sire, you've lost me."

He smiles again, "Listen to those around you. They want you to succeed." He raises himself up, "With every friend, a new bead of water. Let their energy help you form oceans."

Approaching the Prince, he offers him a golden collar with red stones imbued inside, "Put this on Tatchathura once he rouses. It's a special one that will keep him under control."

The Prince nods, "Yes, Father."

I stare at the collar for a moment. Usually the beings that wear a collar have earned it. It usually marks a being who's finished their training and are an Elite Knight. Beings that have these collars might still make mistakes and do wrong things, but they can't become a shadow anymore. The collars must be forged with their spiritual energy. They also take a lot of special resources and time to forge correctly. These collars are for beings that have put in the work to understand Jatali's ways *fully*.

A commitment. It's not a fix-all where we could just slap collars on all the beings of Ituvoh. If only it were that simple. I assume that the King forged this collar with his own magic so that it doesn't require a being's cooperation or understanding. A truly unique kind of collar for a one of a kind situation. The fact that another being will have control over this collar is also unique. Of course, this ruffian is a special case, and the King never reveals all the details—ever.

Indy blurts, "Thank you! I'm sorry."

King Elin-rah gives her a warm look, "Get better, Indy so that you might become an ocean strong enough to change this land."

He gives us all another nod of recognition and then he disappears out into the hallway.

Kyltia is the first to blurt, "The King! He came on *your* behalf. Wow! No offense Azufae."

The Prince chuckles and I roll my eyes. Some beings are just too informal with our Master sometimes.

Indy's eyes are glossy, focused on her paws again, "He did, *didn't* he?"

Indy turns to clamber out of bed.

Kyltia puts up a wing, "Hey, chill—"

Indy brushes her wing out of the way and starts walking across the room.

I say, brows furrowed, "Indy, *stop.*"

She shushes me before stumbling into a chair beside Tatchathura. She presses a paw to his forehead. She pulls back for a second as if he's hot. She stares at the new burn on his forehead. Caused by her no doubt.

I stalk to her side and put a strong paw on her shoulder, "You're playing a dangerous game warming up to—him."

I glance back at the Prince and Kyltia to see if they will be any help but they both seem content for me to take the lead. There's flickers of worry on their faces but not enough to stir them to action.

She glares back at me, her voice full of emotion, "I almost *killed* him. He could've died because of me."

It takes me a moment to recover. Kyltia seems equally puzzled. Even in this moment Indy is more worried about the being that tried to kill *her*. And she wonders *why* I worry about her. The whole reason she went astray in the first place is because she worried about another being *not* worth saving.

I snort at this, "You're being too kind to *it*. It should be back in the basement. Strung up until it cooperates."

"Altikua!" Indy says in a serious way, "He is a being just like us."

"He's dangerous." I lash my tail, lowly growling, "He's not worth saving."

I hear a sound of disapproval from the Prince but I'm too far deep to turn around now. It's too late to stop what's going to be said.

Her shoulders lock with her snout snapped towards me, "Altikua, you have no room to speak. We *all* fall short. Even those titled *the Just*.

Kyltia glances between us. The Prince stoically nods.

Indy stares me down. A twitch on her lips, "If I recall correctly, someone in this room wrongly killed an *innocent* being."

I shoot her a heated look. She's going there.

She's *really* going there.

I suck in a sharp breath, the pain of my past fresh on my chest, "Indy, I don't want you getting hurt in your "old ways" either. "

Her eyes blister for a moment, "This is about doing what's right. The past is behind us."

I'm ready to flare up again. How dare she. Turning my concern against me.

The Prince puts a strong paw on my shoulder, "It's alright. All points have been made."

Tatchathura groans loudly. His eyes are shut as he rustles against the sheets before settling again. His eyes start peeling open. A subtle growl on his lips.

I swallow my pride. It's not worth this fight, not right now.

CHAPTER TEN
You Don't Know Me

TATCHATHURA

There's a pounding in my head as I roll over in bed. For a brief moment I wonder if I had a nightmare. A slight stinging sensation in my forehead ruins any chances of that being true. My head is ringing so loud. A dizzy haze still behind my eyes. Even if I ignored that, there's no way I'd make it out a second time. I couldn't even make it the first time unhindered.

And Indessah's fire. *That* was something to behold. What

a show-off.

I wrench my eyes open. The figure next to me is blurry. Then more figures appear in my view. I shake my head blinking furiously. A bat, Altikua and the Prince fade into view. They all look expectantly at me.

The bat lunges towards me, its claws clacking against the metal bed frame. Its fangs bared, "You **ever** try anything like that again mister, and you're bat chow, you *get* me?"

I give her a bored look, "Sure, Commander."

A rag presses against my forehead. A stinging sensation makes me reel backwards. The bitter smell of herbs wafts past my nose. It's Indessah.

My tongue curls, "***What*** are you doing?"

She continues dabbing my forehead as if I've said nothing.

"Back off, *Jatalian scum.*" I wince and throw myself backwards. My paws are magically chained to the bed so my head hits the stone wall behind me, *Now I've made it worse...*

A small smirk plays on her lips, "You *don't* mean that."

"I tried to kill you *remember*?"

"So?" She says simply. Her gaze neutral as she focuses on my wound.

What is it with her? I stare at her dumbfounded. That's twice in one day that someone has managed to surprise me.

Altikua says, arms folded, "We tried to stop her too."

There is a small chuckle from the bat.

The Prince leans forward and takes a place on my other side, "Have you recovered? Anything feel weird?"

I say, "Besides you all *staring* at me—I can't recall."

Indessah motions for me to settle down. There's something about her I can't place. Just who is this fox?

I ask with a growl, "*Why* are you doing this?"

"We may be enemies now but that doesn't mean we're monsters." Her bright brown eyes meet mine, "Not everyone is kind, but everyone deserves kindness."

I scoff loudly. It slowly turns into a condescending laugh, "Not after some of the beings I've met."

The Prince nods, "It may be hard for you to understand but this is the way of Jatali. Although, it's also true some beings will never understand."

The Prince seems remorseful. I'm not sure why he would care. It doesn't affect his perfect pelt.

Indessah says, "Not everyone is how you are now—"

"And *how* would you know?" I wrench backwards again, *She's just trying to aggravate me...Get inside my head or something...*

Her calm gaze turns sharp, "Orny as a *little baby* too, I suppose?"

"That's *not* what I meant and you know it—" still I seem intent on staying out of her grasp.

How dare she afford me kindness and act like she's doing

me a big favor? If she cared, she would've killed me. It'd be easier that way.

The bat says, "Indy, you're *wasting* your time."

She glares at the bat, "Kyltia, if we don't teach him, *how* will he understand?"

"Some beings **don't** want to learn. That's just how it is."

The Prince says, "She's right to try. We can't give up."

The *Light Brights* seem to squabble amongst themselves for a moment. I grab my head for a moment as I'm reminded by the flash of light she produced. The magic I'd never seen before. A brilliant and white flame vibrantly alive with elegant stripes of blue. Her eyes glowing and the voice that came out of her foreign. It was like she wasn't even there any more. I have no idea what to think of it.

Indessah's voice calls me back, "It took the strength of four healers to undo what I did to you."

Still I won't look at her.

Her ears flatten, brows tilting up, "*Please* let me help you."

Altikua lets out a low groan. Kyltia seems equally displeased.

Guilt. Indessah actually feels *guilty* for defending herself. After I've been terrible to her— and still she's trying— for the Kingdom I suppose.

I finally turn to look at her fully. Her eyes are wide. Still a beautiful brown shade and just as innocent as the first time

I saw her. There's no way the being that took me down earlier was her.

But what was it then?

Begrudgingly, I settle into her attentive paw. She wrings out the rag before replacing it against my hot forehead. The coolness of the water almost makes me forget my predicament.

Almost.

My arms are folded, "I just want you to know that you Jatalians make me sick."

"Actually, I'm from Belaphrium *like you*."

I'm not sure why that surprises me. I raise my brows. The way she's been acting— so dedicated to the Kingdom, I figured she was raised here. You know—brainwashed at an early age.

"What? You don't think the capital can do it's own research?"

"I was *questioning* it." I shoot her a look.

"A simple 'no' will do." one of her canine's pokes out of her lips.

I snort, *What an idiot...*

But even so— it manages to pull a small half-smile out of me. Just barely.

Altikua's fur is ruffled as he casts a hard look over me. He clears his throat, "Alright, time to fill in the blanks. **What** happened?"

I glare at the pompous wolf. My fragment of a good mood soured now.

He throws his large paw, "Well— **out** with it!"

Indessah frowns, "Talik, he's trying! Just be patient."

And for once I see the golden wolf lower his stance ever so slightly. Just who is this Indessah? And how does she have the power to make even this over-sized *mutt* behave?

I glance around at my expectant crowd. My ears flatten. There's a subtle sting forming in my veins as I start to tell them what happened...

I glared at her as she struggled against my grip. This is all so meaningless to me. Such a waste. She couldn't just stand down.

I tightened my grip, "This'll be over soon enough."

Her brows furrowed, and breathing became shoddy as she closed her eyes. I waited a moment and let her fall to the ground. A hot breath on my lips. A sudden wave of flames emanated from her form. Like a radiating star, the supernova exploded. She was panting and almost feral as she pushed herself off the ground.

And then I felt the rage held in her fire. A bubbling frustration that was under that heat. She still has scars from the past that haven't healed. Her words have barely left her tongue before the flames burn hotter still. My fur is practically melting. Clearly I've touched a nerve.

In a flash of strength, I forced my shadow back out.

The tendrils of shadow run along the twisting flames like a braid. Every twisted hook latched violently onto the fire. My shadow overwhelmed her once more. I breathed out focusing every last ounce of strength on her. Her eyes rolled back and her body crumpled to the ground— to believe I was concerned about her.

She's drowning in the shadow and then—

She breathed out a raging cascade of flames that knock me to the ground. I've never been anywhere close to being burned alive— but this might be it. Something in the abyss changed—shifted. I shoved myself up from the ground. A hot glare in her direction. But the being standing there doesn't look like Indessah anymore.

She's turned a brilliant cerulean blue. A fiery white aura flowed around her. Energy itself. Flowing with its own heartbeat. The abyss I made was broken. The trees and skies came into view. Then the sky turned stormy. Currents of various blues channeled through the air cutting through the misty grey before it turned pitch dark. Then its as if all time has stopped.

My eyes widened. Nostrils flared. I couldn't focus anywhere. There's so much energy and light around me—

"Tatchathura Devantum." The voice that comes from her was foreign. It's like many voices at once. An almost ethereal sound to it. Both beautiful and terrifying at the same time, **"You shall not take this cub today."**

I'm not one to fear anything. But that sound— such simple words— and my body started to shake. A growl on my lips.

And then it started to speak words that I don't understand. I'm not even sure they're actually words. Phrases and syllables mashed together into its own language. Words that are strong enough to shake fear into even the darkest of shadows. It seemed my shadow knew what it meant. But I don't have to understand words to know this being's intent. It seemed like such a stupid thing. Words how can they hold this much meaning?

Still I rose from the ground. I force my shadow to claw out of my arm once more. I aim straight for her—

The brightest, most brilliant flame enveloped her whole form. Her paws twisted while her arms make a slicing like motion. Incinerating blue-white flames burst wider. A gigantic shield-like form loomed high above me. It's more brilliant than any fire I'd ever seen! A tendril of fire reached through the shield and crushed me in its grasp.

My shadow shattered as her fire grabbed me. It felt like my fur might burn off. My shadow acted wounded as he completely retreated into my arm— coward.

I stared at my captor. Her pupilless eyes stared back at me.

Sure. I've felt hot coals from the train yard. An ember from a wooden flame has burned my eye before.

I've even felt a Achition's flame down my back. A poison blade slice my neck—

But not one of those fires were as hot or as painful as Indessah's fire.

I never should have underestimated her.

The fire plummeted me into the ground. The shield exploded into a luminous, flashing chorus of lights. Every shade of blue imaginable spiked off in every direction. My legs gave out. I hit a rock and dirt smashed into my face. A trickle of blood oozed down my forehead. The last thing I see is those bright, glowing blue eyes watching me...

I look up from my paws with a heavily glare on my features, "There— *happy* Blondie?"

Altikua glares at me but shifts his focus to the Prince. Azufae seems to be abuzz about what's been said. He's not saying anything yet but his ears are high and tail is swishing happily.

"Hey, don't get *too* excited about it. You didn't get a face full of dirt."

Kyltia starts to laugh hysterically. Throwing her wing to her forehead.

Indessah holds her head, "I-I d-id all that?! I don't remember."

She's frozen in her chair completely confused.

Azufae raises a paw, "Don't get too upset Indy. I think I have an idea of who that might have been, but I will have to consult with my Father."

She nods dimly, gaze still on her feet.

Azufae reaches into his robes and pulls out a golden collar with red gems. Its just as shiny as Altikua's and— it's then I notice that neither Indessah or Kyltia have a collar yet. Interesting. I've heard rumors that maybe its not the Prince's magic but these collar that make beings lose their minds.

He steps closer to my bedside with the collar raised, "I had great expectations for you."

I give him a blank look, "That was your mistake."

"I didn't want to have to do this. You leave me no choice. I must protect those around you." He sounds disappointed.

I say nothing and stare at him venomously. So much for my free will.

His broad paw snaps the heavy metal collar in place around my neck. He leans back and presses the center gem on the collar. It radiates a bright light for a moment before it turns into a steady glow.

"This collar will douse your shadow powers until such a time we've decided that you are trustworthy. Indy, Talik, and I will be the only ones able to take this off at the proper time."

The Prince glances back at Indy with a strong look. She nods meagerly.

I hold my breath. A tense pulse runs through my whole

soul. This is it. The magic is going to link with my mind and overthrow every last thought—

Indy sighs with a bit of chuckle, "You still think we're monsters, don't you?"

I pry an eye open and realize once again, the world hasn't ended. I feel mostly the same save for that shadowy part of me. Somehow his voice is dimmed now.

I stare down at my arm, *He's still there but...I'm sure I could still summon him if I really needed to...*

Kyltia says, "He's so *dramatic*, Indy."

I click my teeth, "Hey."

Even Altikua and the Prince seem amused.

Azufae says, "We don't make anything that controls the will of others. That would be against the Code of Jatali—"

I scoff, "I really want to use my shadow right now. How is that not against my will?"

His lips tilt upwards, "You wish to impose destruction on others which is against the Virtue of Justice. The Magic allows such restraints as long as you're still able to make choices."

I roll my eyes. It sounds like a loop hole to me.

"Now, since you will be without some sort of defense, we shall train you in the Courtyard with the other new recruits." He glances back at the wolf, "Will make sure that happens?"

"Yes Sire, I'll make sure he has full training in Jatalian

Magic."

I say, "*Love it* Chief, but there's a small little problem with your plan." My intense gaze locked with Altikua, "I'm never learning Jatalian magic."

Altikua waves his paw, "We're still have to train you in the Basics."

"Do you even remember the hallway?"

He lets out a low growl and waves his paw again like the discussion is over. He turns towards the others to speak with them.

I glare down at the collar wrapped around my neck. It's ornate and carved with various twisting markings. Some are angular and some are curved. Each gem is handcrafted to fit into the mold. In fact, the whole collar looks as though it's been carved from scratch or something. Did Elin really craft this himself? It's way too nice to just hand out. I wonder if I can crack a stone, or if there's some way to counter the magic in it.

With something like this on me, it's going to be pointless to escape for the time being. Even if I got away I'd be mostly powerless. Sure I have my fists and wit— but with some of the creatures out there—

They've got me boxed in— cornered. Besides, given how well my last escape attempt went. My burns, *have burns*.

Well, this is just *perfect*.

CHAPTER ELEVEN
The Eastern Courtyard

INDESSAH

It's a little while later and I've taken Tatchathura down to the training grounds. Altikua and Kyltia are walking on either side of me.

I'm a little nervous but excited. It's been so long since I've seen Sukua and Heroh. Actually ever since I started working at the Rapsuk school, I haven't made any time to come to the Kingdom. They were my training Captains after the Prince saved me. Sukua is good at the physical prowess and Heroh is great at weapons.

We enter the broad courtyard. It's a giant, wide open space surrounded by side courtyards. There are two in the back wall and one off to the front left. The main pulpit that the rulers address us from is in the center back wall. It's high above the courtyard. There's a rounded balcony dome. A large sweeping archway over it that leads into a triangle roof. Blazing on the front of the roof is a giant red Tash-nev Roch flower. Purple flames surround it. Next to this area on the left is a wide, and higher set of towers. They form a square that's like a mini castle in and of itself.

There are various other towers spread throughout the castle walls and too many winding corridors to count. The walls that hold the framework of the castle have many arches and pillars holding up the overhangs. The castle is glittering and sparkling with bronze stone. It's not really made of bronze. There's just something about the energy here that makes these plain brownstones glow like there's a hidden beauty deep inside.

There's several different groups of trainees. Each group has a couple of Captains putting them through the paces. I don't recognize them. Heroh and Sukua have to be around here somewhere. We pass a few other soldiers deep in training. They keep throwing their arms in sync. They hit the training dummies in a focused repetition. Ah, I remember those days. Unfortunately it seems those days are back again. Altikua was so upset with me he said I'm going straight back to Basic. And no missions until I pass.

(However, I'm sure the Prince will overrule him there.)

I can't believe I let Tatchathura get the best of me. At least he's under control now. Ever since we put that collar on him he's been strangely silent. Oddly enough he keeps searching the far castle walls. I wonder what he's looking for out there? He knows he can't possibly escape now and even if he did, no one can take that collar off but Altikua, the Prince or I.

You would think he'd learned his lesson after I almost burned him to a crisp—

She'd turned a brilliant cerulean blue. A fiery white aura flowed around her. Energy itself. Flowing with its own heartbeat.

"You shall not take this cub today."

Incinerating blue-white flames burst wider. A gigantic shield-like form loomed high above me.

The last thing I see is those bright, glowing blue eyes watching me...

—Well, after *whoever* that was almost burnt him to a crisp. That Magic sounded so strong and in this case Tatchathura didn't have a reason to lie about it. I've never heard of anything like it. Prince Azufae-yoh seemed to know something but defaulted to his "need to research" answer.

I never wanted to hurt anybody — even if he was being a jerk. So what exactly took me over?

Everybody is looking to me and all I can think about is I can't mess this up. Not again. I mean it wasn't exactly the same situation as before— But last time I was here, I let a bunch of beings down— and well— let's just say I'd rather not talk about that right now.

We're finally close enough that Sukua takes notice of us. She waves her arm wide and high. Practically yelling with exuberance.

Heroh turns slightly and shakes his head as if amused by her actions but not fully surprised either.

Sukua is a white jaguar with pink and green rosettes. She has a tail longer than most of her kind and even longer legs. Although she seems lithe, she's got a strong punch underneath all of that. She has a brilliant golden collar with pink gemstones. She's a fun and great friend to have.

Heroh is a black jaguar with green rosettes. They're faint so not as easily seen. His coat is so dark and shiny. He has broad shoulders and a strong stride. His collar is more bronze with rich amber stones. In many ways, he and Altikua are a lot alike. He's slower to approach us.

Sukua runs full force until she bumps into Tatchathura's side, "Hi, newbie!"

Tatchathura pushes her back, "Get off furball!"

Sukua rubs the back of her head, "Sorry, I guess that was rude of me— it's just *always* so fun to have a new trainee!"

Heroh says, "I know, after what happened with the Last One. Any being is a better change of pace."

They both shudder. I'm reminded briefly of how grim our work can be sometimes. There's not always a happy ending.

I motion towards Tatchathura, "This is Tatchathura. All bark and no bite."

He snorts, "Hey!"

"You remember Kyltia? And you already know Altikua."

Kyltia waves her wing, "Long time no see."

Altikua's gaze is focused on Tatchathura.

"Welcome Tatchathura," Sukua points to herself proudly, "I'm Sukua, and this is Heroh."

Heroh *nods,* "Promise we're not all crazy like *this one* here—"

Sukua leaps up and captures him in a headlock, "Heroh!"

He laughs and pretends to struggle.

Tatchathura shoots me a look, "Jatali is just bursting at the seams with **obviously** great help."

Heroh is still struggling with Sukua on his shoulders. I smirk and jump onto his other side. He's strong enough to hold us up easily— so it's a fun game to us. The three of us laughing almost in unison.

Heroh pretends to gasp, "They're too much! I can't go on!"

Sukua says, "That's right. You're our prisoner now."

Kyltia motions towards the castle with a wry grin, "Let's

escort him to where he belongs!"

I'm filled with warmth. It's comforting to know at least some things don't change.

Tatchathura's face is flat, "Okay, I take it back, I'd **rather** rot in that cell for eternity. Thank you."

He starts to walk back towards the castle. Altikua puts a paw on his shoulder to stop him from going too far.

Sukua pouts puffing her cheeks, "Oh Indy, he's so *serious*."

I sigh, "Tell me about it."

Sukua and I slide back to the ground. The four of us stand in a semi-circle.

Heroh says, "You're going to have your work cut out for you, for sure. What a *pain*."

Tatchathura's gaze focuses on us. It seems our words have bothered him.

He's burning red, a growl on his lips, "I'm right **here,** you know!"

I laugh lightly, "But isn't that what makes life so fun? *Challenges*?"

He rolls his eyes.

I give him my best smile, "Prince Azufae-yoh has confidence in me and that's *all* I need."

Sukua and Heroh seem amused. Tatchathura looms nearer me. I startle slightly.

He says, "You really think it'll be that easy? So *simple*?"

I stare for a moment. The other two are quiet.

Kyltia pushes a claw into his chest, "Yes, actually. She kicked your butt *remember*?"

Altikua snorts before recomposing. He focuses his hot look on me, "I know you're feeling *talented* because of what happened a few hours ago, but remember they just said *today*. And I have nothing but time."

I suppress the urge to shiver. It's true. We don't know what might happen next. Was it a fluke? Was it someone really looking out for me?

I shrug before looking away from him, "The Prince has subdued your powers. You have *nothing*."

"Are you so *certain* of that Jatali scum? Shadows have *many* meanings." his snout closer still, eyes like a smoldering fire, "And you're fresh off the farm, just *ripe* for picking."

I suck in a breath, "That's not how I remember our *last* altercation going."

His lips curl into a wicked sneer. A slight chuckle on his lips mocking me as if I'm a rabbit surrounded by wolves with nowhere to run. Nowhere to hide from his sharp gaze.

Kyltia pushes a space between us, "Alright *Spooky*, give the lady some space."

He gives Kyltia an unreadable look before backing up a space. I expect him to say more, but his gaze drifts elsewhere as though we weren't worth dignifying another answer to. His tail shifts along the ground and he forever seems to be searching the courtyard walls. I wonder what or who he's looking for.

It doesn't matter. Whatever it is, Altikua will take care of it. Right?

Altikua leans over me, his voice barely a whisper, "Keep your distance from him today. Please."

I shift to look up at him. His words from earlier echoing the same sentiment—

Indy, I don't want you getting hurt in your "old ways" either.

He still doesn't think I can do any of this. I'm not that same being anymore. I've been made new and will keep getting better.

Sukua voice cuts between us, "Tatchathura if you're gonna work with us, there's some things you should understand."

Tatchathura says, "No thanks. I don't *need* anymore training. I'm just here because my babysitter *Princess Fluff* is here."

Sukua covers her mouth and stifles a snorting giggle, "*There's* his sense of humor."

He's still on the Princess thing...I say, "We were just coming down here to get acquainted with the courtyard again. Altikua says I have to go back to Basic training. So I guess you'll be teaching me some more."

"Oh, that's great! I'm sure you'll pick it back up again."

Heroh nods and motions towards the recruits, "We're gonna get back to our lesson then. Feel free to stick around."

I find a stone bench that's near Sukua's group. I glance towards Tatchathura and wave him towards me. Reluctantly he seems to pick a path towards me. He sits on the far end of the same stone bench as me.

Altikua stands behind me off to one side. He seems to be analyzing the training of the other groups. Kyltia is up close to Sukua and Heroh's group of recruits. Her excitement seems to be distracting to the group. She gets flustered and backs up a little.

I notice that Tatchathura is doing that thing again— the thing he did in the hallway. He's paying attention to everyone around him with intense focus. It's like he's weirdly overanalyzing everything— waiting for a moment to pick us apart. I'll have to keep my guard up. That's how he managed to get away the first time. I wouldn't put it past him to at least cause some more trouble. Given what he just said— he's still not shaken after a literal unknown energy entity tried to destroy him.

What's with this guy? Isn't he afraid of *something*? I know he's working with Zutaom, but still—

I'm reminded in that moment of my duty—

King Elin-rah gives me a warm look, "Get better, Indy

so that you might become an ocean strong enough to change this land."

But no pressure right? I can't believe the King said something like that about me!

And it's all riding on how I do with my current training.

I really have my work cut out for me, don't I?

Sukua assembles her group. Heroh's group falls in line next to hers. I realize they're about to give a speech I've already heard before. It's a speech every being gets when they're in-training. It's our values and remembering to uphold the Code of Jatali at all times—

A recruit raises his paw, "Sukua, ma'am, is all of this really necessary?"

Another says, "Yeah, we learned this as cubs."

"Let's get to the fighting."

Sukua takes it in stride with a laugh, "I get it. But foundations are the most important thing."

Heroh says, paw raised, "Cubs get the basics, but allow us to really *open* your minds about what the Magic of Jatali can really do."

There are some sounds of intrigue among the group. The recruits subtly start edging closer to their teachers.

Sukua raises her paws wide, "A long, long time ago—"

Heroh gives her a look, "We don't have to do a history lesson too."

"I'm setting the scene—"

"Can it be the short version?" he leans in closer, "We don't want to miss lunch again. Today's dessert is pastries and—"

Sukua playfully bats him away, "I get it. I **get** it."

She sighs, "Anyway, after the countries formed, each seemed to embrace a certain Virtue. They became a shining example of these quality traits that are found in the Magic of Jatali: Courage, Kindness, Loyalty, Determination, Charity, Wisdom, Truth, Mercy, Patience, Justice, Faith and Joy."

Heroh says, "Since our magic is based on your will, you will only be able to produce the magic you desire, if your heart can align with the quality that it embodies."

Sukua turns to face the wide open area in front of us, "A Knight of Jatali is like a stream paving the way for what is *right*."

Her paws start pressed together from her chest before sweeping outwards. Green glowing energy sparkles off of her fur. Giant pink and green vines blast through the stone cracks. She's careful not to break the stones.

The recruits let out sounds of astonishment. The vines twist and form spiny pink flowers. Their centers shape into a hard circle-like stone. The leaves sway and sparkle as a faint wind blows through the courtyard. They are semi-transparent almost like crystal flowers.

Heroh walks to one side of the recruits. He tugs his bow and arrow from his back, "Not every Virtue manifests the same way. For example, even though Courage tends to represent as fire or heat, does not necessarily mean that it is constrained to those qualities."

He tugs back the bow and takes aim. He takes a second to breathe, "I will never abandon what's right, even if it costs me *everything*."

The bow and arrows glow a brilliant green. Several arrows form from the singular wooden bow. He lets go of the string and a volley of magical arrows spring forwards. The singular wooden arrow forms a multitude of glowing green and blue translucent arrows. They leave a bright green and blue trail as they shoot into each flower target. As they hit their center marks, a sizzling explosion of vines rupture from the arrows. They twist and grow— multiplying until they wrap their tendrils around every last leaf. The blue light shines and overtakes the green and pink. The magic dissolves and blows away into the wind before completely disappearing.

The recruits seem to be completely stunned. Most of them too shocked to even move. I've seen this display before but it gets better every time.

Kyltia claps vigorously, "Wow! That was amazing!"

Sukua nods to her, "What you all have seen are two Branches of the Patience Virtue. I was displaying Discipline, and Heroh, Obedience."

Some of the recruits shake out of their stupor and start clamoring to understand how they did that. Some of them start trying to make their paws match their motions. Some of them say the words. But none of them produce any results.

Sukua waves them down, "I know you're excited. But learning this magic is more than just knowing the right words and moving a certain way. It's something you have to feel in your heart."

Heroh beats his chest, "It's something powered by your soul. A commitment to something bigger than yourself. The energy of this land that connects us all as family."

"You still have to be careful though. It doesn't grant limitless power. The weapon you carry with you can carry you through weak times. Or times when you can't conjure the right feelings. The more you train, the better your reserve powers will be."

"Training includes reading the Tomes of Jatali, and physical training. Heart, mind and soul. It's the only way a Knight can be whole."

Sukua nods, "We promise after a few more examples—" Heroh looks ready to interrupt her, "And Lunch. We will let you practice."

Heroh is a little flustered so he moves the conversation onwards, "Yes. For another example, to be Courageous can mean many things. The heart of the user who fully understands the power of Courage, can have many powers related to this Virtue. "

Heroh waves towards me. I look behind me hoping he

might be motioning to someone else. Even Altikua seems to nudge me on with an expectant look.

I gulp, *Me on center stage? Fantastic...*

Tatchathura smirks, "I'm sure you'll do *great*. After all, this is all like dress rehearsal for you, *right*?"

I drag my legs across the cobblestone towards the Captains. I settle between the two and they both have a similar expression. I can't believe I'm getting stage fright. I can chase down a wanted criminal but showing off for newbies is what gets me upset.

I glance around the crowd. They are all completely focused on me. Tatchathura seems amused. His eyes are glinting as though he expects me to mess up.

Alright fine. Let's do this.

I take in a strong breath, "I've worked hard to understand the Virtue of Courage. And this is the hardest Branch called Valiant."

I close my eyes and imagine the largest torch I can think of and then the Tash-nev Roch flower comes to mind—

My eyes fly open, "My fire won't be weakened by water nor stone. Let it burn like the love I have for Ituvoh."

My paw shoots straight out. A small red and orange flower blooms into view. I hold it above my paw. I don't want to do anything too crazy or may loose control of it. Considering what happened earlier— did something inside me trigger it? Slowly I let a few more semi-transparent glossy flowers form near my paws. They start spitting a weak fire.

Sukua and Heroh look confused. Altikua gives me a look while raising his brow. Kyltia waves me enthusiastically on. I look away from them all. This is good enough.

Tatchathura condescendingly starts clapping, *"Wow Princess, a pretty garden."*

His words cut me. His tone. My brows set deep. I don't know what it is about him— Normally I'm patient and kind but he's bringing out a side of me I don't like—

The recruits look confused and bored at my display. I try to swallow my doubt. After all, part of why I'm doing this at all is so that others may know the truth.

Fine. Let's really do this.

I say, "A love that only grows. A fire that can *not* die."

From my meek flowers, shards of red and orange flames course out. They glow and sparkle. Flickers of black dance around them until it grows wider. The fire blasts into a mountain hovering over the stones and from it's peak fireheart flowers start to grow again.

Tatchathura says, "A mountain? That's useful in battle."

You see the magic isn't finished— especially not after him teasing me again—

I clench my paw into a fist. Those flowers start exploding. The swelling heat that forms from their bursts turns the mountain into a raging volcano. White hot lava starts spurting down every side of the form. A giant flower has bloomed above the chaos. It explodes into a radiating show of glitter and fragments of what would be fire had I not curbed its power. With another flick of my wrist the forms shrink away. The volcano and flowers are no more but the remaining fragments of glitter and red petals fall down around the group.

The group erupts into applause. They're all so naive they have no idea what they are getting themselves into. That took me so long to learn, and I actually don't know how to finish it right. The fact that I made it not lethal at the end is because I obviously don't want to hurt anyone right now, but also because I'm a failure. It was supposed to be the Valiant Branch of Courage, but I don't even know what that really means. I glare at Tatchathura. He's leaning over his knees with his chin in his paws. A wicked look of amusement on his features. His ears twitching and all.

I flush red and start stomping back to the bench. I realize I let him get to me again. He enjoys it way too much.

He says, "Who knew you were such a *gardener*."

"Shut it."

Heroh claps, "Thank you Indy. See everyone? Don't limit your mind. The more you respect the magic, the stronger you will become." His expression turns pained, "But those who do not follow the Code of Jatali will find themselves lost. That's what's happening all over the continent."

Sukua voice turns somber, "So many beings have been

led astray and turned towards the shadows thanks to the Drake's magic. The shadows he brought to our continent."

Heroh raises his paws and tries to seem brighter still, "However, the great thing about our magic is as long as you can display the qualities that are required for a Virtue, you are not limited to one power. The use of some powers complement each other as well. Like Courage and Determination."

"Indy showed us what you can do when you *really* get it, but we're going to start at the beginning. The Virtue of Courage paves the way for many other Virtues. It changes the world we live in and it is *essential* if you want to be a Knight."

The crowd seems to be abuzz with excitement and a slight bit of worry. They all are probably overwhelmed with the thought of learning all of that. Well, join the club.

Sukua puts her paws on her hips, "We don't need any *cowards* here."

Tatchathura grumbles beside me, "Could've fooled me."

I ignore him and continue listening to Sukua's speech. Altikua seems annoyed beside me. His tail is twitching.

"For as wonderful as Prince Azufae-yoh is, he's still only one being. He can only be in one place at one time. Although everyone in Ituvoh needs his help, there are some situations where he's needed more than others."

Heroh steps forward, his gaze narrow, "That's where you guys come in. Every Knight worth his salt should be able to vanquish a shadow by the end of their training."

There are murmurs of surprise. Whispers among the recruits. Their tails are swishing and ears flipping. When most beings come here, they expect the King or Prince to take care of everything. They don't realize that we're responsible for a lot of the shadows that are banished. You see once our coats start to turn murky, we have a couple different ways we can go. It turns murky when you decide that you're only going to serve yourself. You're not worried about anyone else. When you decide to do bad things no matter the cost— you get murkier until you can no longer turn back to the light.

If you can't speak the truth, your magic will be weak or non existent unless you're willing to give up something like the Zutaomese have been doing. Your actions have sealed your fate and then you turn into what we call a shadow. They used to be like us but now they've traded everything for temporary power. There's no reasoning with them anymore. Once we use our magic against them they're banished to the Abyss of Gareav. However as part of the Promise, one day when a shadow attacks, we'll be able to destroy it for good.

And then our countries can finally be at peace. There's good news for those beings that decide to enrich themselves and help others. Those who want to do good for their families, the community, for everyone— Those are the beings that start to shine. Their coat turns brighter. Their colors more vibrant. Sometimes they even get more magical markings and then they get to a point were they no longer have to fear the shadows. They earn a collar and their souls are too strong to be overtaken.

Not even one little part can be stolen.

But no matter how good they are, no being can be complete without a personal relationship with the Prince. His sacrifice was ordained by the Magic making him the connection to all. The magic will never be fulfilled until he becomes a being's friend. He has the power to make the magic complete and then beings will shine as bright as he does.

It is said that if a being is turning into a shadow, early in their transformation it can be stopped. But only if the King or Prince gets them in time. They are the only ones who can reverse it. So it's safe to say we'd rather help those walking in the shadows turn to the light before they're completely consumed.

Almost as if on cue, the recruits finally notice Tatchathura.

He flips his tail and curls his lip at them, " Don't worry. I'm not your opponent *today*."

Altikua stalks towards him and grabs his scruff, "Or maybe he should be."

"Hey!" Tatchathura growls thrashing in his grip.

Altikua takes him to the front of the crowd and dumps him unceremoniously in front of everyone. Sukua and Heroh back up slightly to allow Altikua to take center stage.

Tatchathura remains on the ground with a look of annoyance still permeating his features. I know that he's a criminal but I can't help but feel like Talik is being a little rough on him for no reason right now. Sure Tatchathura has been making comments— and Altikua is probably still upset about what happened a few hours ago, but still he has no right.

My voice is sweet and calm, "Talik, please. I don't think this is necessary—"

He shoots me a challenging look, "Indessah, stand down. That's an **order**."

I shrink slightly. Maybe it's important for the others. I settle next to Kyltia who seems interested to see what he will do next.

Altikua says, "You see everyone, beings like *this*—" he gives Tatchathura another push, "They're lucky they get a second chance."

Tatchathura looks like he might bite back but lets out a breath instead. His eyes darkening.

Altikua starts to circle him, "They're *very* **lucky** our Master is so merciful and generous. If I had it my way—"

He stops and catches my gaze. My meek look turns

sharp. I know every time we have to work with a criminal it reminds him of them the ones he lost. And after what Tatchathura did—

Altikua clears his throat, "I know some of you have heard the rumors going around the castle. That there have been shadows seen on our far borders."

His look is intense as he combs over the recruits, "We've seen shadows gathering but haven't made their move yet. It's imperative that you all learn exactly how to react in that type of situation."

Altikua grabs Tatchathura by the scruff again forcing him to stand. He lets go and stands a step away from him. Altikua draws his sword. Tatchathura stares him down. His tail is lashing. His lips curling and ears folding back.

"It's alright, Tatchathura. Go ahead and attack me." Altikua studies his sword a moment before glaring at his opponent, "Let's have a little *competition*."

For once Tatchathura seems to hesitate, he glances towards the others. I wonder what he's thinking right now. He probably feels like he's in a glass jar on display so that everyone can see him mess up.

Altikua continues, "Although all of you do not have weapons yet, it will become the most important extension of yourself. Each weapon is forged in the spirit of the Prince. All he has to do is touch it and it becomes enchanted. There are many different abilities that can be forged into a weapon and each weapon must match the user."

The crowd starts whispering amongst themselves. There's a tense feeling forming in the air. Some of the surrounding groups of trainees start to take notice of what's happening and stop what they're doing.

"So don't be discouraged if a sword isn't exactly the right one for you. Maybe you're an Archer or maybe you need something shorter like a dagger. You must treat it with respect or else you risk hurting yourself or others. Or letting the shadow get away."

Altikua's tail starts to lash across the ground.

Tatchathura is still standing on the opposite side of him. He hasn't made a move.

I hug myself. Somehow I realize this isn't going to end well for anyone.

Finally Tatchathura takes off running. Altikua stands still.

Tatchathura runs straight on and then he slides at the last second ducking under his sword. His tail wraps around Altikua's leg and with a violent jerk he hits the dust. Tatchathura spins as he rolls upward off the ground.

Altikua sputters and shoves himself off of the ground. His sword raised as he dashes towards Tatchathura.

Tatchathura twists to face him with his paws raised. The sword crashes towards him. He catches the sword and pushes against it with ridiculous strength. Even Altikua seems surprised at his choice. Tatchathura is only able to resist for a moment before the sword slams him into the ground. A crack of lightning bursts forth from the sword.

It's a form of the Justice Virtue.

Tatchathura writhes for a moment. The stones around him crack as the lightning bursts around him. His tail is slightly charred from the blast.

I cover my mouth. There are other gasps from the recruits. They seem frightened.

Altikua's face is absolutely livid. I can tell he's embarrassed by the fact that Tatchathura was able to get a leg up on him for even just a moment. That split second he was shown to have a weak stance in front of all these new recruits.

Altikua raises his sword again, "So as you'll see, your weapon is an extension of yourself. You must always have perfect control or else you could hurt someone. As you just saw, I wasn't completely ready. I underestimated my opponent and I suffered the consequences. Let that be a lesson to you all."

Tatchathura is winded on the ground. His body completely stiff against the pavement. Some residual crackles of lightning dance around his body. A low groan on his lips.

I breathe some relief. It looks as though Altikua will move on from this demonstration. But then he raises his sword again, the lightning starts to glow and course through the blade.

"Even though my opponent is down, I can see some motion. He's not quite subdued. So we won't give him a chance to recover—"

The sword swings forwards.

I dash to slide between them. I stumble and barely put myself between him and the sword.

Altikua struggles to stop at the last second. His canines fully revealed, **"Indessah."**

I sit up on my paws and knees, the blade centimeters from my snout, "Enough. You've *made* your point—"

Altikua glares down at me, his sword still ready to strike, "You're being too soft on him. Are you **forgetting** he tried to kill you earlier?"

The recruits gasp. A small sound of confusion comes from Sukua and Heroh. I won't look at them. Altikua is just trying to take advantage of the situation to try and prove he's right. That's the one thing I would change about him. Once he's made up his mind about something, he hardly ever yields for a moment.

"We can't give up on him—"

"Shadows don't fight fair. We must always be ready—"

My voice is borderline emotional, "He's **not** a shadow yet!"

"How will he know Justice if I don't show him—"

My brows furrow, a growl on my lips, "This isn't Justice. This is *Vengeance*. A shadow you **never** want to meet."

His eyes widen for a moment before his expression is neutral again. He knows I'm right but he's going to try and save face— somehow.

"*Too late.*" Tatchathura coughs behind me.

My eyes widen, *What is he talking about?*

His claws start digging into the broken stone as he pushes himself half up. His paws are shaky and he can only make it to his knees. His eyes are half lidded.

It seems as though he's trying to glare at me but he doesn't have the strength to, "Your Highness, we're trying to have a fight here. With that *power* of yours, you're kind of making it unfair."

His eyes meet mine for a moment. I figure he means what happened a few hours ago but then he says—

"**Quit** staring at me like that. I'm fine."

If the situation were different, I might have chuckled. I kind of admire the fact that he's able to have a sense of humor even after what just happened to him. He must be crazy.

But I guess you'd have to be to side with the Drake and Zutaom.

Tatchathura pushes himself roughly off of the ground. His legs almost buckle under him as he wipes the blood off of his snout. He steps past me with claws at the ready.

His voice is dark, "I'm ready, *Captain.*"

I scramble to my feet and rejoin the others. Sukua and Kyltia give me concerned looks. They know this isn't right either. But the Prince hasn't intervened so maybe it's supposed to happen this way. They both look ready to burst into a flurry of claws and possibly electricity. It was fairly loud in the Courtyard until they started to fight and now it's almost deafeningly quiet.

Heroh steps forward. His broad paw puts a big space between the two of them. His large head turns to glare at each one of them in turn, "You both have proven your point. Let's get back to the real training demonstration. Altikua, sir, I appreciate your contribution."

Altikua seem startled for a moment. He shakes his head as though he's fully realized that he was out of control. He sheathes his sword. The heavy metal clangs into place.

He looks over at me, "Indessah, I'll be in the library. The Prince has some things I need to look over. Once you're finished here, I trust you to lock him up by yourself?"

I wring my paws, "Of course, Altikua."

As he walks past me, he glances at Kyltia, "Take care of her for me. Make sure he behaves."

Kyltia makes a dramatic and almost comical salute, "Yes, sir!"

Before Altikua gets too far, a Knight rushes up to him. The Knight tells him something in a hushed whisper. Something about shadows forming.

Altikua's tail stiffens before he motions for the Knight to hurry along with him.

Heroh and Sukua start talking to the recruits again.

Kyltia seems to get distracted right away. Absorbing herself in what they have to say. Her eyes light up as she pulls out some paper. She pulls out a pen hidden inside her wing so she can write. I shake my head. Some things never change.

I block it out and turn to look at Tatchathura, "Are you alright?"

He starts brushing his jacket off. He doesn't even look at me when he says, "So, that's *who* you follow? *That's* who you want in charge?"

I stare at the ground for a moment before I level my gaze with him, "Altikua is just angry that you could have finished me earlier. So I guess he felt like he had to prove a point."

Tatchathura raises his brows, "He couldn't find another way to *show* me? At this point I'd much rather be dead."

"You keep saying that, but do you *really* have nothing to live for?"

He pauses for a moment. His gaze set on mine before he says, "I'm just saying if I'm going to get beaten up every hour without a water break— I'm out."

I shake my head, "You're impossible."

He steps closer to me. A mere breath away. I tense. Just what *exactly* is he doing? His tail briefly brushes mine. I think it's an accident—

He says, "*Am* I?"

"Y-yes—"

"I could've pushed you—you know when his sword was

right there—"

"But you wouldn't—" I watch him carefully—

For a moment his grip loosens, and some of my senses return to normal. His gaze turns faintly blue for a moment at he watches me.

I know what I saw.

He hesitated then—

And this was just another chance to hurt me that he didn't take. Sure he was a little weak from Altikua's strike, but I saw him stop his sword mid-swing— no being has ever done that. He's stronger than he lets on.

He seems amused, "Still *not* afraid of me?"

What's his angle? I glare, "Doing what the Prince wants is the most important thing."

He says gruffly, "You're *impossible*— putting yourself between us. He could have fried you."

"He wouldn't."

His eyes seem reflective for a moment, "Thanks for that Princess."

He slowly walks back towards the bench we were sitting on before. He curls his tail around his feet, eyes stoic again and face neutral. It's like he hadn't said anything to me at all.

Yes, I've *definitely* got my work cut out for me.

CHAPTER TWELVE

Tension

CATCHATHURA

Sitting on the stone bench, I rub my shoulder. Roughly my other paw drags across my chest. The sting of lightning still fresh in my veins. That jerk just wanted to be a show off. I'm sensing a trend with these beings. Just before that mutt left I noticed a Knight speak with him. He seemed rushed and urgent. Which could mean there's a spill in the hallway— or something has changed in their perfect little world. I was too far away and the lightning was still messing with me so I couldn't make out what was said. But I'm sure if I listen for the right threads elsewhere I can weave it all back together.

I watch them train these new recruits. They're all tripping all over each other and shaking in their fur. Even though their precious Altikua knocked me down a peg, I can tell that my presence is still making them nervous. I've already heard plenty of the soldiers whispering to each other about the *incident* between me and Indy. And every time I hear it, it gets even more sensational.

The one where Indy blows up half of the North wall is my favorite.

Altikua and Heroh explained to them about needing weapons in case their magical energy gets too low. This means they do have a weakness. Their energy isn't limitless like we thought before. It explains a lot about these weapons. I've only seen a few of them in action before. I figured it was just an easy novelty to carry around.

After all, how are you going to remember books and books worth of words?

Altikua cracking down on me like that I understand. I was waiting for it— expected it even— I'm actually kind of impressed that it took him that long before he decided to have his revenge or whatever.

But I didn't expect Indessah to put herself between us.

Not that I'm thinking Blondie would ever hurt his own

kind but still strange. Why did she even care? I deserved it after all. As I'm watching them, a flash of yellow catches my eye. It's on the far castle wall. I look up and there she is—

Lu-kan...my partner.

She's crouched but I see the flash of yellow on her ears. Subtly she waves her paw. I glance around the courtyard quickly wondering what might happen next. She levels her tail for a moment and then in a quick flash her ears are gone. She must have slid back down the wall.

She's up to something. I chuckle quietly to myself.

You see that's the thing I love about her. She doesn't give up. In fact, she puts me to shame because even if the Drake didn't approve of something— there was nothing that was going to stop her from breaking me out one way or another.

I may have failed my mission but she won't fail hers.

I notice some recruits whispering about something different. I subtly twist my ear, straining slightly to hear what they may tell. Most of the group is distracted by the Captains' instructions. They are working in pairs and trying their best to put the motions to action while reciting their creeds and words.

One soldier turns to two others, "I overheard in the hallway there's been shadow sightings on the border."

I roll my eyes. This again?

But then they say something that catches my attention.

"Yeah, but they said they saw some being *leading* them."

The first gasps and then covers his mouth, "What! Since when do shadows ever let themselves *be led?*"

Another noses his way into the conversation, "I heard it was a grey and yellow fox."

My smirk widens. That's my vixen.

The first waves for them to calm, "See, that's what Zutaom has been doing. Aligning with the shadows so they will obey them."

"I thought they had to join their body with a shadow to get that—"

"Apparently not."

For a moment they all seem to realize something— they turn their hushed whispers towards me. I'm still pretty far away from them so I feign a confused look.

"I bet it's his fault."

"Yeah, that could make sense. I bet he's working with the other one."

One of them throws an arm, "This is all because the Prince keeps showing them mercy."

The other two seem to nod along.

The three of them check over their shoulders to make sure they're still under the radar. A few other soldiers seem to be half listening to them with their ears turned back and face front.

"Yes, I can't believe Indessah stopped Altikua from roasting that *rat*."

I frown. That's not very nice I prefer the term *savage*.

"He had it coming and she showed him mercy." This one gets particularly heated, shoulders hunched, "Why did the Prince bring someone *like her* here?"

Sukua seems to notice their talking. She frowns and waves for them to line up again. They all face front like perfect soldiers.

I groan. Just when it was getting interesting. Who knew the country of light and love had so many gossips?

The first one turns slightly, "I heard this *isn't* her first time here."

A newcomer twists to add, *"She's* the reason we had trouble with the shadows in Luthura a few years ago."

The others seem flustered by that idea, "What? *How*?"

The newcomer glances around for a moment, "She broke off her engagement to a prominent Captain and ran off with a crime lord to get married."

A few cover their mouths. A few more get involved in the conversation. Indessah is at the front of the class next to Heroh and is oblivious to all this chatter about our favorite Princess.

Crime lord? I tap my claws against the stone bench, *Who knew she had it in her? I wonder who though...*

The newcomer seems proud of himself, "There were shadows crawling all over Luthura's borders after that."

"I can't believe the Prince welcomed her back."

A particularly angry one says, "She's probably the reason shadows are on the border. She showed mercy to one and now they're all coming."

I snort in amusement. These fools are two petals short of a flower. The small group that has formed starts to fan. A few others pass the words to each other like a game. Sukua and Heroh are both too fuzzy-brained to even notice they are losing control of half the class now. No wonder these fools are cracking at the seams.

Another agrees, "We should run her off before more bad stuff can happen."

"Yes, we can't have a repeat of what happened *before*."

This makes heat rise against my neck. I was content to let them rattle off nonsense. They can say whatever they want about me or even Indessah but the thing is— I can't allow these half-wits to ruin *my plans*. If I'm trapped here, I may as well get the intel I can. Indy is naive enough to trust me and *even* stand up for me. I practically have a being for a shield. If they run her off, I might not get so lucky a second time.

As I look over each of their coats, I search for their weak points. There are small, dark cracks in each of their perfectly colored pelts. My training has allowed me to see what others can't see. It's just one of the many reasons I'm called the Shadow Fox. You see that's the thing about Ituvoh— if you let your emotions get the best of you— you can invite a shadow in and not even know it. Foster that feeling long enough and you're a prime target for an attack. Most beings turn into shadows for this reason, not because they've made a pact like I have.

I saunter into their midst. They barely notice my arrival they're so buried in each others snouts, "Interesting conversation. Mind if I join?"

They startle for a moment but not enough to alert the rest of the group. They stare at me like I have fire coming out my eyes and shadows are crawling down each strand of fur.

A wry smirk on my lips, "You see— what you **furbrains** don't understand is that it doesn't matter what any of *your* beings do."

They shrink slightly.

I start to loom over each of them in turn, "What *matters* is what the Drake wants. A shadow will follow any being that has my Master's desire in their heart."

Slowly the group is crumpling under my intense gaze. They're lucky Vengeance can't come out, or I would've struck even more fear in their puny hearts for fun.

"And that fox up there, *Princess Indy*— she doesn't have the right stuff."

"H-how would y-you know?"

"Y-yeah, we *know* what we h-heard about her."

I point to each of their coats in turn, "Rage, Vanity, Self-Righteousness— you have them all. Perfect holes to slice and let a shadow through—"

I finally touch one of those marks and the solider squawks and flutters high above the group. She barely makes it back to the ground with an unceremonious flop because she's so worked up.

It's finally caught the full attention of the group. All of the soldiers snap to look behind themselves. Sukua looks flush with annoyance— ears pinned back and tail sweeping. Heroh looks ready to send them all running laps for their disobedience.

Indessah raises her paw to them. Slowly she starts parting the waters of ranks. The recruits all start stepping back a little further than necessary.

And then she pauses—

Her gaze had been facing me, but now it slips towards the ground. Her ears erect and listening to their every word. She's finally heard what they've been saying. Whispers like bugs in the wind. Looks from the others like she's *diseased*.

The expression on her face— I realize she's heard these things before. Small dark energy holes form in her coat.

She bites her lip. A slight hint of water at the edges of her eyes. And then her coat is normal again. It's not something the others can see— only me.

She throws her head up to stare at me again. She stomps over until she's a space away.

She says roughly, "Just what are you doing? If you don't

want to participate, just stay on the bench."

"But I am *participating*. Your comrades here had some facts wrong, just figured I'd fill in the blanks for them."

She glares at me with narrow eyes and flaring nostrils. It's like she's not sure what to do next.

I wonder for a moment if I'm pushing her too hard—

"You see, I figured since you all were about sharing and history lessons, I'd chime in too."

"Don't." Her voice sounds weaker now.

"It's just that you all seem to think other beings have the power over the shadows. But you're **wrong**."

A brave soldier says, "But the Prince, and King Elin-rah —"

"Sure they protect you here in Luthura and most of Jatali, I guess." I dig my paws in my pockets, "But have you ventured *far* outside these borders? Even countries like Esakivh and Ikouvan are crawling with shadows."

"**So**— they broke the covenant with Jatali—"

"So they deserve to *rot* then? I thought you all were about mercy?"

The solider steps back and seems flustered now. A few others whisper.

Indessah finally says, "It doesn't matter. We'll help them how we can *after* we finish training, *please*?"

I raise my paws, "Sure, sure. Just so long as everyone understands that it's Eliayav the Gator from Zutaom that made the deal with the Drake."

Slowly I pretend to walk away. The crowd behind me in upheaval.

"What? The Drake!"

"He's sealed away."

I look over my shoulder, "And I guess Gaphi-tah the Caracal and Mierus the Jackal from Sekulan count too."

They look even more distressed and wide eyed like cubs lost in the woods. Who knew their faith was so weak?

I shrug, "Yup, they all made a deal to burn your glimmering little city to the ground *any* moment."

"You're lying." Indessah says, her tail swishing the dust around, "No one can break the Abyss except for the King."

I smirk, "I'm just trying to follow orders *Boss*. You know, tell the truth."

The look she gives me makes me pause.

She breaks her gaze, paw pointing towards the bench, "That's enough *truth* for one day."

Reluctantly I settle on the bench away from them. There's something about her I can't place. My mind starts to pour over the thing about her I can't understand.

I glared at her as she struggled against my grip. This is all so meaningless to me. Such a waste. She couldn't just stand down.

I tightened my grip, "This'll be over soon enough."

Her brows furrowed, and breathing became shoddy as she closed her eyes.

I waited a moment and let her fall to the ground.

She was down. Completely wiped out. Her energy sapped. I couldn't sense even an ounce of light from her. We were completely enveloped in my abyss.

A sudden wave of flames emanated from her form. Like a radiating star, the supernova exploded. She was panting and almost feral as she pushed herself off the ground.

My eyes narrow. Even in that moment she was still normal— just a like many other beings fighting until the last straw—

Something in the abyss changed—shifted. I shoved myself up from the ground. A hot glare in her direction. But the being standing there doesn't look like Indessah anymore.

She's turned a brilliant cerulean blue.

There was so much light and energy in that moment. I've seen a lot of things, but that was new to me. I noticed Azufae seemed to realize something when I talked about it, but just what does he know? Just who was that being?

***"Tatchathura Devantum."** The voice that comes from her is foreign. It's like many voices at once.*

And it knew my name.

I'm not sure how it happened, or if it was really just her going into overdrive— all that matters is I play my cards right and I can get out of this mess. I'll have to be mindful of how I approach our *dear Indy* or I might just awaken this strange power in her again. However, it seems that annoying her isn't enough. So I should be safe on that account.

Finally their training comes to an end. The sun is slowly setting on the horizon. There was no further sign of Lu-kan after that briefest moment. I wonder if her plan went awry? Or does she need more time? Most of the soldiers have filed away from the courtyard. Even the other Knights have turned to leave the courtyard.

Indessah approaches me slowly. Her tail is drooping and her bright eyes seem glossy. Kyltia is hopping alongside her blissfully oblivious to her struggle.

I look up from my post on the bench, "Yes, Princess?"

She frowns, "Time to go in."

"I don't understand. Isn't night time the best practice time?"

Kyltia gives me a lift up, "Normally I'd agree with ya, but we need shut eye sometime."

* * *

I follow Indessah as she leads the way down some winding hallways. My paws are behind my head and I yawn occasionally. She glances back at me as though confused.

What a weirdo...

Kyltia is following close behind— so I don't get any ideas

she said. As if she could really stop me. Didn't she see me stop Blondie's sword? Sure it was stupid of me since I can't access my shadow, but old habits and all that—

But if Vengeance would've been with me in that moment, things would've gone much differently.

I start to notice that we're not heading towards the dungeon anymore. We're on one of the bottom floors of the castle. She stops in front of a normal wooden door.

She unlocks and pushes the door open wide, "This is where you'll be staying."

I watch her as she walks inside, there's a curl on my lips, "You're kidding, right, Princess?"

"No. It's like I told you— we're not monsters." She folds her arms, "You won't be able to leave. Even if you could, that collar will know what you're trying to do. It's tuned into your soul energy, so any bad thing you try— it will stop you in your tracks."

"I *already* know that. Riddle me this— why even put me down in those stone cells if you're going to move me into an *apartment* later?"

"We always put unknowns down there until we're sure they're safe enough to have inside the castle."

"Safe?" I snort, "Are you sure we're living in the same reality?"

She swallows heavily, "There's been some minor setbacks sure. Just get in here already."

I raise my brow, "My, my *testy*, are we?"

Her glare intensifies, "The soldiers were already scared. You didn't have to say all that stuff in the courtyard—they didn't deserve it."

"I hate to break it to you but a lot of beings don't deserve what happens to them." I shoot her another look as I wander into the open room.

It's got a small bathroom. A little counter space— just enough room to put something down. There's no way to cook here or store food.

She says, "I'll bring you something else to eat in the morning. So don't get *too* comfortable."

I flop onto the bed, arms folded behind my head, and eyes closed, "Whatever you say Chief."

She shakes her head and heads towards the door, "Come on Kyltia."

I sense her undercurrent of rage. A subtle feeling of inadequacy that she always seems to get around me. Although I can't blame her.

I twist in bed to look at her, "I'm surprised you two walked me here by yourselves. No telling what I *might've* done."

"Do you **really** think I'll ever be afraid of you?" She clutches the door.

"Yeah, and that goes double for me." Kyltia folds her wings.

I level my gaze towards them, "Be haughty now, but once you're alone again— far from your sparking palace— You won't be so *lucky* a second time."

"It *wasn't* luck!" She growls, and throws her paw.

Kyltia puts a wing on her arm, "Hey, ignore him already."

I close my eyes and settle into the cot. A self-satisfied smirk on my snout. She makes it too easy. She scoffs and storms out. The door lock clicks behind her.

I let out a heavy breath and stare at the ceiling. This is literally the comfiest place I've ever been in my life— and it feels like the biggest prison I've ever known. I wonder what's happened to Lu-kan. I hope she's okay. I dig into my jacket and pull out a tucked away trinket. It's a glossy grey and black marble stone. It's has tiny flecks of copper glinting just under the surface. It's something she gave me when we were cubs. Something we had when we were back in Zutaom. She has a similar stone that I found for her. A black and purple one. It's got ribbons of silver running through it.

It's supposed to mean that no matter what happens we have each other's backs. She's not my wife but maybe some day she will be— If I ever get out of this dreadful place.

CHAPTER THIRTEEN

No Rest for the Weary

INDESSAH

I lay in a bunk bed staring up at the wooden slats, "I don't think I can do this."

Kyltia and I are staying at the barracks just outside the castle.

"Depends on what you're talking about because if we keep talking like that," Kyltia chuckles to herself, "You're definitely not going to be *sleeping*."

"Very funny." I sit up in bed, "I was talking about being able to keep Tatchathura in line."

"Yes, the *grumbling* one."

"Why do you think this is a big joke? It's a **big** responsibility. And you heard what the High King said? *The King—* Kyltia! How in Ituvoh am I going to accomplish that?"

She leans over her bed to look at me upside down, "Hey, the Prince chose *you* for a reason. Just like he chose *me* to be the **best** journalist this little town's ever seen."

"Luthura is a huge city—"

"You *know* what I mean."

"I'm not sure I do."

She looks down at me again, "I will come down there missy."

I wear a wry grin, before I turn serious again, "Did he tell you that?"

She scratches the back of her head, "Not exactly— **but** I know he will."

I make a sound of disbelief.

"Look, Altikua wasn't called a moment *too soon* was he?"

I think for a moment.

I remember when he was chosen to be Commander that chaos became the standard in his life. He was younger than all of his peers. His training less than a typical Commander. The Prince faced a lot of scorn for that decision.

And what happened next— no being could predict.

He lost his family at the paws of the criminals he sought to bring to justice. They escaped judgment but still he pressed on doing his job the best he could. He grieved them deeply— a wife and his little cub.

And then he had to deal with me ditching my responsibilities at the same time—

But if he hadn't been chosen when he was, corruption deep in the veins of Luthura would still be running rampant in the streets.

I say, "I guess not."

"It's the same for us. He calls us when it's the *right* time so quit worrying."

"I guess so."

"Besides I've been honing my skills ever since I've been at the school. Not my fault if you slacked off."

I smile weakly at her. If only I could be so confident.

But I guess to be fair, writing papers would be probably a little bit easier than keeping a notorious criminal in line and trying to help him realize the error of his ways.

Kyltia waves a wing, "If you're worried about it, like just go talk to Azufae. Maybe he's got some insight, you know."

"I'm sure he's too busy. I don't want to bother him."

"Altikua's here too."

"He hasn't been exactly encouraging."

"That's not surprising." She gives me a blank look, before perking up, "Let's wake up early, go to the courtyard and get in some practice before everybody else gets up."

"Sure. What would I do without you?"

"I don't know— probably crash and burn. Run home with your tail between your legs." She flops back into her bed with a low rumble of giggles in her chest.

It brings a grin on my face. I push up on the mattress playfully. She pretends to be offended. Finally we start to settle down. But once it's quiet in the room, my mind starts to wander again. I stare up at the wood slats in the bed above me.

She's right though.

The Prince chose *me*.

He wouldn't drive me all the way back here for nothing. He always has a plan.

Right?

I shouldn't worry about what anybody else says—

Right?

All I have to do is interact with him for a week? That's not too hard—

Briefly all the interactions with Tatchathura come flashing into my mind. All the frustration in my chest bubbling to the top.

Who am I kidding!?

Maybe that's all the longer the Prince thinks I can last.

Maybe I really am going to mess up like last time. I groan and throw my face into the pillow.

* * *

The sun is slowly peaking over the horizon. It's early morning and I'm in the training courtyard with my sword raised. Kyltia went into town. She claims they have the best drink at one of the local shops. I don't even know how she can think about something like that— we have work to do!

I slice at the dummy once more. I'm winded and my muscles ache. It's been so long since I *actually* trained. I'm kind of annoyed with myself. I let my work at the school preoccupy me— I should've kept training all along. I figured I'd get my sword swinging skills back up before I attempt to learn any more magic. After all a sword won't fail you like a will sometimes does.

My faith in Jatali may be strong but you never know what will happen on a mission. I have to be physically fit. Prepared for climbing the endless mountains— traversing the vast deserts or bottomless seas—anything really! A tingle of excitement runs up my spine. If you'd asked me about this a few years ago—well—none of that matters anymore. I'm ready for the future. I wipe the sweat from my brow. The events of the day before play in my mind.

"I could've pushed you—you know when his sword was right there—"

"But you wouldn't—" I watch him carefully—

Tatchathura says something like that. Why would he

care? It seemed like more than his usual razzing. It was like he didn't understand why I did it. Why I saved him from more pain.

He says gruffly, "You're impossible— putting yourself between us. He could have fried you."

"He wouldn't."

His eyes seem reflective for a moment, "Thanks for that Princess."

For me it's simple, if I see something wrong happening— I try to correct it— At least when it has to do with others. When it comes to criticisms thrown at me— that's a different story.

"But I am participating. Your comrades here had some facts wrong, just figured I'd fill in the blanks for them."

I pause mid sweep. The sword seems too heavy to lift again. I groan. Tatchathura almost ended me. And then strange magic almost ended him— which still would've been my fault. Our rulers have high expectations for me. I can't believe even the new recruits have heard about my baggage. And then they almost saw me cry on top of everything else.

How rotten can my first day back be?

I wonder what exactly they were saying? Why did he feel the need to intervene anyway? I thought he didn't care about anyone. It was almost like he was distracting them from my past to make them focus on the Drake. I level my sword once more. I suck in a deep breath and throw down my sword. It gets stuck in the wooden dummy.

"Sure they protect you here in Luthura and most of Jatali I guess." He digs his paws into his pockets, "But have you ventured far outside these borders? Even countries like Esakivh and Ikouvan are crawling with shadows."

He mentioned some other countries having trouble. I can't believe it. It's really happening. Is the Promise about to be fulfilled or was he just using his leverage to upset the rest of us? And then my mind decides to take it further and flashes back to my confrontation with Tatchathura outside the castle walls. I can still see the look in his eyes...

His shadow strikes my neck. A raw heat unlike any fire. The smog grows thicker still. Slowly it constrains the air.

He sounds empty, "You should've gone back to the castle."

I struggle against his grip but it's useless. My mind growling in agony as the past crashes over me again.

For a moment his grip loosens, and some of my senses return to normal. His gaze turns faintly blue for a moment as he watches me.

He hesitated. I know he did. He had his moment to crush me, and then—

I slice an arm off the dummy by accident—I put a paw to my mouth, *Oops...*

Altikua approaches me, "Destroying things already?"

"Sorry, I didn't mean to." I look up from my sword, "It's heavier than I remember."

The dummy looks even more pitiful now. One arm gone and the other arm half chopped off.

Altikua leans over me to look. He seems amused for once. His tail wagging as he gives me another look, "You know this one's for paw to paw combat right?"

"Is that why it spins?"

He laughs, "Next time let me show you the ones for *swords.* "

"Yes, *Captain.*" I say with annoyance in my voice.

He smirks and takes his own sword out, "Now how about some *real* some practice?"

"As long as there's no lightning." I shoot him a challenging look. The morning may have worn on me, but I'm not letting him get the best of me.

He chuckles mournfully, his head shaking, "Let's begin."

Altikua takes a moment to shove the dummy off to the side. He stands before me with his stance set wide. I look him over and find it odd that he's wearing just his normal leather garb. He usually never takes his armor off. I wonder what could be up with him. For as long as I've known him—

His sword crashes next to my side. It clangs against the stone, "No daydreaming. Your opponent won't wait for you to *figure it out.*"

"I know." I shrug to loosen my shoulders.

He levels his sword again, "How did it go after I left yesterday?"

I bite my lip, sword raised, "Fine."

He narrows his gaze. His sword swings forwards. Basic slice after slice coming towards me. I counter each slow blow easily. He nods and pulls back his weapon for a volley of swings.

I grip the hilt of my sword. The next swing comes so fast I'm dancing to keep up with his swings. I glare at him but he just tilts his head. He's testing me right now. Self-righteously trying to make a point— but that's just it— I already know I'm out of practice.

He says, "I head a rumor that the ruffian was spouting off nonsense about the Abyss seal being broken."

"It's true. He mentioned Eliayav, Gaphi-tah and Mierus." I lower my gaze, "You don't think it's true, do you?"

He taps his chin for a moment, "It's worth looking into. Which reminds me— Tatchathura's collar may curb his shadow powers but it doesn't remove his free will."

I flatten my ears, "I know."

"I know you've been in charge of a classroom at the Rapsuk school but this is a different matter entirely."

"So?" I lower my sword, *What is he getting at?*

He pierces me with his reflective gaze, "Just be careful. I know we're supposed to show mercy, but he's been given plenty."

"I know—"

"I don't want him manipulating you."

"He won't." I throw my arm to the side.

"There's a *reason* he strikes fear into the others." He waves his paw, "He's the kind of being who has no reservations about doing what he needs to survive."

"Maybe now, but he also might be *like us* one day."

His sword collides with mine. I'm barely able to hold him back. His gaze fierce once more, "Interesting *dream* you have."

"You weren't being fair yesterday— and you *know* it."

"Perhaps. But you know I can't afford to lose anyone else."

I lower my sword. There's a fire in my gaze as stare up at him, "You won't."

"Indy, you got *lucky*—" He raises his sword high, "You can't be naive anymore! Not after what's happened to you."

I'm quieter this time, "I know."

His brows tilt, "I know you want save everyone— we **all** do— but you have to remember there are some beings that are just going to drag you back down."

"That was a *long* time ago!"

"A few years ago is *not* a long time."

"Is that all I am now? A big *mistake*?"

He waves me down, "No—"

"Do you trust me?"

"Yes but—"

"Then stop treating me like a cub." I throw my sword to the ground. It clangs loudly, "I don't understand what you want me to say."

He narrows his gaze, "Then don't *act* like one."

"Tell me what *you* want to say." I almost growl.

He sighs, lowering his stance, "I love you Indy, and I don't want you getting hurt again."

I watch him for a moment. My rage is spent. Slowly I walk to stand in front of him.

"I'll get stronger." I hug him tightly around the waist, "I *promise* you."

His paw slowly falls to rest against my back, "I know you will. I'm sorry."

And when I make a promise, I mean it. I can't let him or anyone else down.

* * *

After my conversation with Altikua, I find my mind filled with doubt. I keep thinking about how all those soldiers were talking about me. All they saw was my past. We may say we're the country of mercy but I see now there are still many who need convincing.

I thought I could handle coming back here again.

I thought I could deal with my past but it seems I'm not as ready as I thought.

I finally make it to the Prince's Study. The door is open but I linger in the archway for a moment.

Prince Azufae-yoh has his paws on a book stand. A magical translucent map is hovering above the book. He's completely absorbed in what he's doing. He uses his paws to zoom in and out on certain pivotal moments for beings around the country. Most of it is an overwhelming noise— so many voices and chatter. I don't understand how he's able to make any sense of it at all. Even these brief moments are enough for him to determine whether he's needed or not.

Ever since he laid down his life for the continent, he's gained a connection to all the beings that have been and will be— but only if they stay connected to Jatalian Magic. If they turn away from it, or side with Zutaom, the connection is broken. He may be able to know what most beings may or may not do in general. They are like paths he can see down to a particular future. He watches their steps closely on his map waiting to see which way they will go so he can plan to intercept them if needed. Some paths become absolutes after certain events occur. It causes the Prince great stress because he knows some things can be prevented. But which should he choose? Which will help all beings the most? You could see how it gets complicated fast. That's why we say he's always working. To some extent it's almost as if the Magic has given him more energy to complete his tasks.

Sometimes the Magic reveals knowledge to the King or Prince, but most of the time it's either cryptic or specific. Cryptic with very few details like what we call a "promise". Or specific in the way that the events need to happen. If they don't happen the way they are predicted, adjustments can be made, but it can mean the end of the "correct" outcome for whatever has been said.

So those who've completely severed their connection to the Jatali's Magic, he won't be able to know their inner workings. Unless he touches a being and reads their heart directly, there's still things he and King can't know in this way. They send spies and other military teams to gather whatever intel they can. Until we can reestablish those connections, he's focusing on what we can know and who we can help— at least when it comes to the Magic being involved.

He finally notices me lingering in the doorway and he closes the map.

"I didn't mean to interrupt your work—"

"It's fine. You know I'm never too busy for any being who needs me."

The Prince wears a warm smile and he's completely focused on me in that moment. He waves me on once more, "Please come to me."

I start walking towards him but I can feel every scrape of stone against my paws. I'm barely a step away from him and my tail curls around my paws, "H-how's it going in here?"

He sighs, "Same as usual but I can't complain. I know I've made a difference already for some of these beings."

"That's good." I twist my paws together, *Why is this so hard for me?*

"Please Indy, let us speak about you. You know you can talk to me about anything."

My brows furrow, "I know I just started my assignment, and it's great really—"

"You have doubts about his heart?"

"You could say that. And Talik—"

"Don't pay Altikua *any* mind. He has your best interests but he can't see everything."

"I know my Liege, but I'm not sure I'm the right being for this job. I'm used to cubs, not full grown brutes— brutes who do nothing but antagonize you."

The Prince chuckles, "He didn't get that way in *one* day. Did you really think you could change him in such a time?"

I'm quiet a moment, "No. I'm not sure what I expected. I just don't want to mess this up."

The Prince walks closer to me. His strong paw gently on my shoulder, "One week is enough to change his heart. Stick with it that long and then I have some other ideas for him if you want to quit."

"But Sire, I don't want to let you down—"

"You wouldn't be. I won't force you to do anything you don't want to do. You know that."

I watch his gentle expression. His blue eyes so full of compassion and understanding. I can't believe I can look our Prince in the eye—

I look down, my chest tight, *Telling him I want to quit after one day....lame.*

His brows tilt, "Indessah, we all know the risks we take to make things new, but you're not alone. You can always come to me even if you think it's too simple."

I grit my teeth, my fists clench as I meet his gaze, "I won't let you down. I'll give it my all!"

"You *always* do, Indy." He nods gently, "Please **promise** me you'll come to me if you need anything. You're not alone *anymore*."

I take a sharp breath, "I know, Azufae. Thank you Sire for hearing me."

He gives me the warmest look. A look that could burn through walls and melt even the hardest metal. It gives me the courage to press onwards. He turns to re-open the map and his endless work starts again. Looking, searching, waiting for any being who might need his help. He has such confidence in me but I don't know where it comes from. He's cleaned up my messes more than once and I doubt they'll be the last.

I cut into the hallway and power walk through the corridors. My tail is swishing and the other beings start to take notice. I have an idea. A plan to make Tatchathura see things our way. Prince Azufae-yoh hasn't told me what will happen if I fail, but I guess I just wish I had a clearer idea of what failure looks like.

What step will send us careening off the path of no return?

Will a simple story undo his mind?

Or maybe another blast of fire straight to his heart will change the stars?

CHAPTER FOURTEEN

Negotiating with the Enemy

ALTIKUA

It's a long walk down a long hallway with Tatchathura in tow. For once he's mostly quiet. Usually he's chatting up a storm trying to throw me off my game. I suppose he's figured it was useless after we put that collar on him.

I'm reminded of what my Master has told me...

"I need you to speak with him alone. See what he might divulge to you. I will join you later as there are a few other pieces that need to be in place."

"But why do we need him at all? We're doing just fine."

"He has skills you don't. Skills none of our kind should have."

Normally I'm pretty good at understanding what Prince Azufae-yoh wants, but in this case— the way it was said— confuses me. He has a power our kind *shouldn't* have? I know he didn't mean his shadow counterpart— that much is apparent.

Perhaps it has something to do with the reports I've read about him. The terrible things they've been doing in Zutaom on behalf of the Drake. I shake these other concerns away. The most important thing about this meeting is seeing if we can bargain with him—

I shudder slightly at the idea. Sure we've been accommodating to these criminals and rejects in the past. Plenty have been reformed by Luthura Castle's paw, but never have we cut a pardon-style deal with a criminal.

Ever.

The power Tatchathura has must be valuable for the Prince to even consider it. But still I doubt the Prince will actually let him go at the end of it. It must be part of some grander plan. The Magic must have revealed something to him. So I will stake my faith on this possible fact.

I push open the War Room door. He slinks inside before finding a chair to recline in. Quietly the door shuts behind me.

"So *Captain*, where's Azu?"

"You don't get to call him that." My hackles raise, "It's just you and me right now."

"Do you think I'm blind?"

I suppress the reaction I really want to have but still my tail lashes, "There will always be a little trouble among beings here and there, but the Kingdom can't allow gangs to stick around. At all."

Tatchathura leans back in the chair, "Sounds like a *you* problem to me."

Skills, huh? I lean down near him, "I *know* you know something about all of this."

"Contrary to what you think, not all gangs run with the Drake or Zutaom," he puts a dramatic paw to his chest, "And I'm *offended* you'd lump me into those low level rock-brains."

I sweep my paw in a general motion over the map, "Even though we've done a great job of cleaning up gangs overall, there are still a *few* that evade us."

"Great job Blondie." he claps fakely.

I narrow my gaze, "*Usually* if the leader is taken out, the rest of the gang scatters making them easier to recover."

"Also true."

"We've tried to find these places under stealth or with just a few beings— but they *always* seem to know ahead of time. They vanish into thin air and I can only surmise that someone else— *some force*— is helping them stay covered."

He remains indifferent. His ears strangely still.

I point to a few spots on the map, "These were the last known locations. Medin was towards the north near Behim. Abkan was sighted heading south on route to Nuiat Duah."

As I point to those spots, his ears start to twitch.

"Kileous is more elusive. He seems to favor the border near Deleon. We think maybe the Wandering Timbers are giving him some coverage."

This name rouses an amused snort out of him. But then I say, "Daphoag, is another on our list but we're not sure if he's actually leading anything these days."

For once Tatchathura seems perturbed by this name, "He's a rat out for *himself*."

"A former comrade of yours?"

"A snake-hearted being I wouldn't mind raking over the coals."

My gaze narrows as I lean over him, "So you *know* of at least one of our targets?"

"Let's just say you've got your work cut out for you Captain. He's one of the slipperiest foxes I've ever met."

"Is that so? I believe they are the source of these new shadows forming. You know if you help us, we'll be able work with you."

He grits his teeth, "Even if I wanted to help— which I **don't**— he would be a deal breaker. *No way* I'm capturing that being."

I share a tense look with him. His ears flatten and his claws start clacking on the table next to him. He looks ready to pounce.

My hackles raise. I slam a paw down on the map, "It's not like I wanted to ask you. I'd rather we not get any help from *your type* at all— but I must yield to my Master's wishes."

His pupils are like slits as I stare him down. I was done talking awhile ago. Now I'm *really* done.

Still he says nothing. His stare almost empty at this point.

I huff and brush my fur down, "Fine. Consider it, ruffian. It's the *only* chance you'll get to go beyond these walls."

A moment later the door swings open. The Prince walks into the room with his tail swishing happily. I take a few steps back and hope he didn't hear me lose my temper.

Prince Azufae-yoh says, "How is everything going?"

I say, "Fine."

"What's up Azu?" Tatchathura reclines in his seat, paws behind his head, "We were just talking about what a *great* leader you're going to be once the King steps down."

Prince Azufae-yoh's ears flick to show he's heard but he pays no mind. If only I had that kind of will. He settles down in the chair next to Tatchathura, "How are you settling in? Room cozy?"

"Oh you mean my cubicle? Just fine *Boss*. I should be able to scribe those reports by the end of the week."

He chuckles lightly, "I'm sure the others are treating you well?"

"It depends on your definition of *well.*"

The Prince glances back at me a moment, "I'm sorry if Altikua has been rougher with you than he needs to be. I've had a chat with him already."

I nod. I hate to agree with him about the treatment of prisoners but I will admit I was out of line that day. He just makes all those old feelings resurface. He reminds me too much of the beings who took the most precious things from me.

Tatchathura says, "Why would you care? I'm your prisoner after all."

The Prince says, "I do apologize. I never wanted to put that collar on you. However, I need to do what I must to save my people— to save you all."

The Prince looks at him with such conviction. His eyes burning with a deep blue light. It's nowhere near as strong as the purple light when he reads a heart— but still. I sigh to myself. Prince Azufae-yoh is trying so hard to show this *ruffian* he cares for him, and Tatchathura could care less.

Tatchathura motions to the collar on his neck, "I don't know about that *Boss.* Seems like there could be some budget cuts if using *this* is your idea of saving *anything.*"

He shakes his head seemingly amused, "So has Altikua told you about the mission I have for you?"

"Oh right, *not* interested."

"I need you to do something my Knights can not. At least not very well. The longer you walk in the light the harder it gets to see the shadows. Some can see them, but still they lack proper training."

"I already told Blondie that's a *you* problem." He rests his face against the table and closes his eyes.

Prince Azufae-yoh glances to me with a flicker of concern, "I'd like it very much if you'd to help me find shadows in all the crevices of this land. "

"Yeah, it's pretty crowded in here." He pats his arm, "One is enough for me."

"I admire your sense of humor. But I'm speaking of splitting shadows from beings."

Tatchathura's ears flick around uncomfortably.

My gut clenches. So that is what this is about. You see once a being has made a pact with a shadow, that being gives up parts of their body that the shadow can inhabit. Most beings don't understand that once they commit to that idea, it grows to change their mind and heart. It's no longer about physical real estate, but a battle for their very soul.

The shadow always slowly takes over more of their body and influences their actions in subtle ways. The being is in control and should be held accountable for ultimately their choices, but the darker they go down that hole, the harder it is for them to make the right choices. Until they turn into a full shadow that can no longer be changed back.

Usually if it doesn't get too far, a being can renounce a shadow, but only with the help of a knight, the Prince or King. It takes powerful Jatalian Magic to break a pact fully. Some beings like Xai-ten end up with scars they carry forever like his leaky tail, but at least his soul is safe now. Any pact broken can free a being from their hold. But usually they don't even think of changing as their minds are already polluted with the need for power, greed or any host of negative things.

The Prince is speaking of a magic that allows the user to pull shadows out of beings that have made such a pact before they turn. It's always dangerous and costly to those involved. Since they are being forced apart, instead of the pact being broken with Jatali, the beings that have shadows ripped from them fall into a daze. It's like they aren't themselves anymore. Doomed to shuffle around in a mental haze unaware of anything and never interacting with others save for mumbled or repeated phrases. It ruins their mind and heart.

There are rumors of whole stretches of land in Zutaom that have beings like that roaming around. There's no cure I know of—

I can't believe the Prince would suggest such a thing!

My eyes widen slightly as they fall on the Prince, "Sire, you can't be *serious*?"

He glances at me, "Fear not, it's something that must be

done."

"But Sire, they won't be the same—"

"There is a *way* to fix them."

My heart beats out of control. And Tatchathura's ears flicker as though this is news to him as well.

"It takes the Virtue of Courage to start the healing and then the mastery of this Virtue to unlock the other Healing Branches they need."

Tatchathura rolls his eyes, "Courage has the power to heal? Now I've heard it *all*."

Each Virtue is mostly common knowledge and each one usually has three Branches. And even though I've seen Healing Magic used before, it usually has roots in Patience or Kindness. Courage is a new one on me too.

The Prince twists to face the dark fox fully, "You used to split shadows for the Drake. You're very skilled." His gaze seems leading.

Trusting Prince Azufae-yoh can be challenging sometimes, but I know it always turns out right. If only I could get that through my thick skull about his plans for Indy. I've never had trouble trusting him before but I guess that's what happens when fear clouds your mind.

It seems the Prince's words have finally struck a nerve with our prisoner.

Tatchathura stands up, ears flat, "What do you mean *used* to? The Drake is still my Master."

Prince Azufae-yoh's ears tilt forwards, "But someone like you— it would be very easy to sense. After all you've been walking with your shadow quite some time."

I let out a mock sigh, "Sire, why are we even bothering? It's clearly *challenging* for him."

Tatchathura's tail lashes out of control, "Oh I see what you're *trying* to do Captain— it's the oldest trick in the book. Why don't **you** just teach them?"

I'm itching say more but I have to be patient. I don't like this. Negotiating with the enemy for the slim chance they might change—

The Prince's steel blue eyes never waver, "Unfortunately most of my followers have become lax in seeking this knowledge. It takes many years of study to form an accurate deduction. To see what can't be seen. Years of training you've clearly already had."

"I'm not sure where you're getting your intel. But just because I have a shadow doesn't mean I can see them." He looks away.

This lying furball, I lean over the table and smirk, "Even now you're aware that a few of our new recruits are commiserating with shadows. Does *Rage, Vanity and Self-Righteousness* ring a bell?"

Tatchathura's impatient stance softens as he turns to look at me. His stark blue eyes reveal nothing, but the twitch in his ear tells me all I need to know.

I lean even closer towards him, "Don't be so *foolish* to

think you have all the cards."

He glares at me, "Who cares? I'm not helping you. I'm a lot of things, but I'm not a *traitor*."

Prince Azufae-yoh says, "How about I ask you a different question?"

"I'm all ears." Tatchathura's gaze is traversing the walls. Anything to avoid looking at us.

Prince Azufae-yoh's once gentle gaze turns serious. The faint glittering of blue in his eyes now stormy and dark, "What *exactly* has the Drake promised you?"

The dark fox seems to pause at this question. His ears are twitching and he seems stiff somehow. I'm sure I saw the faintest of a shiver up his spine. So there can be fear in this being after all. Tatchathura turns his back to him with his tail slowly curling around his foot. It's as if to brace himself but for what— I'm not quite sure.

There is bitterness in his voice, "The Drake promised me something **you** won't even share with your **own** beings. So what could you possibly offer me?"

"And what *exactly* is that?"

"If you know the thoughts of beings like you say, then you should *already* know."

That bitterness in his voice. It's almost as if he's taking such a question like a personal attack. It's odd to me.

Prince Azufae-yoh sighs deeply, "What has happened to you— *can not* be changed."

"You think so?" he pretends to be surprised with an obnoxious expression.

"Don't pretend you had *no choices*."

Tatchathura snarls at this.

I click the hilt of my sword. He glares at me and settles.

The Prince calms his voice, "I ask you to consider what I'm offering. Help me root out this bad blood— these criminals that are tearing our continent apart. And I'll grant you a full pardon."

"Wow, *full* pardon." Tatchathura rolls his eyes.

The Prince's eyes are like steel now, "The only *condition* I have is that if you offer to help me, you have to do it without complaint, follow my rules and listen to my Knights. Only then will I grant your full pardon. I should mention I can't put a time limit on how long this mission might take. I'm sure you understand."

He twists away from my Master's gaze, "Not gonna happen."

Prince Azufae-yoh stands, his shoulders stiff, "It takes a special kind of soul to do what you can. It's time for you to use your talents for what *I* intended them to be."

Tatchathura looks completely livid but he's strong enough to bite back his full reaction—(I guess he's not completely stupid), "And if I still *refuse*?"

"I'm sorry but I'll be forced to send you back to the prison so you can serve your time there. It wouldn't be right to let you walk free after everything you've done."

"Oh, so you do *know* me?" His gaze almost wild, "And still you'd risk trusting your beings to *me*?"

Honestly that's a concern I share. It's one thing to have to work with criminals around the castle and town, but to have to go on country-wide trips with this fool?

Prince Azufae-yoh nods calmly. His gaze resolute and fiery.

Tatchathura's words sound like poison, "I'm not gonna play **your game.** You might as well take me back to my cell. I'd rather **rot** before I'd help the Kingdom of Jatali."

The Prince says, "Very well. Let me know if there's anything else I can do for you."

Tatchathura turns like he's crazed. His eyes wide like he can't believe it. He half-snarls and stares at the door. His tail swishing violently.

The lion nods towards me and I understand his desire. It takes only a moment to call some guards to take him back to his cell. I make sure his cuffs are on tightly and put an extra heavy tail lock on him so that there won't be any shenanigans like the other day.

The guards walk into the War Room. A panther and a rhino walk in. Still they shake. It seems that the rumors I've overheard in the ranks are growing in power. We've faced worse than Tatchathura. I'll have to have a pep talk with the troops later.

I put a firm paw on the panther's shoulder, "Don't speak to him—" I ignore Tatchathura's groan of disappointment, "Like most of his kind, he feeds on that chaotic energy. **Ignore** him at all costs."

The soldiers bow their heads a moment before taking each of his arms.

"Also set up a meeting for everyone this afternoon. Around three. We have things to discuss."

The rhino nods meekly while keeping his sights on the Shadow Fox.

After they take him away, I turn towards the Prince, "Master?"

The white lion turns slightly. His gaze seems worn, "Yes, my faithful friend?"

"Why didn't you question him about the Taoah-lut Glove?"

He shakes his head, "That is a conversation for another time."

"We already know they seek it for power, but to what ends?"

"I'm sure it has something to do with those rumors in the East. About uniting the Thirteen Relics."

I nod evenly. I can see why he'd put that off. Even if a being wanted to unite all the Relics, he'd be searching for a lifetime. Most of them are lost with unknown powers and origin save for the Glove that was kept here.

I say, "I just *don't* understand— why him? What makes him so different that he gets a deal? If you would've let me use Honesty for another minute in the Great Hall, he could've told us *everything*! I'm sure of it."

The Prince sighs, "I know it's unorthodox of me, but it's the way things *have* to be. Besides in his case, he needs to feel like this is *his* idea. That he's helping because he views a gain from it. If we force him to help, he's just going to be more obstinate."

"So the magical collar is just for show then?"

"The magical collar works—"

"Forgive me Master, but I just don't see the point."

"The Kingdom has grieved him greatly."

My ears flatten, *He's never said that before about any being...*

For once, Azufae-yoh's ears flatten, "It's hard but you're just going to have to trust me. This is the best way to save his soul from the shadows."

I sigh, a deep rumble in my chest, "You know, I could just hang him by his toes off the tower. It'd make it way *faster*."

He chuckles, "Stop it, Talik."

"Sire, please forgive my hesitation— After our dealings with Daphoag—"

He faces me fully, eyes ablaze, "They may seem the same to you but it couldn't be further from the truth. Daphoag walked the path he had to take."

"How can you be so sure? I know you read his heart—"

He seems deflated now, "The only path I saw he might change involved letting him escape, but even now my heart is not sure he will ever change."

"I know you don't want to let any being suffer the fate of the Abyss, but surely *some* of this isn't worth our time?"

"If even one being is changed for the better, it's *always* worth the commitment."

There's a low growl on my lips, "Tatchathura **won't** work with us. Even if agrees, he'll just be plotting a way to escape the whole time."

The Prince smirks, "You know, you two might even be friends by the end of this."

I sputter, a heat under my collar, "Never. I'm sorry but I don't see why Indy has to be a part of this either. She's— *naive* to put it nicely. How can I protect—"

"She doesn't need your protection." He says flatly, tail lashing, "Do you think I'd give her more than she's capable of? Are we not all tested to grow stronger?"

"She's going to get killed from trusting him too much. You know what happened the *first* time he tried to escape."

He raises his paw, eyes steely calm, "That collar is linked to her soul and your soul because you're the only ones who can change him enough. To lead him to me. To Jatali's purposes."

My tail lashes while my paws grip the table next to me.

That heat rises in my gut making my stomach turn. I've seen a lot in my days as a plain solider and even more as a Commander, but the thought of losing another so close to me— my sister-in-arms— it's hard for me to grapple with.

The Prince has a knowing look and puts his paw on my shoulder, "I have already seen what they will do. They are still on the path they need to take. I will be watching them closely so they don't shift. "

I snort, "Wish you'd tell me what path I should take."

There's a small smirk on his lips, "If I did, you wouldn't take it."

He gives me another friendly nod before heading towards the door. I watch the Prince leave. My brain turning over the possibilities. My way of life has already been shifted so much in a short amount of time. I can't imagine a path worse than this one.

And a path that I wouldn't obey?

I may question from time to time, but I'm loyal to the Kingdom until the bitter end.

After all, I owe them everything.

They were there for me even in my darkest hour. A moment I can never take back and will always regret. It's something that haunts me every night. It's been three long years since I lost them. With the line of work I'm in, I was prone to make enemies. And in my case, the one day I fell short, the target on my back finally exploded.

My family and I always lived on the outskirts of the city. It was a quaint little farmhouse. My wife loved the view and my little cub loved climbing the trees. I was promoted to Commander way ahead of my time. Within weeks I'd managed to root out almost all of the gang activity in our city. I suppose that made my bright golden pelt stand out a little.

On my path for justice— to clean up the city— I made enemies all over. I didn't just make enemies with Zutaom's henchmen, or random gang lords— I made some enemies within my own commanding officers. Those who were jealous or frustrated that I was promoted over them. Those that had illicit dealings with the gangs I rooted out. After all, if you ruin someone's way of life, there's bound to be consequences.

One of them became vengeful and must have sold the location of my house to our enemies. I came home one night. The door had been ripped off. Windows shattered. Clearly there had been a struggle. My wife was a strong fighter but there's no way she could have possibly defended herself against what was most likely a group. I did everything to try and weed out the attacker or group. But on my quest for Justice, I almost let the shadow of Vengeance take me.

The Prince pulled me back from the edge of that dark path. He kept me seeing the light when all I wanted was to drown in my misery. I didn't deserve a second chance— but he gave it to me freely. He knew my struggle. The pain in my heart.

I won't soon forget the love my friend has for me.

* * *

I walk briskly down the corridor. The hallways are filled with Knights and other soldiers. There's a scattered energy as I head to the main War Room. A few of the captains are already seated around the large table. Prince Azufae-yoh isn't here yet but I know he'll be there soon. A few of the captains greet me. Few others look concerned already. I know exactly what they're worried about. It seems the ruffian was onto something when he goaded us about the Abyss's seal being broken.

After my morning chat with Indy, I'd informed the captains to send teams to investigate our borders. All of those teams have come back now with reports. Prince Azufae-yoh finally comes in. He seems happy enough but I can tell something new is bothering him. His forced optimism for the sake of the others. I've known him long enough now to know better. He's always worried about accidentally starting a panic. I think the others shouldn't be so soft. We're at war aren't we?

The Prince catches my gaze for a moment. He waves for me to commence the meeting.

I stalk to the head of the table, "Has everyone gathered their reports from their quadrants?"

All of the captains offer up their paperwork. I shuffle through them quickly. As I scan each paper, there does seem to be a consensus that Luthura is about to be under attack by the biggest shadow force we've ever seen. Gravely I lay the papers down on the table. There's a giant map in the center. It has all the detailed roads, foliage, all of our side passages and hidden tunnel systems marked with different colors.

I lean over the table, "Tephus, what exactly did your being see on the southern Ridge?"

Tephus, the gazelle, stands up, "There's only a few Commander, but they're just *waiting* at the southern border. My beings left a few sentries to keep watch. They were worried if they engaged too early it might cause calamity for the rest of the city."

I nod, "That was wise of your team. I'm assuming they are still on post?"

He nods, "I told them to send word immediately if anything changes."

I spread the papers in front of me. Shadows usually work alone and attack whenever they have a weakened, lone prey in sight—but these shadows are coordinated. The light of Luthura keeps the city protected from their presence for the moment. But if too many of them decided to gather and attack— then the barrier would be weakened. Which tells me they're waiting because they've been told to wait. Normally we'd just root out a few on sight. Just be done with it. But every report says there are pockets of three to five shadows on every border about every hundred feet or so. Even if I wanted to engage them, it'd be risky to the civilians. They'd probably even hop over our heads and wreck havoc on the city.

I nod to Tephus. He settles back in his chair. Some of the others seem anxious at the news. I keep a strong stance and go through each report with them. A few different sightings get more attention as they are even more troubling. The easy part is initiating evacuation plans as soon as possible. Getting as many innocents out of the line of fire is always top priority. The tricky part is— *when* will they attack? *When* does it make the most sense? Will we have enough time to get everyone out?

I pinch my brow and look at the Prince, "Sire, what would you have us do?"

He narrows his gaze scanning the map. He bites his lip with ears twitching, "Increase the forces here and here. Let's start the evacuations in this sector of town first. It's the closest to the border where the most shadows seem to be forming. Then fan out and start evacuating the others."

A few of the captains nod their agreement and start writing down notes. I'm taking mental notes.

Prince Azufae-yoh stands, "We need to be discreet about this evacuation. If we make too much ruckus, then the shadows might attack earlier. Every second counts but be smart about it. You'll need to make sure everybody is in the bunkers as soon as possible. But I don't want our forces spread too thin or else we may not be able to push them back."

There is further agreement among our forces.

I wave for their attention once more, "Also, keep a lookout for a grey and yellow fox with a torn ear. She's a little on the smaller side, but I've seen her several times rooting around the castle walls. None of our forces have been able to capture her yet." I pinch my brow, "We have the suspicion that she may be working with the Shadow Fox."

There are a few hushed conversations of concern. Nervous whispers between them— but it's more of a nervousness of what to do rather than fear of our enemies. For the time being, Jatali has blessed us with strong captains.

The Prince says, "Everyone, communication is key. Let's work together and keep our city safe. Dismissed."

There's a rumble of approval in the room before the captains start to file out. I watch them with a stone weighing down in my chest. My heart is tightly twisting in my chest— stabbing like a pain cutting me to pieces.

Any mistake—

Any mess up—

One little crossed path could mean losing someone else I love—

I'm not going to have that happen— Not on my watch ever again.

The Prince rises slowly. He looks worn as he gazes upon me, "Altikua, my old friend. I know you're worried. But you must understand— everything that is going to come to pass — **must** happen this way."

I grit my teeth and force down the reaction I really want to have, "Sire forgive me. It's not that I don't trust you, it's just painful for me— hard to understand all of this."

His eyes seem glossy at this remark. He nods slowly, "Of course I understand it. To think that any of our beings might suffer because of these shadows. But my Father has already explained it to me. Soon things will finally be changing into the way they were supposed to be all along. A world without suffering. We'll finally be rebuilding our continent. That's something happy to look forward to, don't you think?"

He wears a small smile but I can tell that he's struggling with his own insecurities—the thoughts of losing *even one* being to the shadows— The Magic we follow may reveal itself to the King and Prince, but still it's sometimes hard to swallow the finer details.

That's the problem with having faith— you're walking in blind— sometimes it's so dark and there's no candles left—

But if you're surrounded by beings you love—

Words you trust—

Feelings you can't shake—

You have no other choice but to charge in headstrong and start a fire all your own.

CHAPTER FIFTEEN

Around Town

TATCHATHURA

It's the next day. I'm stuck in the courtyard as the Rainbows discuss their plans. Indy has a piece of paper out. She is talking to Heroh, Sukua and Kyltia in a somewhat hushed way. They all seem to be in agreement about something—

Like I care what they're talking about.

However, I don't mind making time to annoy her.

I saunter up to peer over her shoulder. It's not hard because she's that much shorter than me, "What are you doing?"

She jumps slightly hugging the paper to her chest, "Does it really matter? You're stuck with us either way."

It's amusing, honestly. So short but such a powerful, fiery punch. My chest still hurts after her collision with me. If she wasn't serving Jatali, I'd be more impressed with her.

She's nothing like my Lu-kan. Ferocious, powerful, and deadly. Someone I miss very much right now.

But I know I'll see her again. Even now I know she's working hard to figure out a way for me to leave this glimmering place. She's never been one to leave anyone behind. That's what's rare and beautiful about her. Most Zutaomese only worry about their own skin. She and I share a past much different than that. Even before we were together, we were taking care of each other. We were only cubs after all.

My lip quirks to one side, "That important, huh?"

"I'll explain it on the way." She glances over at me with those soft brown eyes *still* taunting me. Like she's really *that* innocent. I know she's trying to play me for a fool too. Liars. All of them.

I wouldn't be surprised if that was their plan all along. The Mutt to intimidate me and the Princess to make me feel like I have nothing to hide—that I'm *loved* or some nonsense. Azufae to swoop in when I get "vulnerable".

Not gonna happen.

Sukua says, "We've got some important business to attend to in city."

I manage to snatch the paper whenever Indy is distracted again. She scoffs and yelps about giving the paper back.

I glance over the list. It's contents are weird to be sure. I half-expected a happy face or hearts at the end. But nope just a standard paper—

She snatches it back, "Let's get going while it's still light."

"Really, I'm flattered, but I don't need to participate in your menial to-do list from your pompous Prince. Just lock me back up—"

Indy turns with a wry look, "You'd like that wouldn't you?"

Heroh says, "Best get a move on."

I say, "You **weirdos** *really* want to go shopping with a criminal?"

Sukua says with a giggle, "You're not a criminal anymore, *silly*! You're *one of us*."

I stare at her with a blank expression on my face. She really is the most air headed of them all. At least Indy has some common sense.

Indy flashes them a hot look, "Hey, we're just fulfilling our duty as Knights. Let's not get it *twisted*."

Kyltia raises a wing, "Knights-in-training."

"Whatever! Can we just go already?"

Heroh shrugs, "Just kidding. You're no fun Indy."

"Forgive me for not rolling out the welcome wagon for that—*fluffbrain.*"

I smirk, "Of course not *your Highness.*"

She ignores me and starts heading towards the castle gates.

* * *

As we wander into town just past the castle gates, Indy is already fumbling with the paper. Sukua waves her down and takes the lead. I'm ushered towards the front as Heroh and Kyltia take their spots behind me. I'm boxed in.

Sukua turns to say to Kyltia, "I can't believe Prince Azufae already had something lined up for you."

Kyltia says, "I guess he's good like that. I'm kind of embarrassed that he figured I would tag-along anyway."

Indy shakes her head, "It's probably for the best. Sooner or later you would have shown up. He's probably had it ready for months now."

Kyltia folds her ears, whispering, "But they only caught the Shadow Fox a few days ago."

"Oh, he's just as *predictable* as you are."

They all laugh. My ears flatten shooting her a look but I say nothing. My mind wanders back to the conversation I had the other day with Blonde and Azu...

Azufae's once gentle gaze turns serious. The faint

249

glittering of blue in his eyes now stormy and dark, "What exactly has the Drake promised you?"

There's *something* about the way he looked at me that sent a shiver up my spine. It seems my suspicions are correct— there is a darker side to Azufae that he is suppressing. The beings have no clue. It's not like I *never* expected him to talk in a more serious tone— after all *I* was at the throne room when he practically ripped me apart and put me back together.

I'm not even sure if all the pieces were put back in the right place.

Azufae calms his voice, "I ask you to consider what I'm offering. Help me root out this bad blood— these criminals that are tearing our continent apart. And I'll grant you a full pardon."

They want to offer me a deal for my freedom?

What a joke.

Don't they realize sooner or later I'm gonna get out of these confines? I'll find a way to break this collar. No one cages me for long. I look down at the glimmering gold tight around my neck. The red gemstones are so beautiful and elegant.

But it's the mark of my oppression.

The girls are now all ahead of me. I tune them out. Their endless chatter about nothing makes me want to cut my ears off. Besides, none of them really understand the things I've done.

I can't even forgive myself.

They *honestly* think that the Prince is gonna forgive me?

That fuzzy fluffball doesn't know *half* of what I've done—

I say, "And if I still refuse?"

"I'm sorry but I'll be forced to send you back to the prison so you can serve your time there. It wouldn't be right to let you walk free after everything you've done."

"Oh, so you do know me?"

I glance down at my paws. The paws that have left so much destruction behind. I never said I was proud of being the Shadow Fox, but in some ways it's all I have anymore. That and Lu-kan. No other friends, and no family. He was talking about the way I split beings from their shadows. The ultimate punishment for failing in Zutaom. Beings who have a shadow torn from them aren't the same afterwards. Rock-brains roaming around endlessly. The shadow is usually fine. I can only assume it's because the shadows entwine themselves into our very core.

I clench my fist. My hot gaze at the arm that holds Vengeance. I've only failed twice as a whelp. I have the scars they gave me to prove it. This would be the third time I've failed them. I always figured my ability would keep me alive even if I failed— but I wonder— what will the Drake do to me if I can't undo this failure?

I'd like to say I can't believe the *Prince of Light* would do the same thing the Drake is to other beings— he was even bold enough to say he has a cure!

Everyone in Jatali thinks their rulers are just too perfect.

But I know *exactly* what their *Prince* is doing. He puts on that nice persona— looks inviting and kind— like he really *actually* cares—

Azufae says, "Very well. Let me know if there's anything else I can do for you."

But I know what he's *really* like. He's just as manipulative as I am. He's kind to get what he wants— to have everyone fall in line. But his father is waiting just behind him for you to slip up. The Great King strikes down any being that won't listen to his son.

They can lie to themselves all they want— but I'm not a cub anymore. I've grown out of that dumb *fantasy*.

I don't need anyone's forgiveness.

Besides, when I bring my parents back, all this pain will be worth it— If I live to see it that is—

As we walk through town, I look over the civilians. Most of them are unaffected by my presence— blissfully unaware of who's in their lovely little garden. I look them all over in turn. Cracks here— more holes there— all of Jatali's beings are crawling with imperfections. It seems the land of love is on hiatus. No wonder Zutaom is itching to attack these fools.

One of the civilians whispers to the others as we pass, "Wow! Knights of Jatali. They must live such charmed lives."

"I wish I could use magic like them."

This seems to catch the ear of our faithful Indy. She turns with a bright smile. As she heads towards them, they start to fluster.

She takes one by the hoof, "You see that's what's great about our kind— anyone can do magic!"

The horse retracts her hooves, "No way. You need training and will." She flushes.

Heroh says, "That's true. Lots of might and desire. But the Prince is more than willing to train anyone who desires it."

The horse shakes her head again, "I wouldn't want to go to war."

Her friend is wide eyed, "Can you imagine taking on a shadow!? Well, I guess you can." She chuckles awkwardly.

Indy's ears flatten and tail brushes the dirt. It seems to have gotten her thinking.

Heroh says, "That's the best thing. We'll train anyone in self-defense. You don't have to become a soldier."

Again they both fluster and meekly decline.

A small smirk forms on my lips, *So that's what it is...*

I expected to walk these streets and see magic on every street corner. Bastions of light and ingenuity from every paw—

But the commoners are afraid of their birthright. Every being who can align their heart with Jatali or a shadow can have great power. But it seems most won't take it. That figures.

You see that's the thing about magic in Ituvoh, it's based on strength of will. You may be able to learn any type of magic that you want, but if you don't have this will to back it up, then you're dead in the water. That's why most of the beings in this world have all the potential but never fully utilize it. I know the Magic of Jatali has aligned itself with them. But Indessah went so far to say that Azufae and Elin have the magic of hundred beings. I have yet to see that myself. If it were true, it just seems like the Prince would have done something about the Drake by now. If either of them was so powerful, all they would have to do is snap their paws and end the war.

But they haven't done it.

They sit in their cozy castle and force everyone else around them to do their bidding.

After winding down various cobblestone roads, past the bakery and host of other small shops, we finally see a hanging sign that sticks out from the others. The building is smaller than I would have expected. A broad golden sign hangs down shaped like a present box. A glittering purple fireheart flower sits in the middle. There's a magical sparkle that flickers around the wood like a firework. Twisted curls of red are carved into the golden sign with words that read: FIREHEART PAPERS.

Heroh steps ahead of us to open the door. He waves his

broad paw allowing us in before him. They all thank him separately besides me. I walk inside and it's bustling with the activity of many kinds of animals. Most of them seem to be customers looking over all of the books and magazines. Some parents are huddled with their cubs trying to pick the best toy from the shelves. There's a worker behind the counter who looks flustered trying to ring up the many orders. Annoying. We *had* to come to come place like this.

In the middle of the chaos, a puma cuts the sea. She settles next to the cashier for a moment. She speeds up the process by using both of her paws with lightning precision. As she finishes another batch of customers up, she notices our group towards the door. Her eyes light up, "I had no idea you'd all come! Come. Come."

She dashes around the counter and starts waving us with a quicker motion. They all seem to giggle and get closer to overenthusiastic giant cat. "My name is Zelenah Ta-nela. So nice to see you Heroh and Sukua."

Sukua grabs a hold of Indy, "Yes, and this is our pal Indy. And that grumpy one is Tatchathura."

I roll my eyes while the others are amused at my expense again.

Zelenah lowers her paws onto the Kyltia's shoulders, "So you must be Kyltia. Prince Azufae-yoh has nothing but good things to say about you."

Kyltia's face flushes and waves her wing, "Aw shucks. I'm just here to do my part."

The bustle of the crowd starts to intensify. More patrons try to squeeze in the door and some start bumping into us. I suppress the urge to give them a full growl.

Zelenah seems to notice at the same time, "Let's head to where we can talk."

Our group starts filing in line after the puma. We pass the counter and then disappear through a door into the back room operations. A few other beings are busy working on printing the papers and magazines. A few other beings are speaking through Soul Links to presumably field agents. The ones behind the screen seem to be regaling stories about what's happening in the country and possibly other countries. Zelenah leads us through another set of doors before letting us into her office. The others start excitedly looking around her heavily decorated room. It's spacious considering the front of the shop is so tiny. She's got seemingly every report, clipping and photo she's ever published. Colored crystal chimes hang from various posts in the ceiling. A bright lantern with a purple flame sits on her sweeping grey desk.

She settles behind her desk. Her paws clasped as she looks up at us, "Now Kyltia, when will you be able to start?"

Indy pushes Kyltia towards the front of us. Kyltia flashes her a look of annoyance before putting on a show, "Of course, immediately!"

Indessah smacks her own forehead, "The Prince said you had to finish your training first."

The bat deflates, "Fine. Sorry, but I'm guessing sometime next week."

Zelenah snaps her paws as if disappointed, "Well, I guess it will have to do." She starts rummaging in her drawers before pulling out a stack of papers like it's a pile of treasure, "This is what I want you to get started on— after you finish some training with us as a reporter."

Kyltia starts hopping in place with the paper clutched in her wings, "Really! Already!?"

I can't imagine being so excited about nothing.

The puma nods, "You see— for a long time the Prince has wanted me to run reports on the shadow sightings—"

Kyltia blurts, "Can you believe some beings don't believe in shadows!" She covers her face in embarrassment.

Zelenah's smile only grows, "It's crazy isn't it? But the problem is— most of our staff is too sheep-hearted to go out into that field."

Kyltia watches her with eyes practically glowing, "Yes! Yes, I'll do it!"

There's a wry grin on the cat's lips, "He told me you would. I can't believe you were ready to take on Tiphanrah."

Kyltia scratches her head, "He told you that, huh?"

She raises her paws, "Just that much. No worries."

The two of them start talking about more assignments and other shadow sightings. It's almost like the rest of us aren't here. Indy pulls out the paper and glances towards the others.

Sukua says, "As great as this has been, we have a few other things to attend to—"

Kyltia moans, "Really— already?"

"You can stay here if you want. Just be back at the castle for tonight."

"Oh Sukua! You're the best!" she hugs her tight before twisting to face her new boss once more.

The others are amused and start filing out. I scoff. What a waste of time.

* * *

We file out of that stuffy place and back onto the busy city road. They start to look over the paper before heading south.

Heroh glances at me, "Some day, huh?"

I don't need small talk on top of everything else. I raise a brow at him and keep walking. We don't get very far before the cries of "Fire! Fire!" meet our ears. Indy and Sukua take off at light speed with the two of us following shortly behind. And now running on top of it. Yay. The girls look the situation over as if they actually know what to do. The building is ablaze. It's smoking out of control and all the beings around it can't do anything to quell it.

Sukua glances at Heroh, "You up for some Loyalty magic?"

Heroh stares up at the raging fire, "I'm a bit rusty—"

A few other beings cry and fuss that their loved ones are still in the building. It's starting to catch fire to the other buildings beside it.

Indessah looks back at me, "Do you think we can use fire magic to draw it out?"

I glare, "Why are you looking at me? Do you honestly think I have any ties to Jatali?"

She snorts and turns towards the building. Some of the floors crash into each other. More pleas of despair are let out.

Then all at once— a controlled burst of water rains from inside the building. A golden aura wraps around the structure. The floors that fell lifted up. The golden threads pulse through the broken stones mending them until they're new. Waters rush with a life of their own carefully quelling the fire and missing the beings in their paths.

Another flash of gold radiates from the doorway and out walks Azufae carrying the two beings who were still trapped inside. The waters quell and all the buildings are stable. The beings all rush to lump praise after praise on top of him.

He shakes his fur and some water spatters about. The beings all laugh about the situation as if nothing has happened. As if they haven't just lost all their material possessions.

I turn sharply towards Indy, "Don't you Jatalian scum

have some beings for *this job*?"

Indessah bristles— when is she going to learn?

"True," she says, "We do but he must have sensed it before them. The damage would have been much worse if he hadn't come. He has a soul connection with all of the beings of Jatali. He goes to those who need him the most."

"Then why take so long? Couldn't he have helped them *before* the fire started."

"It doesn't work exactly like that."

We start walking again. Sukua and Heroh take either side of me while Indessah takes the lead.

She keeps talking while looking up at the clear blue sky, "Those who are hurting, weak and sad. His connection to the other beings of the nations has weakened significantly. That's why he's striving to bring them all back together again."

I snort at the very idea, *Where was he when **my** beings needed him? Belaphrium practically supports the Kingdom single pawed. **They** should be in charge if anything...*

I take a second to glance back. The beings are all still cloistering around their *Prince*. Making such a fuss because he was able to put out a fire. So what? He's not the only being with water magic. So what if his fur wasn't even singed— just wet.

But it's odd to me. He's royalty and he leaves the castle

for such a menial task? I was under the impression he left everything up to his subordinates.

Maybe they all have rocks in their heads. Besides he wasn't there when we needed him, so what does it matter how he treats beings *now?*

You can't make up for the past.

* * *

It's the next day. I expected to see Lu-kan again by now, but still silence. Given her track record that's a day too long. The rumors of shadows on the border is my only comfort for the moment. So I'm stuck sitting outside in the courtyard while the Rainbow Brights run around. There is a guard on each of my sides. For once they seem competent— shocker. The others are playing some kind of game but I still don't understand the rules. They could be making things up at this point— knowing them. All I know is that it involves a ball and some tiny flags.

Bunch of *weirdos.*

Indessah, Sukua, and Heroh form a team of some sort. A pack of cubs from seemingly every nation bounce around them full of excitement. Got to start the brainwashing young after all. On the other side Azufae, Altikua, and Kyltia form a team with their own pack of cubs.

Indessah bounces the ball on her knee and taunts the others. Altikua seems to take the bait and dashes straight for her. I had no idea the mutt was even capable of smiling. A few cubs chase wildly after him. Their paws are raised ready to snatch away the ball. But Indessah is faster. She smacks the ball across the field into Sukua's waiting paws.

She darts around the other cubs before passing the ball to one of the smaller cubs. The young ox stumbles a little. He doesn't have a chance to hit the ball before flopping onto his face. A tiger from the opposing team darts ahead.

A couple of the cubs cheer. The tiger seems to be making a lead of some sort. Her belt is full of flags as she runs full force towards the Azufae. The lion takes off at a full run laughing right along with them.

In fact, there's so much joy on this field right now it's making me sick. The energy is so bright and strong. It's like a new glow has formed. Glad I'm 'stuck' on the sidelines.

Suddenly Azufae pretends to slow down in an exaggerated way. His steps stilted and stiff, "Oh no, don't slow me down! I was going to win."

A rooster at the head of the pack laughs, "Not anymore!"

The group of them tackle him to the ground. In a flustered rush, they all grab flags from his belt.

The other adults just stand by laughing at the ridiculous display.

Azufae throws his paw dramatically against his forehead, "I've been defeated— the end is *nigh*."

I shake my head. If only it could be true. It would solve *all* of my problems.

Another chorus of laughter erupts from the group. The

rooster has been hoisted up onto the Azufae's shoulders. His paws wrapped tightly around the young bird's legs before taking off into a sprint.

The rooster yells, "I'm King of Ituvoh!"

The view of it all stirs something in me.

Something ugly and violent.

How dare that Azufae act like he upholds us *all*.

How dare he act like he *actually* cares!

They're *literally* playing when war is at their castle stoop! He doesn't take us seriously at all. Now I'm questioning how come we haven't won this war yet. If this is how they spend their time, all we need is one really coordinated attack. Strike at the heart of Luthura. His army blown to pieces and town a wreck.

I'm so focused on what to do next about this predicament I'm in, I barely notice the ball roll up to my feet. One of the cubs yells that they'll get it but all of the adults seem to have the same response.

Indessah says, "Wait, let me get it."

The cubs seem confused and turn to look at me.

"Why? He's just a being like the rest of us?"

"Yeah, why isn't he playing with us?"

"He's your friend, isn't he?"

Ah, nativity of cubs.

I grab the ball in my paws. It feels foreign to me. I'm

reminded of the deserts of Sekulan where I was trained. A ball was a rare commodity there.

Indessah approaches me. She threads some of her long, blonde locks behind her ear.

I give the cubs a playful look, "I'm not playing because then you would *all lose* for sure."

She watches me a moment— like I'll lash out at her. I offer it up. Her paw brushes mine as she takes it. Her gaze still uneasy.

Isn't this the same being who chased me down a castle wall?

I ask with a growl, "Why are you doing this?"

"We may be enemies now but that doesn't mean we're monsters." Her bright brown eyes meet mine, "Not everyone is kind, but everyone deserves kindness."

I scoff loudly. It slowly turns into a condescending laugh, "Not after some of the beings I've met."

Azufae nods, "It may be hard for you to understand but this is the way of Jatali. Although, it's also true some beings will never understand."

The being that almost *died* by my paw and still threw herself in front of me in the courtyard?

She dashes to slide between us. She stumbles and barely puts herself between me and the sword.

*Altikua struggles to stop at the last second. His canines fully revealed, **"Indessah."***

264

"Enough. You've made your point—"

*"Are you **forgetting** he tried to kill you earlier?"*

*"We can't give up on him—He's **not** a shadow yet!"*

I don't understand her.

Why worry about me?

One of the cubs says, "Oh, he doesn't *know* how to play.

Another pipes up, "Let's teach him!"

My tail lashes, "That's *not* what I said."

Indessah covers her laughter. The others seem equally amused.

I guess that's what I get for being *nice* to the little brats.

There's another flash of exuberance from the cubs. This time Altikua stops them. His long, broad tail blocks their path.

His gaze is absolute, "Let's just get back to playing. That *friend* of ours doesn't know how to *play nice*."

As though to hammer the point home, he shoots me a look of pure loathing. I roll my eyes dramatically. My tail swishes against the ground. I could care less. The longer I spend with them, the more annoyed I become and the further away my salvation from this place feels.

* * *

The game I thought would never end, finally wraps up. The whole group gathers around Azufae and they start saying their goodbyes.

My ears twitch, *Did they just say goodbye?*

The lion nods and gives them all parting greetings. He even takes a moment to pat each of the cubs on their head. He turns from us. Drawing his paw back, he lets out a whistle.

The next moment a large creature comes galloping into the courtyard. It has long slender legs covered in fur. It's front feet webbed like a duck. It's back paws like that of a fox with claws. It has two sets of bug-like crystal colored wings that are pointed and wide, and then another set of wings that are narrow. It's tail is long and slender like a lion's tail. On the end of its tail three circle like fins. It's whole body is a beautiful blending of fur and feathers. It's mostly white with a translucent undercurrent of blues, purples, and copper. It has a narrow snout with broad nose. Two eyes that are wide and bright shining like crystals. It snorts and shakes its head full of fluff and spines. Azufae greets it in a warm way like it's a cub even though it towers over all of us. He hugs its leg before the creature lowers its neck down so he can pull himself onto its back.

He says, "Take care. Let me know if anything comes up. I'm never that far away."

He leans down to whisper to it. It tilts its head and lets out a sound like a trumpet before thundering off. It's running faster and faster until it lifts off the ground. The wings glow golden and flutter against the breeze in the courtyard. A giant, magnificent whoosh and then they're high above the courtyard sailing through the sky. The rest of them are stuck waiting for their precious Prince to return. I wasn't aware that he ever left. I know that sounds stupid but considering the rest of Ituvoh doesn't see him, and it's just so gosh darn *perfect* here—

They all seem mesmerized by the creature. I'll admit I've never seen such a thing. I'm curious and wonder if they have more. Indessah and Sukua are still distracted.

I place myself between them, "Must be nice to *run off* whenever he wants."

Indessah shoots me a look, "He's allowed to take a break —"

"So the hour long match of ball was *work* then?"

Sukua says, "Besides, more than likely, knowing him, he's off to help some other being in need."

"So what *exactly* was that creature?"

Indessah and Sukua share a look as if trying to find the right words.

Sukua finally says, "We're not really sure what she is but her name is Ashtevah. And she is the Prince's faithful companion."

"Are there more of those *somewhere*?"

Indy chuckles, "Nice try Tatchathura but unfortunately she's one-of-a-kind. He rescued her a long time ago."

Sukua says, "I think he said something about finding her abandoned somewhere in the Eastern continent. But it's been so long, so who really knows?

"Right."

Why did I expect them to be *anymore* helpful **than that**?

CHAPTER SIXTEEN

Late Night Fire

A L T I K U A

It's late when we finally settle down around the campfire. There are a few logs for benches. We're not too far from the castle walls and at our vantage point we will be able to see anything coming from the wide horizon. There are other patrols that cover the other corners of the castle. Having a "camp out" with a criminal under the moonlight seems like a foolish thing to do. And most of them go about how you'd expect a group of enemies to interact. But there are those rare times, and moments where our enemies get a flash of clarity. The briefest understanding of how they've been wrong.

How they might change. What they've been given.

The girls settle onto a log together. Heroh scouts the perimeter before rejoining their side. Tatchathura settles onto a log as far from the group as possible. His tail flicking in annoyance. I stay standing off to the opposite corner from the group. A cool night air buffets against my thick fur.

Sukua is already bouncing about the logs. She bounds towards the ruffian with her paws raised like she wants him to hit back, "First guard duty Tatchathura!"

He glares at her and as if to spite her, tucks his paws under his arms to completely obscure them from view.

Sukua shrugs and bounds back to the others, "This is so exciting!"

Heroh raises his paws wide, "I know!"

Sukua smacks his paws instead. The pair of them erupt into giggles like they're cubs again.

Tatchathura snorts, "I'm beginning to see *why* they spend time together."

Indy smirks at him, "Be nice."

Heroh says, "Sukua and I thought that we might share some of our lives before we came to Luthura. So you could feel more at home."

Tatchathura looks towards the forest at the base of the hill, "I'm good."

Indy seems uncomfortable. And I can only imagine why. Her past isn't pretty— none of our pasts are pretty— but hers least of all. Kyltia puts a wing on her shoulder.

I glance towards Sukua, "Since you're so eager, how about you go first?"

The other beings nod.

Sukua leaps up, tail lashing happily. Her words come out in a jumbled mess.

Indy waves for her to slow down, "We have plenty of time. The night is young."

"When I was younger, I lived in a small town named Rizuagh. I lost my parents when I turned seven. But because I was a stubborn child, I never asked anyone for help. Had no relatives to turn to— My parents were pretty secretive after all."

She holds her arm over the bottom of her face like it's veiled, "Even though I was living in Jatali and I knew someone would probably help me— Instead, I took to stealing from others."

Tatchathura raises his brows, "You a *thief*? I'll believe it when I *see* it."

She sticks her tongue out, "That was me a long time ago. I don't even know if I have those skills anymore."

Heroh pats her shoulder, "You still have the *important*

skills."

Her cheeks flush and tail curls around her feet, "You see what started as my ploy for survival slowly turned into a game for me. And then turned into how much I could steal."

The crackling fire seems to reflect in her eyes. This story isn't something she enjoys telling but it's as much a part of her as is all of our pasts. You can't escape it.

She hugs herself with ears flat against her head. Her paws rubbing her arms, "As I got older, I got better and better at stealing. I had quite a stockpile of items in my cave. When I was about eighteen, I had my eyes set on the next big thing."

Indy and Kyltia lean in closer to her as if to comfort her.

Sukua sighs, "I knew I probably wasn't fully prepared, I'll admit. But it was just something that I couldn't ignore."

Tatchathura narrows his gaze, "You went after the Taoah-lut Glove in the castle."

She nods solemnly, "I was *so* close. I almost had it in my paws— but then the guards ran in!" She mimics an explosion, "And Altikua burst in with all his glowing glory. I was **so mad**. I'd heard about him before."

I chuckle quietly watching her. She's very friendly now, but at that time she was a stubborn live wire— much like Indy.

Kyltia's claws cover her mouth, "I knew you were a thief but I had no idea that you actually met Altikua that way!"

Indy chuckles, "She still complains about it too."

Sukua shoots them a look before standing up dramatically. Her paws spread wide and the fire flickers up higher as though joining in, "So he dragged me to the Great Throne Room. And I'm coming face to face with the King and Prince."

She pauses for a deep moment. The shadows on her face seem ominous. The others are leaning in. Tatchathura seems to be grumbling and more invested in the tree line than anything else that's going on.

"I figured they would be furious with me. But instead they were both amused at my attempt. It enraged me more. They didn't take me seriously at all!" She practically beats her chest at this point, "They were just gonna turn me loose on the streets and tell me not to do it again. Like I'm a cub. Oh, I'll *show* them."

The girls start laughing.

Indy says, "You did **not**."

Kyltia spreads her wings wide, "No, it was more like this —Hi-yah!" she kicks her short legs high before following it with a wing swoop.

Sukua just grins, "Just when I think I'm flying the coop, Prince Azufae-yoh says 'Would you like to work for me?' Like *yeah sure*, I'll steal the royal slippers— *good* plan."

I smirk at her, "As if you wouldn't be *watched*."

"Yeah yeah, I'm getting to the best part—" her eyes

dramatically wide, "I said, 'Oh you want me to work off the damages?' Nope. A job that pays for real. I figured he was *tricking* me. You know? "

Slowly Sukua pretends to sneak behind the group on the log bench as the girls giggle out of control.

"But I agreed with the crazy idea. I was going to take what I could and then slowly dip out around the corner." She takes a dive under a nearby bush. Her white fur completely masked.

She's silent for a moment and it's almost as if she's completely disappeared.

She pops up next to Tatchathura and he startles for once. His rump half off the log and ears flattened as he glares at her. She seems pleased with herself, "Of course, you all see how well *that* worked out for me."

Tatchathura says, "You're an annoying furball, you know that?"

She giggles in her usual way before she falls silent. Crawling onto the log next to the dark fox, she starts staring at her left paw. It's always wrapped in a cloth bandage.

Slowly she unwraps it, "The scar on my wrist is from that day. It kind of never healed the way it should have. I suppose it has something to do with our magic— as if to remind me of what I'd been given."

Indy leans over to hold her paw, "That's so beautiful, Sukua."

"Yes, truly." Kyltia nods motioning to the scar on her wing. I know it well.

I glare at Tatchathura, "See? This isn't my first time dealing with *incompetent* thieves."

The ruffian grumbles something under his breath. He moves to another log with his ears focused on the sounds of the woods nearby.

I've heard her too.

I'm sure it's the same grey fox from the day I almost fried our *new best friend.* I gave the order to capture her that day but she's slippery like the rest of the criminals on our most wanted list. So I'm waiting to see if I can trap her at the right moment. As long as we have the Shadow Fox in our possession, it seems Zutaom will keep coming our way.

Kyltia jumps up, wings flailing, "Me next! Me next!"

As if anyone was going to stop her. I shake my head in amusement.

Kyltia clears her throat in a comical way, "From a very young age, my brother and I used to sell herbs to other beings. They were herbs that helped beings relax among other things— at least that's what I told myself. But they truly are bad herbs that help no one. But one day a trade went south taking my kin with it."

Her wings are already flapping around a mile a minute. The fire is licking the air with every burst of her uncontrolled energy.

"There I was-- high on the mountain peak! Ready to strike. Typhan-rah, the gryphon king, would pay for what he'd done to my brother." She clenches her claws tight, her glossy eyes beady tight.

Tatchathura snorts with a lazy eye on her, "This ought to be good."

"But just as I'm ready to swoop in— a daring beacon of destruction! The Prince appears in the bushes next to me." She takes a few more steps. Dramatically she pretends to fall backwards, "My whole plan ruined!"

She slops into a startled Indy's lap. Her wing on her brow, "Then the Prince put me on guard duty at the Rapsuk school and promised me a new job in the future."

She's focuses on the stars. There's something in her voice that seems to make the rest of us look up too— save for Tatchathura. The cool night air fills my lungs. A brassy glow punctuates the night through every star.

Kyltia says softly, "I was a bad being. And he chose me anyway. He saved me when I didn't deserve it."

Then she suddenly sits up perky as ever, "Alright, enough of that. Heroh why don't you go next?"

Tatchathura looks towards Heroh and says in his usual sarcastic tone, "Yeah, been through anything *exciting*?"

Heroh leans forward filled with hesitation. His giant paws clasp together, "Like all of us, I didn't have exactly the best start. The difference with me is— I knew exactly what I was doing. I should've known better."

"Ooh, this should be good. Everyone loves a story about a *bad boy*."

Indy shoots him a look, "Like you're *anyone* to talk."

He folds his paws behind his head, "I'm just trying to get *invested* in the story here. Now quit interrupting *Indy*."

Indy can't seem to choose between being amused or annoyed with him. And honestly he confuses me too. He shifts back and forth between being obstinate and then suddenly interested at the most random moments. It must be some kind of ploy. I'll have to keep my ears open.

Heroh gets up and crosses the distance of the campsite. He settles on the end of the log near Tatchathura. He shakes his head, a curl in his lip as he starts to tell the story of how he came to join us.

"I'm not originally from Jatali. I used to live on the border of Belaphrium and Atayip. There's actually quite a lot of gang activity that goes on around those parts."

Kyltia says, "That doesn't surprise me. The gryphons can be quite brutes."

Sukua nods along, "They're greedy too."

Heroh sighs, "Not just gryphons but other big cats are there too. And I was more than happy to run with them. They said we were carving our own path. That the King had lost his touch when choosing rulers."

"This was before Tiphan-rah took over Atayip. The ruler there was weak and the rulers in Belaphrium equally so. Or so we said— that we could do better. We convinced ourselves we were doing it for the good of everyone and that the Kingdom would realize their mistakes."

He kicks the dirt, his tail lashing impatiently. This story isn't easy for him to tell. But he knows he needs to tell it— if only for the ruffian's benefit.

"We knew Belaphrium a little better so we figured that would be our first strike. We spent many late nights patrolling and scoping out the Cinnasuk Stronghold. This was before they put in that new fortification at the front—"

Tatchathura raises a brow, "Were you *there* when it was built, old timer?"

Heroh gives him a rough but playful shove, "I'm not that old— even though I feel like it sometimes."

Another oddity. My ears flatten. Since when is Heroh so friendly with a newcomer? Sukua always is because she's a little oblivious— bless her— but Heroh?

Heroh says, "Anyway, it may have been *our* plan. But I'm the *one* who shot the arrow into the king's heart."

"So that was *you*." Tatchathura says clapping in a mocking way, "That story's pretty *famous* in Zutaom. Take a *bow*—the whole country almost collapsed after that."

Heroh's ears flatten, and tail curls around his feet, "Yeah. Needless to say, it brought down forces from the High Kingdom very fast. My comrades were content to leave me behind. Some other soldiers strung me up. I could tell they wanted to kill me on the spot, but that Great King Elin-rah wouldn't allow it. I wasn't a shadow after all."

"Hold on—" Tatchathura raises a paw, "You're *kidding* me?"

Indy says with a wry smirk, "Now *who's* interrupting?"

"This is important context. You killed a ruler of a country and they *weren't allowed* to retaliate on sight?"

"I guess you wouldn't understand it—"

"You think I ask questions *for fun*? I knew you guys were weird—"

I wear a wry look, "Am I going to have to separate you two?"

Kyltia bounds up to the center of our campfire, "It is said that those who do such a thing offend the Magic. But it's not right to persecute without a trial no matter how vile the act — unless they are already a fully formed shadow. So says the Code of Jatali."

"Thank you Kyltia." There's a groan in my voice as she seems pleased with herself, "Don't get any ideas *ruffian*. Your trial already ended when the Prince's paws left your heart. You've been judged and given this ruling—"

"Aright, calm down Blondie. I just think it's *stupid*. They didn't know he wouldn't kill anyone else there—"

Heroh stands up, tail lashing, "I **did** my time in the dungeon but I could never work off my guilt. Prince Azufae-yoh has always been patient with me. Somehow he *cared* about me. It was weird. I was a murderer. I killed a being—" he bites his lip, "I didn't have remorse back then—but now I think about that king all the time."

Tatchathura pretends to write, "Alright, Heroh's weakness is—"

"I'd take it back if I could! But that's not how things work around here." Heroh gives Tatchathura a sharp look, "I'm just further proof that **anyone** can change. I've been in charge of the weapons for almost eight years now. I always thought the High Kingdom didn't know what they were doing. But they showed me mercy and gave me a job when they had no reason to—"

He throws his paw and shakes his head again. His tail lashing out of control. He takes a few steps away from the group heading closer towards the forest. My eyes narrow slightly. He always gets like this when he has to tell the story. I understand his pain because my *"perfect"* golden fleece— is not so perfect— but it's not a story I'm going to share tonight.

Tatchathura yells after him, "Where are you going? Why not stay and relish your glory days. It takes a lot of strength to take down a king at the Cinnasuk Stronghold."

Heroh waves this paw as though telling him to give it a rest. Tatchathura leans back on his log. His head rests against the rock next to it, "Well, so far, his story is the most interesting one of the bunch. At least he has the guts to take someone out and admit it."

A wave of irritation passes through us. Hackles raise, and

tails swish. Kyltia lets out a small hiss before she covers her teeth again.

Sukua folds her ears back, "I should go talk to him."

I sigh, "Best not. You remember what happened last time."

She watches me with a forlorn gaze but nods slowly accepting my decree. Her tail wraps around her feet.

Kyltia says, "Now that we've shared with you. What kind of work were you in Tatchathura?"

Tatchathura curls his lips in amusement, "Oh you know picking off furballs like you, selling drugs to innocents and raking in a massive profit for my Master. Only the *best* kind."

Sukua and Kyltia blister at his admission. Heroh seems perturbed even at a distance. His ears flickering as if he wants to rejoin, but can't muster the strength to—

Indy snorts, "You don't have to act so proud about it."

He responds, "Why not? Does it make you *uncomfortable*?"

She lashes her tail, "If I were you, I'd think about the second chance you've been given. You can't really *enjoy* doing those things to other beings."

He leans back against the rock. His paws smugly folded behind his head, "And if I *do*? Would that make you go against your precious *Prince*?"

"Never." her eyes are ablaze.

"Would that make you think he made a *mistake*?"

"He didn't make a mistake saving you!" Indy's paws clench at her sides.

"You're *right*. He made a mistake long before I got here—with that *Last One*." he closes his eyes as though the conversation is over.

Indy starts huffing. She looks ready to strike him down. Kyltia puts a claw to her shoulder. She looks up and catches my gaze too. I nod quietly for her to calm down. Indy sighs and settles on a rock away from the group.

Sukua speaks up, "Well, I think he's way better than the last one."

I see what she's doing and agree wholeheartedly (also realizing it will annoy him), "That's true. He's definitely got a sense of *humor*."

Tatchathura's tail starts lashing, "So tell me, who exactly is this "last one" you keep talking about? Does he have a name?"

"Oh right." Sukua looks towards me and I nod, "I guess we tend to forget their names once they do what he did. His name was Daphoag."

I smirk, "You remember our conversation from the other day, right?"

Tatchathura stomps a foot, "I *know* him."

The others seem interested at the idea.

Sukua presses him, "Former co-worker of yours?"

The fox narrows his gaze, "It doesn't matter."

They wait a moment but I already know he won't say more. The silence becomes too much for the moment.

Sukua sighs, "It's not a perfect system—"

Indy puts a paw on her arm, "We have to give them a chance even if they betray us. It's what's right."

Tatchathura puffs his chest out, "Interesting. I wonder *why* you lose so many if it's what's *right*?"

Sukua seems lost for a moment. I keep my gaze focused on the castle wall. I'm striving to keep my temper under control. He doesn't have a clue. My ear twitches. Motion from my left side draws me back into the conversation. Indy has left her rock and is standing in the center of the group.

The campfire blazes in her gaze as her tail swishes violently, "It does work! We—"

"Oh I'm *sorry*, I thought 'right' meant '*functional*'. You have a castle full of beings too afraid to even *say* his name. All it takes is for me to look in their direction and they run. They're **cowards**."

"That's not true! Many beings lost their souls to fight off Daphoag!"

Tatchathura pushes off of his log. He stalks towards her. The others tense. I click my sword hilt. My body already twisted and slowly stepping in that direction.

His ears flicker and he settles slightly. His gaze sharper

still as he stares her down, "You're a fool."

She butts her forehead into his, "I'm NOT afraid of you!"

His intimidating sneer melts into a knowing smirk. He turns on his tail and settles against a his rock again. He watches her with a gleam in his gaze and a chuckle in his voice as he says, "Well it doesn't *matter much* if you're not afraid of me."

Indy seems frozen in place.

"If the rest of your Rainbow Brights crumble in fear, there isn't much of a guard *is there*?"

Her voice is quiet, "Even when all seems lost, a light can still shine in the darkness."

The girls seem to perk up at what she's saying. Even Heroh stops pacing for a moment. All of their bodies slowly turn to focus on what she might say.

Her voice raises, "Even if the whole world faded, the tiniest star will be enough to turn everything back."

He snarls, "It'll never go back to the way it was. **Never.**"

The fire flickers in her gaze, "Watch. You'll see what was promised come true."

"You all believe that fairytale?" He glances around us, "It's a bedtime story."

There's silence as the group looks at each other. There is some doubt seemingly from the others but Indy is resolute.

I level my gaze with him, "You can revile the truth all you want— but you can't change what is." I nod subtly to Indy.

She takes a deep breath, "If all the nations can't embrace the true ways of Jatali, then we shall all fade to darkness."

He scoffs and starts to study the tree line.

"Every negative thought, every hateful thing a being does just helps it grow. The root of the darkness that grows in our land came from a lack of love. The inability to care about others. Senteia pushed his beliefs so far as to crush everyone in his path. To convince our comrades to betray each other so that he might be exalted over our land."

He says smoothly, "If they betrayed you so easily, did really they have any good in them at all?"

But it's too late— Indy won't be swayed. She'll say what we all know is right.

"When a heart is weak, when fear grows there— or pain— it's easy to believe in lies."

For a moment, there's a deep silence between us. Even the ruffian seems to be considering what she's saying.

Tatchathura finally says, "Why follow him? He's just like ever other ruler. He sends you to do the dirty work while he lives in his cushy, protected palace."

"So putting out the fire was just a convenient publicity stunt?"

"It's just *one* thing."

Indy levels her gaze at him, "The reason Prince Azufae-yoh has the power he has is because he gave it all away."

"Gave it away?" Tatchathura cackles, "Yeah, *right*. The

golden castle is just for show then? There are beings living in the dirt with no tent over their heads."

The others get uncomfortable. I narrow my gaze. It does seem he is an expert in finding "flaws" in our Kingdom. The fact is we have been neglecting some of our duties to the other nations. The War has affected us all but we hope to change that soon. They look to Indy.

She glances at them, "If he's going to be with us, he may as well learn."

Tatchathura scoffs again.

"Long ago the continent of Ituvoh was mostly whole..."

The capital of Jatali was thriving. Many new cities were being built all around our land. Some beings started find that they had more in common with their own kinds rather than the diverse group but still there was peace. This was the beginning of forming the nations.

That was until Senteia came.

Even back then, the Drake was good at manipulating and dividing our beings. And then when he found the Great King's hidden magic— it was the final stone that toppled our nation into pieces. The King may have banished the Drake to the Abyss but the damage had already been done. So much destruction from a simple lie.

"King Elin-rah doesn't care for his beings because he's been keeping such powers a secret."

The differences the nations already found amongst

themselves too great. But as the new nations formed, it still wasn't enough power for some. There was a War coming against the High Kingdom. They wanted revenge for the ways they'd been "wronged".

As the Jatalian troops surrounded the castle, the other nation's armies filled the far ridge. King Elin-rah had consulted the Magic of Jatali. That he might be given a wisdom to counter this threat but to also save the beings lost to Senteia's lies.

The Promise he received was heartbreaking...

"Allow the one which you love the most to lay down all that they are so that the others may live. Become a medicine to your beings so that the shadows have no soil to grow in this fair land.

Keep to my ways and your nation shall prosper. Fall away and the malaise will poison every last soul."

With a heavy heart, the King sought council with his young son.

"My dear Azu, what might you give up to save our beings?"

Azufae-yoh said, "I will do whatever you ask of me Father, no matter the cost."

Elin-rah said, "Even at the cost of everything you are?"

He was merely eighteen years old with the burden of a nation on his heart and mind.

The Prince hesitated, "Might there be another way?

Something else to counter the growing darkness?"

The Great King sighed, "It is what the Magic has Promised us."

Prince Azufae-yoh's eyes were alight with determination, "If it is what the Magic has spoken, then let it be so."

The Father's heart clenched tightly. A stone weighting down every beat as he embraced his precious son for the last time.

Our forces were at the ready. The other nations were rallying against us. No attack had started yet. Every being was on the edge awaiting the very battle call.

But as the Prince cut the ranks, our forces grew in confusion. So many were ready to perish for their cause. He walked out onto the battlefield with no weapons. His eyes on fire as he crossed the field. Our armies slowly started to fall in line behind him. Our enemies confused at his sudden appearance.

No one dared touch him. The silence on the field deafening as he made it to the center on display for all. He bared his soul. Pleading with the other nations to understand.

"There can be peace. Come together and know stillness once more."

Indy's ears flatten, eyes glossy, "What happened next— I can't even imagine how I'd feel."

The others are hanging on her every word. It's as if they'd never heard the story before, but perhaps some of these details they do not know. Tatchathura is strangely quiet and listening for once.

"The Leader of Ikouvan pushed to the front of the pack..."

*"I've heard **enough**." He squawked thrusting his sword straight into our ruler's heart.*

Before anyone could help the young prince, the other rulers had made sure he would fall. A dark shadow fell on all of those rulers' hearts that day— For what being could attack a defenseless being and call themselves just?

This caused the Great Sea to form. A split straight down the middle of the continent. The nations as we know them today formed from this rift. For even our allies had decided it was better to stay apart for a time.

A brilliant light erupted from the center of the battlefield. The forces of both sides thrown back from each other.

The young prince rose from his spot. His coat should've been bloody and tattered from his wounds, but it had been turned from tawny to pure white. His mane flickered in a golden light. Never had such a brilliant white light ever been seen until that day.

For the first time ever, the Magic spoke with another. The Prince had now been given a new Promise to fulfill.

"As sure as this heart beats in my chest, so too will the

lifeblood of this continent beat once more. The Peace we lost will re-form, and the flame of Love will burn hotter than ever."

Many hearts were changed that day.

The light that came from him washed over all the beings of all the Nations. The other forces fell to the wayside. Not able to stand up to the light. The hate crept away into the darkness...

Indy focuses a hard gaze on Tatchathura, "Every wound was clear from our Master's body save for his heart where Ikouvan struck first. And his arms where the others struck. The scars are still there. A reminder of how he suffered and risked everything for us."

"Pure love." Sukua says in a dreamy way.

Tatchathura half-growls, "He threw himself into the middle of a battle with no weapons and you call that *brave?* Sounds stupid to me."

"The authority to decide the fate of all rests on the Prince's shoulders because of his sacrifice. He's been working ever since then to fight back the shadows."

Indy adds, "Less and less beings believe in the Promise so that's why the shadows are growing in strength."

He says, "Good."

"You're rotten to the core." She swishes her tail.

"He's a Prince. Why give up his throne? He had all of you fools to fight for him."

Indy levels her gaze with him. It's brimming with a fiery, determined love, "Because that's the kind of Ruler he is. Everyone is the same in his Kingdom."

"You weren't even there. How do you know that's *how* it happened?"

Indy steps back a space, her tail flicking back and forth, "It was what was told to me—"

"Told to you by who *exactly*?"

"A Leon Elder turtle. He said he was there."

He snorts.

She throws her paw, "No one can explain the power he has otherwise, so it *must* be true." Her paws fold together, gaze downcast, "We were all broken in one way or another. Unfit to be citizens of any Kingdom, but he forgave us anyway. He gave us a new purpose and we cleaned up our acts."

He narrows his gaze, "You're slaves to the Kingdom. He caught you in a moment when you owed someone something and he turned it around on you. And if that's not manipulative, I don't know what is. Why not execute you? Or keep you in prison? Why does he keep showing mercy to all these bad beings?"

There's an almost a chilling silence in the group. The girls seem lost as to what to say. Heroh's too far away to care about the conversation anymore.

My ears flatten as I stare him down, "None of us were

forced to continue serving the Kingdom. All of us were given a sentence to serve after which we could walk free. All of us stayed because we realized how wrong we were. Our rulers care only about bringing all of us to peace. How are we to survive if we never forgive anybody for *anything*? Answer me that."

"You're delusional." Tatchathura looks away.

"If they didn't care for the beings of this world— What kind of King gives up his son? For beings that hate him no less? What kind of Prince is willing to lay up his life for others?"

Finally Tatchathura seems sore about the subject. A strange silence coats the group. I can tell he's frustrated. He doesn't have an answer. None of the criminals ever do. My gaze is still hot on him.

He shoots me a side look, before his tail starts wagging, "So Princess, *nothing* to share?"

Indy snorts, "The Prince saved me. That's all that matters."

"You're afraid to face the truth. That's why you won't say it."

"No. I just— you don't need to know everything about me."

"Why not? I thought we were sharing so we could all be *best buds*?"

I grip my sword hilt, "Indy, you don't have to tell him

anything."

"You're *afraid* that deep down you were **never** worthy and that he made a mistake. That everything is riding on you, and you're going to make a *royal* mess of things again."

Indy looks ready to lunge, but crumples into herself. Her ears flat, "I don't know what you're talking about."

His lips curl into a sneer as he tells us what he heard in the courtyard a few days ago...

This one gets particularly heated, shoulders hunched, "Why did the Prince bring someone like her here?"

The first one turns slightly, "I heard this isn't her first time here."

A newcomer twists to add, "She's the reason we had trouble with the shadows in Luthura a few years ago."

The others seem flustered by that idea, "What? How?"

The newcomer glances around for a moment, "She broke off her engagement to a prominent Captain and ran off with a crime lord to get married."

"It's *interesting* to me Indy. You think everyone should follow the rules but you went against him too."

She stares at him. A look of terror fills her usually soft gaze.

Kyltia hisses, "That's enough."

Sukua covers Indy into a hug, her voice a low growl, "You don't know **anything**."

It's tense for a moment.

He's taunting her. He's just pieced together what he's heard to punish her for it. It's causing our strong Indy to falter. The girls are ready to pounce— and as much as I'd like to push him off the log too—

We have a job to do.

I turn slightly, my voice strong, "So what about you? You still haven't told us your *real* story?"

Tatchathura lazily pries an eye open to look at me but shuts it again before he speaks, "I already told you furballs enough. The only reason I'm here is because the Drake needed something and I was more than happy to oblige him."

"You're here because you made a mistake. Same as *everyone* else."

He clicks his teeth at me, "Mistake is a matter of opinion. Besides with all of your loose lips, it's made it more than *worth* it to get caught."

This lying fool...I bristle, "I think that's enough sharing for one night—"

"Finally—"

I glare at him knowing it won't make a difference. He's already got a smug look on his face. I glance towards Indy and she's still upset and perturbed by their argument.

I call, "Heroh, care to take the girls back in? Shift is done."

Heroh glances back at me. He's still a fair distance away, "What of you? Can't leave—"

"You think I can't handle one measly fox? One washed up cub with a superiority complex?" I look down on him from my snout, *"Shadow?* More like a speck of dust."

Tatchathura bristles slightly but I can see he's holding back— trying not to give me the satisfaction.

Heroh nods and walks back up the hill to the girls' side. Indy seems as though she might protest but follows anyway. Once they are out of sight I stalk closer to him.

My paw is tapping on my sword hilt, "So any chance your *friend* will be joining us today?"

He looks confused but I'm sure it's a ruse, "Isn't it time to head inside, Captain? It's not like you're gonna *do* anything if you found a bad guy anyway."

I lean over him, "How do you know I wasn't told to *keep* you alive? For whatever reason my Master needs your skills, so for as long as that time exists, I shall uphold his wishes." My sword slowly clicks out of the hilt, "But don't be so confident that those conditions won't change at a moment's notice."

He scoffs, "Do it Blondie. I'm itching for it."

"Pathetic." I stand upright, my glowing green gaze piercing his, "You're nothing but a coward hiding behind an empty title. Now get inside."

A wicked smirk plays on his crooked smile. He slinks off

the log and walks ahead of me. The sun slowly starts rising on the horizon. I sigh deeply. I just hope Indy isn't too discouraged. I'll have to visit her later.

But what am I going to do about him? And how will we catch his partner?

CHAPTER SEVENTEEN

Reconsider

INDESSAH

We spend the next day training and making preparations for the pending danger. I'm exhausted but still a part of me yearns to do more. A part of me is trying to fix what I think is broken. After all, what good is a Knight-in-Training if she can't even conjure magic at the right moment?

It's late now. I'm in one of the side courtyards. The only sounds around me are the soldiers patrolling the top wall. The main courtyard is empty. I say the words of Valiant

297

once more. My paws clasp together for a moment before I shoot them forward. Once more red and orange flames jump off of my paws. The fireheart flowers start to appear and the mountain slowly emerges into the air before me.

I grit my teeth and try my hardest to think about the most courageous things I can think of— I picture myself sliding down the castle wall after Tatchathura—

I edge closer to him even though every fiber of my being is begging me to cut my losses. But there's just something inside me. Something that won't quit.

He cracks his wrist, "Couldn't just stay in the castle could you, Light Bright?"

"Tatchathura, you don't know what you're giving up—"

*"So what you're gonna do, **Indy**?"*

I shake those thoughts away and try something else— I'm in the courtyard with Sukua and Heroh. In the middle of training, and Altikua is on the attack—

It looks as though Altikua will move on from this demonstration. But then he raises his sword again, the lightning starts to glow and course through the blade.

"Even though my opponent is down, I can see some motion. He's not quite subdued. So we won't give him a chance to recover—"

The sword swings forwards.

I dash to slide between them. I stumble and barely put myself between him and the sword.

*Altikua struggles to stop at the last second. His canines fully revealed, **"Indessah."***

I sit up on my paws and knees, the blade centimeters from my snout, "Enough. You've made your point—"

"Shadows don't fight fair. We must always be ready—"

*My voice is borderline emotional, "He's **not** a shadow yet!"*

But still— my fire is not strong enough. It's still fizzling. The flowers are staying dormant on the mountain. I close my eyes and start to think what else I'm missing. What am I supposed to feel *exactly*?

I literally faced down the Shadow Fox of Zutaom and *lived*— what the heck am I afraid of exactly?

I let out a hot breath and wave my paws to the side. The magic dissipates. I guess it was silly of me to try this right now. Even in the dark of night there's just too much on my mind. And after our conversation the other day around the fire— all it's done is put more knots in my heart. Tatchathura voiced all of those concerns I've been trying to bury in my heart. I wonder if it's because his shadow touched me that day. Does he know everything about me now?

*"You're afraid that deep down you were **never** worthy and that he made a mistake. That everything is riding on you, and you're going to make a royal mess of things again."*

I hear a branch snap behind me. Twisting violently I

raise my paws expecting the worst. The Prince comes into view.

He raises his paws, "Now, now, I'm not ready for *combat practice.*"

I lower my stance, "Sorry Prince Azufae-yoh, I'm just a little upset that's all."

"I noticed." he says walking to a bench. He sits down and pats the space beside him.

Of course he would know. Another sigh leaves me. But I stay stubbornly where I'm standing. I raise my paws again. The words for Valiant coming out fast. A weak burst of fire flows off my paw. This time even the flowers won't form. He nods slowly. I already know he has full understanding before he even came down here— and yet I'm intent on 'saving face'. How can he be so patient with someone like me? A stubborn being who won't ask for help.

He says, "So the Valiant Branch doesn't seem to be working out for you?"

I throw my arms, "It's so simple! It should work—" I notice him watching me in amusement. I look away from him, burning red, "So you've noticed *that* huh?"

He really has been paying attention to my lack of ability. My failures.

I brush my hair behind my ears, "I just don't understand what I'm missing."

"I think maybe you're forgetting how each of the

Branches of Courage form to make a tree. Guts is the foundation. Sliding down a castle wall was a great example, but still not the choice you should've made."

My ears flatten. I want to disappear.

"It was Daring of you to stand up to those who frighten us. You took steps to try and rein in Tatchathura outside the castle walls. It wasn't wrong, but lacked in Wisdom."

It feels like there is a pit in my gut and it's just getting deeper. I have made some foolish decisions since I've been here. But I just wanted so badly to show I had changed—that I'm committed to the Kingdom now.

His gaze softens, "Being brave isn't just about dashing into danger no matter the cost. Being truly Courageous is asking for help and understanding that others sometimes know better than us."

I clutch my paws tighter. It's hard to tell if I'm in trouble right now or if it's my mental state that's making me feel that way.

"You probably don't realize it yet, but you're already found the core of the Valiant Branch."

I twist to stare at him, "What? When? I can't even make the flowers bloom now—"

"That's because your mind is cloudy with doubt. Which causes—" he glances at me expectantly.

I sigh, "Doubt is the enemy of Courage. Yes, Sire. But it's hard to find the path in the dark. Every way looks right."

He nods in an understanding way, "There is something Valiant you've done. But maybe you hadn't thought of it that way."

"What's more Valiant than throwing myself in between Talik and Tatchathura?"

He half-laughs, "I can see how you might think that. Although it was very Daring of you, it was not completely Valiant because you knew that Talik would listen to you in that moment. I'm glad you made that commitment but there's something else."

I pour my mind over. Still I'm not sure what he means and shake my head.

He says, "The root of Courage is self sacrifice. Most beings can find the other two traits easily, but there is no loss in them. The true strength of Jatalian Magic is the loss of something precious to the user, or the risk of loss."

I shake my head in disbelief, "But doesn't that make it just like the Osekou Magic? They have to give up parts of themselves—"

"That is a perversion of the Magic. The loss here is more figurative or emotional. And sometimes even relational for the benefit of others and not oneself like the shadows." He seems somber for a moment, "A Valiant act is one where a being is willing to do what it takes to change hearts and minds no matter their personal cost. To be willing to show others the way even if it seems hopeless while knowing it's for their benefit that you experience pain."

The wheels start turning in my head. I start piecing together all the time I've spent with Tatchathura since he's been here.

His voice is more excitable now, "In the Med Bay, your sentiment of Kindness to Tatchathura—"

"What about it? It didn't change his mind."

"Focus on how you felt in that moment. What was it that caused you to say such a self-sacrificial thing after all he'd done to you personally at that point?"

"It was my duty— the responsibility you gave me—"

"Lay that all aside. You know in your heart that no one leaves the castle without my say so. I could've had him back in an hour if I so chose— Why did you feel compelled to say such a thing to him?"

I purse my lip. My gaze falls to my paws. I try to think back to that moment.

"We may be enemies now but that doesn't mean we're monsters." My eyes are wide as I stare at Tatchathura, "Not everyone is kind, but everyone deserves kindness."

He scoffs loudly. It slowly turns into a condescending laugh, "Not after some of the beings I've met."

I stare at the Prince for a moment, "He didn't believe me when I said that."

"And still you stood for your beliefs. And still you keep trying to convince him because you know the truth. And still you put yourself in front of him in the courtyard when he was against Altikua."

The Prince watches me expectantly. I'm starting to get what he's saying.

I say, "Then why didn't the magic form in that moment? Why didn't it rise to protect me or something?"

"You know it doesn't work that way. And to be fair, there was still a considerable fear in your heart when you intervened."

He's right. And if you're heart isn't aligned, then it can't work. That and I didn't want to hurt Altikua anyway.

I say, "I'm perfectly focused and not afraid right now, and still it didn't produce the results I need."

He raises his brows at this.

I flush, "Alright maybe I have a tiny fear— but still it should go further than it has."

"That's because you are still thinking of these branches as separate things. All three traits work together to form the Virtue of Courage. The highest Branch Valiant can only form when you understand that."

Something burns inside my heart. A new emotion. I close my eyes trying desperately to blend all of the feelings I had in all those moments together.

But still the fire fizzles, and doesn't come out fully. I frown.

"Let's talk about that fear buried in your heart." He motions for me to sit again, "It's a hard Branch to understand, but I have confidence in you. You still know the other two Branches fairly well—"

"What good is that if I can't use it in battle?"

"You just need some more time."

Slowly I walk to sit on the other side of the bench a space away from him. I stare at my paws. He pats my back gently as I settle.

"So tell me—" he glances at me, eyes wide and attentive as usual, "What's *really* on your mind?" His tail starts swishing with anticipation.

"It's just— I know you didn't mean to— but you and the Great King put so much pressure on me. I just don't know if I'm going to add up to what is expected of me."

His ears swivel forward, "And what *exactly* have I expected of you?"

I narrow my gaze slightly, "Well, you expect me to reform Tatchathura and you've seen how he's been a total jerk."

His paw goes thick into his mane, "I can see how you might think that. My apologies, but your role in all of this is *not* to reform him."

My full attention snaps to him.

"*Reforming* him is **my** responsibility. Just interacting with him is all I require of you— if you're still able?"

"I'm fine. Really. I guess I got into my head a little bit."

He puts a comforting paw on my shoulder, "You, like

Talik, want to do your best always. But know that as long as you keep trying, you will never fail me. Even when all seems lost, a light can still shine in the darkness."

My eyes widen. I've obviously heard the story passed down, but to hear our Prince speak the words out loud sends shivers down my spine, "Even if the whole world faded, the tiniest star will be enough to turn everything back."

He smiles brightly, "Indy, the reformation of one soul can be affected by one light, but one light can't burn alone forever. Tatchathura's awakening— if he *ever* comes to one — will be the might of the love *we* show him. Nothing less, nothing more."

"I guess that makes sense, but why me, Sire? I've been asking myself over and over again."

His gaze is still tender, "When I spoke to the Magic of Jatali, he told me; *Like a Fireheart flower turns to ashes in the wind, so too would another fire make a heart bloom new*. He explained that you were the one who would start to change his heart. That it *had* to be you."

"The Magic said that about **me**?" my ears twitch in excitement.

He glances to me with raised brows, "However, he never said anything about you turning blue."

I chuckle. That's still an oddity even in a land of magic.

"I have a few theories but nothing concrete."

He pulls a book out of his robes and offers it up to me. It's blue with gold trim pages. The whole tome is dusty like it's been hidden away for a while. It's so ornate and beautiful that some part of me worries about it turning to crumbles the moment I touch it.

He nods for me to take it.

The book is heavy in my paws. I crack the spine lightly. The bronze colored pages are thin but strong. Some of our ancient writing is there. He points to the symbol in the center of the page. It's a squarish mark with winding spikes flowing below it. Each one looks like a sword that's on fire. The top of the symbol looks like a sturdy shield protecting it.

"That is the symbol for Determination. One of the Virtues of the Jatali. Although Courage and Determination go paw in paw, I think it's worth a shot for you to look over a different Virtue."

I start nicely flipping through the pages. Most of it is in our modern script, but I notice that some of it is still written in the ancient language. I give him a half-hearted look.

He glances down at the page. His paws run over it again. A small burst of golden lights up the pages, "Sorry, I thought I got it all. It should be fixed. Just let me know if you find more later. Determination is a Virtue not easily found by many beings."

"Then what makes you think *I* can do it?"

"Because I know you Indy." He's amused again, "There's not much that stands in your way."

I'm flustered for a moment. If only I could see myself like he does. I stare at the book. My eyes light up and heart races out of control. My tail swishes on the ground. New magic—

You see when we're cubs they tell us all of the different Virtues. We go through test and trials to see which one fits us best. Kind of like a personality test. And for most beings, it ends up being Courage, Kindness, Joy or Charity. They also are the easiest to learn. The others are usually a little more rare and take more skill and time.

He puts a paw on my paw. I look up at him and he gives me a warm smile, "I'm just trying to help. I don't want you to think that this is just another task that you might fail."

My heart clenches erratically at the thought. There's a tenseness in my voice, "How can you say that? Tatchathura almost got away the first day! And then my past— the other soldiers— they know *somehow*."

"We can't let our past define us any more than we can let others define who we are. Just by doing the things that you've already done for me, you've already won."

If only it were that simple.

He raises his paws wide, "No matter what you do in life it will always take time to grow. That's all I can ask for— that and we'll figure out the rest in due time." He stands up, his look more resolute this time, "Promise me this won't grieve you?"

"It won't." I say honestly, "I'll start reading right away—"
I return to flipping through the pages. Some of it seems
familiar— like I recognize the motions are similar to
Courage but there's something different about it that I can't
quite place.

He gently puts a paw over the page, "Please, Indy,
consider getting some rest first. There will be time."

I look up at him. His eyes are gleaming in amusement
and warmth, "I appreciate you talking to me, Azu."

"Always. Just let me know if I can help you in any other
way."

I stare at the book for another moment. Maybe this is
exactly what I need, "No Sire, I think this is more than
enough."

CHAPTER EIGHTEEN

On the Horizon

ALTIKUA

It's hard to believe that it's been almost a week since that ruffian tried to infiltrate our walls. He's been nothing but trouble and has brought more of it with him. I stare out at the horizon from the castle walls, it's evident the shadows are coming. Normally our country is bright and shining even under the dark of night. But now there's a haze. A vicious darkness bubbling at the seams. I've never seen anything like it. They look like wispy dark fire with flecks of red smoke and ash.

A solider comes to my side, "Any ideas Commander?"

I glance down at him. He's putting on a brave face for me but I sense his unease. His tail is hugging the ground and ears are twitching.

I grip the rough stone wall, "Are all of the beings evacuated from their homes?"

"They are rounding up the stragglers as we speak."

"Good. Ready the troops for impact. Surround the castle on all sides. Leave no flank unguarded. We need to have every solider here as soon as possible."

"Understood."

"And make sure every criminal is locked up. Even the ones on good behavior or those who have shown progress. I don't want there to be any *rescues* today."

He hesitates a moment, "Sir, doesn't that mean— the Shadow Fox too?"

"I said *everyone,* didn't I?" my lip curls, *What's with this disobedience?*

He presses his paws together, "Well it's just that Prince Azufae-yoh—"

"Let me guess, he wants him by his side."

"Yes sir! How did you guess?"

"Well, besides your demeanor solider, I *know* him. And I had a feeling he might do something like that when things started to heat up." I sigh, "It doesn't matter. Lock everyone else up. Leave the Shadow Fox to me."

The solider nods furiously and then scampers off. My claws dig into the stone. It's like flint striking a stone. And the fire is just getting started.

I've already sent various groups of our soldiers into town. Each group has around three to four Knights. There are several bunker location sites under our city. Although we've rarely had to use them, we knew this day would come soon enough. The day when Zutaom was bold enough to stomp into our country. To think they could take what's ours.

But they'll be sorely mistaken.

* * *

I have a few ideas of where he might be right now but it's a big compound and I don't have time to search every corridor. I open up my soul communicator. It takes a few moments for the transmission to come through.

The Prince's warm smile shines through, "Yes, my friend?"

"Where are you?"

"Are you finished dispensing the troops already?"

"Sire, please."

"We're in the Southeastern Side Courtyard. Everything okay?"

*It's the place he goes to think so it makes sense...*My ears are burning, "Stay there."

I cut the communication off. I'm a little out of line to speak to him in such a way, but he's understanding of my tendencies.

Besides, he knows how I feel about his abrupt plan changes. It's not like he has to tell me everything but when it involves that— Shadow Fox— I'd prefer he not go off script.

* * *

It doesn't take long for me to get to the Southeastern Side Courtyard. In the midst of a volley of soldiers, there stands Prince Azufae-yoh giving out commands. He takes his time with each being making sure they fully understand their responsibilities. Sukua, Heroh, Indy, and Tatchathura are a few steps behind him as though waiting for him to finish. Some of the soldiers practically trip into me they're so distracted. They start apologizing but I wave them on.

"It's fine. Just get back to work." I pinch my brow, *He's up to something...*

Prince Azufae-yoh looks up from a recruit and gives me a warm smile, "My friend. What ails you?"

The last two soldiers scamper out of my way with their assignments in paw.

"Sire, I refuse to allow your plans to commence. That ruffian will only make you a target for the shadows—"

"Aren't I *already*?"

Tatchathura says with a smirk, "Yeah, don't you have a

counterattack to mount or *whatever*?"

I shoot the prisoner a look, "Everyone already *knows* their place. Your Highness, I request that Tatchathura is left in my care. It will be too dangerous once the fighting starts—"

Prince Azufae-yoh seems amused, "You doubt my power?"

"No Sire, I just fear for your safety."

He looks distraught a moment, "I'm sorry my friend. My Father told me it was important for it to happen this way. Tatchathura *has* to be with me. You can't change it."

"You could've told me sooner."

Indessah's tail bristles as she says, "I'm sure he had a *good* reason."

Tatchathura sneers, "Yeah, know your *place*."

I shoot him a hot look— but I don't have time to get dragged into his nonsense.

Prince Azufae-yoh walks towards me, "It's alright for him to ask questions. I'm sorry I didn't tell you sooner. We've both been busy trying to protect our beings."

"I just think having him right out in the open is going to make them converge in one spot." My ears are flat against my head, brows heavily creased, "And then they will be too strong—we won't have the power to drive them back."

His gaze is solemn, "Talik, I can not die. What better place is there for the shadows to come then?"

I turn my head, "Just because you can't die, doesn't mean I want to see you torn apart."

I can sense that our comrades seem to have a similar concern but were too afraid to say anything.

"My dearest friend, I'm sorry to have caused you grief. But sometimes the Magic doesn't make sense— what my Father has seen— the things to come to pass— they must be *this* way."

The others seem entranced by his words save for Tatchathura who seems distracted as usual. Just waiting for one of us to mess up and give him an out. I'm sure he's absolutely *giddy* to see shadows on the horizon.

I say, "I don't even want to think about it."

Indy softens at my admission, "Talik, it's going to be alright. We *must* trust him."

The Prince puts his paw squarely on my shoulder, "Tatchathura has to stay with me for the time being. He and I are the ones they want. And I need to be in the right place for when that time comes. And I need you to be where you can protect those that need it *most*."

I suck in a sharp breath, "I understand. I'm sorry."

"Don't be." He says strongly, "Never apologize for fighting for those you love."

* * *

For the moment, the Prince has gone to his study with the Ruffian and Indy. He told me that he and the King have to watch for the right moment to intervene. My main goal will be to keep the shadows in the courtyard and out of the towers. Of course that's easy to say.

Most of our forces are lined up in the main courtyard. A few on each perimeter to watch for their convergence. I stand at the front of our troops. Sukua, and Heroh each take a corner. Kyltia hovers near me. She's the least experienced of the group but insisted on doing what she considered "her part" anyways. It's no wonder her and Indy are friends. There's a magical golden shield overhead. I draw our troops' attention to it.

I say strongly, "This forcefield will be able to delay the shadows for a time. This force will only hold as long as we keep our hearts strong. Have faith that Jatali will prevail and that the Magic is with us."

A few of them start cheering. Others let out battle cries in an effort to keep morale high. The golden shield shows a reflecting wave sliding across it as if it's being strengthened.

Kyltia flutters down by my side, "The shadows are halfway through town. They aren't even stopping to view the scenery."

My chest tightens, "Very well." I project towards the crowd, "Keep up your morale. Strengthen each other. And if the shadows break through before the proper time, at all costs keep them away from the Prince's Study."

I say that, but I know these creatures have a one track mind. Destroy. Even if they're given instructions by another force, they will most likely tear all of us apart first before they even look around the castle. They expect us all front and center.

"Kyltia, can you keep watch on the northern gate? Tell me when they hit Gutah Road."

She gives me a salute before flapping upwards. I watch her as she disappears over the castle gate wall. Another tense feeling radiates through my gut. I still don't like my Master's plan. He assured me that the collar around Tatchathura's neck will keep him in line even if the light of Luthura falls. But it's hard to put so much faith in one item. Sure it's imbued with the King's magic, but what if it does *break*?

What if enough shadows converge on that dark fox that he's let *free*? If the Shadow Fox isn't constrained in the heat of battle, then I fear we will lose for sure. I watch the shield a moment. Small flickers of light radiate across it like cracks forming. The troops are starting to whisper amongst themselves. Even through the tinted shield we can see the sky is turning darker by the minute.

All of our citizens deep in their bunkers are surely feeling as anxious as we are. The light we share is through a combined hope. The faith that the Magic will protect the beings aligned with the heart of its energy. But what good is that hope if we crumble under the first sign of trouble?

Just as the soldiers seem to be festering in their own self-doubts, an uplifting song starts floating through the ranks.

In the far corner Sukua has them singing one of our national tunes. The group that's focused on her is lively and bright.

Good idea Sukua. I motion to the the troops closest to me. I'm not much of a singer but I start to join in with the ranks.

Those troops join and soon the whole courtyard is filled with an uplifting and jaunty tune. The shield reflects the waves of positive energy. It's no longer glossy but thick and hard to see out of it. It's been strengthened by our energies.

The moment of calm is immediately squashed. Kyltia flies over the ridge and crash lands into the space beside me. Her eyes are wide, "They got down the road so fast! And they're huge!"

I glare at her.

Shadows start crashing into the shield. There's a terrible sound ricocheting off the front castle door. The singing in the courtyard abruptly halts. There's a collective sound of weapons being drawn as everyone stares up at the shield.

Each monstrous shadow keeps smacking and crashing into the energy. Some of them cry out as the magic burns them. Despite their pain they press onwards. Leaping and bounding against the energy like it's glass. A carpet of darkness covers the light. A stronger force than them all weighs down on it.

It's quiet a moment before— CRASH!

It's like a floodgate has been opened. The weakness in our faith has caused the shield to break early. The dark mass wriggles into the open spaces until the energy is dispersed. Shadows that can't fly crash into the pavement. A chorus of roars and growls overtakes the light. The clanging of swords is heard throughout. Blasts of fire and water fly through the arena.

Random shots of light slice through the shadows. Vines grow everywhere restraining and tugging the beasts into submission. Kyltia is near me her wings raised. Some of the shadows take notice of us and start closing in.

I glance to her, "You think you can get me up high?"

She looks me over a moment, "I can try."

She pushes off the ground and puts her feet on my shoulders. Her broad wings start flapping in long strokes. She winces before flapping wildly. Finally lift off. She takes us high over the courtyard swiftly dodging the random flying shadows. My sword slices through those close enough to pass us. Strings of lightning jolt through those that are hit and then cause a chain of damage through all those in the sky. A collective screech is heard as more electricity is channeled through them.

Kyltia says, "As great as that is— I'm not sure I can do this much longer."

"I'm right where I need to be." I look down at the bubbling masses in the courtyard, "Go ahead and drop me here."

"Drop you! Have you lost your mind?"

"It's okay. I have a plan."

She stares down at me a moment. Her lips quirk to the side, "Okay." She lets me go.

"A warning would be nice!" I half-tease, as I start to plummet towards the ground. She gives me an embarrassed look before smacking at the new wave of shadows.

I raise my sword high, "Let my sword ring true. Bring forth the light of balance!"

I sweep downwards. A glowing rage of light courses around me. It forms a sphere like a comet crashing to the ground. Two streaking tails of fire and debris follow behind me. The energy obliterates waves of the shadows in the sky. As I crash into the murky pool, an electric storm blazes forth from my blade. Rings of energy blast in every direction. It tears apart every shadow in it's way clearing half of the courtyard. Some cheers from our forces are let out.

I level my sword, "Stay courageous! Don't back down to this darkness."

A new force of shadows burst through the wooden castle gate door. I narrow my gaze in their direction. An elephant-like one is leading the charge. He's got four long necks with a head on each end. Legs like trees crashing through the jungle of shadows. It's body dwarfs the rest of us. A vicious snarl echoes from its many mouths. It levels its smoggy green gaze at me. It starts charging full force. The smaller shadows scamper out of its way.

"It seems I have a fan." I tighten my grip on my sword ready to leap—

Vines spring up around its legs. It cries out enraged. The vines climb higher and start dragging it to its knees. Sukua dashes up to my side with Heroh on my other side.

I say, "Shouldn't you be helping the others?"

I dash forwards without waiting for an answer. I slice and weave to avoid the shadow's heads. More vines wrap around their necks dragging their faces to the ground. I leap up and crash my sword full of lightning down into its back. It screeches wildly before bursting into heated blasts of green smog.

The shadows nearby hiss at the loss of their comrade. Four of them leap towards me. My sword barely misses them as vines drag them away.

I glare back at my comrades, "I have this under control. I don't need help—"

Sukua says, "And so do we."

Heroh says, "We're in this together, remember?"

I take a look around the courtyard. Heroh and Sukua are back to back. Their vines are growing everywhere taking over so much of the battlefield. Most of the shadows can't seem to counter their combined efforts. Kyltia is near them using her claws and wings to fend off what she can. Even without a weapon she's holding her own. I spot a pocket of soldiers who seem to be struggling.

I race through all the shadows. Violent bolts of lightning crash and split the sea of shadows. Splashes of darkness fizzle into the air as my light explodes in the courtyard. Some of the shadows go screeching into the sky. Others go racing away before they can be next. Some slither back under the cracks in the rocks. The sky grows darker still. The match seems to be an even draw for the moment. I glance back at the Prince's Study. I hope they get finished soon. With our rulers' powers, this battle will be over in no time.

The haze on the horizon causes a twist of concern in my gut. I wonder have they really been able to release the Drake from the Abyss? Surely no one but the King can break the seal?

But the faith of those lands died a long time ago.

The coastline near the Abyss is filled with darkness and those who've forsaken the Magic of Jatali. He was sealed so long ago. It wouldn't surprise me that after all this time the seal has enough cracks to finally break.

I slice another shadow into bits. My energy level is okay, but still— *Hurry Prince Azufae-yoh...*

CHAPTER NINETEEN
No Matter What

INDESSAH

I'm high in one of the castle towers looking down as the courtyard fills with shadows. From the moment the battle began, I kept my gaze focused on Altikua. If anyone has a chance of keeping those monsters at bay, it's him.

I press my paws against the stained glass, "Surely we won't be long?"

The Prince is quickly looking over his almost transparent map, "I know in moments like this it's hard to wait— but our timing must be just right."

I glance to the side. Tatchathura is leaning against the wall and looking out the window that is next to mine. He's stoic and it makes my stomach turn. Just what is he thinking?

I glare at him for a moment, "You called them here— didn't you?"

"You see, I did— but not really."

My frown deepens. I think it would kill him to give me a straight answer.

"I didn't call them here but you keeping me locked up—" he smirks self-righteously, "And they'll just keep coming until you let me free."

I stare at him while my gaze drifts to the collar. I look out the window again and see the masses of shadows overwhelming pockets of our forces.

"If I were you, I'd give me up now. You wouldn't want more of your precious friends to get stolen away—" he offers the collar up as if to tempt me.

My heart is swayed for the briefest moment. But I fold my arms and look away from him.

Prince Azufae-yoh says, "Nice try Tatchathura, but I'm afraid you're stuck with us a little while longer."

He snorts as if amused, "I just wonder when you're gonna figure it out. We don't play fair Indy." His gaze now focused on mine, "We're trying to *win* this war— not make *friends*."

My ears flatten as I stare out the window once more. My tail is stiff against the cold stone floor. I just can't believe what's happening! Shadows have never been able to breach the castle walls like that. And there is so many of them. Light and love that's what our country is supposed to be. It's supposed to hold everything together and keep things like *that* out.

It must really be true.

It's finally time for the Promise to be fulfilled—

Or is this just the beginning of everything?

And *why* are we still up here!?

"Sire, is it time *now*? They need help."

Another rush of our forces fill the courtyard driving back more of the shadows. Its like the ebb and flow of an ocean. A victory and then a defeat. I sigh. The faintest sound of an insult is on Tatchathura's tongue before King Elin-rah hustles into the doorway. The Prince twists to meet him with ears held high.

"It's time." The King's gaze is worn, more grey than it was before, "Our old enemy is on our doorstep. It's time to finish what we've started."

The Prince's ears flatten, "They were able to break the seal."

"That seal was never meant to last forever."

My full focus is on the King now, *Wasn't meant to last forever?*

The King hold his paws out to draw his son near. The air is tense as he speaks, "You have doubts?"

The Prince glances back at us, "I just wonder Father. Maybe it is best to retract our claim to the Shadow Fox. We can always—"

Tatchathura is staring out the window but I know he's listening to every word.

King Elin-rah grips his paws tighter, "No my dearest son. The Drake promised war to our country a long time ago. It matters not who we've taken."

"I suppose that's true—"

He puts a strong paw on his son's shoulder, "No matter what happens don't give up. Don't yield even one soul to that evil. Never forget how important one piece can be to build a glimmering castle."

Prince Azufae-yoh glances down at the ground before meeting his gaze once more, "I trust you Father."

"Promise me." The King's eyes are glossy now.

I can tell my friend is a little confused for the moment, but he says, "I promise to keep him in our custody. No matter what."

The Great King hugs him tight. There's tears in the old lion's eyes. He clutches his son as if they might fall. The Prince returns the hug but his tail is twitching and brow is furrowed. He's confused by this behavior too. The King has never been one to back down from a righteous cause nor avoid a fight that needs to be had.

He nods and glances towards us, "You two go on ahead and then we shall be quick to follow."

The Prince looks unsure and my tail is in knots. Me— go downstairs with Tatchathura *all by myself*? In the middle of that chaos? What if he runs away from me the minute we get down there? What if we get into another fight?

"Hurry! The moment is right."

His voice startles me before I take off running towards the door. Surprisingly Tatchathura follows— abet more slowly— after me. I start sprinting down the corridors. I glance over my shoulder every so often to see him keeping pace with me. He must be thrilled. He'll finally be at home in his element.

Oh Jatali, keep me safe!

* * *

My feet fly down the stairs. My paws have barely hit the last stair before the screeches reach my ears. A sound like hundreds of souls calling out at once. It takes all my strength to not cover my ears.

He nudges me slightly before walking ahead, "It's worse than this in Zutaom."

The two of us reach the edge of the courtyard just below one of the archways. It seems our forces have been able to keep them preoccupied but it's obvious to me that our light is growing weaker. I start to step towards the battlefield and a wretched cry catches my ears. My gaze forced in that direction. Heroh has put himself between a shadow and Sukua. He slams into the ground. Her paw juts out to pay retribution to the shadow. It stumbles but takes a few more hits from her deft paws before it is finally quelled.

She dashes back and crashes to be by his side. Altikua is too far away to notice at this point but Kyltia comes flapping over.

Sukua stares up at her with watery gaze, "He's hurt really bad."

Tatchathura snorts, "Sure you still want to go out there, Princess?"

Heroh tries to move but curls in agony. His paws clutching his chest. Violent twitches run the course of his limbs.

Sukua says, "Help me—"

Kyltia scoops him upwards, "I'll take him. You're a better fighter Sukua."

The jaguar hesitates. She stares at him a moment before tearing herself away from them. She launches herself into the fray once more. Kyltia flashes past us without noticing us. With Heroh gone, their vine defense is weakened. More soldiers hit the ground. Some others help them out of harms way. There's just too many and it's happening too fast. Sukua's vines have become sloppy. Her movements look more like a cub's than a trained warrior.

The shadows are closing in. It seems every corner is filled

with their filth. Seeing them injure a big being like Heroh has my stomach turning. I'm nowhere near as physically strong as Sukua nor is my magic strong like Altikua's.

Tatchathura nudges me again, seemingly amused, *"Any time Indy."*

Our powers may be based on the strength of our will but sometimes it's hard to keep up with that when you're surrounded with so much doubt. I guess that's the struggle with our beings— you have to believe in yourself and others in the Kingdom or your magic is weak.

I thought I could do this.

I thought I was ready for all of this again.

Sukua is driving back a pack of shadows with a volley of vine whips. Flashes of pink flowers burst around their every side. Her explosions of light poke holes through them. Wounding them gravely.

Altikua shoots bursts of a lightning everywhere. He seems to be making the biggest impact on the forces against us.

The shadows just keep coming. There's no end in sight and the hope in me fades a little—

A massive beast charges through the crowd with Altikua at it's helm. The beast flings him backwards and he lands awkwardly. One of his hind paws makes a snapping sound as he lands. The wolf growls and clenches his sword tighter. He's panting while down on one knee.

The shadow grabs Altikua. It's tendril wraps around him and holds him high above the others, "Aw you poor loyal dog, your *Master* has left you to die in his place."

Lesser shadows gather around and start chanting. It makes me sick to think this is *entertainment* to them.

Altikua groans, "That's a death I'll gladly take if it helps him for even a moment."

A small light forms from this statement of faith, and the other soldiers notice but all of them are too afraid to help even their Commander.

The beast snarls at the show of resilience before slamming him into the ground. The chanting grows louder. He raises a claw high— ready to strike. Altikua writhes against his grip. Sparks of lighting try to form but for naught.

Tatchathura is complacent to stand next to me— as I foolishly stand still.

It's like all of the fire in my heart has been snuffed out. How can I possibly approach any of these intimidating creatures? When I can't even deal with a simple criminal?

The only reason that I was able to subdue him in the first place was because I got *lucky*. Nothing more and nothing less.

Altikua cries out.

The beast's tendril flies towards him.

"Stop!" I yell lobbing a spurt of fire at it's head.

The shadow's claw crashes into the ground next Altikua. It's nostrils flare. The red in its eyes contain a thrashing golden flame. The other shadows protest— it seems my intrusion has embarrassed the beast.

Tatchathura says, "Well, that's *a choice.*"

The shadow lobs Altikua away from his claws. A pack of lesser shadows bound after him like they've found new prey.

I grit my teeth as the creature comes crashing towards me. It's spitting fire and a wicked dark smog. Venom seems to drip from it's fangs.

I just *had* to pick on the big monster.

My paws are frozen to the pavement. I've fallen into quicksand and with every attempt at movement, I just sink deeper and deeper into my concerns.

That violent, twisting and sinking feeling that's dragging me into the Abyss—

I had to help— Altikua was in trouble—

But now what?

What if I do help and my fire doesn't come out right—

The words are stuck in my throat.

What if I hurt someone like I did Tatchathura—

Everything starts to fade and it's like I'm not even here anymore. My sight is blurry, sounds are dim. A trance has been put on me. The ocean sucking my head below the water—

Then a burst of sound and light— an explosion of darkness overtakes me. My eyes are wide and wild now. Everything's clear—

The shadow that wanted to devour me— his fangs run deep into my shoulder. I cry out and find myself limp for a moment—

And then Tatchathura levels a blow against it's jaw. It hisses and releases me. I slop to the ground as Tatchathura stands in front of me. The creature shakes its head and rears back to strike again. Another flash of light and shadow boom from their collision. The arm with his own shadow crackling against this new foe.

My body is still tense against the pavement, *What's even happening? What is he doing?*

He growls, face contorting in pain. His arm is fighting against the magic of the collar.

I can tell it's really hurting him. Lightning is shooting up and down his arm. Sparks of fire that aren't his own. They burn both shadows. The attacker squeals throwing itself backwards for a moment. Tatchathura doubles over holding his arm to his chest. A sinister snarl on his lips.

The other shadow's claws dig into the ground scraping violently against the stones. It's soulless golden eyes pierce us. The other shadows are even more confused. Some of them start to slither backwards as through afraid of Tatchathura—

Tatchathura's arm is half mast with a low growl on his

lips, "Don't you know **who** I am?"

My body is still frozen to the pavement. The pain of the bite wound courses through my veins. Luckily, I don't seem to be poisoned.

I can't believe he put himself between me and a shadow. What's going on with him?

"We're trying to win this war— not make friends."

Doesn't he want us dead?

The shadow has a gravelly voice with words that come out garbled. It's a collection of voices speaking over each other that make one hardly discernible.

It lowers its snout to be a breath away from Tatchathura, "I **do** know. But we're here to **take over**, not **spare** them!"

Tatchathura uses his good arm to push the creature out of his space, "I command you—"

"**Why** aren't you doing **your** part?"

He pops his shoulder, "*This one* is **important** to our mission for the moment. Don't *forget* your place. I'm still your **boss**."

The shadow is reviled at his words. Those fiery copper eyes blazing with a new energy, "We **all** serve the Drake. You're nobody and **not** above me."

The shadow lunges towards him again. Tatchathura's arm flies up to brace for a new impact. The shadow's claws fly down onto his paws. The power of Tatchathura's shadow slowly screeching and tearing its way out of his arm in an attempt to fight against the magic that binds it.

Again the shadow is burned by the magic of the collar. It howls stumbling backwards. Tatchathura is slammed into the ground. He hugs his arm to his chest and glares over at me, "Feel free to jump in at **any** time."

"*Me*? What can I do?"

"So that fire of yours was *only* for me? I'm *flattered* truly." His paws slip against the ground as he tries to stand again.

I clench the ground, "No, I *just—*"

The large shadow has shaken off its wound and charges towards him again. The lesser shadows chant and jump up and down wildly. The large shadow scoops the dark fox up and crashes him into the ground.

Tatchathura cries out and slams into the ground. He's crumpled into himself. His wounded arm completely limp.

The large shadow hovers over him. A crazed snarl on its lips. It's toying with him.

Tatchathura yowls, "*What* are you so afraid of?" His gaze slits, "**Get** him."

His harsh words startle me to attention.

What am I doing! I have to help him.

The beast starts reaching for him again—

I start pushing against the current of the tide. The ocean that was slowly drowning me. I've found a plank in the vast waters. Those words are just enough to throw myself forward— break through the ocean current and into the misty stormy air. As if a simple wound was what was holding me back, when I know it was just my mind and my soul in tatters.

I shove myself to stand. My bitten shoulder wants to limp but I force it to act. I breathe out harshly, "My fire won't be weakened by water nor stone. Let it burn like the love I have for Ituvoh."

I've never felt such burning—such a fierce feeling piercing throughout every fiber of my fur. It's uncontrollable—out of paw. It's just like when I overwhelmed Tatchathura out by the forest.

Fire is going everywhere. Exploding, and burning every shadow in its path. It envelops the shadow that's before us. The shadow that was ready to devour Tatchathura is suddenly consumed.

"TRAITOR!!" It roars.

It screeches violently but it's trapped. It's helpless. It can't fight against the fire. This isn't like an ordinary fire that just scorches the ground in every direction at once. This fire has a soul of its own. Its direction knows my heart. It follows my will. It's the Fire of Valiant! I'm glaring, and completely focused— even though it feels like I'm being ripped apart from the inside out.

My paws seem to comb the fire together even though I'm a few feet away from it. And like that, once my paws meet in the middle—

SMACK.

The fire bursts like a volcano and explodes skyward taking the shadow with it. Flowers bloom and singe all the straggling shadows around him.

The shadows that were chanting have scattered screeching in every direction. Some of them singing— *All hail the Shadow Fox— he commands us!*

I totter backwards for a moment. My head is swimming — my gaze blurry. I grip my feet into the ground and my tail tries to hold me steady. A dull pulse of pain ebbs from my shoulder.

Another burst of light springs from Tatchathura's arm and he growls. He face plants into the ground. His arm mangled and bruised. His eyes clenched shut and his body doubled in half.

Altikua comes dashing to my side. I see that he was able to recover his energy a little but even his pelt is faded. We may have this life force beating within us but we're not infinite. Kyltia is hot on his tail. She throws her wings wide to give us a moment free of shadows.

Altikua kneels beside us, his gaze focused on me, "Are you alright? You're shoulder—"

My eyes are wide and I can feel the water behind them, "I'll be fine. It's him."

He tears his gaze from me to search over Tatchathura,

"The idiot tried to use his shadow—"

"He did it to protect me." I say softly.

Altikua's face snaps to mine, his eyes darting, "Impossible."

"I wanted to help you, but I choked—" I hold back tears. The battlefield is no place to cry.

Kyltia calls, "Hey— they're getting closer!"

He rubs my back for a second, "Don't think about it now. Let's jolt him back to life, shall we?"

He puts a paw on his chest and his hip before unleashing a jolt of electricity. Tatchathura's body springs up for a moment. It takes another bolt before he pants awake. He clutches his gut and watches us through veiled eyes.

Altikua stands up, "Try to be more careful next time."

Tatchathura sputters, "Train your recruits better." He starts to hack up a little blood.

My brows furrow and before I can ask, the wolf calls back — "He'll be fine." His sword is raised and a small blast of lightning springs forth once more. Kyltia glances at me a moment before springing back into action again.

Tatchathura is still panting and clutching the ground. Any shadows that edge near, notice him and sprint the other way.

I lean down to offer him my good paw (even if I'm not confident about my strength to help him up).

He glares up at me. The arm with his shadow looks

mangled and beaten. His other shoulder is drooping, "Took you long enough."

With a strained pull, he fumbles to his feet. He almost crashes into me— his paws twist to help him stand again. A paw clutching my shoulder as he winces again.

I say, "I saved you, didn't I?"

He chuckles darkly before leaning against me. But he's heavy, so I stumble before we're awkwardly steadying each other.

He says, eyes glinting, "You're a mess."

"You're the one who jumped in the way—"

"So I should've *let* you die?"

I half-mock him, "We don't play *fair* Indy."

"Didn't know I needed to *convince* you *to* live, Sunshine."

I snort, ***"Whatever!* We need to help the others."**

He says gruffly, "A life for a life, right?"

I glare at him, "What do you even mean?"

"The courtyard training with Blondie's lightning. I figure I owe you that much." He looks over his shoulder at me, "Besides, they reassign me to someone else and I might not be able to manipulate them as well."

I don't have time to process what he's said.

A rain of light and fire bursts from a range of clouds. Our attention drawn to the sky as the King and Prince come charging through the masses. Shadows are obliterated left and right. Some go screaming towards the castle gates in the hopes of escaping. Just as most of them are sliced to pieces, the sky turns sickly dark. For a moment its as if there is no light. The castle fades. Our troops take the moment to circle around the middle of the courtyard. The sparse leftover shadows pace near the castle front gate.

King Elin-rah gazes towards the sky. His regal snout troubled for once, "It's time."

CHAPTER TWENTY
Born from Darkness

INDESSAH

A dark green fog starts to descend onto the castle. The shadows in the courtyard all rattle to a halt. Their crooked faces twist to look towards the front castle wall. There's a jarring silence as if time has completely stopped. A screeching chant forms from the stones below. The shadows start swirling near the wall. Our forces start to fall back towards the center of the courtyard.

More fog covers the courtyard and blocks out the sun.

Our blue sky completely darkened by the haze. A black circle forms on the front castle wall. Black tendrils spring forth breaking the circle and a giant claw reaches forward. A murky crimson and black talon comes into view.

The shadows are chanting wildly. Loudly proclaiming: *King of Darkness! Come! Come!*

The shadow energy projection crushes the center of the wall. The glittering stones crash down leaving flashes everywhere. The crashes like blasts of fire.

The Drake's long snout comes into view. Eyes empty like soulless pools of lava. His whole body is shrouded in darkness and crimson flashes. His long, smoking arms look like more shadows are bleeding out of him and being born into the continent. Every breath of fire and sulfur creates a scorching heat raising the temperature. His body a raging volcano.

Dark tendrils flow down the rest of his body slowly settling into the wall. A murky tendril forms into a long tail that's spiked in every direction. There are remnants of what might have been a regular tail at one point. Every tendril twists and curls with a mind of its own. Little crackles of lightning can be seen writhing under his scales. He flaps his wings dusting us with more of his smog and heat before they settle.

Each taloned claw grips piles of the stone like the arms of a throne. The stones under his tail a crushed seat. Each broad wing is large enough to span a part of the castle wall.

Slowly the chanting fades downward like a wicked whisper — a hushed hiss into the air like every breath has been twisted into this madness and tainted with evil muck.

His teeth are mangled into the shadows of his snout as he bellows loudly, "I'm finally **HOME**."

Every being covers their ears. An enormous force presses us down as the Achition settles in. My shoulder seems to sear in the pain of my bite wound. My paw clutches it tight. Even Tatchathura seems to wince under the pressure but I can tell that a part of him is pleased. His tail is twitching like he's ready to bound off at a moment's notice.

It causes a fire in my heart. How *dare* he? How dare he destroy half of our castle and claim this is *his* home!

The Drake will never rule Ituvoh and especially not here.

King Elin-rah and Prince Azufae-yoh slowly stride to the front of our group. The King waves his paws wide and then smashes them together. A bright golden orb surrounds our whole army. It's shielding us from all of the energy the Drake has brought with him. Sighs of relief come from our forces. A few of them sound like they can breathe again.

King Elin-rah glares up at the arrogant beast.

A wicked smirk forms on the Drake's lips. His mangled shadowy teeth forming a snarl, "Hello, *old friend*."

"Senteia."

"How *adorable*. That old fool died a long time ago."

"You arrogantly show up with a *fraction* of your power

here? That will be your *downfall.*"

"Well, I have other matters to attend to you know—" the Drake flips his tail around like he's bored, "Beings to meet, towns to crush. You know how it is— *Elin.*"

The shadows laugh and praise him as though its the funniest joke ever told. Our forces bristle and keep their fighting stances at the ready.

The King says, "This ends now."

"My hatchlings need to eat too you know."

"Have you become so arrogant—"

"Me, **arrogant**?" a laugh molten with spite falls from the Drake's jagged jaw, "You've allowed even *Vengeance* into your midst. You think you can tame a force such as that?"

There is a tense moment in the courtyard but our rulers don't waver. I curl my tail around my feet. I was barely keeping up before but now with my injury— and Vengeance is *here* too?

And then I remember something from the first time we were training Tatchathura...

Altikua raises his sword again. Tatchathura is winded on the ground. His body completely stiff against the pavement. The sword swings forwards.

I dash to slide between them, "Enough. You've made your point—"

Altikua glares down at me, "How will he know Justice if

I don't show him—"

*My brows furrow, a growl on my lips, "This isn't Justice. This is Vengeance. A shadow you **never** want to meet."*

"Too late." Tatchathura coughs behind me.

My eyes widen as I focus on the dark fox, *That's what he meant! He's Vengeance. I can't believe the Prince— or Great King...they had to know and they let him in anyway!*

They've dealt with other beings that have shadows before. (Kind of comes with the territory of reforming criminals.) But there is a collection of shadows that even Jatali won't mess with— Of course to be fair— beings who carry those kinds of shadows usually don't stay beings for very long.

It makes me wonder—when did Tatchathura get his shadow anyway? And how much longer does he have before he completely turns?

Altikua shoots a heated glare in Tatchathura's direction. He tugs me closer to the center of the group. A few of the soldiers start backing away from him once they realize who the Drake is talking about. Tatchathura does nothing. His paws still in his pockets and gaze on the Drake.

The Great King finally speaks, "Every being that's not a shadow deserves a chance to redeem themselves."

There are roars of laughter that come from the Drake's side. The Achition himself spews fire at the idea, "Still clinging to *your idea* of Justice I see."

"True Justice is giving every being his due and upholding the law." He slowly pulls out a great sword, "Now I will send you back to where you **belong**."

"Send me back? I should be **thanking** you. I've been able to grow in those festering shadows. And now even with a **fraction** of my power I will crumble your glittering city to the ground! And I'll **destroy** you Elin-rah. And by the seasons's end, I will make all your beings bow to me. I will make the Prince watch before I crush him on display. There will be nothing left for any of you to defend and then I will **crush** the rest of your beings into the dust."

A flash of golden light glimmers off of the king's coat. His eyes are gleaming with a terrifying orange light. His brows set deep, "Enough."

The silver lion slips through the shield. The rest of us still trapped and left behind in his magical force.

Prince Azufae-yoh hits a paw against the shield, "Father, let me help you!"

He glances back, "This is my fight, my Son."

Shadows make a carpet across the ground. Some of them rise up out of the cracks in the stone. Claws of pure smoky energy. Some with multiple heads. A volley of screeches break out. Then there's chaos in the courtyard.

King Elin-rah slices his sword into the new rage of shadows, "Uphold the weak, and balance the strong. The storm of Justice upon them all!"

The glowing light from his coat burns to consume his form. The light radiates outwards and overpowers all the shadows next to him. The blaze burns straight into the sky. All of the fog is fizzled into a haze. The golden light pulses all of the darkness away making the sky blue again.

Still more waves of shadows claw their way across the ground. The Drake stays on his "throne" waiting with a sinister curl on his lips. The King dashes through the crowds and no claw can stand against his blade. He's pure lightning. A storm cloud grows overhead. Just like my fire, it takes on a soul of it's own. Clouds glow a vibrant blue as they rain down more lightning from the skies above.

The sword slices through the remaining ground forces. His paws start pounding towards the Drake with his sword raised once more. For once, the Drake seems unsettled. He finally moves and shuffles back from the first swing. But the swipes keep coming. The King's sword slices through a limb. A vicious roar bellows from the Drake.

The sword and lightning crash all around their bodies. Each strike slamming into a part of his shadow. Blasts of gold and green crash into a burning smoke. Growls and roars rise from them both filling the courtyard with a terrible sound.

The King raises his sword high, a new ethereal, blue-silver glow overtakes his body, "The Magic of Jatali reigns over all!"

The sword swings down. The Achition claw grabs the

King mid-sweep. A vicious crush is heard. The King gasps. His powers recede on contact. All of us press to the edge of the golden shield. What's happening? How could the Drake —

A bellowing roar thunders from the Drake's throat. He fills the space with words of his own. Evil whispers of the Osekou Magic. More shadows emerge form the ground. The mist starts reforming around them. The King is tightly bound in his crimson grip. He struggles for a moment as his storm clouds reform.

A flicker of frustration crosses the King's face. The glow in his body seems to fade. His expression turns resolute.

The Drake's injured arm starts to re-form. A red flame erupts from his mouth. The fire spreads to all of his followers. They cry praises as they rise up in strength.

King Elin-rah glances back at us with glossy eyes, "It's my time. But my Son, I will give you the strength to overcome."

Prince Azufae-yoh slams his fists into the shield, "Father! No! Let me help you—"

The King closes his eyes. His paws pressed together and then it's completely dark in the courtyard for a moment. All of the light of the castle fades.

And then the smallest light from the King bursts forth into a raging sun. The white orange light blinds us all temporarily as it flows over every crevice of the stones. The light yanks every hidden shadow from the ground into view. It takes them screeching into the fiery light. Waves of lightning pass through the Drake slicing his scales into the pavement. Bursts of green and red erupt from his wounds and more gassy essences swirl around.

In the King's final moments, the lights take out almost all of the Drake's forces and wounds him severely. Still the Drake clutches the King and the light finally snuffs out. King Elin-rah's body hangs limply in the Achition's talons. The Drake sounds winded as he leans against the crushed castle wall.

The golden shield around us finally fizzles out. The warmth of the magic gone and replaced with the cold of the sickly air.

"Father!" Prince Azufae-yoh calls ready to run—

Altikua puts a paw to his chest, "Wait. We don't know what's happened."

Somehow the Drake was able to hold onto the King through it all. All of his forces in the courtyard were obliterated but still the Achition stands— barely. A snarl on his lips as he glares at his wounds.

I stare up at the half-beaten Drake— but why hasn't the Magic destroyed the Drake? How can it not be his time? Has his reign of terror not drawn on long enough?

It's deathly silent in the courtyard.

It's as if all life has been snuffed out of the castle's light. Luthura grows dim. The sparkling energy fades. The sky is ripped in two and a new wave of shadows descends from the air. They swirl and twist around the edges of the Drake so much so that it's hard to tell which being is which. A terrifying mass of ebony and crimson that paints the pastel sky ocher.

The new forces bring about a new pressure to the air. Some of our forces seem trapped in place again. More chaos blurs my mind. Shadows scoop up some of our forces. Volleys of magic blast past other capture attempts. Some Knights break others free and they flee back towards our center group. Shadows start swarming around their master once more. The Drake's wounds slowly start to heal as his followers sacrifice themselves into his ebony mass.

He lets out a victorious roar and stands up straight again. His energy back in full force. Waves of negative energy press us all down again. Groans and cries raise around us again as we're crushed into the stone.

I start pushing against the force that's bearing down on me on all sides. The fog seems to have a mind of its own. Its like the stories I've heard about Zutaom— the now desolate wasteland filled with poison. Shadows start pouring in waves towards us. A wicked laugh bellows into the once pristine courtyard. A smoky red fires blazes around the air making it harder to breathe.

I thought I was ready for all of this—

But my soul is a mouse. Tiny and frozen in place.

The Drake's talons toss the Great King across the courtyard not far from the Prince's paws.

The Drake snarls, "What of your father **now**?"

Any shadows that were near us slither across the stones to join their master's side. There is an eerie moment of calm as our forces are allowed a moment of peace from the onslaught.

The wound on the King's chest is permeated with dark particles. A smoggy haze over his once glimmering body. Prince Azufae-yoh crashes to kneel beside his father's body. His paws cupping his father's face. Giant tears fall down my friend's face.

Altikua and the soldiers sprint quickly to cover them. They've formed a new semi-circle around them. There's trembling and shaking in most of their forms as the weight of the Drake's presence grows stronger still.

The King said it was his time. He was giving himself up—but for what? It was supposed to drive the shadows away—to wound the Drake— but still they come! There's so much panic behind me. Most of the soldiers start urging the others to fall back. To regroup—

Bubbling forth from the shadows starts to form more figures. A vicious caterwaul starts uttering from the pit of their gloom. Hissing and screeching fill the courtyard walls. Some of the more eager beasts start sliding closer. They're impatiently waiting their master's request— the Drake is arrogantly gloating over it all.

The Prince wipes his tears roughly. He stands with his tail lashing. Altikua sees his movement and twists to block his path.

The Prince tries to slide past him but Altikua puts a strong paw to his chest and growls, "We can't afford to lose you **too**!"

The Prince's eyes are glossy, "I won't stand back—"

A shock wave like force emanates from the Drake— drowning in hatred— the weight of the skies start to press down around us. My legs start to buckle. Cries of anguish fill the smoggy green sky. My gaze darts around to see our forces practically pinned to the ground from the weight of it all— save for the Prince who is stubbornly able to resist. I can tell even his light has been weakened. Stiffly. he still stands near his father's body as the chaos around us grows again. A few more shadows pick soldiers off and there's nothing any of us can do about it.

Tatchathura is near me now. He slowly seems to walk through the shadows but I can tell he's stalling. He's silent. No laughter— gloating— nothing. Shouldn't he be happy? He's been tearing us down since he got here and now when they're winning— he doesn't care?

My claws scrape the ground. I should be trapped by now. But every shadow that darts near takes notice of the Shadow Fox and diverts their path. He's not doing or saying anything— but his presence many be the only reason I'm still alive.

"A life for a life, right?" he says gruffly still offering a paw.

I glare over at him, still feebly trying to crawl, "Are you happy now?"

He levels his calculating gaze over me but still he's quiet.

The Drake bellows, "**TATCHATHURA!** *Come forth.*"

For once I see Tatchathura's ears flatten. His tail rigidly still.

"**TATCHATHURA!**" the Drake crushes more of the castle wall.

The shadows reconvene with their master and let out terrible shrieking noises of pleasure. They're so self-satisfied they aren't even going to finish trying to crush us for the moment—

So arrogantly believing they won already—

Tatchathura doesn't pass me another glance as he walks through our midst. He starts to pass the Prince—

The Prince says, "You don't have to go to him."

Tatchathura snarls at this and shoulders his way past our still half-paralyzed troops.

For some reason this makes my heart hurt. I know I shouldn't care about someone like him— but we were all lost once.

What will happen to him? I've heard stories— the things the Drake has done and continues to incite among his followers. I just can't imagine following a ruler who would sacrifice his beings for a minor mistake— what happened to Tatchathura that made him so willing to follow such a wicked being?!

The Prince seems to break the energy's hold on him. He stumbles forwards a step. A pant on his lips. There's a fire in his gaze—

But without the Great King Elin-rah— what can we do?

CHAPTER TWENTY-ONE

A Golden Calvary

TATCHATHURA

The ebony and crimson sky drifts onward. It'd be a comforting reminder of home if I wasn't here. The Drake is crouched proudly on his makeshift stone throne. The shadows all dance and shift around him. Singing and gurgling praises of the *true* king of Ituvoh.

I've walked to stand in front of the group of Jatalian scum, but I stop short—

"You don't have to go to him."

I glare back at the group. They're all still trapped by the Drake's influence. Most of them are watching me with hatred— which they should—

But Indy watches me with fear all over her innocent face. Her paw still gripping her injured shoulder. Clueless—

The Prince is watching me like a father who doesn't want to let his son leave— what a weirdo! What is wrong with these beings!?

Their panicked hearts made my shadow excited— thrilled even— but I feel nothing. This world is full of suffering after all.

The Drake's thundering rich voice calls, "Tatchathura, *my son*, why do you linger over there? Come see your **Master**."

Another shudder runs up my spine. The other shadows all focus on me at once. A subtle chant seems to start among them. *Tear him, rip him! Break him, burn him!*

This is it.

One mistake is all it takes—

Tear him, rip him! Break him, burn him!

It's going to cost me everything.

The Drake slams a heavy talon into the ground. The stones shatter in his wake. A sinister hiss on his sanguine forked tongue.

I start to drag myself across the courtyard. Every step is agony and it's not the Drake's influence. I've torn other beings apart for lesser transgressions on my Master's behalf. It'll be a miracle if he doesn't maim me right now.

I stand a few steps in front of him. My legs slowly crumpling to kneel before him. My front paws hit the ground and I dare not look into his empty molten eyes.

"M-master. **Forgive me—**"

A booming roar erupts from his chest. So deep it fills the air and weighs me down. His talons sweep the ground and snatch me up. He squeezes me tightly as he brings me to his eye level.

His voice timbre, "Watch me **hatchling**."

It takes all of my strength to meet his horrible gaze.

Somehow Indy's gasp sticks out to me. She only saw a fraction of the kind of power a true shadow has. The power to make you re-live every horrible thing that's ever happened to you— over and over again until you've gone completely rock-brained.

I've never been one to run away from anything. I've faced down monsters even as a little cub— but the Drake—

A familiar voice calls up, "You can't have him. He belongs to me now."

The Drake violently turns his attention to the newcomer. I wince against his vice grip to look down. The Prince is standing only a few steps away from my Master's claws. What a fool.

The Drake roars, "Just because you've put a collar on this

mutt doesn't make him **yours**! His heart is far too *wicked* for that."

The Prince holds steadfast, "Tatchathura was captured on castle grounds. He belongs to me *now*."

The shadows at his feet detest this comment so much they start chanting again. *King of Darkness! Slice him! Burn him!*

The shadow Achition slithers down to wrap some of his form around the Prince. A tiny light almost drowning in the murky crimson. The Drake clutches me tighter still. I'm sure I felt a bone break— but I've had worse.

"You're just like your father— **weak** to the very end. Naively inviting in every wayward soul as **your own**." The Drake shatters more of the castle structure with his tendrils, "Have you learned **nothing** all these long years?"

"Tatchathura has my Father's seal. Not even you can break it."

The Drake snarls. A red eye pierces the collar. Then a wicked smirk plays on his crooked lips, "You're still about choice aren't you Azu? Well, let's see what Tatchathura thinks."

Azufae nods simply. His look is expectant as if he already knows the outcome.

I flatten slightly in the Drake's grasp, *What's with this dumb lion?*

The Drake narrows his gaze, a puff of heated sulfur blows

into my face, "Do you know *why* you were captured here?"

"I made a mistake—"

"I gave you an impossible assignment." There's a twisted amusement in his gravely voice, "**I** put you here, so all of this could happen."

A sharp breath thrusts from my lungs. A shuddering sigh of relief on my lips. I'm not dead— *today* at least.

Heated grumblings rise from the others below. They want me punished. They literally heard it was part of *our* Master's plan and *still* they want me to suffer. This is how it is in Zutaom all the time.

He squeezes me tighter, "Do you know *why* I chose you?"

"No Sire."

"All of those hatchlings, so much potential. But none held such a vengeance for Jatali as you." His laughter tainted with a vile sludge, "That's why I gave you the power you have. A power that's **detestable** to Jatali."

The Drake lowers his gaping jaw towards the Prince. He's barely a snap away from his face. Still the Prince stares him down. His blue eyes holding a faint purple glow. A tense energy passes between them.

The Drake dangles me closer to the Prince, his tight grip all but crushing me completely, "So Tatchathura, *where* does your allegiance lie?"

I glance at the Prince. His gaze has softened for a

moment.

It's disgusting.

All of this fuss over me. Why is he fighting so hard over me? I've tried to kill his soldiers, steal stuff from the castle and have been actively rude to that fuzzbrain—

He could've saved me when I was a cub— but he didn't.

"I don't want *any* part of it."

The Drake rumbles in self-satisfaction, and offers me up again— taunting the Prince, "You see? All your kindness brought you **NOTHING!** He doesn't want you."

Azufae watches unfazed by this declaration, "Kindness is never wasted."

My Master starts to bristle at this. The chanting starts again, "The land of Jatali has it's true ruler— the one who *should* sit on the throne." His snout level with the white lion once more, "Tell your beings to bow to me or I'll crush you all. **NOW!**"

"Senteia, you will **never** rule Jatali." A subtle purple glow surrounds the Prince.

The Drake's scales raise off his neck. Even a strong being like him can feel the energy shift— *"Still* you press **for him**?"

"My Father said not to yield even one soul to your darkness. So I *won't*."

The amusement in my Master's rumble fades. A small snarl starts to form, "Have it your way."

He slinks to tighten the ring around the Prince. A small light in the darkness. Cries of protest erupt from the Jatali group. The Drake's focus is completely on the foolish lion. His talon goes closer to the ground before he slops me into it. I crash roughly. My face scuffs against the rough stones. My ribs are sore and a little blood is on my face. I push up on my paws. A weak tremble barely keeps me from the cold ground.

The Drake bellows, "Go my hatchlings. **SNUFF OUT** every last bit of light in Luthura. "

The shadows let out raucous cries of exuberance. All of them pouring outwards in every direction. Slithering across the pavement to sink below the ground again. Some dart ahead to crash against me. I can feel them through my clothes. It's like they're scraping against my fur.

I shove myself to stand. My body half limp.

I wish he would've just finished me off.

I forgot for a moment that he's just a projection of himself. A fraction of his true power. He was strong enough to take out the King even if he seemed to give up. The thought of it makes me shudder.

Blasts of radiant purple light start exploding from the center of the achition's coils. Another wave of radiating golden energy follows it. The pressure and chains on the Jatalians break. The shadows protest against their freed prey. The courtyard blazes to life with bursts of light and waves of shadow. Every being seems engaged in combat—

giving it their all. Save for one fox who seems out of her element *again*. Indy's back pressed against Altikua's. That wolf is more than happy to keep her out of trouble but it won't last. The shadows are closing in.

The remaining soldiers are surrounded and the Prince's light seems to be intermittently snuffed out. Fools. All of them. The Drake gave them a chance to save their hides— fight another day— but this dumb lion is too prideful. Senteia may have been a foreigner to this land but he exposed the very problem with Jatali. They hide things from their beings. Azufae could've saved all the beings at the castle but instead he chose to fight.

But I guess I don't blame him too much— the being who unites the thirteen Relics will have the power to live forever. The power to turn back death itself. A scythe to reap back the souls to this realm and make them breathe again. It's no wonder to me the lions would hide it for themselves. They wouldn't want any other beings living forever like they have—

But with the death of the King, the spell is broken. What could the Prince hope to accomplish? To die fighting? Noble I guess. When he couldn't die, I'd say arrogance—

It is also said that the Magic will obey their every move. The being who accomplishes this will no longer be under Jatali's rule— Free to live out their heart's desire without fear.

The Drake raises upwards. His large talons spread wide.

His broad wings cloak the courtyard. More smog starts to fill the air. A rich haze seems to gobble up every last scrape of air. Some of the Jatalians start to buckle under the pressure.

A wave of despair on their master's face. He closes his eyes. Is he finally giving up?

Each of his paws clasp together. The words he speaks are foreign to me. It seems as though they may be part of our ancient tongue. And then his eyes are open wide again. A pulsing golden energy flashes off of his white coat.

A wave of magic startles the Drake. He growls lowly.

The Prince says some more words. His paws making a different form. A stance like any fighter would make. The gold and purple light surrounds his form. It strengthens the magic around the groups and then new magic starts to spring forth from his paws.

My eyes are alight with the brilliant golden flame that covers the Prince. It's almost as if he's a turned into a ball of brilliant energy as radiant as the sun. A glistening planet full of light and righteousness.

Faith Magic!

The exploding lustrous light is a shock wave that ripples through the courtyard. Every single shadow is ripped apart from every castle stone. The intense shrieks raise all the way to the broken sky. The crimson and red haze starts to ripple away into a faint pastel blue again.

Just as Azufae might unleash more magic, the Drake

snatches him up viciously. The lion cries out in anguish. The Jatalians protest.

The Drake bellows, "I should've **crushed** you when you were a cub."

My ears pin back. The Drake would've been sealed at that time. What does he mean?

The achition's talons clench tighter. Azufae struggles against his grip but it's futile. There's a subtle crack. The lion looks winded now. His gaze dim as he slumps into the Drake's claws. There's more gasps in the courtyard. Altikua practically drops his sword. Indy covers her mouth.

The Drake yowls triumphantly. Azufae's magic wasn't enough. Surprise, surprise.

Just when I figured it would go dark again, a brilliant blue light fills the courtyard stones. A light that seems very familiar to me. I step back a space as if I have anywhere to go. The entire courtyard ground is shimmering blue.

The Drake snarls down at the pavement. His feet start moving rapidly against the warmth of this light. A shining golden and ghostly energy shoots out of the ground. It's Elin-rah's soul! Back from the Void? A thing that's never happened before. The golden lion phases straight through the Drake's claw. Azufae takes in a breath like he's winded.

Enraged the dragon drops him to the ground. Azufae is too weak to move. His breathing erratic. Altikua rushes across the courtyard to kneel by his side. The others are too shocked to do anything.

The Drake roars, "What sort of **trickery** is this!"

Elin-rah's soul hovers in front of my Master. Slowly more souls start rising out of the glowing pavement. They are all different animals from every country. Each one is a different color on a rainbow spectrum. Some of them are dragging shadows from beneath the ground with them. The shadows burst into nothing in their paws. There are calls that seem to come from around the city of Luthura. More souls and lights are seen throughout dragging every last bit of darkness from it. Hints of pink and purple swirl through the ground. Even the clouds seem happy. Glimmering flickers of light start to race out of every crevice and every hill near the castle. Their positive force is smothering the dark influence of the Drake. Fantastic.

The Drake tries to swipe at these newly formed souls but his claws phase right through.

Golden globes roll across the courtyard to cover up his followers in a crystal golden shield. Even one rolls to capture me. I snarl at this. The shadows shriek if they are caught inside and then they wither away. The others outside the globes violently try to claw their way back in.

The shadow tendrils of the Drake fly down to try and break each of them apart.

Elin-rah folds his arms, "Long live Jatali."

In an radiant burst of light and color the souls all crash through the Drake. His projection is viciously beaten by each wave of light. Blast after blast breaks each piece of his form into a shriveling shadow. A weak mass of red and black slowly being frittered away.

His wicked growl is ear shattering to the those left in the courtyard, "Tatchathura— **FINISH** the job."

My gut twists. He wants me to stay here in the middle of this mess? *Really?*

And for a moment there is silence. Another eerie calm. The other soldiers all seem to collectively crash to the ground. Separated and startled from the massive amount of energy that's been loosed here. Indy is a little ways off from the group. A paw thick in her mussed hair.

The rainbow lights are fading into a pristine blue sky. There is gleaming pockets of white lights like stars in the daytime. Elin-rah is still hovering in the courtyard. His form slowly floats over to where Azufae and Altikua are. There's a small delay before two more lights come flying onto the scene.

The first light courses through the sky from beyond the far horizon and lands in front of Kyltia. The bat seems startled a moment before she tries to hug this light. Her eyes are watery as she mentions his name. It must be some close relation of hers.

Indy says, "It's your brother!?"

From below the stone of the courtyard, the Queen of Jatali rises to meet her family.

Altikua helps the Prince sit up. The lion's eyes are still dim—Let's see him properly recover from that—

The King places his broad paw against his son's heart. A blast of blue goes coursing through the lion— because of course it does! They can't even be wounded for a second it seems.

Azufae reaches for his father but his paws seem to go through him, "Father, what's happened?" he rubs his head, "Mother?"

She calmly nods her head. Her gaze full of love.

Elin-rah puts his paws on his son's shoulders, "This is what we've been working towards my dear son. A beautiful place for our souls to go to live forever. Just like your sacrifice birthed a new era for our land. My sacrifice with the Drake has helped birth this place the Magic has been preparing for us."

Azufae's eyes go wide, a small shimmer to them, "Does that mean—"

"We are in the final stages of the Promise of this land. Those who never aligned with the Magic have been banished to the Abyss for good. The beings that were in line with the Magic now have a paradise to live in for eternity."

"I still don't understand it all."

"You won't understand everything right now, but you will in time. Finish the work that we started. Reunite the countries and banish the rest of the shadows for good."

"Yes, of course Father." There's tears in his eyes. It's about time he's lost something important to him, "Mother, I miss you."

The Queen leans down to drawn him close, "How I have missed you Azu. But we will be together again."

The King kneels to embrace the three of them together tightly. A flash of glowing light seems to emanate from their display and course over the land around us. The light of Luthura castle seems to burn brighter.

The scowl on my brow deepens.

Elin-rah starts to float upwards, "I have to leave you now, but I know you can do it. The Drake will be wounded for a time. It should be enough to get a head start."

Altikua helps Azufae to stand. Azufae says, "I won't let you down."

"We know." He smiles brightly before shooting off into the sky. She follows his tail like a comet of her own. They enter a misty blue and white pocket of light much like a gate. As they enter in, it dissipates into a regular sky once more.

Well isn't that all just fantastic! Just when we thought our goals were clear— that blasted Magic of Jatali goes and changes the rules. The Jatalians all seem to gather around their Prince. There's so much fussing and big feelings it makes me sick.

I put a paw to my chest. It still hurts from the Drake's assault and fragments of lightning from the collar seem to rattle the shadow still inside me. I snort at the absurdity of it all. We were so close. *We* should've won.

I remind myself that it was only a small part of his power.

I also realize this is why it's so important for us to gather the Relics. With the thirteen Relics in my Master's talons, it will give us control over the Magic of Jatali and then no being in Ituvoh will be able to stop us.

The Prince got incredibly lucky. But as long as I'm around, I'll be able to make sure he doesn't have that chance again. Just as I am about to start walking towards the group, a paw tightly grabs mine. I twist ready to strike — my paw stops as I recognize the golden gaze staring back at me. Her lips twitch upwards for a moment before she starts urging me onwards. I realize that everyone is too distracted by the events to even notice us. I glance at the chaotic courtyard for another second before darting with her.

* * *

Lu-kan and I climb over the castle walls. We slide down the other side and land in the lush grass below. A part of me is ready run far away from this place. Escape to some other continent in our vast oceans and never come back to Ituvoh again.

After all, the Drake is too busy trying to fight this war to come after just one fox, right? But he has so many shadows ready to do his will— I'd be running for eternity—

*"Tatchathura— **FINISH** the job."*

She yanks on my paw to keep me moving. A beautiful look of confusion on her face.

I let out a harsh sigh, "I'm not going."

She glares at me and tugs again, so I tug her towards me.

She barks, "What? We have to go **now**!"

"We still have work to do—"

Her gaze is wide, and ears fly forwards, "They've brainwashed you! The Prince touched you, didn't he?"

I put a gentle paw to her lips, "He doesn't have the power we thought he does."

She pushes my paw down, "I don't believe you. What's my middle name? Do you still hate Jatali?"

Before I can answer, she throws both paws down on my shoulders hard, "Tell me your boss's name!"

I wince slightly under her metal enhanced grip, "Atiness, Jatali can rot, and Re-kivah."

"Oh no, *now* you're lying for **them**!" She grips her head and shakes it back and forth.

I chuckle slightly. Who knew she'd be a mess without me? I tug her in close and kiss her quickly. Gently, I push her back so I can look into her eyes, "*Darling*, Lu, do you really think the place of endless rainbows and sunshine is going use magic on me that lets me **lie**?"

Her gaze softens, "Tatch, you're—"

"I'm me, more than ever. Now will you *listen* for a minute?"

She breathes out, "Fine. *What* work is left?"

"It turns out Jatali is full of soft heads who trust way too easily. Just give me two weeks and I'll know everything we need to find the other Relics—"

Her ears flatten, tail brushing the ground slowly, "You got captured *on purpose*? That wasn't the plan. How did you get past Altikua's Honesty?"

I wave her down, "No, getting caught was an accident but the Drake said it was part of his plan all along."

"And you believe that?"

"He has no reason to lie about that. He knows more than we do."

She bites her lip. Eyes like daggers as she scrutinizes my every motion. She should be able to trust me— she glances at the collar around my neck.

I shake my head drawing her closer, "Even after *all* this time— you don't trust me?"

"Well, you are *you*." She snorts, "Fancy *piece* you picked up."

"Yeah, another reason I can't exactly leave. The Prince or one of his cronies has to be the one to take it off."

She tenses at the knowledge with her tail lashing violently.

I put a comforting paw on her shoulder, "If it's what the Drake has said, we have to follow it. Besides we'll never find all the Relics on our own. The Prince *has* to know."

She shoots me another disbelieving look, "So if the Drake really said that? That you being here is his plan? Will Azufae *really* let you stick around?"

"They wanted to cut a deal with me before the Drake showed up. I doubt that much as changed. Besides—" I jangle the collar to emphasize the point.

"He could be leading you astray. I don't like this."

"Look, I don't think he's any more trustworthy than you do, but this lion had the chance to take his beings and go when the Drake showed up— but chose to fight for his *claim* over me." I shudder slightly, "No rational being does that without cause. I still have something they need."

Lu-kan's ears twitch, but she seems to get the idea. Her breathing is shallow, "Okay."

I press my forehead to hers. She startles and looks up at me, "I will never abandon you Lu-kan, but I'm staying here for the moment."

She shakes her head, "I thought I lost you. If they ever *changed* you, like that—"

"I'll die before this place changes me." I walk back towards the castle wall, "Tare care. I'll contact you somehow. Stay close."

She watches me, "I'll try. Be careful."

"Just do what you do best, love, and leave the rest to me." I give her a confident wink before climbing back over the wall.

I stand at the top for a moment. Looking back down, she's still watching me— uneasy with the idea of letting me out of her sight.

*Be safe Lu-kan...*I wave her onwards and jump back into the courtyard without another look back.

I hate to leave her too but we're too close to our objective. The Drake put me here. I have another chance for our mission and I won't mess that up.

CHAPTER TWENTY-TWO
A Task for Many Knights

INDESSAH

The lights finally fade into the horizon. There is so much excitement and wonder blooming in the courtyard. Most of us are still watching the skyline hoping to see more of those that we've lost over the years. I can't believe it— it was promised so long ago. A new place for souls to go instead of the Void and the Abyss. The Magic of Jatali has been faithful to its beings indeed.

As I gaze skyward I can't help but think: *Thank you.*

The others around me are bustling to help each other. Some are taking off towards the Med Bay. Others seem ready to head towards their homes or barracks. The Prince and Altikua are caught in a heated conversation. It's mostly positive but there's a concern there. Sukua is still looking over her soldiers to make sure they get the care they need. I can tell she's probably anxious to see Heroh again. Kyltia is darting around trying to take notes on any being that will speak to her about their experiences. She's so unphased sometimes I envy it.

Tatchathura is nowhere around. I figure he's run away in the middle of the chaos. I'm not surprised. I would've done the same if I were in his fur. Through the bubbling masses still trying to recover, a dark fox cuts a path. He saunters towards me with his paws in his pockets. His tail dusting the ground. My eyes must be wide as I stare at him. Now that the danger is gone, I have a moment to think about what's happened not only did Tatchathura put himself in danger's way for me, he got injured for me too.

Why help me in that moment? Their forces were swarming us. It was such a perfect opportunity for him to leave me alone.

It makes me wonder what he's up to.

He said its so he can manipulate me.

But some part of me doesn't believe that.

He's been nothing but crass since he's been here. Sure, he's bonded by that collar but that wouldn't make him put himself in danger on purpose.

Let alone for me.

I know *what* he said. That I was valuable to him for the moment. But I just find it hard to believe—

He saunters near me. I glance up at him, "Not running for the hills?"

He jangles the collar as though that explains everything. He digs his paws into his pockets again. A sour look on his face.

"It's because the Prince was willing to *save you*. Isn't it?"

"What? He didn't save me from anything, Princess."

"How's your arm?"

"I was almost crushed by the King of Darkness and you're worried about my arm from a few hours ago? *Priorities* Indy."

My hackles raise. I'm ready to barb him back but then I see him inspect his arm as though he'd truly forgotten. I mean a lot has happened— but I would remember if I mangled my arm like he did.

It sends a shiver up my spine. What other pains have they inflicted on their beings?

He stretches his arm and flexes his paw. A slight wince on his features, "I'll live."

"I don't understand you."

"There's a lot of things you don't understand."

"I mean—" My ears flat, "I don't understand *why* you jumped in front of me."

He glares at me, "I told you. The Kingdom wants to cut me a deal. You're valuable to me alive. When the conditions change, so will my charity. So don't get used to it, *Your Highness*."

"Noted." I narrow my gaze, "We should get you to medical bay. They'll be able to fix your arm."

"I'm fine." He scoffs.

"Don't worry. They won't be able to extract your shadow. When you made a covenant with the shadow, you're stuck with him until you renounce him completely. And we all know you're not going to do that *ever*."

He raises his eyebrows, a smirk of amusement on his lips, "So Indy does have a brain after all."

At that moment, Altikua, Sukua and Kyltia walk over towards us.

Sukua's brow creases, "Let's go check on Heroh."

The others seem to subtly agree. Sukua starts leading us towards Medical Bay. I can tell she's more agitated than usual. Heroh and her are close friends and do almost everything together. I can't imagine if something had happened to Kyltia.

As we walk, I glance around at our other comrades. Most are still shaken, and exchanging possibly helpful information from the battle. I shake it away for the moment. There will be plenty of time to finish processing these events.

Hopefully Heroh has recovered. For all our sakes.

* * *

We all walk into the bustling Medical Bay. There are still a lot of wounded soldiers to tend to. One of the staff takes notice of us lingering in the doorway and directs us down the hall to the Resting Ward. That's good news. Whatever happened to his arm and shoulder has been fixed. They also mentioned that many of the beings who were captured by shadows have been found. They are also recovering down there. I turn the corner and enter into the Resting Ward. Most of the beings are sleeping as you'd expect but Heroh is sitting on the edge of his bed trying to see the events of the courtyard from the tiny arch window.

I call, "Heroh! You've recovered."

He almost falls out of his cot, "So good to see you guys. Sorry I got myself knocked out." He seems flustered at that fact.

"You were protecting Sukua. Any one of us would've done it. In fact, you were probably the only one who'd be able to survive an attack like that."

I find myself frowning at that thought—

The shadow that wanted to devour me— his fangs run deep into my shoulder. I cry out and find myself limp for a moment—

And then Tatchathura levels a blow against it's jaw. It hisses and releases me. I slop to the ground as Tatchathura stands in front of me. The creature shakes its head and rears back to strike again. Another flash of light and shadow boom from their collision. The arm with his own shadow crackling against this new foe.

My body is still tense against the pavement, What's even happening? What is he doing?

He growls, face contorting in pain. His arm is fighting against the magic of the collar.

I can tell it's really hurting him.

Somehow he managed to get through it. Did his inhabiting shadow help him? Is that how he's able to withstand so much pain? The Prince said he tears shadows out of beings for the Drake. So maybe that was nothing compared to what he's done before?

Sukua rushes to his side. She tugs him into a tight hug, "Don't ever do that again! I would've been alright."

He half-growls, "I wasn't going to let you get hurt."

She pulls back to look at him, "We could've stopped it together—"

Altikua waves for them to settle, "It's over. Everyone is safe that's all that matters."

Sukua frowns at Altikua and Heroh in turn as though she might say more later but she quiets for now.

Heroh says, "So, what happened down there? Don't leave

anything out!"

I wave him down with a half-smile, "I'll start at the beginning."

Kyltia bumps into my shoulder, "And I'll help."

He sits cross-legged like a cub ready to hang onto every word. Sukua sits at the end of his cot. Altikua starts wandering towards the door interested in what the med staff are saying. As I start to tell Heroh what happened, I glance over to Tatchathura. He's leaning in the small window staring down at the grounds below.

At the beginning of the week I was terrified of the idea of him. I was more stressed than I let on to the others— Every argument I'd had with him up until this point had torn down my confidence. But this one battle alone has changed my view of him so much.

* * *

The next day starts with a dreary morning. Even though we know the Great King and many of our loved ones are in a glimmering place now— still a fog hangs over the castle. I'm in the Great Hall with Tatchathura at my side. He looks bored and annoyed as usual. Prince Azufae-yoh and Altikua are here. They keep periodically discussing the plans for the future. Just when they started to get some progress, the giant wooden doors are thrown open. The council of Elders make a quick procession into the room. There's some confusion in the room until they all settle around the Prince.

A deer with a cane says, "Sire, we should make the arrangements for your coronation immediately. The beings want to know that you are our king now."

There seems to be a joyous energy to that thought. Some of the other Knights in the room hit their staffs against the ground to voice their approval.

Prince Azufae-yoh rubs the back of his head, "I understand your concerns but unfortunately before my Father passed he explained to me that I need to remain a Prince until the Promise is filled. Only then will it be my time to be the true King over all."

There's a murmuring among the group of Elders. An evident confusion that passes between them all.

An elk says, "It's impossible! We can't wait. The beings need *some* kind of hope."

Another says, "All the Providences are restless and the shadows rise more each day."

The deer with a cane says, "You can't possibly hope to unite the Kingdom under one banner with so much chaos. I'm sorry your Highness it's too much even for your power."

The Prince sighs, "You're right, old friend. Still— I must honor what my Father has left me. I will explain it to the beings. Send out a summons. I'll address them tomorrow."

* * *

It's around lunchtime the next day and the rain hasn't let

up. Altikua, Sukua, Heroh, Tatchathura, and I are waiting in one of the high towers. The Prince is preparing to go out for his speech. He's flustered for once and keeps pacing.

Altikua says, "Your Highness, our beings understand our circumstances. In fact, some of the beings don't even believe that the Great King Elin-rah is dead at all but merely planning a new strategy."

"Oh, how I wish it were true. I've listened to him so many times and yet still— here's this moment."

Tatchathura sulks as he leans against the far wall. I can tell he wants to make a comment but for whatever reason is holding it in.

Sukua puts her paws on her hips, "Sire, the people love you and whatever you say they will understand."

Heroh puts his fist up in an encouraging way, "That's right! Our country may have some issues to work out but there's no better time than the present."

Altikua says, "If anything, the shadow attacks woke everyone up to the fact that things aren't right here. That things haven't been right here for a while now."

My brows tilt, and tail wraps tightly around my leg. I know he's upset about the things that have happened and he's worried about messing up but we know he can do it.

I know he can do it.

In many ways, he had already been dealing with everything the Great King used to do in preparation.

Prince Azufae-yoh nods to us, "Thank you, my friends."

Although he seems calmer, I can tell something is still bothering him. His paws are rubbing together and tail twitching back and forth almost running circles across the floor.

I know it's kind of bold of me and normally I wouldn't even consider it—

But the Prince has been so kind to me. He's always been there for me—even in the moments when I never deserved it.

I have to try and be there for him—

Even if the one thing I say makes a difference it'll be worth it to look foolish to the rest of them. I step closer to the Prince. Each step feels like it's taking forever. He stops pacing to look at me.

I reach out my paw onto his shoulder, "I know that the Elder said the beings don't have hope but he's **wrong.** Ever since you first walked onto that battlefield, you've always been our hope."

His concerned expression turns brighter as his lips tilt upwards.

"Everyone in our country knows that you're going take over. It doesn't matter what your title is." I throw my arm dramatically, "What matters is you care about your beings so deeply. You've always been here for us— even in our darkest moments."

He's smiling and shaking his head as if he can't believe it.

"A wise lion once told me that you're *not* alone anymore."

His face is full of mirth, "Did he now?"

"Azu, we're your Knights— and Knights-in-training. We took an oath. We may not have the Great King to rely on anymore but you learned everything you could under him. The Magic of Jatali speaks with you and now we have to impart that knowledge onto the rest of the country so there can be peace again."

The Prince warrants me a warm look. I tug him into a hug. It's the least I can after everything he's done for me— for all of us.

"Here, here," says Altikua putting his paw on the Prince's shoulder, "You're making the rest of us *look bad* Indy."

It only takes another moment before Sukua and Heroh join our hug. It's a tender moment for us all. A hug we all seemed to need after experiencing such loss. Not only the King but our other comrades that fell that day. I can hear Tatchathura groaning at the display but I ignore him.

Maybe one day he'll understand it.

Reluctantly we all pull apart. Prince Azufae-yoh gives me another nod before he heads out to the balcony. Altikua is at his side. A few of the Elders are waiting alongside some other Knights. The Prince and Altikua stand in the front row of the balcony. The crowd is a huge bubbling mass in the courtyard below. A quiet roar bounces off the walls.

I linger a few steps behind them.

Tatchathura saunters up to me. His paws buried in his pockets, "Who knew you were such a *speech writer.*"

"Do you have something *important* to say?"

"Actually, *I do.* You can make as many speeches as you want but it's not going to stop Zutaom."

"Don't you think I know that? Everyone *knows* that."

"Just figured you needed a wake up call."

I narrow my gaze at him and say nothing.

He raises a brow, "I guess I just figured I'd give you a pep talk too— in case you thought those *pretty* words worked on us."

"They work well enough— besides I **don't** need validation from **you.**"

He makes a sound like he's amused but his face doesn't change.

A quiet hush comes over the courtyard as the Prince spreads his paws wide, "Citizens of Jatali, my friends."

The crowd settles until it's almost pin drop quiet.

"I know that you expect me to take the crown of my Father today but I'm here to explain that it will not be so."

There are gasps of confusion in the crowd below. The murmuring turns into a quiet roar again. Altikua motions for the crowd to settle.

The Prince continues, "I am still your ruler. Titles matter

not. What does matter is that we stick together. We've been through worse. We built this country up and weathered many wars from our enemies. Most of us have been so caught up in the wars happening around us, we've forgotten to fix the war happening inside us."

"So I'm asking you all today— spend some time with your neighbors. It's good to know the weakness in your own heart and refresh yourself with our teachings so that you may be strong. So that you may uplift the others around you. And then we shall become unified once more into the country we were always supposed to be."

"It's easy to say there's nothing wrong. It's easy to push those feelings down but I'm urging you look deep inside to find any weak points. Fortify them. We can't afford another shadow attack. The further we're divided, the stronger they get."

"So that's why, in addition to this, my Knights will be working overtime. Going far and wide to root out any destructive forces by bringing them to justice."

There are exuberant cries in the crowd. Many of them throw their hats and their arms. Some start dancing a jaunty jig in a circle. It's true the Knights have been helping in little ways here and there, but most of them don't venture far past our own borders unless they're on a military assignment in a different country.

In many ways, we've neglected who we are and have suffered the consequences. The Prince's speech is just the kind of hope this country needs to hear. We might just be able to rebuild.

Prince Azufae-yoh raises his paw and the crowds settle once more, "I've sent word to all of our cities and towns to let us know any issues they might have. We are erecting a Community Board in the center of town. I have enchanted it so that anyone may post to it but once it is placed on the board it can no longer be tampered with. I'll know exactly who wrote it. So take caution when writing on this board because if we try and make a joke—I'll know who you are."

There seems to be some chuckles from the crowd below. It's as if we all thought the same thing— the young ones making silly requests and all that.

Prince Azufae-yoh waves us all forward. The five of us stand in line with him. There's a fluttering in my chest. My tail is suddenly restless. I cling to the stone in front of me. My claws start to scrape against it.

This is really happening.

I'm really gonna be a full-fledged *Knight*—

Soon.

All of these beings are *depending* on us.

Prince Azufae-yoh says, "Thank you for having listened to me. I urge you all to take my words to heart. I'll be here for any being who needs any extra support. My Knights will help you with any issues— you need just ask. Jokan, Mutiem, lus Haoyut tav Jatali!"

It means: *Justice, Peace and Glory to Jatali!*

As the Prince starts to chant, the rest of us join in. The courtyard is so filled with love and joy, it makes my chest swell. A grin spreads across my face—

But even in all that happiness—

That we're getting back up again—

My gaze is drawn to Tatchathura and I see nothing but sadness there. The murkiness he carries permeates his soul like he can't feel anything at all.

But then again I guess he wouldn't be happy right now— he's trapped among beings that he believes are his enemies. Far from home and his family—if he has one. I just wonder if he's every truly happy?

If only he knew we were all like him once.

Whether we came from this country or another, only through the Kingdom of Jatali are we made new.

CHAPTER TWENTY-THREE

Underneath a Starry Sky

INDESSAH

It's been a few days since the castle siege. It's late and quiet in the castle for once. The only ones still up are those on night duty. It might sound silly to some but on nights like this, our group likes to go up to the tallest tower in the castle and stand on the balcony. We watch the stars, the moons and all the night creatures come out. I'm leading the way up the stairs. Kyltia is by my side seemingly proud of herself. The others behind me are talking. Sukua and Heroh are chattering on like they always do. I can't imagine giggling so much in my life. Bringing up the rear Tatchathura and Altikua are bickering about something. I'm not surprised about that. What's weird though is there's a small tone in their voices that isn't exactly hostile.

If I didn't know any better, I would just say they're two brothers trying to figure out the best way to do something.

I push open the wooden door. A cold night air blusters against my face. The soft cries of the Tize-khan fill the air. The buzzing of bugs pierce my ears. Our world is alive both day and night. Every day I'm always in awe of the beauty and wonder we get to live in. If only the shadows didn't exist anymore, then our world truly would be paradise. One day when the Promise is fulfilled, it finally will be.

I lean against the edge of the castle wall. I dig my claws into the stone and stare down at the glimmering city before my gaze is drawn to the forest. Kyltia settles next to me. She wears a warm smile. Her presence helps buffer the winds from being too cold. Our gazes drift skyward. It's dark with muted grays and purples. The stars are twinkling faint green. The three moons are glowing each with their own light in red, blue and green.

Sukua butts her shoulder into mine. There's a playfulness in her voice, "So how's your week back been?"

"As if you *even* have to ask." I grin at her.

"I know pretty exciting compared to a school, huh?"

"Yeah, it's different. I wonder if the kids are okay. Hopefully Betavon isn't driving the new teacher crazy."

Sukua giggles, "I'm sure he'll put that drive to good use one day and become a great warrior."

Kyltia lolls her tongue, "Or be a great nuisance to his commanding officer—"

"Kyltia." I frown at her, "He's just tenacious."

"That's a word for it." She folds her wings.

"Maybe he'll see the day where he doesn't have to fight at all." I hug myself, "I've been away from the shadows for so long I forgot how terrifying they are."

Sukua softens, her paw wraps around my shoulder. She hugs me tight, practically crushing me to her chest. I lean into her hug. She's so warm and I feel safe. My arm is loosely wrapped around her. Kyltia may be my best friend, but Sukua is like the sister I wish I had—

I actually have a sister but she and I— well— we don't exactly get along. In fact, if she were here she'd tell me to get over it. That it's no big deal.

Sukua says, "Still you're alive and in one piece. *Mostly.*" Playfully she points at my shoulder.

I cover it with my paw, "Don't remind me."

"So how's it been going with Tatchathura?"

Kyltia glances at me, ears raised, "And what about the courtyard? I heard a rumor that the Shadow Fox saved you from *certain doom!*"

My ears flatten as I rush to cover her mouth. I glance over my shoulder to make sure he's not listening. He's caught in a conversation with Heroh and Altikua, "It's not a big deal. It was the heat of battle."

"That's odd— isn't it?"

"He said I'm his valuable asset or whatever."

Sukua narrows her gaze mischievously, "*Sure.*"

"You kidding me right now? He's *the reason* I have this mark in the first place."

She looks coy, "He's also *the reason* you're not dead too."

I grip my shoulder tightly. My mind flashing back to that moment...

The shadow that wanted to devour me— his fangs run deep into my shoulder. I cry out and find myself limp for a moment—

And then Tatchathura levels a blow against it's jaw. It hisses and releases me. I slop to the ground as Tatchathura stands in front of me. The creature shakes its head and rears back to strike again. Another flash of light and shadow boom from their collision. The arm with his own shadow crackling against this new foe.

My body is still tense against the pavement, What's even happening? What is he doing?

He growls, face contorting in pain. His arm is fighting against the magic of the collar.

I can tell it's really hurting him.

And when I confronted him about it all he had to say was —

He says gruffly, "A life for a life, right?"

I glare at him, "What do you even mean?"

"The courtyard training with Blondie's lightning. I figure I owe you that much."

"Yeah, I don't get him," I stare up at the sky, "He's had all these opportunities to let one of us die. I don't know what he's waiting for."

Kyltia waves a wing, "You kidding me Indy? He tried to kill you before that collar was around his neck." She pretends to be trapped for a moment, "Once that baby comes off, I'd watch my back."

Sukua waves us down, "Kyltia's right. If you think about it, it doesn't make any sense for him to try and take you out right now. Or any of us for that matter. We have him outnumbered and surrounded in a place that he can't use his full power. He obviously wants to live. It sounds like from what you told me— his only mission was to get the Taoah-lut Glove— which you told me his partner grabbed."

My mind pours over it for a moment. At least for now, injuring us doesn't make any sense for him. His soul is locked with that collar and he obviously wants to escape back to his own home country.

So maybe I am reading too much into his moments of kindness.

After all, most of Zutaom are beings like us with some good still in them or we wouldn't be trying to save them.

I watch him out of the corner of my eye for a minute more, *Not killing us outright I get, but I just don't understand why not just let the shadow finish me? Is it because he said I'm naive? He always seems to act like I'm a cub or something—*

She says, nudging my shoulder, "You're thinking **too hard** again."

Kyltia laughs, "She's always like that."

"And there's nothing wrong with thinking about stuff." I stick my tongue out, "But if what you're saying is true, then he must be just like all the others?"

Sukua nods, "See? Isn't that much easier? You've been worried about nothing. Besides you have your best friends here help you. Heroh and I have dealt with more than enough of his kind. And strangely enough, all of these criminals have their own rare moments of kindness or whatever. Sometimes I think it's hard to remember that they are beings like us. And that something in their past is causing them to make these choices. I'm not saying it's right— it's **definitely not**."

"I know what you mean. I guess I just don't like the back and forth and I just wish I knew that he was going to do next."

"Don't we all? But if we all had the power of the Prince, I think we'd all go nuts."

"Yeah, I don't know how he handles knowing so much. It would be overwhelming to know what so many beings *might do*. I'd never be sure. I guess sometimes it's better to just hope for the best and expect the worst."

"One week back and she's already a *wet cat*."

"Hey! You love water for one—"

"Jaguar." she sticks out her tongue, "Not like other cat species."

I give her a playful push, "And for two, we've been through *some* things this week."

"That's true but you heard the Prince. More negativity that grows here, the more problems we're going to have with the shadows." she seems reflective and calm for once.

Kyltia puffs out her chest, "We just have to do our part to keep building up the Kingdom. We'll get the rest of those shadows out of our country. Then we'll start working on rebuilding the other countries."

"I know that's what the Prince wants to do but it just seems so *daunting*. All of our countries are so broken. How will we ever repair them?"

Kyltia deflates a little, "I wonder how Atayip is doing."

I sigh, "Or Belaphrium."

We stare at the stars for a moment. There's a few shots of light across the sky. Some kind of creature makes a faraway sound. The guards on the lower level can be heard chatting with the fire in their paws lighting their way.

Sukua dons another bright grin, "I guess it's a good thing that we just have to listen to Prince Azu and just help him whenever we can."

"Yeah." there's a pit still in my gut, *I feel better about most of this now. But what if I'm still not enough?*

She puts a strong paw on each of our shoulders, "You also have to remember that no matter what good we do, there will always be someone, somewhere who doesn't like what we do— who doesn't want to do the same thing we want to — and that's okay. You just have to do the best you can and keep pushing forward."

"I know." a small smile finally forms.

Keep waking up.

Drag your paws across the floor.

Keep opening that door.

Never back down.

* * *

Altikua walks up to us, "Can I speak to you for a moment? *Alone.*"

Sukua and Kyltia look at me for just a moment. I nod to them. They make their way towards Tatchathura and Heroh.

Altikua leans in next to me. His brows tilt, "How are you doing?"

"I'm fine." I twist towards the wall, "It's not like I've *never* been hurt before."

"I wasn't saying that—"

"It's just *been a while*." I say in a mocking tone, *He's still being overbearing...*

"I'm just looking out for you."

"I knew what I was getting into." I shoot him a fiery look — ready to wind up further—

Altikua hugs me tightly, "I'm glad you're safe. Truly."

He pulls back to look down at me. His gaze is glossy. Even though the courtyard battle was a few days ago— he's still thinking about it.

I soften my stance, "I'm sorry I worried you. I just couldn't let that shadow take you."

"I know. I'm grateful. And you destroyed it as good as any." He backs up to lean against the stone ledge. Slowly I follow suit.

"Prince Azufae-yoh has already told me my contract is up. All I had to do was interact with him for a week."

His brows raise, his tail almost happy, "So you'll be heading back to the school then?"

"Don't act *too* excited." I smirk, "Of course I'm going to stay around as long as I'm needed."

He sighs, "I was afraid of that. I know you can handle it but *please* remember we're here for you."

"I know." my gaze softens, "It's just I ran away when things got tough before and I'm not *that* being anymore."

"So you'd *really* rather stay here and babysit him instead

of get back to those cubs that love you?"

"I've made my mind up Altikua. That's what I need to do to feel like I'm forgiven—"

He sounds wounded, "He's already forgiven you."

I wring my paws together, "You *know* what I mean."

He buries his head slightly, "I know what you mean, but — you can't undo the past. You *know* that."

I stare out at the green and navy starry sky, "I know but that doesn't mean I can't try. And if I can keep someone else from making the same mistakes I did— I'll do it."

"You know sometimes beings have to make those mistakes for themselves."

"I'll keep that in mind."

He gently pats my shoulder, "Make sure you get some rest. We've got training in the morning."

"Of course, Talik."

CHAPTER TWENTY-FOUR

A Somber Sky

ᴛᴀᴛᴄʜᴀᴛʜᴜʀᴀ

I've seen a lot of things in my life— good things, bad things, strong and weak magic— but I've never seen anything like what happened in the courtyard a few days ago. It's almost borderline impressive how the Prince's grief was used in such a way.

And then the King had a host of fallen beings of Ituvoh rising back up as pure light?

Who knew such a power exists?

The Magic of Jatali as we call it has always been an unusual entity. Some beings claim to have spoken with this force— that it has a mind of its own. I always believed it was just an idea. An abstract concept of their proposed unity. Stronger together and all that noise.

But if the Magic does really have a will of its own— is it just biding its time? Will its power destroy the Drake for good?

Probably not. I've seen the power the Drake has. The achition that was in the courtyard yesterday was only a reflection of his *true power*. *He* wasn't even fully present and still they struggled and lost their Great King on top of it. The only being who's ever sent the fully formed Drake running. The only being that could stand between them and the darkness is now gone.

Even the Magic's parlor trick of bringing all those beings back was easily a one-time thing. No way it would keep dragging souls out of their "paradise" to fight their battles on the mortal plane.

Indy leads me down the corridor to the Prince's War room. He's apparently in a meeting with the other captains and Blondie. She said they're going over the schematics of their next move. We reach the door as they start filing out. Azufae looks worn and weak as he waves us in.

It should be the perfect time to strike— but the Prince's powers destroyed a good chunk of our forces. There's no way they'll be coming back anytime soon. They all care too much about their own hides even when an opportunity presents itself.

Azufae takes a seat next to Altikua. Indy is still at my side watching to see what I will do.

I look the lion square in the eye, "I'm ready to make a deal."

He seems pleased at the notion, "And what deal would that be?"

"I'll find those gang leaders for you and any other rogue you want— but you have to *promise me* that when it's all said and done— that I'm free, no strings attached or additional fees. **Done**. And my partner gets a full pardon too."

"Does your partner have a name?"

I fold my arms, "I'll share that with you when my contract is complete."

He looks down a moment before meeting my gaze again, "I promise that I will give you both a full pardon. But remember the time limit—"

"Yeah, yeah *time*. I'm pretty *efficient*. So when my time is up, you ***better*** pay up."

Altikua stands and smacks the table, "Enough. You've made your point. If that's all you wanted to say, be *on your way*."

I glance at Indy who's been strangely silent throughout the whole thing. I start walking towards the door.

The Prince says, "I do appreciate your change of heart—"

I twist to face them again, "*Nothing* has changed. Don't get it twisted."

His gaze softens, "You will be a great help. Please let me know if there's anything else I can do for you."

I shake it off and walk through the doorway. What is it with him insisting on saying things like that? *Help* me? Indy is on my tail as we head back down the hallway. Although it frustrates me that I have to help them at all, I don't see much of a choice either. I can rot in a cell here or travel the country with the Rainbow Brights and maybe find another way free.

It's simple really. Any information I need, they're naive enough that I can manipulate it out of them. I'm sure the Prince has to know more about the Relics we're searching for. What better way to find them than the source? There's lot of beings in Zutaom counting on us to find these items. To keep searching for what was lost but has never been ours to keep. So we'll just have to change the cards so we can have the power that Jatali doesn't think anyone should have.

Besides, now that I've seen the power the Jatali has, there's a small chance he might actually destroy the Drake

—

And if that happens, then Lu-kan and I will both be free —for good. Either way we win.

* * *

It's late and noisy in the castle. You would think these beings would sleep sometime. I was very content in my cubicle until these fools came and checked me out— and since I'm at their mercy, I had no choice but to follow them up here to the roof of the highest tower in the castle.

The girls quickly break away from us giggling and tittering like they're still in school. Altikua and Heroh are nearby. They seem more solemn.

And they should be.

I didn't agree to help them out of the goodness of my heart. The only reason I'm helping them so I can get this stupid collar off my neck and so I can pry the information for all the locations of those missing Relics. Plus my Master wants me here for some specific reason.

I figure I'll probably start in the morning. Indy is naive enough that she might even take me to their library. Sure I could start snooping around on my own and find exactly what I'm looking for. But if I listen to the right soldiers— plenty of them have loose lips. Who knows— maybe I can get cozy with the Prince and he'll just blab all his secrets. That seems to be the way these beings are around here. Truthful to a fault. I guess in a way they're making my job that much easier. I *should* be thanking them.

Heroh leans on the stonewall next to us, "I had no idea the shadows had grown so much in our country."

Altikua leans over the edge of the wall, his claws digging in deep, "I guess I can't really blame the beings. It's been so long since that Promise was spoken."

"Still I thought they had some hope left but after seeing all those shadows. How broken are we?"

"Don't give up hope—"

"I'm not. It would be kind of counter intuitive right?"

"We just have to keep pressing forward. However, I do worry for the Prince. The spell was broken. He's vulnerable at a time when we can't afford to lose him."

"That's true but you underestimate him. He's got more power in his paws than we have in our whole body."

Normally I would scoff at the notion or roll my eyes but after witnessing the power myself— I'm inclined to agree with them.

I know. Crazy.

I didn't think any being could stand against the Drake, let alone hurt him— besides the King. But it was like a crashing force of pure light and pure shadow that ended in destruction. I wonder where the Drake is now. I had no idea it would turn out like this. I watch these other Rainbow Brights chat and comfort each other— I miss Lu-kan. We've always been there for each other. I have to make quick work of this job so I can get back to see her.

The Drake narrows his gaze, a puff of heated sulfur blows into my face, "Do you know why you were captured here?"

"I made a mistake—"

*"I gave you an impossible assignment." There's a twisted amusement in his gravely voice, "**I** put you here, so all of this could happen."*

I thought I'd messed up the Drake's plans. I figured I was dead— but he put me here on purpose. I almost don't believe it.

Heated grumblings rise from the others below. They want me punished. They literally heard it was part of our Master's plan and still they want me to suffer. This is how it is in Zutaom all the time.

Even though the Drake said it was *his* plan— if I don't finish the work— if I don't collect the Relics and take care of that mutt Altikua then I'll be on the chopping block next. I bet Re-kivah has ripped his scales out over the news. I can hear him now— *My best assassin stuck in the land of light! What rotten news!*

He should be happy he doesn't have to deal with me for awhile. I snort at the very idea. As if *that being* could ever be happy—

An obnoxious laugh cuts through my thoughts. Sukua and Indy are practically hysterical with each other. Kyltia is in the middle of it attempting to be funny. They're all hugging and carrying on like the last week hasn't happened.

It's just been so long since I've felt anything that caused me joy it just seems strange to me. I'd never admit it to her face but there's a few things about Indy I don't understand.

I should give up even worrying about it.

How can she stay positive towards me when all I've done is treat her like garbage? Sure we have to work together but that doesn't mean we have to be nice.

Even then I could probably get that— land of light and love. Belch. But putting her life on the line for me. Trying to save me— the Prince did the same. Facing down the Drake on my account? Of course that's probably his arrogant ambitions—

But Indy? She doesn't have stake in this match. What does she gain by helping me in that way? Because her *Master* told her so? I'm not buying it. He's let plenty of these other furbrains quit at a moment's notice.

I suppose she's just a fuzzy headed idiot with no world experience. Blindly optimistic.

In fact, as I look around me I'm surrounded by these fuzzy headed idiots. I may be an expert at what I do—

But this is definitely a new kind of mission. And I've got my work cut out for me.

CHAPTER TWENTY-FIVE

One Last Request

INDESSAH

The next day Altikua and I are preparing the new missions for the Knights. He and I are quietly chatting but it's nothing of note. Tatchathura is in his cell right now because honestly I needed a break from his attitude. That fox is gonna be the death of me.

A few moments later Prince Azufae-yoh comes rushing into the room. Both of us look up as he shuts the door in a flustered rush.

406

His eyes are wide and tail is lashing, "A letter. I found another letter from my Father!"

He walks to be next to us. He unfurls the parchment onto the table and quietly the three of us read it...

My dearest son, Azu.

You have always made me proud even if you felt like you weren't living up to my expectations. I want you to know you've *never* failed me. I've always loved you and I always will.

There was one more thing the Magic revealed to me, but it had to be told to you like this. I hope you understand. I wish I could have told you directly.

The Magic revealed a new prophecy. A new Promise to be fulfilled:

"An act of Pure Love will keep the Shadows bound,

Until a Fire burns the lush land,

And the place with no scars is downed.

The Prince of old can't rise again,

until the Twelve can be perfectly intertwined,

Then Ituvoh will be bathed in a Light so that all wounds will mend."

Remember the Virtues of each country? Take your time finding your way back to them. The way things happen are meant to be that way.

Timing is a tricky thing. So don't be upset with yourself if you don't get it right the first couple times because I know that every time you put your head to something you will succeed.

Keep your friends close to you and know that I'm always watching. Even though I want you to enjoy your life, your mother and I'll be eagerly awaiting your return and when you do, we'll throw the biggest party!

I love you Azufae-yoh Zintah, my *precious* son.

The Prince covers his mouth. The tears are falling freely as he slowly falls into the chair. Altikua puts a paw on his shoulder. I lean down to hug his side. In that moment— I'm reminded of my own parents.

It's been so long since I've seen them. Or even spoken with them. I wonder if they worry about me? Do they even think about me anymore? Or am I just their forgotten reject of a daughter?

The Prince takes another moment before composing himself. He springs out of his seat and heads towards his magical book. The one he uses to check on his connections throughout Ituvoh. The book springs open and an ethereal glow fills the small space. Everything seems so small whenever this book is opened. The overbearing light of so many souls in one room.

The Prince's paw slides over the connections his face shifting to look over the various beings in turn. There's a small spark in his gaze. He slides the book close. He looks to each of us in turn, "I have some ideas about this Promise. But I'll need some time."

Altikua says, "Of course."

I nod, "Is every week *this* exciting here?"

They both seemed to chuckle 'No' at the same time.

"Because forget about the Daybreak Resort, I might have to book an extended stay here."

They both still seem amused but I can tell their minds are working overtime. Some of the Promise seems obvious, but other parts of this might not be what they seem.

After the Great War, the King tried to extend a peace offering of sorts to the other Nations. A way to try and form solidarity with them despite all that had happened. It seemed at the Magic's urging, twelve relics were made for the twelve other rulers. A thirteenth for Jatali— the Taoah-lut Glove. It is said that it has the power to bind their use together for unspeakable power.

The other Relics all mean something to each country. They each had a unique power that represented what was great about each country. Each item had a power of the core Virtue Magics— Courage, or Loyalty for example.

All the Virtues are what every leader should have but that each country represented more than the others. However, those Relics were meant to bring us together soon made them targets for rogues and bandits. All of the Relics were scattered. Some were lost, others were coveted and traded, some even hoarded by our enemies. It's been many years since anyone has seen any of the other relics.

This new Promise definitely wants us to work on

reuniting the countries and it's always been our number one priority anyway. But how can we ever traverse an ocean and drag the countries back? How can all wounds even mend when there are so many scars still on our hearts? I want to believe the things Azufae-yoh Zintah says, and I've always trusted the Great King Elin-rah Ventash, but it just seems more and more impossible as the years tick by.

How can such a great Promise be fulfilled?

CHAPTER TWENTY-SIX

Last Chance

LU-KAN

I'm just outside the castle walls. There's still more waves of light radiating off of that place. I may not have a shadow in me but that warm, fuzzy happy energy is making me completely nauseous.

Unbelievable. Absolutely unbelievable!

All this time I believed the Prince didn't have any kind of power at all. *Why else* would he stay in his ivory tower all the time while his Knights swarmed everywhere? Heck, I even thought that their power was a greatly exaggerated myth to make them seem more important than they are.

I twist to look back over the rock. The castle is glimmering and bright on the horizon. All of the shadows have disappeared— banished from this place back to the Abyss until they recover.

I slide back down the rock and fold my arms, *It's frustrating. Tatchathura was supposed to be done with this mission. He was supposed to be back with me...*

I take a few moments to let my body calm. I have to make a call that I'm not looking forward to. Once I'm no longer shaking, I reach into my vest and pull out a metal clip. It has a small piece of glass in the middle. There's a button on the side to turn it on. It's basically Zutaom's response to the Prince's soul link. Anyone who has a coordinating piece can communicate through a shadow link.

I swipe my paw around the screen to find the one I want to speak with. Re-kivah, my boss, an armadillo who doesn't take kindly to failure—

Even though we've gotten him off his back more than a few times.

It only takes a few moments before a grizzly voice answers. The screen flashes into view. He's sitting behind his desk as usual. One of his mangled claws scribbling down furiously on a paper.

One of his bloodshot eyes focuses on me, "Well— **out with it!**"

"I have the Taoah-lut Glove."

He turns slightly as I hold out the Relic. A simple leather glove with gold stitching. It faintly glimmers in the sunlight. It doesn't look like much but it's just the first piece in this multi-layered puzzle. The power to control life. To turn back time for those who are lost. And I'm biting at the bit to get the rest of the pieces.

He comes closer to the camera, "Is that right? At least you did **something** right. What else?"

"It's complicated." I wince.

"I don't have **all day**."

I take a breath, "We failed to take the castle. The rulers of Jatali had a trump card we weren't aware of. They destroyed half of our forces and wounded the Drake. He will have to recover."

Re-kivah growls and flips his desk. The wood clatters against the muddy ground. He waves his arms around wildly. Papers go everywhere. I silently wait for it to pass.

"The Drake was injured? *Impossible*. Have you seen him?"

"His shadow completely vaporized with the rest of them but I'm sure he went somewhere into hiding to rest. Maybe a cave or something."

He lets out another growl, "**What** of Tatchathura?"

"That's where it gets complicated—"

"**Girl**—"

"Will you let **me** speak? I'm surprised the Drake hasn't made you into a hat yet." I glare at him. He gives me a hateful look back, "Tatchathura was captured—"

"Are you **kidding** me right now? He's not like those other idiots who get captured. He's the **best** one I have!"

Before I can speak, he starts going on another rant yelling and throwing his arms about. I wait letting him get more of his frustration out. Even though he's angry right now, I know there is some concern in his voice. After all, he took care of us when we were younger.

I wouldn't exactly call myself his daughter or anything. I still have a family somewhere but that's a different story for a different time.

But Tatchathura is like a son to him.

Re-kivah says, "That means that **mangy mutt** Altikua is still alive then! Do you have any more **bad news** you'd like to tell me?"

"It seems the Prince has been watching over him *personally*—"

"I **don't care** who's watching over him! You stop at nothing to retrieve him. He's too valuable to be stuck behind bars—"

I glare at him again and he finally seems to get the picture. He covers his mouth and waits for me to finish, "The Drake said he put Tatchathura here. This was part of his grand plan. The Drake said he intends for him stay until he gets the information we need."

"WHAT! How can it get even WORSE? Him hanging around with those Light Brights." He puts a claw to his brow, "And Tatchathura told you this? Or you heard it *yourself*?"

I pause for a moment. It's true I didn't hear what was said. I'd only just gotten to the courtyard. My last minute attempt to free my love.

I fold my arms, "Tatchathura told me."

Re-kivah lets out a cuss, "Tayaeme— If the Prince has touched him, he might already be **brainwashed**."

I tense at the thought of it. A strong burning forms at my back.

I won't let them take him. He's mine. We're never supposed to be apart.

And I won't let Jatali take *something* else away from me. They've taken **enough**.

"I'll die before this place changes me." He says, his gaze fiery.

I'll have to trust him for now. Trust that he wasn't changed— because if he was— wouldn't he have turned me in after that conversation? It's just hard to accept that the Prince might not have the power to change minds like we thought he did.

I say, "I trust him. And he has no reason to let me go after telling me such a thing."

He pauses for a moment before he looking at me again,

"Never mind it. The plan goes ahead just the same. Do what you can to keep an eye on Tatchathura. In the meantime, work on finding those other trinkets. I've got intel about locations in Rusim and Mutamay."

"Sir, I don't mean to be rude but Rusim is going to be a hard nut to crack. The Valfium Timberland is a magical place where beings get— lost."

"So **what?!** If there is no risk, no reward. Until I hear from the Drake, I've got all my beings out searching for all these pieces. Hang onto the Glove for now— it's useless without the others. I'll keep in touch. And Lu-kan—"

"Yes, Sir?"

"Don't **fail** me again or **don't** bother coming back."

That's how it is in Zutaom. I accomplished my objective. But in Re-kivah's eyes since I lost sight of my partner— I failed. It doesn't matter if it was part of the Drake's unspoken plan. Tatchathura still failed the objective of getting Altikua out of the way.

"Of course not." I click a button on the clip and our magical projection ends. I shove it back into my vest. Standing up, I straighten out my outfit and brush off the dust. I take one last moment to glare at the castle.

My paws clench tight, *I'm trusting you for now, my love. Be safe...*

COMING UP NEXT IN THE SERIES...

#2- A Burning Heart

The magic in his paws brandishes his heart with darkness...

Tatchathura has never been ordinary. Their kind may be born with magic in their paws— but the marks of disobedience against the Magic were on him from the day he was born.

The Knights are called away to a mountain called the Lonely Summit. Rumors of beings disappearing runs rampant there. The idea that the crystals within the cave have powers is unsettling to most—

While the Knights are called away at the Summit, criminal activity in Luthura explodes. A past that haunts Altikua is torn to the surface of his cool veneer as this news reaches his ears.

The rescue mission becomes desperate in the caverns as the darkness grows. Altikua and Tatchathura keep challenging each other for dominance. Indessah finds herself stuck in the middle of their feuds with no end in sight.

Amid twists and turns, these new found comrades will have to rely on each other if they ever want to see the light again...

Thank you so much for reading Knights of Jatali. It was a joy to write. I hope you got as much enjoyment out of it as I did.

If you'd like to help spread the word, here are a few things you can do:

1. Write a Review.

2. Sign up for our email list for Updates and Release schedule.

3. Bookmark and share our Website so others can find us!

4. Share with anyone who likes Fantasy as much as you do!

And thanks again!

Want more of Ituvoh?

Website: https://swanheartpress.com
Email List: https://swanheartpress.com/join-our-mailing-list
Youtube: https://www.youtube.com/@swanheartpress
Tiktok: https://www.tiktok.com/@swanheartpress
Facebook: https://www.facebook.com/SwanHeartPress
Instagram: https://www.instagram.com/swanheartpress
Pinterest: https://www.pinterest.com/SwanHeartPress

Characters

Great King Elin-rah Ventash Gantus- Ruler of the High Kingdom of Jatali; He is a lion with a perfectly gold coat, and silver mane and tail tuft. He is mostly quiet and observes other beings. His is the Founder of the Magic of Ituvoh and knows all of it's secrets. Secrets which have not been revealed to the populous and only a few have been shown to his son.

Prince Azufae-yoh Zintah Gantus- Ruler of the High Kingdom of Jatali; He is a lion with a perfectly white coat, and golden mane and tail tuft. He spends all of his time watching over the beings of Ituvoh in various ways with the hope to reunite them all.

Ashtevah- the Prince's flying mount; unknown species; It's whole body is a beautiful blending of fur and feathers. It's mostly white with a translucent undercurrent of blues, purples, and copper. It has a narrow snout with broad nose. Two eyes that are wide and bright shining like crystals.

Altikua Talous- Elite Captain of the Guard; *also known as Talik by his friends;* He is a golden wolf with lighter cream patches. He has one magical marking that can be seen on his forehead that looks like a comet. He oversees all of the military functions of Jatali, and spends most of his time at Luthura Castle making sure every being is in line. He is extra protective over Indessah whom he views as a younger sister.

Indessah-yah Brantum- Former teacher at the Rapsuk School of Jatali; *also known as Indy by her friends;* She is a purple fox with darker purple markings and blonde hair. Her magical markings are triangle stripes. Although she's had her basic combat training, she has a long way to go before she's ready to be a real Knight. Currently her task is to keep the criminal Tatchathura in line.

Kyltia- Former Guard at the Rapsuk School of Jatali; She used to live in Atayip. She is a salmon colored bat with pink magic markings and a violet blue chest fluff. She is Indy's best friend and moral support. She's often times not serious and hopes to be a prominent journalist some day.

Sukua Allutiauh- Combat Training Specialist (Physical Strength); She is a white jaguar with green and pink spots. Her magical markings include leaves and flowers. She is one of the prominent trainers at Luthura Castle. Although she may seem small compared to the other big cats, she packs quite a punch. She is often giddy and jokes around with Heroh a lot.

Heroh Flintiv- Combat Training Specialist (Weapons); He is a black jaguar with green rosette markings, and his magical markings include leaves and branches. He is another prominent trainer at Luthura Castle. He is great with a bow and light hearted most of the time. Despite this, he harbors something of a dark past that he rarely speaks of.

Tatchathura Devantum- Former thief and assassin for the country of Zutaom *(Also known as the Shadow Fox of Zutaom)*; Currently a criminal under the care of Jatali. His temporary collar gives Indessah the power to subdue him. He is a black fox with red and yellow markings and dusty ginger hair. His magical markings include the fireheart flower, and other flame-like markings. His soul is so corrupted that his coat is what they call 'murky' and not glossy like the Jatalians at all.

He has been tasked with aiding Jatali in discovering the locations of specific gang members that are running rampant within their borders but it's hard to say if he's actually helping them or just helping himself.

Lu-kan Atiness Eslaf- Thief and assassin for the country of Zutaom; The partner to Tatchathura and the being that stole the Taoah-lut Glove. She is a grey fox with yellow and gold markings. Her magical markings are yellow and grey diamonds that are split with jagged lines. She has murky purple hair with gold accents. Her right ear is torn, and like Tatchathura she has many scars. She's determined and ruthless to get what she wants.

Re-kivah- Tatchathura's boss from Zutaom. He is an armadillo with many scars, one eye and a mangled arm. Similar to Tatchathura he is coated in darkness. He will stop at nothing to get his prized assassin back and works for the Drake of Garaev.

Typhan-rah- the self-proclaimed gryphon king of Atayip; the longest ruler of the region since he is so ruthless.

The Drake of the Abyss of Garaev- The Self Proclaimed Ruler of the Eastern Continent (*Formerly a member of the Achition species with the given name of Senteia Rakous*); Every time he reveals himself he's covered in a smokescreen so his true form and colors are unknown. All of the beings in the Eastern Continent fear the ruthless Drake and will do as he tells them to protect themselves.

He intends to overthrow the High Kingdom and any being who stands in his way. He is so strong only Great King Elin-rah has every been able to get a mark on him. He is currently gathering his army and uses beings like Re-kivah to run smaller groups of recruits to do his bidding.

Locations

Jatali- *The Land of the Great Cats;* The main country of the continent Ituvoh. This country used to be the only country before the Great War.

Luthura Castle- The Capital is Luthura, and the castle held here is the stronghold for the Rulers. It is also a Training Grounds, and Criminal Rehabilitation facility.

Fireheart Papers- This is the new stand store that houses one of the main forms of media for the citizens of Jatali. They have plans to expand the print distribution to the far reaches of every Nation.

Belaphrium- *The Land of the Great Dogs;* This is Jatali's closest ally. They are the country to the west of them and where the majority of the army is trained. The forces trained here are used to reinforce all of their territory points through out the Nations. They also help reinforce their allies' borders such as in Mutamay. They also have a Navy, an Air Division, and Special Forces branches.

Rusim- *The Land of the Reaching Forests;* This is the nation to the north of Jatali. It is a heavily forested area with a magical enchanted woods called the Valfium Timberland. They are one of Jatali's close allies. They revere the Knights greatly and are more than happy to help in anyway they can.

Lueon- *The Land of the Endless Waters;* They are very faithful to the Kingdom of Jatali. Many of them train to be an adviser to the King. If that dream falls through, they are still very useful as scribes helping the King spread the message of unity. Their land may seem small compared to other countries but the rest of their nation is underwater in the Sparkling Sea.

Mutamay- *The Land of the Unicorns;* Although it's been dubbed the Land of the Unicorns, pegasai, horses and donkeys have also made their home here. They are a divided kingdom. Many don't think the young queen is qualified to rule but they have exceptional support from Jatali.

Zutaom- *The Land of the Once Great Savannah;* The country that started the conflict with Jatali and where the Drake calls "home". They have been amassing an army for some time now and frequently send beings to plunder and wreck havoc on the neighboring countries

Common Phrases

Eatiref!— **good tidings;** a greeting and also parting phrase

Jokan, Mutiem, lus Haoyut tav Jatali!— **the chant at the end of training;** Justice, Peace and Glory to Jatali

Tayaeme— **rats/curses;** something has gone wrong, sound of frustration

Artivah— **That's it!;** sound made when breakthrough is made, like Eureka

Zellum Yus— **get well;** akin to prayer, that the recipient will be blessed with good health once more

Other Nationalities

Rusim- Rusimians
Lueon- Lueonese
Nidah- Nidahmaic
Belaphrium- Belaphrians
Mutamay- Mutamaic
Sekulan- Sekulanese
Ikouvan- Vanaic
Esakivh- Esakivhians **Guth-**
Guthic
Zutaom- Zutaomese
Deleon- Delie
Atayip- Taphi
Jatali- Jatalians

The Code of Jatali

Honor the Ruler of Jatali above all.

Help every being that you can, no matter the cost.

Treat every being like family even when they are your enemy.

Honor the family you're born into, and also treat the community likewise.

Do not steal, for all trinkets serve to bring life to another.

Do not murder, for all life has value.

Beware, Jealousy will make your heart and soul rot.

Other Concepts

Achitions— or a upright walking lizard-like beings. They are a kind from another land. This is the original species that the Drake was.

Bulzatin— A Bulzatin is a native creature to our land. Giant, slimy, and full of teeth and fangs. Definitely not a creature you'd like to meet ever. Luckily for us they've mostly died out.

She puts a paw to her head, "Like a Bulzatin ate me for breakfast. Ug."

Cekantus— or the large, scaled titanic beings of the southern oceans. Giant water creatures with many tails, and leather skin. Too many fins to count and holes in every side that allows the water to shift through them. It's as if they become one with the ocean. Lightning fast and silent. Although they belong to other lands, we see them from time to time.

Magic of Jatali- The energy force that powers their magic. It's based on a users will and intent. Those will foul intent will not be able to use this magic. They will be forced to bargain with a shadow or give something of themselves up to gain the power they want. The Magic is mysterious to most beings here and is said to converse with the Great King and Prince.

Osekou- This is the Shadow Magic that was founded by the Drake. He cultivated it's negative energy and with his commitment lost his soul to the shadows. Other beings can commit to this way of life if they're ready to part with some of who they are.

Taoah-lut Glove- One of the thirteen mystical relics; These relics were part of the foundation of the 13 nations of Ituvoh. Each item had a specific power and was given to each Nation based on the Virtue Magic they represent.

The Taoah-lut Glove represents the Virtue of Justice. A magic that seems to be exclusive to the Prince and King of Jatali. It is said that when all thirteen are gathered together, then untold powers will be revealed! But the true nature of the power contained in the Glove is unknown at the moment.

Tash-nev Roch- Also known as the "Fireheart Flower", is

prominent around their nation specifically. It blooms purple until the end of its life and then turns red-orange as it dies surrounded by sparkling dust. In its death many more flowers are born.

Tize-khan— are nocturnal mammal like creatures with long snouts, furry body, scaly legs(lizard-like), and scaled "fins" on back with two larger blade like fins that are used for attracting mates and warding off predators. They have four arms and two legs, they have multicolored spots/patterns and are able to glide from tree to tree with their fan scales. They also are avid swimmers.

The 12 Virtues of Jatali

There are twelve qualities that represent the a ruler in Ituvoh. Each country personifies a specific quality over the others. These are the main Magics that permeate the land. Each Magic has what are called Branches. There are three branches per Magic. The third Branch is always the strongest and hardest to learn. It is said there are other unknown forms that were lost during the various wars in Ituvoh.

Courage- strength of mind to carry on in spite of danger
Branches: Guts, Daring, Valiant

Indy Guts Example: "Jatali lights my way. Like a fire, my light will shine even in the pitch darkness."

Indy Daring Example: "Jatali will never leave me."

Indy Valiant Example: "My fire won't be weakened by water nor stone. Let it burn like the love I have for Ituvoh."

Determination- firm or unwavering adherence to one's purpose
Branches: Fortitude, Tenacity, Nerve

Patience- the capacity to endure what is difficult without complaining
Branches: Obedience, Discipline, Gallant

<u>Sukua Obedience Example:</u> "A Knight of Jatali is like a stream paving the way for what is *right*."

<u>Heroh Discipline Example:</u> "I will never abandon what's right, even if it costs me everything."

Loyalty- adherence to something to which one is bound by a pledge or duty
Branches: Allegiance, Dedication, Fidelity

Charity- the giving of necessities to the needy
Branches: Generosity, Benevolence, Altruism

Truth- agreement with fact or reality
Branches: Verity, Honesty, Rigor

<u>Altikua's Verity Example:</u> "Jatali knows the Truth inside us all. There's no heart he doesn't know."

<u>Altikua's Honesty Example:</u> "Let the stonewalls of Jatali stand forever. Let no brick be so weak that it makes the rest of us collapse. Honor your comrades, and speak truth *no matter* the cost."

Wisdom- the ability to understand inner qualities or relationships, a body of facts learned by study or experience
Branches: Discernment, Perception, Brilliance

Kindness- sympathetic concern for the well-being of others
Branches: Compassion, Affinity, Grace

Joy- a feeling or state of well-being and contentment
Branches: Felicity, Bliss, Elation

Mercy- kind, gentle, or compassionate treatment especially towards someone who is undeserving of it
Branches: Empathy, Favor, Tender Soul

Justice- the practice of determining what's right; lack of favoritism toward one side or another
Branches: Righteous, Honor, Valor

Great King's Valor example: "Uphold the weak, and balance the strong. The storm of Justice upon them all!" The Magic of Jatali reigns over all.

Faith- firm belief in the integrity, ability, effectiveness, or genuineness of someone or something
Branches: Devotion, Steadfast, Assurance

About the Author

CEO & Author of SwanHeart Press

Kelly has been writing ever since she was a child. She even won some poetry contests back in the day. She was recently set on fire with inspiration to go back to those roots and start writing stories again (like she always wanted to do). Devout follower of Jesus Christ the Son of the Living God. The World's Savior and the only hope for mankind to make peace with God. John 3:16, Romans 10:9-13

She's always loved stories that feature strong protagonists and a moral message at its heart. Stories that feature fantasy, friendship and protecting those we love are my favorites. She lives with her husband, daughter and three cats (who are like her other children).